Outcast

Orgoru had grown up knowing that he was useless as a peasant. He had struggled to please, tried harder and harder with every complaint, but no matter how hard he tried, his mother always found something wrong with what he had done, his father always demanded to know why he couldn't be like the other boys—until one night Orgoru went to bed weeping, feeling as though his little heart would break.

Then it was as though a light exploded in his mind, and Orgoru suddenly understood. He was so different because he was so much better! He must be of a higher station, the son of parents who were gentry at least, but more probably noblemen, such as the ones who figured in the stories grandmothers told their grandchildren.

Once he realized that, it all made sense. Of course his parents resented him—they knew what he really was! Of course he didn't fit in—he was different indeed! One day they would come back for him—or he would find out where they had gone, his real parents. Then he would go to them, and no silly law or magistrate's command would stop him! He knew what he really was, and one day he would know who!

A WIZARD IN PEACE

Christopher Stasheff

A TOM DOHERTY ASSOCIATES BOOK
NEW YORK

This is a work of fiction. All the characters and events portrayed in this book are either products of the author's imagination or are used fictitiously.

A WIZARD IN PEACE

Copyright © 1996 by Christopher Stasheff

All rights reserved, including the right to reproduce this book, or portions thereof, in any form.

Cover art by Peter Peeples

A Tor Book
Published by Tom Doherty Associates, Inc.
175 Fifth Avenue
New York, NY 10010

Tor Books on the World Wide Web:
http://www.tor.com

Tor® is a registered trademark of Tom Doherty Associates, Inc.

ISBN: 0-812-56797-8
Library of Congress Card Catalog Number: 96-8452

First edition: October 1996
First mass market edition: May 1997

Printed in the United States of America

0 9 8 7 6 5 4 3 2 1

CHAPTER I

Miles fled swiftly through the forest—or as swiftly as he could, in the dark. That was still fairly quickly, for he knew the forest well, this close to home. Nonetheless, fear chilled him, and the thought of turning back flitted through his mind—but through it he went, with all his heart helping it on its way, for he fled from Salina.

Well, from the magistrate, really. The thought brought the man's face instantly before his mind's eye, heavy-jowled and hard-eyed, glowering down from behind his high bench against the paneled wall of the courtroom, with the clerk looking on from his desk in front of the bench and the other petitioners watching from their stools. The magistrate orated, "Salina, daughter of Pleinjeanne, and Miles, son of Lige, I have given you each five years and more to find mates, and you have found none."

"But we don't fancy one another, Your Honor," Miles protested.

Didn't fancy Salina, indeed! He glanced up at her—quite plain, rawboned and scrawny, with squinting eyes, a long, sharp nose, and a tongue quick to insult and blame linked to a mind that could find every fault unerringly and instantly. She was only five years older than he, but was a shrew already.

"Salina, you came of age ten years ago," the magistrate intoned. "Miles, you came of age five years ago. If I leave you to find your own partners, you never will."

"Give me time, Your Honor!" Salina glared at Miles in a way that made it clear she was as appalled as he at the thought of marrying, for he was no prize. He was short, a full head shorter than she, and so stocky that he seemed fat. He was round-faced, with too strong a chin and too short a nose, quiet and reticent—too quiet for Salina's taste. She proclaimed far and wide that she loved a good quarrel. Miles hated them.

"Give me time," she said again, "and a permit to travel, and I'll find a man before I'm thirty."

"By thirty, fifteen years of childbearing will be past! Eight children you could have borne in that time—and you have already wasted ten years, forgone the bearing of five more citizens for the Protector."

Citizens and taxpayers, Miles thought sourly.

"But you, Miles." The magistrate frowned down at him, puzzled. "You've always been a good boy, never any trouble. You haven't broken a single rule in your whole life, never even gone poaching!"

Miles winced at the thought of the public punishments the reeve meted out to anyone the foresters caught. No, he had never gone poaching! He shuddered at the memory of the last flogging he had seen—a man from two villages away hanging by his wrists from the pillory while the cat-o'-nine-tails smacked across his back. His whole body had convulsed with every stroke; he had cursed at first, then begun to scream, and finally mewled before they cut him down. Miles had heard that he had lived, but hadn't walked straight again for six months.

"What has made you so stubborn now?" the magistrate demanded. "You know the Protector decreed long ago that everyone over eighteen must be safely bound into marriage, so that the men won't make trouble for the reeves and the women won't raise havoc among the men. Salina shouldn't waste her life in spinsterhood when she can bear many healthy babies—

nor should you, when you could be earning a living for a wife and family."

"But I don't love him," Salina snapped, glaring at Miles.

"Love!" the magistrate snorted. "What has love to do with it? We speak of marriage and child-rearing, and since you two have *not* spoken nor been spoken for, you shall marry or go to the frontier farms, so that the Protector shall have *some* use from you!" He banged his gavel on the bench, and that was the end of it.

Until nightfall.

As he ran, Miles wondered if perhaps he should have chosen the frontier farms after all. He remembered what he had heard of them, those places that the Protector wished to see used, so that people wouldn't become crowded in their homelands as they increased. Some were in the north, where it was cool in summer but frigid in winter; some were in the western desert, where people broiled by day and froze by night. They were prisoners, those folk, lawbreakers—waste people for the wastelands—turning the desert into a garden or the frozen lands into oatfields for a few months of every year, making the land livable for their children, if they had any, or for settlers whom the Protector would send when the land was fertile. Then the prisoners would move on, always in the wastelands, always where the work was backbreaking and constant, always where life itself was a punishment.

But could it be worse than the punishment for trying to leave the village without a pass?

With the thought came the memory of Lasak in his shackles, the long chain stapled to the side of the courthouse, dressed in rags and striking blow after blow with sledgehammer or pickax, trimming blocks to shape for the magistrate's walls, smashing broken blocks into cobblestones, fourteen hours a day, gray-faced and haggard, his eyes losing luster with every sunrise. He had stayed at that labor for a year, and when the magistrate released him, he did whatever he was told, looking up in fear at the slightest word from the Watch, cringing at a word from the magistrate, going when he was told, coming when he was bidden, marrying the worst shrew in town as he was ordered, and going almost eagerly out to hoe all day in the fields, glad to be away from her. His spirit hadn't just been broken—it had been extinguished.

And here was Miles, daring to leave the village without a pass just as Lasak had, courting disaster just as Lasak had—but bound and determined that he would escape, as Lasak had not. He resolutely put the memory out of his mind—he would rather hang slowly than marry Salina. She might feel insulted at that, but she would thank him secretly, and who knew? The next husband the magistrate chose for her might be more to her taste. At least she wouldn't be sent to the frontier farm for disobeying, not when the crime was his.

So here was Miles, fleeing through the wood, though the punishment would be far worse if he were caught, far worse than for either refusing to marry, or for poaching, or any of the hundred other things the Protector forbade. Still, the difference between giving up a few hours' sport and a week's meat on the one hand, and sacrificing a whole lifetime's chance of happiness on the other, wasn't worth thinking about.

He slipped between trees, went down almost-hidden game-trails at a trot, for, poacher or not, he knew the ways of the forest well. He, like every other village boy, had hunted every fall during the open season. He didn't doubt that he could escape if he could be far enough away before the magistrate discovered he was missing and sent the foresters after him.

But hang, emigrate, or grind, Miles was leaving the village, and Salina would thank him for it. He would live a bachelor all his days, stay free to marry for love as the minstrels sang of it—or die trying.

The two men sat in soft chairs that tilted back and molded themselves to their occupants' bodies. Each had a tall, iced drink on the table between them, and sipped now and then as he watched the pictures changing on the huge wallscreen in front of him. The lounge in which the men sat was lit with subdued splashes of light that illuminated the copies of great paintings hung on the walls, and other pictures the great artists had never painted, although each painting looked as though they had. The subdued light that spilled over from those pools gave a glow to the thick wine-red carpet and the golden oak of the walls.

"All right, Gar, so they all could be better off—but I haven't seen a single one where I'd say the people were suffering," the smaller man grumbled. "At least, not most of them."

Actually, he was fairly tall, by the standards of his home planet—but his companion was seven feet from toe to crown, and wide-shouldered in proportion.

The picture changed, and Gar said, "This one does look fairly standard, Dirk—like a picture from old Earth. They've built up plant life and oxygen, enriched the soil with fertilizers and carbon, and seeded it with Terran lifeforms."

Dirk nodded. "It's been settled for a few hundred years, then."

"I'd guess a thousand, if Herkimer is right about there being walled cities in the middle of the forest. People don't build that way."

"I know—they chop down the trees and plant crops. Besides, he said his sonar probe showed that the biggest of them was built over the buried hull of the colony ship, and they wouldn't have tried to land it on top of all those trees. So you're pretty sure those cities are abandoned?"

"Herkimer is," Gar answered, "and a ship's computer that size is almost never wrong. He'll plead ignorance sometimes, but when he doesn't, he has so much evidence that it's no use to dispute."

"Of course, there *could* be a fact he doesn't know about," Dirk said sourly.

"Yes, and he doesn't know anything about the current government on this planet." Gar frowned as the picture changed to an overhead view of a town. "There isn't that much we can tell, sitting up here inside a spaceship."

"What do you know about the people, Herkimer?" Dirk asked.

The computer's mellow voice answered from all about them. "Nothing, Dirk, except that their parents were Earthmen who left to escape crowding, and to gain fresh air and sunshine."

"That's very strange." Gar frowned. "There's usually *something* in the database."

"Well, he's got the best one around, when it comes to lost colony planets," Dirk agreed. "Absolutely nothing about what happened after Earth withdrew all support from the colonies, huh?"

"You *know* we don't even have an idea whether or not the people survived," Gar reminded him.

"Well, we just found out." Dirk gestured at the screen, where they seemed to be descending as the camera expanded the picture. They found themselves looking down on people walking fairly quickly along the streets, wearing dark clothing. The women wore bodices and skirts and bonnets; the men wore knee pants, tunics, or short robes, and some wore conical hats with flat tops and wide brims. "These pictures are live, right?"

"Yes, Dirk," the computer answered. "Of course, I am recording them, and will store them for you."

Dirk frowned. "Odd to see the physical layout so similar on every continent, especially when none of them are very big."

"True," Gar agreed, frowning thoughtfully. "Every single one shows a lot of small towns in expanding rings around a few big cities with a network of roads and canals tying them together. No huge forests with occasional villages in clearings, no vast grasslands with tiny tribes following great herds, no wide-open spaces broken into patchwork fields around Neolithic villages . . ."

"And no medieval castles on hilltops overlooking collections of villages ringed by more patchwork fields," Dirk finished for him. "Not what you'd expect of a colony that crashed when it couldn't get spare parts, or trade with Terra for new machines."

"Still, it's scarcely modern," Gar pointed out. "There's no sign of automobiles or electricity, not even steam engines and railroads."

"So it crashed, but not very hard," Dirk inferred. "At a guess, the political system kept some kind of infrastructure going."

"If that's so, then there may not be any need for us." Gar

sounded almost gloomy. "Not if their government fits their needs."

"Don't rush to judgment, there." Dirk held up a cautioning palm. "Just because it kept them alive, doesn't mean it made them happy. Besides, after the crisis was over, whatever command structure saved them, might no longer be needed."

"True," Gar agreed, his eyes coming alive again, "and the look of the land does seem to indicate a strong-arm government of some sort. The layout being so much the same everywhere indicates a common social and political structure."

"Probably," Dirk cautioned his friend.

"But what kind?" Gar asked. "I've never seen a lost colony that looked so organized from space!"

"At least those people on the screen look well-fed and healthy," Dirk said.

"Not very many of them look happy, though," Gar said, "and *that* is enough to arouse my suspicions."

"Mine, too. Definitely we want a closer look."

"I'm also suspicious because there's no sign of king or noblemen, even though the culture seems to have regressed to late medieval."

"Or early modern—take your pick." Dirk shrugged. "But what strikes *me* as strange is that there's no sign of clergy or churches."

"Most unusual, for a culture in this stage. Yes, I'd say we have reason to investigate." Gar rose from his chair and strode off toward the sally bay. "Down we go, Herkimer! Down to the nightside!"

Orgoru trudged homeward, his hoe over his shoulder, his face wooden as they came into the village and Clyde whooped to everyone who could hear, "Three! Orgoru only cut down three stalks of maize in his hoeing today!"

"Only three?" Althea looked up from snapping beans by her mother's door. "Better and better, Orgoru! Maybe we'll actually have corn to grind this fall!"

Orgoru took the gibe with a straight face, but he could feel his treacherous skin growing hot.

"Hear how they mock you, boy!" his father growled beside him. "Must you shame me every day of your life?"

The angry retort leaped hot to Orgoru's lips, but he held it within; he knew from bitter experience that talking back would only win him blows and kicks—and, full-grown or not, with the vigor of youth on his side or not, he knew that his father was stronger than he was, quicker than he was, in all ways a better fighter than he was.

"Can't even manage a hoe!" his father grumbled. "Thank heaven we never trusted you with a plow or a scythe!"

He'd certainly never taken the trouble to teach the use of them to his son—but Orgoru shrugged off the older man's complaints, telling himself once again that it was no wonder he was so useless with peasant's tools.

He had known he was clumsy since he was five, struggling so hard to please his mother in drawing water for her, sweeping, gathering kindling—but always she scolded him for spilling some of the water, for gathering too many rotten sticks, for missing a spot in his sweeping. His earliest memories, and his latest ones, were all of such scoldings, such blaming:

Little Orgoru tripped, stumbled into the table, and his mother's only vase crashed to the floor. "What was that?" she cried, and came running. Orgoru flinched away from her, trying to make himself as small as possible; but it did no good; she screamed, "My vase! You clumsy, stupid child!" and began beating him, beating and beating and beating. . . .

Papa's fist caught him on the side of the head, making him sit down hard. Through the ringing in his ears, he heard the man shout, "You've left half the weeds in that row still standing!"

Orgoru whined, trembling. "I didn't know they were weeds, Papa."

"Stupid boy! Anything that's not corn is a weed!" Papa's big hand came around to slap his head again. "Do them again now, and chop down the weeds, but leave the corn!"

Orgoru had tried, had really tried his best, and he had chopped down all the weeds—but a quarter of the corn, too.

There was no dinner for him, and his father beat him with a strap that night. He cried himself to sleep lying on his stomach.

He didn't have a hoe in his hands that fall, when the children came running after the grown-ups, who were tired from reaping and binding sheaves all day—but in spite of having done their share of binding, the children still had energy enough to run and shout.

The blow took Orgoru full in the back. He stumbled, nearly fell, but managed to catch his balance in only a few steps. He turned to see who had struck him, fighting down anger. . . .

Clyde grinned down at him, a head taller and two years older, with his friends laughing behind him. "Sorry, Orgoru," Clyde said. "I stumbled."

Orgoru scrambled to his feet, knowing what was coming, dreading it. . . .

The kick took him in the seat and sent him sprawling on his face. "Aw, now you stumbled! Get up, Orgoru! Can't you get up?"

Orgoru tried to stay down, knowing their rules, knowing they wouldn't hit him if he didn't stand up, but two of the boys yanked him to his feet, and they all took turns giving him a punch or two.

Finally they ran off; finally he heard the heavy tread, and looked up to see his father's face wrinkled in disgust. "Can't even fight back, can you? All right, come along home—but cowards get no dinner."

He had missed so many dinners that it was amazing he had grown up at all. It was completely unfair that he had become chubby—he hadn't eaten that much!

So Orgoru had grown up knowing that he was useless as a peasant. He had known it because his father growled at him for being too clumsy to throw a ball, for losing every fight, for always being the butt of every prank. He had struggled to please, tried harder and harder with every complaint, but no matter how hard he tried, his mother always found something wrong with what he had done, his father always demanded to know why he couldn't be like the other boys—until one night, whipped for knocking a loaf of bread onto the dirt floor, then denied his dinner for having shouted at them for the injustice, Orgoru went to bed weeping, feeling as though his little heart would break—and suddenly understood.

All at once it burst on him—why he was so clumsy at peasant's chores, why he couldn't even talk to the other children and be liked—because he *wasn't* like them! Wasn't of their kind! So unlike them indeed, that this man and woman couldn't possibly be his true parents! They didn't love him, they were ashamed of him, they behaved every day as though he were a burden they had to carry, but only grudgingly—so he couldn't actually be their child! His real mother and father must have left him with these surly grouches for some mysterious and important reason—and would come back for him someday!

Orgoru fell asleep that night hoping that they would come back soon, and wondering what they were really like. He mulled over the question whenever his mind had time free, and his mother soon took to scolding him for his daydreaming, too. But Orgoru didn't mind—he had found a much better world than hers, in his imagination. He daydreamed of parents who were wise and kind.

When puberty hit, and he began to notice how lovely some of the girls were, he shyly began to try to talk with them, but they only laughed, amused, or let him talk long enough to find something they could mock in his words. The other boys began to pick fights with him even more often, which always ended in disaster, for if he ran away, he was too slow because his legs were too short—they caught him and pummeled him all the worse.

Then Mayday came, and the boys stood in a line, waiting for the girls to each choose a boy for the dancing. The young men stood waiting, and one by one they went to step to the fiddle. Althea chose Burl the handsome with the boyish smile, her bosom friend Nan chose Arn of the broad shoulders and bulging muscles, their crony Seli chose Gori who won all the races, and so it went, the prettiest choosing the most handsome, the strongest, the most skilled.

Finally Orgoru remained standing alone and turned away quickly, for Ciletha was chatting and giggling with two older girls but glancing at him with concern, and he didn't want her choosing him out of pity. Truth to tell, he had no great wish to dance with her, either, for she was almost as plain as he, though not so misshapen.

Misshapen! Who was to say he was shaped wrong? So he had a long torso and short legs, whereas the rest of them had long shanks and short waists—what of it? He stumped up to the village pond and stood glaring at his reflection. Yes, his face was round where theirs were long; yes, he had a snub of nose where they had long, straight blades; yes, his eyes were too large for a man's but too small for a woman's, and dark brown where theirs were blue or green or gray—and yes, he was plump, but that didn't make him worse than they!

Then it was as though light exploded in his mind, and Orgoru suddenly understood. No, it didn't mean he was worse—they were! He was so different because he was so much better! After all, they were only peasants, all of them, but he had known for a long time that they who raised him were not his real parents! He must be of a higher station, the son of parents who were gentry at least, but more probably noblemen, such as the ones who figured in the stories grandmothers told their grandchildren, those who were lucky enough to have grandmothers.

Once he realized that, it all made sense. Of course his parents resented him—they knew what he really was! Of course he didn't fit in—he was different indeed! Of course none of these peasant girls would choose him, for he was so far above them that they couldn't even recognize him for what he was!

He turned away from the pond a new man, vibrating within at the wonder of it all, aching to tell someone—but of course, there was none he could speak to, not about this.

There would be, though. One day they would come back for him—or he would find out where they had gone, his parents.

Then he would go to them, and no silly law or magistrate's command would stop him!

He went back among the roistering, the drinking, the singing. The other boys shoved him, yanked the last tankard from before his reaching hand, sneered at him, mocked him, but he smiled up at them with an amazing new serenity. He didn't care what they did, these peasants, these lowborns. He knew what he really was, and one day he would know who!

CHAPTER 2

The huge golden disk glided down in the darkness, its outer edge revolving around a stationary center that held gun turrets, sensor dishes, ports—and people. It spun down into a meadow just beyond a forest, a few miles from a town whose lights had blinked out several hours before. It sat immobile for a few minutes as its guiding computer sampled the air, analyzing it to make sure there was enough oxygen for its passengers—and no toxic gases or microbes to which they weren't immune. The ship's edge spun more and more slowly until it hissed to a stop; then the ship extended a ramp, and two men came down, dressed in broad-shouldered jackets over bell-sleeved shirts, and balloon trousers gathered into high boots. If worse came to worst and some poacher saw them, he wouldn't think their clothing odd, though he might wonder about their transportation.

"The ruling class on this planet *would* wear robes," Dirk grumbled. "They're very awkward when it comes to action." He glanced down at his loose-fitting, square-shouldered jacket and equally loose-fitting trousers, both garments gathered tight at wrists or ankles. "At least the military dresses sensibly. A little extravagantly, but sensibly."

"Don't let the clothes worry you, Dirk," Gar said soothingly. "We'll probably wind up naked, filthy, and pretending to be madmen again, anyway."

"Well, it works on most planets," Dirk admitted. "I keep hoping, though, Gar, that we'll find a planet where they keep the mentally ill in decent housing of their own."

"If they did, we wouldn't need to be there," Gar returned. He gazed at the countryside about him. "It looks peaceful enough, and the people certainly have their physical needs fulfilled."

"Yeah, but once they're well-fed and well-housed, they have time to pay attention to other needs," Dirk sighed. "We're a very ungrateful species as a whole, Gar."

"Yes, we keep wanting unreasonable things like happiness and love and self-fulfillment," Gar said with a wry smile.

"No government can guarantee those."

"No, but the wrong kind of government can certainly block them." Gar took a firmer grip on the pike he carried as a staff. "Let's see which kind we're dealing with here, shall we?" He stepped down off the ramp. Dirk followed suit, and the metal walkway slid quietly back into the huge gleaming hull.

Gar pulled a locket from inside his jacket and said into it, "Lift off, Herkimer. Wait for us in orbit."

"Yes, Gar," the locket replied, and the huge golden disk rose slowly, then shot up into the night until it was lost among the stars—but the locket said, "I will keep you under surveillance whenever I can."

"Yes. Please do," Gar said. "After all, you never can tell when I might lose my communicator."

"Surely, Magnus. Good luck."

"Thank you, Herkimer. Enjoy the rest." Gar tucked the locket away, ignoring the difference between his birth-name and his professional name, and turned toward the forest.

"Lose your communicator?" Dirk scoffed. "What difference would that make? You were born with one!"

"Yes, but it's so demanding, sending thoughts on UHF frequencies," Gar said mildly. "Do you think we can find a road, Dirk?"

"There's a pathway over there that might lead to one." Dirk pointed. "You don't suppose we could land during the day sometime, do you?"

"Of course, if you enjoy attracting a great deal of attention."

"Uh . . . no, I think not." Dirk gave a somewhat theatrical sigh and asked, "Why do we do this, Gar? Why do we hunt down planets where the people are oppressed, just so we can go in and free them? What business is it of ours, anyway?"

"I have the perfect reason," Gar said, somewhat smugly. "After all, I'm an aristocrat, and our occupational disease is ennui. I'm fighting off boredom. What's your excuse?"

"Me?" Dirk looked up. "I'm an exile. You know that—you landed on my planet and linked up with me so you could start the revolution there!"

"Yes, but you're a *self*-exile," Gar corrected.

"Speak for yourself," Dirk countered, "and I think you do. Me, I was born a serf, you know that, and when the other escaped serfs helped me get away, they recruited me into their high-tech, space-cargo company, to spend my life the way they did—working from off-planet to free my fellow serfs. But once I gained some education and became part of the modern world, I lost touch with the people I'd been born among—and lost my home." He looked up with haunted eyes. "I have to find a new home now—and find a woman who's enough like me to fall in love with me, which isn't going to be easy—a lowborn lady of culture and education."

Gar nodded, eyes gentle with sympathy. "Which is more important, Dirk? The woman, or the home?"

"I suppose it comes to the same thing in the end. How about you?"

"I?" Gar shrugged and turned away, seeming suddenly very restless, though he took only a few steps. "I have a home, at least, but I have no purpose there—no woman for me, I found that out the hard way. Besides, I'd always live in my father's shadow."

"But you don't really think you'll find another home," Dirk said softly.

"I don't." Gar turned back, meeting Dirk's gaze. "I don't think I'll find another home, and I don't think I'll find a woman who can be gentle enough to trust but strong enough not to be afraid of me. But a man has to have some purpose in life, Dirk, and if I can't find love and can't rear children of my own, I can at least spend my days trying to free slaves and make it possible for them to find their true mates and be happy."

"As good a reason for staying alive as any," Dirk said, "and better than a lot I've heard." He grinned. "So we're just like boys hanging out on a street corner in a modern city, aren't we? Trying to find some way to pass the time while we wait for the girls to come by."

"I suppose." Gar smiled in spite of himself; Dirk's optimism was catching. "And as long as we're helping other people, we aren't wasting our time."

"They aren't going to thank us, you know."

"Yes, we found that out the hard way, didn't we? But gratitude doesn't really matter, does it?"

"Why, no," Dirk said. "I suppose all we really want is to feel we've put the time to good use."

Miles came panting up from the stream's ford, careful to walk on the gravel of the road that led down to it. Dogs might pick up his trail, but no one would see footprints—and the hounds would have a long time casting about for his scent, since he had waded and swum for almost a mile.

Now, though, every muscle screamed with fatigue, and his feet felt like lumps of lead, so hard did he have to strain to lift them. His head ached, and spells of dizziness took him now and again. He had jogged all night and traveled all day, alternating between wading, swimming, and walking the gravel of the riverbank. But there was no sound of pursuit—either no one in his village had noticed his absence, everyone thinking he was at some other chore, or the foresters were being uncommonly merciful, pretending to take even longer about finding his trail than was necessary. He had heard rumors that they would do that, if they thought the fugitive's cause right and just—and Salina's cousin was a forester. Still, it was only a matter of time before the thrill of the chase caught them up and, sympathetic or not, they would be hunting him in earnest.

They probably were already.

But he was so bone-tired and weary that he felt as though he couldn't take another step. The thought penetrated the murk in his brain enough to make him realize that he would have to sleep soon, or he wouldn't be able to run anymore—he would fall down where he stood, and lie unconscious till the dogs found him.

So, when he saw the haystack standing high in the field, he felt a surge of relief that washed him up onto its prickly sides and left him beached, to burrow his way in. With the last strands of consciousness leaving him, he pulled a few wisps of hay down to cover the hole he had made, then collapsed into sweet and total oblivion.

Gar and Dirk strolled down a broad road, lined with thick old trees that shaded the sides well. The traffic was light, but they were scarcely alone—there were two others going their way: a hundred feet behind, a woman driving a cart with a man walking beside it, and a hundred feet ahead, a lone man with a pack on his back and a staff in his hand. Both men wore trousers, scuffed boots, and smocks belted at the waist. The woman wore a long, dark blue skirt and a light blue blouse under a black shawl.

"Working men—farmers, at a guess," Dirk said. The others were so far apart that there was no chance of being overheard.

"I'd place the one ahead as being a tradesman of some sort," Gar mused. "No clay on his boots."

"Sharp eyes," Dirk said. Then, a little more loudly as another traveler passed them, "No, the storm clouds are too far ahead—it won't rain before sunset."

"Oh, I think it might," Gar said, equally loudly. "Stiff breeze in our faces. It'll bring the thunderheads sooner."

The carter looked up, startled, and frowned at them as he went by before he had to turn back to tend to his team of oxen.

"Not too hard saying what he is," Gar muttered. "Full-scale wagon crowded with barrels—he's a delivery boy for a vineyard."

"Or for the wine seller," Dirk said. "Of course, those barrels *could* hold ale."

"They could. At least we're both agreed he's not the merchant himself."

"Of course—not well-enough dressed." Dirk nodded at another man with a wagon, a hundred feet farther down the road and coming toward them. "Now, *he's* a merchant."

Gar looked; the man wore tight-fitting trousers and a tunic, like the carter, but his were clearly of better fabric and livelier color—deep blue for the trousers and light blue for the tunic. More importantly, he wore an open coat over them, and it was of brocade. "Yes, I'd say he's a bit more affluent, but still has to be on the road with a wagon. Besides, he has hirelings."

Two other wagons followed, each with a driver wearing the usual earth-toned trousers and belted tunic.

"O-ho! Here comes somebody important!" Dirk pointed.

Around a curve in the road ahead came a small closed carriage, square and Spartan, painted a somber black. Before it rode two men on horseback with another two behind, dressed alike in dark red jackets and trousers with broad-brimmed, flat hats of the same color. They carried spears stepped in sockets attached to their saddles and wore swords and daggers very obviously at their belts.

"Soldiers, wearing the livery Herkimer used as models for our costumes." Gar frowned. "Presumably, ours being brown only means we work for a different boss."

"Yes, but ours isn't here, and theirs is inside the carriage," Dirk pointed out. "This might be a good time to see what the backs of the roadside trees look like."

"I think we'd be a little obvious," Gar replied. "We'd better brazen it out. I hope they speak our language."

The thought hit Dirk with a shock. "My lord, we *did* come down here unprepared, didn't we?"

"Not hard, when we didn't have any information," Gar said dryly. "But their ancestors spoke Terran Standard, so there's no reason to think they don't."

"Yeah, and it'll give us a way of guessing how restrictive their culture is," Dirk said, smiling. "The worse their accent, the more permissive the culture—the closer to Standard, the more their authorities insist everything be done just right."

"We should be in an excellent position to study the authorities," Gar said, "considering who's in the coach."

As they passed, the soldiers saluted them. Each held his arm straight out to the side and bent up at the elbow, hand a flat blade. Gar and Dirk copied the gesture, careful to smile no more than the real soldiers did. As the coach passed, they caught a glimpse of a man in his thirties with a square black hat, and a robe that matched the color of his soldiers' livery. He had spectacles on his nose and was trying to study some papers in spite of the coach's lurching and swaying. Then the rear guards were saluting, Dirk and Gar were returning the salutes, and the coach was rumbling off down the road.

"Well, we passed the first test," Dirk sighed.

"Now we know how the local military salute works," Gar said. "Not much more than a ritualized wave of the hand, I'd say."

"I'll view that as a hopeful sign, if you don't mind. What do you think of the local ruling class?"

"Professional administrator, by the look of him—not a part-timer, like the merchants of Venice or the Athenian citizen-assembly."

"I think I prefer amateurs . . ."

"Oh, give this one the benefit of the doubt. At least he's probably trained for the job."

"Yeah, and has figured out how to hand it on to his son, definitely *not* his daughter. At least the amateurs don't have a vested interest in bloating the bureaucracy."

"You're being unfair," Gar chided. "One look at the man is scarcely enough proof to convict him of so many crimes."

"Why not? He's old enough to have children. And if he's a trained paper-pusher, he's part of a bureaucracy."

"Aren't you using a rather broad definition of 'bureaucracy' . . . ? Wait, what's this?"

The torrent of babble from the curve ahead had finally become loud enough to force itself on their attention.

"A crowd," Dirk said. "Don't look at me that way—somebody had to state the obvious. They don't sound threatening, anyway."

"No, rather happy—a holiday sound, in fact. Let's see what's going on."

They rounded the curve and saw peasants lining both sides of the road, chattering and gesturing to one another, smiling, bright-eyed, excited. Some had packs over their shoulders and were sharing food and drink with one another. There was a sprinkling of merchants, carters, and other wayfarers among them, laughing and sharing their own provisions.

"You were right," Dirk said, "it *is* a holiday. When does the parade start?"

"Let's join them and see if we can overhear anything." Gar stepped off the roadway, leaning on his staff and looking about with a gentle, interested smile. Dirk followed, growling, "Why do I feel conspicuous?"

The peasants glanced up, and conversation muted for a few minutes—benign smile or not, Gar was still a scary figure. But he offered no harm, only spoke quietly with Dirk—so quietly that none of them could hear—and the people went back to chatting with one another. Dirk could almost see Gar's ears prick up, and wondered what his own looked like—but he was hearing words that he recognized. Yes, there was an accent, broader vowels and lazier consonants, but he had no difficulty at all eavesdropping.

"I can understand them," Gar muttered.

"Me too," Dirk said. "That's not a good sign."

"No, not at all," Gar said, with a casualness that made Dirk's skin crawl. "It bespeaks a very rigid government, one that's stonily conservative."

That raised several interesting possibilities, none of which Dirk really wanted to think about at the moment. To put the unpleasant implications of this out of his mind, he paid attention to what the nearest people were saying.

"The Protector himself! What would bring *him* so far into the countryside?"

"I don't know, but they say he travels around when folk least expect it, to see that his officials do as he tells them and don't cheat."

"Cheat him, or other folk?" The woman who had asked the question grinned. "I know, I know—neither."

"But are they sure he's coming?" a carter asked, frowning. "How do they know?"

"A crier came riding, calling out to all to clear the road, for the Protector would be passing!"

"I *told* you we should have made an earlier start," Dirk growled. "We might have heard the leather-lungs ourselves."

"He must be riding quite far ahead," Gar said, surprised. "We've been on the road an hour already."

"Oh, he came through last night," one woman was telling the farmwife from the cart. "The Protector is kind enough to give us all a chance to see him."

"And mobilize public support by making sure there's a cheering throng all the way along," Dirk muttered.

Far down the road, trumpets sounded. The crowd oohed and aahed, but didn't start cheering yet.

"So much for the fanfare," Dirk said. "When do we get the overture?"

The trumpets sounded again, then again and again, each time closer. The oohing and aahing became louder and louder. Then horsemen appeared, trotting down the road and calling out, "Make way for the Protector! Make way for he who guides and judges all the Commonwealth!"

Guardsmen in dark blue livery followed on horseback, lances low to push back peasants who were beginning to strain toward the road. Behind them came a severe, black-and-silver open carriage. Two men in charcoal-gray gowns rode in the backward-facing seat, watching a lean, grave, unsmiling man who waved to the people, turning from side to side. He wore black robes with a huge, weighty silver chain, a flat, broad-brimmed black hat, and a black beard shot through with gray.

The people cheered. The people went crazy, throwing their caps in the air, waving frantically, crowding forward so that the two guards who followed the carriage had to ride by its rear wheels, their halberds down to push the crowd away. Dirk and Gar craned their necks with the rest, very interested to have a look at a high executive, or whatever he was, of this strange backward planet on which they had landed. The leading guards came up, their pikes low, and Dirk and Gar leaped back with the rest.

Then the carriage spun by, and for a second or two, the Protector was looking right at them, waving rather wearily. He looked away, turning to the other side of the road, and the rear guards came up. They passed, and the crowd moaned with disappointment—though whether it was at the briefness of the Protector's appearance, or at having to go back to work, Gar and Dirk couldn't guess. They certainly stretched the holiday out as long as they could, turning to one another and talking excitedly.

"He was so lofty, so commanding!" one woman burbled to another.

"But so weary!" her companion replied. "The poor man, with the weight of us all on his shoulders!"

"I have lived all my life waiting for this day," a man sighed, "and I shall tell my grandchildren of it!"

"Was he not grand to look upon?" a youth asked Dirk, eyes glowing.

"Very impressive," Dirk replied. "You've never seen him before, then."

"I?" The youth laughed. "I haven't even seen twenty summers, sir! It would have been rare good fortune for me to have seen him!"

An older man looked keenly at them. "But you have seen him before, have you?"

"One of the benefits of being in arms," Dirk answered, smiling, "and of being sent on missions now and again."

Vague as the answer was, it seemed to satisfy the man—perhaps because it was so vague that he could read into it whatever he wanted. He was turning away to exchange exclamations with a friend, when a clarion voice called, "Hear ye, hear ye! Listen to the magistrate!"

The companions turned and looked. A man in a dark red robe stood in the center of the road, hands folded across his stomach and almost hidden by his long, full sleeves. He was young, perhaps in his late twenties, but already had an air of authority that seemed to assume no one would even think of disobeying. Gradually, the crowd quieted, and the magistrate called out, "You have seen, good people! It has been a wonderful morning for us all, for rarely indeed are we fortunate enough to see the man who is Protector of all this land, Reeve of all reeves, Magistrate of all magistrates! Treasure the memory, and speak of it to one another, the more surely to engrave it on your hearts! But the time for gazing is past, and the time for your work has come again! Go now, to your homes and fields and shops! Talk still about the delight of it all, but go!"

The buzz of conversation started up again, and the people turned away, some back into the fields that bordered the road but most away down the cobblestones, presumably to the lanes that led to their villages.

"I think we'd better go with them," Gar said.

"Yes, as far from that red robe as possible," Dirk agreed. "I smell authority, and I'd just as soon avoid it until I know whether or not the aroma is poisonous."

They set off, quickly working their way into the center of the throng. The magistrate's guards glanced briefly at the tall figure in the brown livery, but didn't seem to think it all that unusual, for they turned back to attending their young master as he mounted a tall roan. They set off down the road, and were soon far enough away for Dirk and Gar to feel safe. They dropped back from the peasant throng until they were out of earshot.

"So," Dirk said, "it seems we lucked into getting a look at the chief executive after all."

"Yes, but is he only the executive, or the whole government?" Gar asked.

"They did call him 'Magistrate of all magistrates'," Dirk said, "but they didn't say anything about who enforces the laws."

"I don't think he's a king of any sort," Gar said, "though he might serve one."

"Could be, but I think the herald would have mentioned that among his other titles," Dirk said thoughtfully. "Apparently the guy in the red robe is his local representative."

"Yes—very young to be a magistrate, don't you think?" Gar asked. "I thought the office usually went to a minor local aristocrat, or a businessman who has managed to build up enough of a fortune to build himself a big house and spread a few bribes."

Dirk shrugged. "Maybe he's just finished law school, and this is his internship."

"That seems unlikely," Gar said slowly, "but the idea of having finished some sort of training does strike a bell."

"Let's just hope it's not the alarm," Dirk replied. "You know, I'm beginning to feel a little too visible in this soldier outfit."

"So am I, but we don't know if it would be safe to travel in any other disguise," Gar said. "We need information, Dirk, in a bad way."

"Yes, and I know what that means," Dirk sighed.

Gar nodded. "A local, preferably one who's in trouble with the authorities for the right reasons."

"Yes, for doing what his conscience tells him when the magistrate tells him not to. If we don't find one, can we declare this planet to be well-governed, and leave?"

Gar was silent for the next few paces, then said, "The Protector did seem to be very popular—but that might have been simply because he was the head of the government, and a rarity. Still, if the only outlaws we find are the kind who have no conscience, or are just out for themselves no matter who gets hurt—well, yes, I suppose that will be proof enough."

Dirk loosed a huge sigh of relief.

CHAPTER 3

The youth dashed from cottage to cottage, hammering on the door and calling, "A minstrel! A minstrel! Come and hear!"

Orgoru looked up from the cane chair seat he was weaving—badly, his mother was sure to tell him—with his heart hammering. A minstrel! News of the outside world, songs of the great days of old! But Orgoru couldn't let his fellow villagers see how excited he was—they mocked him so often for his plumpness, his moon-face, and his clumsiness, but most of all for his fumbling attempts at conversation and his unerring knack for always saying the wrong thing, that the only way left for him to have a shred of dignity was to seem bored with everything that went on in his village, even though, in his heart, he yearned for Althea, the brightest and prettiest of the girls, for her sparkling laugh and bright eyes, for her sheer delight in life that surely must catch up any man who was lucky enough to win her favor.

But she had mocked him too, and scorned him. They all had, all the young folk of his own generation, and most of the elders—even some of the children! So he ambled nonchalantly toward the village center, even though the shouts of surprise and bursts of laughter told him that the minstrel had already begun to tell the news, and in a way most entertaining, too. Besides, he told himself, he didn't really care what happened in the world today. All that really mattered was the singing, the glorious stories of the days of old, of brave knights in shining armor, of tournaments and quests and beautiful princesses to rescue. By the time he came to the village square, he believed it himself.

And he was in time! As he came up, he saw the minstrel swing his lute from his back and begin to pluck it. He watched between the beefy shoulders of two other young men, Clyde and Dale—but Clyde glanced at him, made a face, and nudged Dale, who looked up, saw Orgoru, grinned, and stepped closer to Clyde, shoulder to shoulder, blocking the troubadour from his sight. Orgoru ground his teeth, but managed a look of disdain and stubbornly refused to give them the satisfaction of seeing him move about, trying for a look around them or for a better place among the other people—who would only do the same, anyway. Orgoru knew from bitter experience that everyone would deliver the riotous joke of blocking his sight, unless Ciletha or one of the other, plainer girls took pity on him and pulled him in to share her looking-place—which would be even more embarrassing. Besides, Orgoru knew that their motives weren't just pity—they were worried about marrying, and thought any husband would be better than none. Orgoru couldn't bring himself to accept either reason for their friendship—both were too humiliating: pity and being last choice.

So he stayed where he was, pretending not to notice that Clyde and Dale had blocked his view. After all, with a minstrel, the music was what mattered—and even more, the words! He held his place, and listened.

"Prince Arthur dwelt, unknown, obscure," the minstrel began, and Orgoru's heart leaped.

"Sir Ector and his good wife raised the lad from a babe with their own son Kay, and he grew to be a fine, strapping youth. Now and again the wizard Merlin came to teach him, and to bring some hint of what passed in the great world outside—but how was Arthur to know that the slain king of whom Merlin spoke was his own father, that the lost prince of legend was himself?

"At last the wizard came with news of a tournament. . . ."

Orgoru listened, unable to see the minstrel, but with his head ringing as he heard how Sir Kay had insisted on going to the Christmas tournament, and Arthur had gone as his squire, heard how they had come to Glastonbury and seen the sword locked in the stone to prove which man was rightful King of England. The lilting voice told him how Kay had forgotten to bring his sword, and Arthur, in a hurry to arm Kay in time for the joust, had pulled the sword from the stone instead—and been acclaimed King of all England!

The minstrel sang on, but Orgoru turned away, his head ringing, dazed with the wonder of it.

"Can't see, Orgoru?" Dale gibed. He had been watching for signs of defeat. "Aw, too bad!"

"Want to sit on our shoulders?" Clyde offered.

But Orgoru scarcely heard them—though he did hear one last minstrel's verse:

"He built his court, to withstand time,
And for all courts be paradigm!"

Light exploded within Orgoru for the second time, and he staggered, nearly falling. He caught hold of a sapling in time to hold himself up, not even noticing the mocking laughter that rose behind him—for he knew now who he was! Not only what, but who! Like Arthur, he was a prince raised in secret, hidden among the common folk until he could understand his true nature, discover his true destiny! The minstrel himself had just told him his name—he was the Prince of Paradime!

He walked around the pond slowly until his legs were no longer weak, his breath no longer ragged, the light in his mind dimmed enough for him to notice other things. What wizard was this minstrel, this herald of destiny, who had brought him this understanding? Suddenly, Orgoru felt a clawing need to hear the man's voice again.

As he neared the knot of listeners once more, he heard an older man scoff, "A city in the forests? You tell wild tales indeed!"

"I should think so, too," the minstrel replied, "but the man who told me swore he had seen it himself—stone towers rising above the treetops, and beyond them, turrets even higher!"

"But who would build a walled city inside a forest?" one of the older men objected. "Wouldn't the forest be wall enough?"

"Ah!" The minstrel held up a forefinger. "But what if they built the city on an open plain, so long ago that the forest has grown up about it?"

A murmur of awe went through the crowd, at the notion of buildings so old—but a grandfather called, "Nonsense! Could they have been such poor householders that they let the woods grow to cover their fields?"

"No," said the minstrel, "if they were alive."

It took a minute or two for the significance of his words to sink in, but when it did, a murmur of fear went through the crowd—the delicious thrill of fear that doesn't threaten—and a frisson of superstitious awe. "Do you say it's deserted?" a woman asked.

"Not 'deserted,' exactly." The minstrel's voice sank low. "For the man who told me of it camped by its walls that night, and swears he heard thin voices, distant laughter, even music so faint he wondered if he had heard it at all."

A moan of delighted terror ran through the crowd. "Do you say they are ghosts?" the grandfather asked.

"Perhaps. Who knows?" The minstrel affected disdain. "He didn't look, after all, for the walls were too high to climb. But he heard, he heard. Who knows? Perhaps the lords and ladies who lived in that city in its proud youth dwell there yet, alive and deathless!"

"Impossible!" the grandfather scoffed.

"Ghosts," somebody said with full assurance, and the word ran through the crowd like a ripple: "Ghosts! Ghosts!"

"Ghosts of princes and princesses," the minstrel agreed, his voice low and thrilling, hand gesturing to show them invisible royalty. "Ghosts of kings and queens! And at night they come out to feast on phantom food and listen to enchanted music, to dance their airy rounds and court one another with wraithlike grace."

The murmur shivered, and so did the crowd that made it.

But Orgoru didn't shiver; instead, his eyes glowed. He listened through the tale, hanging on every word the minstrel said, drinking each in and letting them all together build a picture of courtly refinement, of beautiful and gallant people, in his mind. But when the minstrel was done and paid, and the crowd, disappointed that the delights must end, went off to their beds, Orgoru turned away with fire in his eyes and hope singing in his heart.

"Why are you so excited, Orgoru?"

Orgoru looked up, startled. Could one of these village girls at last have realized the excellence of his hidden qualities? But he was massively disappointed; it was only Ciletha, plain and skinny—the only village maiden to treat him with civility, even friendliness. If only Althea could have seen him so! But he was grateful for kindness, whatever its source. Ciletha was, after all, the only person in the village with whom he could share his thoughts, though he didn't dare chance his secrets even with her. "Who wouldn't be excited by such a tale, Ciletha?"

"No one, but with the rest of us, the excitement goes when the tale is done," Ciletha said. "Why are you still filled with fire, Orgoru? I've never seen you like this!"

Orgoru looked around in one quick glance, to see if anyone was close enough to overhear. "Anyone else would think I was crazy. . . ." He turned back to Ciletha. "You're the only one I would tell—but you have to promise not to tell anyone else." What did it matter if she did, though? By sunrise, he'd be gone!

"I promise." Ciletha's eyes were wide and wondering.

Orgoru took a deep breath and plunged. "I've always known I'm better than these cloddish people in this village, Ciletha. In fact, I know my real parents must have been people of quality!"

Ciletha halted, staring at him in fright. "Your real parents? But, Orgoru . . ."

"You don't think these shallow fools could be my true mother and father, do you? No!" The words came in a rush now. "They must have been a magistrate and his wife at least, who had to hide me here out of fear of their enemies! But even that shrew and her husband don't know what I really am!"

"Orgoru!" Ciletha gasped. "To say such things about your parents!" Then curiosity overcame her: "What are you?"

"Tonight, listening to the minstrel, it all became clear to me—I'm a prince, sent to be raised in secret where my parents' enemies would never think to look for me—among peasants! He even told me my proper name—the Prince of Paradime!"

"He did?" Ciletha stared. "When did he say that?"

"Early on, when he had just begun to talk! And he must be a courier in disguise, sent by my true family, for he even told me where to find my own kind—in the Lost City in the forest!"

"The Lost Place!" Ciletha gasped. "But Orgoru—he said it was filled with ghosts!"

"Oh, that was for the lack-wits." Orgoru didn't even try to hide his contempt. "The courier knew full well that those were no ghosts the woodcutter had heard, knew that if he had climbed a tree by that wall, he would have seen actual lords and ladies dancing!"

"How could he have known that?" Ciletha asked, eyes huge.

"Does that matter?" Orgoru demanded with a flash of irritation. "He knew, or should have—that's enough. Of that I'm sure, completely sure! That story of a man who overheard the ghosts—bah! I'm not taken in, like the rest of these clod-heads. It wasn't a woodcutter who found the city and heard the lords and ladies—it was the minstrel himself, and they brought him in and made him their courier to me! I've heard that tale he told before, only it was about the Little People who are supposed live within the Hollow Hills, and now and again take a human prisoner to watch their feasting and dancing, then give him so much wine that he falls asleep and wakes up outside the hill twenty years later! No, I'm no fish, to take such bait and let it hook my soul! I know what I know!"

"Why, the tales *are* somewhat alike," Ciletha said in surprise, "though the minstrel didn't say he'd gone into the city and seen the gh—them."

"He couldn't very well, could he? Letting everyone know why he was really here! No, he came to give me the message in secret, and knows I've found it! I'm going to find that Lost City, Ciletha, and be with my own kind of people at last!"

"Will the magistrate give you leave?" she asked in wonder.

"Magistrate? Bah! What right has he to interfere with a prince born?"

"Orgoru!" Ciletha gasped. "You don't mean to run away?"

"I shall escape the prison of this village!" Orgoru shouted. "They have no right to hold me! I'll go this very night!"

"But the punishment—" Ciletha protested.

"Punishment? Bah! What matters their chain and labor when I've endured it all my life? Surely they can't hold a prince of the blood royal, or find him if he doesn't wish it! No, I must go now—now, for the magistrate and his hounds won't dream I'd go so quickly!"

"Tonight?" Ciletha stood a moment in shock, then all at once threw herself upon him, clutching Orgoru's tunic and pleading, her face turned up to his. "Oh, Orgoru, take me with you! I would never have the courage to go by myself, but with you I dare! Maybe you're right, maybe you do have some charm that will keep you safe from them!"

"You come with me?" Orgoru stared, taken aback. "But, Ciletha, this is your home, you've been happy here!"

"Not since Father died last winter!"

"Yes, the poor soul, pining away for your mother!" Orgoru muttered. "Why, he didn't outlive her by a year!" They'd been one of the very few couples he'd seen who were really, truly, in love.

"But now that he's dead, the magistrate has warned me that I'm going to have to marry soon, or he'll choose a husband for me!"

"Choose one for you!" The faces of Tan and Bork flashed before Orgoru's eyes—the ugliest boys in the village, who would surely never find wives by themselves. "No, Ciletha, that mustn't be!"

"The magistrate says Father's house is too big for one, woman alone, and that no woman can be trusted with his wealth—but I know that none of the boys are attracted to me for myself. Oh, they treat me politely, but only because Althea and Shara are my friends, and all the boys hope to win them someday."

"But they'd marry you if the magistrate made them, and gladly, too, since house and money would go with you." *Yes,* he thought, *then treat you like a dog they had to keep but didn't like.* Gentle Ciletha, kind Ciletha, shackled to a brute who would make her life one long torment!

"I don't want them!" It was almost a wail—would have been if Ciletha had dared raised her voice. "I don't want any man who doesn't love me! They can have the house, they can have the money, so long as they leave me my heart!" Her hands tightened in his tunic again. "Oh, please, Orgoru, take me with you! I've been aching to leave the village—there has to be some life better than this! Ever since the magistrate told me I'd have to marry a man who despises me, I've been in a panic to escape! But I've been terrified to try—even if the bailiff and his foresters didn't catch me, there are highwaymen and forest bandits—and men who'd be honest enough at home, but who might want to take advantage of a woman traveling alone. With you beside me, though, only the outlaws would be a threat. I'd have no chance by myself, but with you I just might!"

Well, what could Orgoru say? The one person in the village who had been willing to talk with him, to be his friend, to see some good in him? How could he leave her to misery? "Well, two might have a better chance than one."

"Oh, thank you, Orgoru!" Ciletha threw her arms about him and hugged him close. "Oh, thank you, thank you! You won't be sorry!"

Orgoru put an arm around her, and fervently hoped he wouldn't be sorry indeed—for two might stand a better chance than one alone, but they also might stand worse.

The dogs bayed in Miles's dream, huge dogs with flabby dewlaps, long ears, and sad eyes, sad that they must chase the fox, though their voices rang with the delight of the hunt. The poor fox ran panting and trembling with weariness, blown and on the verge of collapse, but it didn't wear a fox's long nose, it wore Miles's face, and as he looked back at the dogs, he saw that the foremost bore the magistrate's face, contorted with anger, mouth yawning wide to show long, pointed teeth. . . .

With a shudder, Miles came awake, thrashing about in panic for a minute, then realizing that the firm walls about him were made of hay. He went limp, burying his face in his arm, trying to put the nightmare aside, but it wouldn't rest, the dogs' howling still echoed in his head. . . .

And in the rest of the world too. He finally realized that he was really hearing them, though their voices were faint and distant. The hunt! He scrambled out of the haystack, heart thudding, and saw with a sinking heart that he had slept the night through, and that the sun burned on the horizon. It was dawn, very early dawn, but he was lost if he couldn't find some fortress, some safe bolt-hole for hiding. He set off down the gravel path, pulse thudding in his ears, hoping that he would come to a main road, where his scent might be lost in the thousands that lay upon the stones, where he himself might find a crowd in which to lose himself. . . .

He found it. Panting and disheveled but with his staff still in his hand, he hurried down the cobbles, trying to catch up with a dozen travelers ahead.

Then he heard the voice behind him. "Slow down, lad! What's your hurry?"

The voice sounded so friendly that Miles looked back, hope leaping high—

—and falling into a pit. The friendly face topped a soldier's livery, and the huge man beside him wore the same. Miles turned and ran.

"Ho! We mean no harm!" But if they didn't, why were the heavy boots thudding closer and closer behind, why was the huge heavy hand catching Miles's shoulder, whirling him about—

"If you're in trouble with the law, lad, you may be just what we're looking for," the giant rumbled, looking down at him with compassion. "My friend and I aren't quite what we seem—in fact, we're not soldiers at all."

"If you're running for the right reason, we'll be your friends," the smaller man said—smaller, but a good head taller than Miles himself. "Call me Dirk. Why're you fleeing?"

"I won't marry Salina!" Miles panted. "I'd rather hang!"

"They're going to force you to marry a woman you don't love?" Dirk stared. "What did you do to her?"

"Nothing! But she doesn't want me, and I don't want her!"

"So they ordered the two of you to marry anyway?" The giant frowned. "Who ordered you?"

"Our magistrate, of course! If he catches me, he'll drive me to hard labor until my spirit's broken and I marry Salina anyway!"

"Even though she doesn't want it, either," Dirk said grimly. He nodded at his huge companion. "This is Gar."

"I—I am Miles, sir," Miles stammered.

"Only Miles?" Gar asked. "No last name?"

"Of course not, sir." Miles was astounded that the man should even ask—everyone had a public name, but only magistrates and their families had private names, and only other magistrates knew them.

"How close are the ones who are chasing you?" Dirk demanded.

"Listen! You can hear them!"

The two false soldiers stood still, heads cocked, eyes blank, listening.

"Hounds," Gar pronounced, "but still far away. That gives us time. Are you sure they're after you, though, lad?"

"Who else?" Miles asked, honestly bewildered.

Gar shrugged. "Anyone breaking the law."

"Who would be so desperate as me?"

"You don't have to be really desperate to break the law," Dirk pointed out.

Miles just stared at him as though he were insane. Hadn't he seen men punished, flogged to bloody meat, only for a barbed joke about the magistrate?

"All right, so you do have to be desperate," Dirk said

impatiently, "but are we really close enough to your home for those hounds to know you? Okay, their noses would, but how about their handlers?"

"What matter? Whether they recognize me or not, I have no travel permit. They'd know me for a criminal by that alone, and hold me while they sent messengers to all the magistrates in the county."

"Travel permit, huh?" Dirk exchanged a glance with Gar, then turned back to Miles. "They don't exactly leave you a sporting chance, do they?"

"Sporting?" Miles was amazed that he could still laugh, no matter how bitterly. "Yes, it's sport for the bailiff and his men, all right. Not for me."

"Oh, I think it could be a great deal of fun, losing yourself so thoroughly that they can't find you." Gar caught Miles about the shoulders and turned him away, toward a barn a hundred feet off the road. "Come, lad."

"A whole village uses that!" Miles protested. "They'll see us for sure!"

"Not a soul will notice," Gar promised. "Dirk, did you bring the brandy?"

"On this early a world? Of course!" Dirk pulled a bottle out of his pouch and turned to walk backward after them, sprinkling the ground where they had walked.

"The dogs . . ." Miles warned.

"Believe me, once they sniff that brandy, they won't notice your spoor at all," Gar assured him.

A breeze blew Miles a sample, and he saw the truth of what Gar said. It smelled sweet and strong, of almonds and summer. Sweaty as Miles was, he didn't think the dogs would notice anything but that lovely scent. He led the two strangers toward the barn.

They followed Miles, having a silent conversation—for although Dirk could not read minds, he knew that Gar could. He stared at the giant and tapped the side of his head to show he was giving Gar permission to read his thoughts. Gar gave an infinitesimal nod, the silent equivalent of *Receiving. Go ahead.*

Aloud, Dirk said, "I'm tired of stewed jerky. Think we can catch something fresh for dinner?" Silently, he thought, *We've caught us a fish—but can we trust him?*

Gar gave another abbreviated nod while he said, "I think there's time. Of course, we don't know what's in the streams around here. You can't tell if a fish is any good until you eat it."

You can't tell either, huh?

"I'm willing to try a new fish," Gar said, "if it seems to have all the qualities we need. After all, if it's the same kind of fish you've caught before, it's probably just as good. Bass are bass."

Yeah, we've teamed up with peasants on the run before, and they've proved trustworthy, Dirk thought back, *and this one does seem to have the qualities we're looking for—enough courage to run away on a matter of principle, and enough intelligence to avoid capture. No way to say if he can be a good leader, of course, except by watching him. But trustworthy? We can't know until we've tried him—and after all, I suppose he's wondering the same thing about us.*

Gar smiled and nodded again. "Fish should never trust anglers."

Right now, we're the best thing that could have happened to him, Dirk mused. *Pure self-interest will keep him looking out for us.*

"Trusting or not, the fish still gives in to temptation and strikes at the bait," Gar said. "Selfishness is very predictable."

But you can never be sure what an altruist will do, huh? Well, you should know. But it goes beyond that—I get the overall feeling that he's a good man, solid and dependable, and on the wrong side of the law only because his bosses pushed him too far.

Gar's nod was emphatic.

You thought so, too, huh? Well, I always did consider myself a good judge of character. In fact, I had a course in it—kind of necessary, when you're trained as a spy.

"But when you're fishing, you read only physical signs,"

Gar said, "the rock where a fish might hide, the branch shadowing a deep pool." ·

Or when the fish is human, the look in the eyes, the twist of the mouth, the set of the shoulders and spine. Nonverbal language, huh? But you can read thoughts. Thought you didn't do that without permission, or a really pressing need.

Gar only smiled at him.

Oh, Dirk thought. *Sizing up potential allies is a pressing need, huh? Of course, but how deeply do you read him?*

"I always did enjoy watching the play of the light upon the water," Gar told him, "but I like to watch the fish that move beneath the surface too. Of course, the water is rarely so clear that you can see the bottom without effort."

So you go past the surface thoughts to what the person's really thinking, but you don't probe down to the intimate secrets and the buried memories that make them what they are? Dirk nodded. *Well, I suppose that's deep enough to figure out whether or not a man's a police spy—unless he's deliberately trying to deceive you.*

"We really should stop talking and start baiting a hook," Gar told him. "Grilled trout, perhaps. Plain, simple, honest fare is sometimes best."

Okay, I get the point, Dirk thought. *Miles looks to be a plain, simple, honest farm boy. But I've known some farm boys who were very good at looking honest when they were really devious, Gar.* Aloud, he said, "The only honest trout is a grilled trout."

"They're honestly greedy," Gar pointed out. "There's something immensely honest in a fish taking the bait."

Our protection is the bait, hm? Well, I suppose we can grill Miles slowly, over a period of days. If he's hiding something, it'll show sooner or later. He gave Gar a narrow glance. *At least, if you're listening with your mind as well as your ears.*

Gar gave him a look of withering scorn.

Oh, Dirk thought. *You always do. Well, I suppose we all do, metaphorically at least.*

Gar shook his head.

Not even metaphorically? Well, I have to admit I've known a lot of people who hear without listening. Aloud, Dirk said, "Okay, fish it is. But do we really have time to bait a hook and wait?"

"We may have to use a net," Gar admitted.

Miles wondered why the two men took so long trying to decide whether or not to go fishing. For his own part, the decision was simple—if you were hungry and had time, you fished. Of course, they didn't have time right now—unless the fish bit quickly.

It also never occurred to him to wonder whether or not the two men were trustworthy—he knew they weren't. They were strangers, weren't they? But for some reason, they seemed to think it was in their interest to protect him, and he would have been a fool to turn down such assistance. After all, there was something in it for them—he could tell they really were foreigners by their accents, and really did need help in local customs. But he wasn't about to trust them farther than he had to—unless he happened to travel with them long enough to get to know them, which wasn't likely.

They came into the barn, and sure enough, a villager was harnessing his ox to a plow. Miles shrank back, trying to keep Gar between himself and the peasant, but the man didn't even look up until Dirk stepped up on his far side and said, "Good morning, good man."

The peasant looked up, surprised—and his back was to Gar and Miles. "Good morning, guardsman." His tone had so much deference as to be almost dread—no wonder, Miles thought, for reeve's guards might be sent to do anything, even to arrest innocent peasants for nothing worse than wild talk when drunk.

"Am I on the road to Innisfree?" Dirk asked.

"Innisfree? Never heard of it!" The peasant frowned. "Did your reeve truly tell you it lay in this direction?"

"Down the east road, he said, but we seem to have taken a wrong turning." Dirk frowned darkly. "Are you sure you've never heard of the town?"

"Never." The peasant's eyes widened with apprehension; he sidled around to put the ox between them.

"Ask among your friends, then, will you? See if any of them have any notion of the way. I'll wait here for you to send word."

"Indeed, sir! I'll see to it straightaway!" The peasant ducked his head in a sort of bow and called to his ox, shaking the reins. It slogged into motion, ambling out of the barn. The peasant followed it, plow rolling ahead of him, with an air of relief.

"Innisfree?" Gar asked from the shadows of the hayloft.

"Why not?" Dirk shrugged and started climbing the ladder. "I heard an argument about how to get there, once. Seemed like a good place for getting someone confused."

"I suppose it would be," Gar agreed.

"Now what do we do, sir?" Miles asked in a half-whisper.

"We wait," Gar told him, "and we lie quietly."

Dirk came to lie down near them. All three lay back and rested as the day aged and the heat grew. A fly came buzzing to see what they were and, finding them unappetizing, buzzed off. After a while, they heard footsteps below, and a quavering voice called, "Guardsman?" It waited, then called again, "Sir guardsman? Reeve's man?" It waited a longer while, then sighed with relief. "He didn't wait."

"Praise heaven," the peasant's voice replied. "I wasn't looking forward to telling him we couldn't find his precious Innisfree."

"What do we do now?" the younger voice asked.

"Forget about him and get back to work," the peasant said with the firmness of experience. "Don't borrow trouble, lad— you'll earn enough of it in your own time."

"What's that?" the younger asked.

They were both silent, and Miles could hear the dogs, much nearer now, and coming even closer quickly.

"Hounds," the peasant said with a shudder. "Pity the poor soul they're chasing! Come, lad, let's hurry back to our field! Remember, we know nothing!"

Their footsteps faded away. Trembling and hollow-bellied,

Miles nonetheless couldn't help himself. He squirmed over to the wall and peeked through a gap between boards. Behind him, he heard Gar say, "Sorry, Dirk. I've developed doubts about the government here after all."

"Oh, that's all right," Dirk answered with a martyred sigh. "So have I."

CHAPTER 4

The moon gave enough light for Orgoru to steal from hut to hut with an eye out for the Watch. Admittedly, in so small a village as this, the Watch was only one man, but he was almost as old and sour as the magistrate he served; both plainly resenting having been sent to so small a village toward the ends of their careers, and were therefore all the more likely to vent their spleens on young folk they might catch trying to slip away to a greater chance of happiness.

On the other hand, being as old as he was, the Watch wasn't likely to be able to catch them, either.

Orgoru tripped and stumbled twice on his way to Ciletha's cottage, but fortunately didn't make too much noise either time. He walked past her kitchen window slowly, and that was signal enough; she was waiting and watching, and slipped out the door only moments after she saw him pass, her pack over her shoulder. He gave her hand a squeeze, then turned his face toward the forest.

Moonbeams managed to pierce the canopy here and there, so the gloom wasn't quite complete. They felt safe enough to talk, and Orgoru said, "We have to make sure we don't leave them a clear trail to follow."

"How shall we do that?" Ciletha quavered.

"Why, as folk of high station should do—by taking the high road, and leaving the low road to the lowly!" Orgoru reached up to a tree with low branches and clambered up, ungraceful and panting, but up. "You now!" He reached down and took Ciletha's hand.

"I'll fall," she objected.

"We aren't going high enough for it to hurt you much," Orgoru explained, "and we'll go very carefully. Come now—or would you rather marry Bork?"

Ciletha shuddered and reached up.

They went very carefully indeed, edging out along the lowest limb until they were able to climb into another tree, then inching along its lowest branch to a third.

"We'll never get very far," Ciletha protested.

"True, but they'll never find us, either," Orgoru pointed out. "Their hounds won't be able to catch our scent, up here."

Finally they came to a tree that overhung a brook, and Orgoru passed his pack to Ciletha while he dropped down into the water. Since it didn't come above his shins, he reached up and called, "First drop our packs, then drop down yourself!"

Ciletha seemed glad enough to do that, surprisingly. They splashed off together, making much faster progress than they had before—until Ciletha caught Orgoru's arm and pulled back, pointing with a trembling finger. Looking where she indicated, he saw the glowing coals of a campfire, and near it, a figure wrapped in a blanket.

Ciletha put her lips next to his ear. "We must slip far from him!"

"No," Orgoru breathed back. "I see no dogs—and he's left his clothing in a pile!"

"What of it?" Ciletha asked, frowning.

"It has his scent! If we wear clothing like that, the dogs won't know who to chase! Come now, stay quiet while I steal away!"

Ciletha almost reached to pull him back as he slipped off, but held her hand, heart pounding. It was a bright idea, far brighter than she would have expected of Orgoru—but the dear boy was so clumsy, so fumble-fingered, that he was bound to wake the forester and bring down his wrath. Moving silently, Ciletha followed him and caught up the nearest stick of wood for a club. Orgoru was all she had now, and she wasn't about to let the forester take him from her.

But she didn't need the stick. Amazingly, Orgoru managed to be deft for once in his life. He found a long stick and lay flat at the edge of the firelight, reaching in to pull the forester's clothes to him one piece at a time. Holding the whole pile under an arm, he turned away to creep off into the night, back to the brook. Ciletha joined him again, heart pounding, but they were a hundred yards downstream before she dared talk. "How clever you were, Orgoru!"

"Why, thank you." She could almost see him expand in the darkness. "I did manage it pretty well, didn't I?"

"But shouldn't you have left him your clothes? The poor man will be naked!"

"Then let him go bare," Orgoru said grimly. "The longer I'd stayed near, the greater the chance he'd have wakened—and If I'd left him my clothes, I might as well have told him who did the stealing. This way, he just might put it down to a badger or a bear, and thank the Protector for his life."

"Wise," she said slowly, "but I feel sorry for the poor man."

"Would he have felt sorry for you once the magistrate told him to catch you?" Orgoru demanded, then answered his own question. "Yes, he might have felt very sorry for you, but he'd have chased you anyway. Besides, it's not as though he was hurt, Ciletha." He halted in a patch of moonlight, looking about him. "We've come far enough. Let's change clothes now."

He gave her the forester's boots, but they were way too big, so he had to settle for cutting the shirt in two and tying it over her own shoes. He wore the leggings and the boots himself, and together they slipped off down a gametrail, hoping the forester's clothes would cover their own scents.

The hounds bayed, closer and closer, and Miles, looking through the crack between the two boards, saw them come trotting down the road, their handler holding one leash in each hand and trotting himself, to stay near them. Behind him marched six men dressed in brown and green, with a seventh behind them who wore maroon, with a hip-length robe and chain of office—the bailiff of Miles's hometown with half a dozen foresters. Miles stiffened, and Dirk hissed, "Company?"

"Be ready for drastic measures," Gar muttered.

Surprised, Miles glanced at him, and saw him pull a piece of right-angled wood from his shirt—then two pieces of wood that tapered on the ends. He turned back to the spyhole, suddenly thinking he didn't want to know what Gar was going to do with the strange objects. He heard clicking and slithering noises behind him, and knew Dirk was doing whatever Gar was, too. He couldn't look, though—he was fascinated by the hounds trotting a hundred feet away. They came to the pathway to the barn and stalled, milling about, their voices turning querulous. Miles held his breath and hoped.

The hounds cast about in larger and larger circles, but their barking stayed confused. The foresters called to one another, growing angry and frustrated—but they kept their hounds where they were, sniffing in an expanding spiral.

"They'll hit our trail sooner or later." Gar rose and went to the ladder. "Time for a bit of misdirection."

"Stay where you are," Dirk told Miles, "and don't worry— we've confused harder cases than those guys."

Miles stared, speechless, as they scrambled down the ladder, then ran for the barn's back door. They slowed to an easy stroll as they went through. He spun back to the crack between the two boards and stared, watching. It seemed a year before Gar and Dirk ambled into view, and when they did, they came from far off to his left. They had circled around to come from the trees along a stream that curved through the pasture. Dirk called out and waved; the foresters looked up, then turned and waited for him, frowning. As they came closer, the hunters looked them up and down and seemed to relax a little. The bailiff stepped forward, fists on hips and chin thrust out. Miles held his breath; with the bailiff come himself to lead the foresters in pursuit of the fugitive, it was no wonder they hadn't let the search lapse. Still, he had to admit they had dawdled as much as they could, to give him a decent lead.

As Gar and Dirk came closer, the bailiff called out, "Which reeve do you serve, and why have you come?"

The two companions halted and glanced at one another. Miles gnashed his teeth—if he had known they were going to talk to the bailiff, he would have told them to say their master was the Reeve of Ulithorn! That was far enough away so that no one here should know anyone there, except perhaps the magistrate—but by the time the bailiff reported back to him, Gar and Dirk would be long gone and, hopefully, Miles with them.

The companions turned back to the bailiff. "We're between, just now," Gar said, "ordered back to the Protector."

Miles released a breath he hadn't known he'd been holding, and the bailiff stiffened. To be ordered to the Protector meant they would become part of his army, and everyone wanted to stay on good terms with the Protector's soldiers.

"There is certainly no need to see your travel permits, then," the bailiff said, forcing a smile.

"No, certainly not," Gar agreed, returning the smile. "We're growing tired of walking, though, and wondered if you could tell us where to find horses."

"I'm surprised you weren't given them—"

"None available," Dirk explained. "We'd just rounded up a band of outlaws, but we'd lost five horses in the fighting." He shrugged. "No men lost, though a few of our friends will be some months recovering. That didn't leave our reeve any mounts to spare, though, so he gave us the wherewithal to replace them when we could."

"An order to supply you, or gold?"

"Gold," Gar said, "but we haven't found anyone with horses to spare, and it would have been unkind to commandeer them, especially since we weren't given a date for reporting."

"Ah, some unofficial leave, eh?" The bailiff nodded. "Well, there's a farmer named Landry hereabouts, who raises horses for the magistrates. His farm is seven miles that way." He pointed northeast, past the barn where Miles hid.

"Thank you for the information," Gar said, inclining his head. "May we return the courtesy?"

The bailiff gave him a sour smile. "Only if you can tell us where to find the runaway we're hunting."

"Runaway?" Dirk and Gar exchanged a glance, then Dirk said, "What did he look like?"

"Not short, but not tall, either. Round-faced, dark-haired."

"So that's why he seemed so nervous!" Dirk said to Gar.

Miles's heart dropped down into his boots. His mind screamed at him to run, but he was too stunned to move.

"You've seen him? Where?" The bailiff seemed almost to pounce, and his men stiffened.

"Back at the ford, carrying a huge fish on a string." Gar's nose wrinkled. "Dead since dawn, at least. He walked with us to this very place, where he told us we might find horses for sale at a village yonder." He pointed toward the copse from which he and Dirk had come. "We hadn't gone but a quarter mile, though, before we saw there were no horses pastured. We came back to give the fellow a good thrashing for his lie, but we see he's gone."

"Don't worry, I'll give him the thrashing for you," the bailiff said grimly. "No idea which way he went, then?"

"No but if he sent us east, I'd guess he'd have gone west." Gar pointed out across the fields.

"Likely enough." The bailiff looked off toward the outcrop of woods, frowning. "How'd he disguise his trail from the hounds, though?"

"Remember that fish I told you of?" Gar asked. "Well, I suspect he dragged it behind him. It's quite dead by now, and in the sun, it's probably giving off far more odor than he is."

"Yes, probably enough," the bailiff growled. "Cunning rogue! All right, men, set your hounds to questing west!" Then, to Dirk and Gar, "Thanks for your information, guardsmen!"

"Our pleasure—and thanks for telling us where to find horses." Dirk raised a hand in farewell, then remembered to stiffen it into the salute he'd learned the day before.

The bailiff imitated the gesture, then hurried off after his foresters. Gar and Dirk started off toward the northeast.

Miles sagged, and lay back against the boards with his heart thumping. He'd never heard such adroit lying in his life.

But how would Gar and Dirk come back for him?

Time enough to think that through later. For now, he needed to catch his breath—and let his body stop screaming at him to run.

He was almost calm when he heard their voices as they came into the barn. "Well, yes," Gar was saying, "they did seem to have the hunting down to a routine. But that could be from being drilled in it, not from practice."

"Yeah, and I might be good at speaking Standard because I studied it in a book," Dirk retorted. "Of course, it *could* also be from having spoken it all my life."

"Well, we'll let Miles tell us." Gar smiled up at the wide-eyed peasant. "Come down, Miles. I don't think you'll need to worry about that official for a while."

"The bailiff?" Miles asked, round-eyed. "Do you really think he'll stay away?"

"No," Dirk told him. "He'll be back in half an hour or so, when he finds his dogs don't strike any trace."

"I expect they'll give them a dead fish to smell," Gar added, "but when they can't find *that*, the bailiff will come storming back, looking for blood. We'd better start hiking."

Miles scrambled down the ladder, and they set off toward the woods along the stream. "Where are we going?" he asked.

"To Farmer Landry's, first," Gar replied. "The bailiff and his men will be at least half an hour on their wild-goose chase, more likely an hour. We can have three miles' lead on them in that time."

"Time enough to buy horses and be gone before they catch us," Dirk said. "By the way, Miles, settle an argument for us. Were those guys good at hunting because they've been trained in it, or because they've done it so often?"

"Not 'often,' I would say, sir," Miles said slowly, "no more than two or three times a year."

Dirk looked up, startled, and Gar's face became a mask. "So you've met some other people running from the bailiff?"

"Only before they ran, sir," Miles said, "or after they were punished. Not a year goes by without some young fellow giving in to the temptation of poaching, and I know most of them."

"They don't get away, then?"

Miles shook his head. "None from my village. I've heard rumors of highwaymen and forest outlaws, but I've never seen them myself."

"But knowing they might be there ready to pounce, makes you think twice about running away," Dirk said with irony, "and the punishments are enough to make you think three or four times."

"They are indeed, sir, and I don't know of any other runaways who are free. Even the bandits and highwaymen are caught by the reeve's men sooner or later."

Gar frowned down at him. "You must really feel strongly about not marrying Salina, to dare all those dangers— especially since you seem to be sure you'll be caught sooner or later."

"Killed, I hope, sir." Miles shuddered. "But I'd rather face death than a life of misery with a woman who hates me—and hates me all the more because I make her miserable, too. But yes, I am sure that if I don't fight to the death, they'll catch me. They all get caught, all the runaways I've known. The watchmen or the foresters bring them back." He shuddered again. "The flogging and the forced labor aren't pretty, and the shunning must be torture."

"But they make you watch them, all the same," Dirk inferred.

"That they do."

"Doesn't anybody ever get angry at the bailiffs, or the Protector?" Gar asked.

"No," Miles said very quickly. "Anyone foolish enough to let others know he's angry at the Protector, or even the magistrate or the reeve, disappears very quickly, never to be seen again. Old Jory—well, he loved his wife, but when she died, the magistrate ruled he must marry again. He didn't even say to whom—but Jory got drunk that night and swore they were all a pack of bullies and thieves, the magistrates and their bailiffs and watchmen, even the Protector himself—before he passed out. But the next morning he was gone, simply gone in the night, and no one ever saw him again." He shuddered.

"Horrible," Dirk said, eyes wide. "How old was he, by the way?"

"Old enough, sir—in his forties, at least."

"Your magistrate doesn't seem to have heard of common decency," Dirk growled.

Miles shrugged. "I suppose he felt that if the Protector made him marry so many times, he should make a widower marry again, too, sir."

"So many?" Dirk looked up. "*Have* to marry? Why?"

"Because the Protector won't let a magistrate stay in one town more than five years, sir," Miles said, surprised they should even ask. "Part of an official's job is to marry and beget sons who may become magistrates in their own turn—but when he is sent on to his next town, the marriage is dissolved, and he must marry again."

"Practical, anyway," Dirk said with a shudder. "What does his ex-wife do for a living?"

"Oh, the Protector sees that she and her children are well-housed, well-clothed, and well-fed, sir—or the reeve, I should say, doing it for the Protector."

"Yes, I can see that might make a man want to inflict marriage on other people," Gar said, "especially if he fell in love with a wife he'd had to leave."

Farmer Landry was quite willing to sell them horses, even though their gold was only in little bars, not in coins. His eyes went huge when he saw them, and Miles elbowed Dirk and gave his head a little shake to tell him the price was far too high—but Dirk only winked and gave him a reassuring smile. Miles shrugged his shoulders and stood back to watch his friends be cheated, then walked beside them, feeling helpless, as they rode off on their new mounts.

But as soon as they were out of sight of the farmer's hut, they reined in, and Gar said, "We'll never outrun the bailiff if you keep walking, Miles. Up and ride, now!" He seized the peasant's arm and swung him up on the horse's rump. Miles clung for dear life, his stomach turning as he looked at the ground, so far below. It had never looked so hard.

"Now for a hiding place," Gar said. "Is there some wild land where nobody lives, Miles?"

"You must be from far away indeed, sir," Miles said, "not to know that the Badlands are only four days' journey from here."

"Probably only a day and a half, on horseback. Hold tight, Miles." Gar clucked to his horse, then urged it into a fast walk. Miles clung, swaying and staring—and gradually, the fear subsided. In half an hour, he was surprised to realize he was actually enjoying it.

All that time, Gar and Dirk had been talking, alternating between things that were so obvious he would have thought they were half-wits, and matters that sounded very complicated, but which Miles couldn't even begin to understand.

"So the government is a dictatorship," Gar said, "only the dictator is called the Protector."

"Shades of Oliver Cromwell," Dirk muttered.

"His shade certainly seems to be alive and well here. He has the country people intimidated well enough—but there might still be rebels in the cities."

"Oh, I think city people can be scared as thoroughly as country folk," Dirk replied. "Pardon my skepticism, but these 'disappearances' Miles told us about smack of a secret police. They might not go by that name, of course. . . . Miles, what do they call watchmen who work in secret, so secret that nobody knows who they are?"

"Protector's spies, sir."

"Well, that's clear and plain enough! I'll bet they arrest dissidents before they worry about anybody else."

"Still, they might not be entirely successful," Gar pointed out. "If the watchmen and foresters actually did manage to catch every bandit sooner or later, the peasants wouldn't have rumors about outlaws and highwaymen."

"Big forests *are* notoriously hard to police," Dirk sighed, "and I take your point—so are the warrens of alleys in a big city."

"Big city, yes." Gar looked back at Miles. "How big is the capitol, Miles?"

"Capitol, sir?" Miles frowned.

"The Protector's town," Dirk explained.

"Oh! Milton?"

Dirk and Gar exchanged a glance. "Cromwell's secretary," Dirk said.

"Old Olly's ghost *is* alive and well." Gar turned back to Miles. "Yes, how big is Milton?"

"Oh, so very big, sir! Why, I've heard it holds fifty thousand people!"

"Yes, immense," Gar sighed. "I hope they don't all work for the government. . . . Well, let's see what the Badlands look like."

"Bound to be an improvement over Milton," Dirk said.

Miles could only hold on and stare, scandalized.

CHAPTER 5

They went under the canopy of leaves, Ciletha and Orgoru, amazed that it could be so far overhead. "Thirty feet and more above our heads!" Orgoru marveled. "Why are there no leaves closer down?"

"Because the sunlight can't reach them," a hard voice said, amused.

Orgoru's gaze snapped down to the leathery face before him, and the bow the man held casually at his side, arrow nocked and ready. Ciletha gasped and clasped Orgoru tightly, trying to edge behind him for protection. The half-dozen younger men behind the leathery man eyed her lasciviously, chuckling deep in their throats. Ciletha stared in sheer surprise—no boy had ever looked at her with lust before—then began to tremble when she realized what sort of courtship they had in mind.

They wore an assortment of ragged, threadbare clothing, but what chilled Orgoru to the marrow was that two of them wore the livery of watchmen, two more the livery of reeve's guards, and the last two the livery of foresters. The leathery man wore a bailiff's breeches and short robe, though not his chain of office. He saw the horror come into his victims' eyes and gave them a gloating smile. "Yes, they had to be dead before we took their uniforms, these Protector's men. Well, we have protected ourselves against the Protector, and ask no man's leave to come or go, to wed . . ." His eyes flicked over Ciletha, and his voice grew husky. ". . . or not to wed." He nodded to one of his henchmen, who advanced, hand outstretched. "We don't see women very often," Leatherface explained. "It gets so a she-bear looks pretty."

Ciletha cried out in indignation, but the outlaw's hand touched her arm, and she shrank away behind Orgoru with a gasp that was half a sob.

The sound galvanized Orgoru. He shoved his fear into the back of his mind and held up a palm, looking down his nose at the man and proclaiming, "Stop! I forbid you to touch her!"

"Oh, you do, do you?" the young outlaw snarled, and shook a fist right under Orgoru's nose. "Who do you think you are, to forbid me anything?"

Terror shrieked through him, but Orgoru held his ground, only pulling away from the fist with a look of disgust, as though it stank. In his most haughty manner, he commanded, "Don't dare to come near my exalted person! Know that I am the Prince of Paradime, and that one so lowly as you may not touch me!"

"Lowly, am I?" the outlaw cried. "Well, touch you I will, fellow, and very hard, too." The fist lashed out and cracked into Orgoru's face. He fell back with a cry of outrage and fear. Ciletha cried out with him and dropped to her knees, cradling his head to her. The young outlaw snarled in jealousy and lifted his fist again, but Leatherface stopped him with an upraised palm. "Let them be," he said in disgust. "Don't even bother with her, for he's another one of them, and what he is, she likely is, too."

Disgust showed on all the other outlaws' faces, but the one who had hit Orgoru snapped, "So what if she is? We're talking bodies here!"

"It might be catching," one of the other outlaws muttered,

and the disgust flooded the young one's face too. "Aye, leave them alone indeed!" He turned away.

"When will we get one with some wits?" another outlaw grumbled as he turned away, too.

"If a woman had wits, would she come this far into the wood?" Leatherface retorted, as he led his band back into the trees. They stepped in among the trunks, strode a step or two—and were gone.

"Oh, thank you!" Ciletha gasped with a catch in her voice. "However did you scare them away, Orgoru?"

But Orgoru was glaring after the outlaws, quivering with anger. "How dared they call me 'another one'!" He scrambled to his feet, storming, "I, the Prince of Paradime! How dare they. . . . " Then his voice trailed off and his eyes widened as realization struck. "They recognized my quality! They knew me for my kind!"

"What . . . what do you mean?" Ciletha stammered.

" 'Another one,' they said!" Orgoru spun to face her. "They must have been speaking of other noblemen and princes whom they dared not touch! They have seen them, they know of them!"

Ciletha's eyes widened as she realized what he was saying. "We must be near them, then!"

"Yes, near the lords and ladies and their Lost City!" Orgoru caught her hand and turned, hurrying deeper into the forest. "They must be here, they must be near! Only a few more hours, Ciletha! Then, surely, we'll find them!"

Miles couldn't understand why, when they took the first of their brief rests, Gar took out paper and ink and spent a fair amount of time carefully drawing. Miles glanced over his shoulder and saw no picture, only lines of odd shapes that he knew were letters. He couldn't read them, though, so he shrugged and left his new friend to his amusements. But half an hour later, when two reeve's guards hailed them and flagged them down, Miles was amazed to discover what Gar had done.

"Greetings, fellow guardsmen!" the first guard cried. "What brings you here?"

"Greetings," Gar replied with a smile. "We're being sent to Milton Town, friend."

Miles stared, and fear gibbered flailing up within him.

The reeve's man stared, somewhat taken aback, then said carefully, "Your pardon, but you know our duty. We must see your travel permits, friends."

"Of course." Dirk took out one of Gar's papers and held it out. Gar held out two.

The guard took them and studied, frowning. "These don't have the look I'm used to."

"No," Gar agreed. "Our reeve was rather cross at having two men taken from him, and told us that our orders would have to do for travel permits."

"Well, they should do that," the guard admitted, "but I'm not used to a scribbled note as an order. Not even the Protector's crest, hey?"

"No," Gar agreed, "only the signature and title of the official who wrote them. It seemed odd to me, too, but it's not my place to argue."

"No, nor mine," the guard said, with sudden decision, and handed the papers back with an air of relief. Then he nodded at Miles. "What about him?"

Miles felt his heart stop.

"He's the third letter, though the clerk who read it to me said it didn't give a name—only that we could take a servant. The reeve was even more cross about that, I can tell you."

"Yes, I'll bet he was," the other guard said with a grin. "When are you supposed to be in Milton?"

"They didn't give a date." Gar returned the grin, and they were off into ten minutes of idle chitchat. Miles, sweating, noticed that Gar and Dirk managed to stay very vague about everything they said, though they certainly sounded open and forthcoming. After a few minutes, though, they were doing most of the asking, and the guards most of the answering. But soon enough the reeve's man said, with regret, "Well, we'd better be on our way. Can't exactly go drinking your health at a pub while we're on patrol, you know."

"I certainly do," Gar said with a smile. "Good riding to you!"

"Odd greeting, that," the second guard said with a smile of his own, "but it has a good ring to it. Yes, good riding to you, too, strangers!"

And they rode off, with loud farewells on both sides. As soon as they were out of earshot, Gar said, "Interesting that the guardsmen can't read."

Miles looked up, startled. "Of course not. Only officials, and students studying to be officials, can."

"Even more interesting," Dirk said.

"You didn't know that? Then how did you guess it?"

"Because the guard didn't say anything about what the note said—only about how odd it looked," Gar told him. "Risky, putting a man in his job who can't sound out the words. I could have handed him someone else's travel permit, and he never would have known it was the wrong name."

Miles stared in amazement. "But how could you get some-one else's permit?"

"I'm sure the outlaws have lots of chances," Dirk said dryly.

Miles realized what he meant; his stomach sank.

"Why aren't the guards taught to read and write, Miles?" Dirk asked.

"Oh, it costs a great deal, sir, far more than any peasant can scrape up! Our village didn't even have a school, and we're almost big enough to be a town."

"So." Dirk scowled. "Expensive, and even if you can afford it, you have to move to a town that has a school."

Miles shrugged. "The schoolmaster has a right to a living, too, sir."

"And the government doesn't provide it for him," Dirk replied. "Interesting, eh, Gar?"

"Fascinating," the giant answered from a granite face.

The towers rose majestic in the golden light of late afternoon, smooth-surfaced and slightly tapering, their sheen nacreous, as though they were made of mother-of-pearl. At their tops, they were pierced with windows under pyramidal roofs. For half their height, creepers and vines cloaked them so thoroughly that they might have been dead and decaying tree trunks.

"Oh, Orgoru!" Ciletha clutched his arm.

"Yes." He clasped a hand over hers. "Beautiful, isn't it? My rightful home! I feel it within me! Never was there a place so right for me! Hurry, hurry! I ache to see them, these noble men and women who must live here!"

It was hard to hurry through a forest, where trees roots bulged up unexpectedly to trip the passersby and thorns leaned out to catch clothing—but they went as quickly as they could, stumbling as often as they strode, until they parted a screen of brush and beheld a blank expanse of pearly wall. They froze, staring, then stepped forward to gaze upward with wonder.

The wall was only six feet away, but it rose high, high, thirty feet or more, with the towers rising that much higher again, a hundred yards apart. Looking down, they saw a tangle of weeds and vines, of ivy and fallen saplings that had tried to take root and tumble the wall—but the strange, pearly substance had tumbled the saplings instead, and repelled the ivy.

Marveling, Orgoru stepped forward, reaching out.

"Oh, no, Orgoru!" Ciletha cried. "It might . . ." Her voice trailed off.

"Hurt me, as it has hurt these little trees?" Orgoru shook his head. "It has only repelled the hurt they sought to give it, Ciletha, by being too smooth to gain a hold—and too deep and hard for their roots to burrow under. It won't hurt me—I feel that deep within, I'm sure of it!" His hand touched the wall, and he let out a gust of breath. "It's smooth, it's warm, it feels as though it might yield . . ." He pressed hard, harder. "But it doesn't."

He looked up, wondering. "Where could the vines have come from, that cloak the towers? . . . Ah! There!"

Ciletha crept forward, craning her neck to look upward. For two long strides, the ground was clear all along the wall except for spreading, shade-loving plants like clover making a lawn. But huge trees rose beyond that range, spreading thick limbs toward the wall and over it. Ivy climbed along bole and bough, wrapping from leaf to leaf about the tower. It rose as high as the trees could reach to the strange pearly stone, but no farther.

"No seams," Orgoru whispered, eyes alight.

Ciletha looked down and saw him running his palm over the wall. She stepped forward and mimicked him, feeling nothing but smoothness. "They have joined the stones so cleverly that we can't even see the cracks!"

"If they used stones." Orgoru stepped back, looking upward.

A thrill of dread encompassed Ciletha. "Of course they used stones! How else could they have built this wall?"

"Maybe they poured it, as we pour pewter into a mold." Orgoru shrugged. "Maybe they grew it. We can't know how, Ciletha. This is a magical thing, made by the wizards who first came down from the stars."

The dread gathered and coiled down her spine. "That's only legend, fable, an old wives' tale!"

"I don't think so." Orgoru brought his gaze down, smiling at her, but she almost recoiled. There was something uncanny about the way his eyes burned, something eerie about his excitement. "They told us it was just a story, Ciletha, but they told us that about this city, too, and the others like it that legend spoke of! Let's go find the rest of the truth!" He caught her hand and set off along the curving strip of lawn.

Ciletha stumbled, then had to run to catch up with him. "Wait, Orgoru! What truth are you talking about?"

"Why, the rest of the city, of course! There must be a gate, a door, a way in! Aren't you burning to see what's inside?"

Ghosts and bones, she thought, but only said, "What will you do if you find the gate?"

"Why, knock, of course, and demand to be admitted!" Orgoru cried. "I have a right to be in there, after all!" And he strode on down the path.

Ciletha hurried to keep up with him anyway, though the dread was mounting.

Finally they found it—a gate twice as tall as either of them, or a gateway, rather. The portals themselves were only a mound of dust and crumbling wood along the threshold.

"This magical wall, and they had to build the gates out of

ordinary wood!" Orgoru breathed, his eyes shining as he stared inward. "See, Ciletha! The buildings are of mere stone, ordinary stone! You can see the joins between the blocks!"

Ciletha looked. Sure enough, the buildings within were made of courses of stone, though cut so exactly like one another that she marveled at the masonry. They were all of stone, taller than the wall, each wide as a village, with huge dark portals and staring, empty windows. Several had rows of pillars holding up projecting roofs; others were perfect domes, held up by . . . magic? She shivered, awed, thrilled, and fearful, all at the same time.

"I had meant to announce myself and demand to be let in," Orgoru said, "but there are no gates to keep me out, and no one to bar me."

"You may go in whenever you please," Ciletha whispered. She felt a trembling within. "Oh, Orgoru, I'm afraid to!"

Orgoru took her hand and stroked it gently, reassuring her. "I'd have to go alone anyway, Ciletha—it's me who's their kind, not you. Wait for me, though. I want to come back and tell you how wonderful it all is."

"Of course I'll wait," Ciletha assured him, tears in her voice. She hesitated a moment, then lunged up on tiptoe and kissed his cheek. "Go now, and good luck!"

Somewhat dazed, Orgoru turned toward the gate. Then, heart pounding with excitement, he went in.

They stopped for lunch, and for a few minutes every two hours to stretch their legs, but other than that, Miles rode with Gar and Dirk all day, his legs aching worse and worse with every hour. How could soldiers stand it?

In mid-afternoon, they were challenged a second time, and this guard didn't even comment on the "permit" not being on a standard form. He only looked at it and said, "Gar Pike? That really your name?"

Gar stared in surprise, then recovered quickly and said, "My parents tried to be funny now and then."

"The rest of it looks good enough," the guard said, "though I wish this 'Jonathan Esque, Clerk' would have said who he was writing for."

"You can read!" Dirk blurted.

"Can't I just, though," the guard said bitterly. "My parents scrimped and saved to send me to school. Much good it did me, though."

"They must have been well-off," Gar said.

"Only peasants, friend, same as you and I—but the magistrate thought I had promise, so the whole village went without and scraped up enough to send me to the school at the reeve's town—and what came of it? I failed the examination! They've forgiven me, though—I think."

"Failed?" Gar frowned. "Odd, when you had the talent and so many years' schooling. What happened?"

Miles stared at him in surprise. Surely he had to know he was asking about something painful! He was startled that Gar should be so rude.

But the guard didn't seem to mind talking about it, though his mouth twisted with bitterness. "Oh, I knew the law well enough, had high marks on that day—but the second day was essays, and though I did well enough explaining why we need a civil service, and why peasants mustn't have weapons, my explanation of why we need a Protector didn't satisfy the judges. Odd, because I only said what the books did, with just one idea of my own to show I could think."

Gar, frowning, said, "That's odd. What was your reasoning?"

"Why," said the reeve's man, "that we needed a Protector to protect us from kings and noblemen, who might too easily grow weak and corrupt, because they inherited their titles and power instead of earning them, so didn't know their true value."

"Good as far as you went," Gar said judiciously, "but you ignored the reason why there must be a head of state in the first place."

"Oh?" The guard frowned dangerously. "Why is that?"

"Why, because without a head of state, the reeves and magistrates would keep things running along, but their superiors would wrangle and debate and never decide anything. After a while, they'd grow so frustrated that they'd order their armies to take the field against each other, and as their men killed one another off, they'd conscript peasants out of the field, then more peasants, and more, until there was no one left to raise crops—and famine would stalk the land. Then the few peasants who were left would charge the armies, crazy with hunger, and die fighting—and the whole commonwealth would collapse and dissolve."

The guard shuddered. "You paint a horrifying picture, sir, but you may well be right. What you're saying, though, is that a government without a head is no government at all."

Miles looked up, alert—the guard had called Gar "sir."

"You can make a good case for it, yes," Gar said. "I'd hate to try it in practice just to find out, though."

"Wouldn't we all! But why are you and your bailiff disguised as reeve's soldiers, sir, and your clerk as a peasant? For you must be a magistrate yourself, to have such knowledge!"

"Not yet," Gar assured him. "I've been studying during my free hours, and haven't taken the examinations. I was about to, I'll admit, and my reeve encouraged me—but this order came a week before I was set to go."

The guard turned away, his mouth working, and swallowed hard—to keep curses in, Miles guessed, and felt sorry for the man; those curses would fester, and ruin his health. When he turned back, his face was grim. "You must have been sorely disappointed, sir."

"Not altogether." Gar smiled easily. "There are examination stations in Milton, after all."

The guard stared, then burst into laughter. As it eased, he nodded, wiping his eyes. "Oh, yes, there are, many examination stations indeed! What a surprise you'll hand them, on your first leave!" He sobered suddenly. "You don't suppose your reeve reported your training to the minister, and he ordered you to Milton so you'd be handy for assignment when you passed your examinations?"

"That would be pleasant," Gar said, straight-faced, "but surely it would be too much to hope for. Still, friend, if I've done it, you can, too—and do it again and again until you finally pass."

"Yes, they can't keep me from taking the examinations, can they?" The guard's voice grew hard. "An inspector-general might come by in disguise, talk to the townsfolk, then demand to see the examiners' records, and if he found a man had come to take the examinations and been turned away, he'd report it to the Protector himself—and the Protector would fly into a rage if he heard of it. Yes, thank you, sir. There is still hope, isn't there?"

"A great deal," Gar said. "Back to the books with you! Go study!"

"That I will! Pass, sir, and good luck to you!"

"And to you," Gar returned, and rode on.

As soon as they were out of earshot, Miles let out a very long breath.

"It wasn't that hard to fake this time, Miles," Gar told him, "not once he told me about the examinations, and thought I was a magistrate because I knew enough to pass them."

"You surely do!" Miles exclaimed. "You mean that was all guesswork? You sounded as though you knew!"

"I didn't actually lie about anything except my imaginary reeve—and the rest wasn't hard to guess. Besides, I've given him hope."

"Hope that will be dashed, sir," Miles said bitterly. "Unless you're really brilliant, there's no chance that the magistrates will let you pass the examinations and do one of their own sons out of a place."

Dirk looked up, surprised. "Is that a fact?"

Miles shrugged. "Everybody knows it, sir."

"It could be just a rumor," Gar said slowly, "started by a few failures making excuses."

"Or it could be true," Dirk countered. "Nepotism will out. It wouldn't be the first time civil-service officials have made sure that only their own sons would succeed them."

"The human drive to protect and foster their children is a very good thing, within limits," Gar protested. "It's just that it goes beyond those limits very easily." He turned to Miles. "So you're governed by a Protector who makes all the laws and orders his ministers to enforce them—and each minister gives orders to his own set of reeves, who each commands a few hundred magistrates."

"That's so, sir." Why did Gar have to state things that everyone knew?

"And each magistrate has his own squad of soldiers, only he calls them 'watchmen' and 'foresters,' and has a bailiff to command them."

"I suppose you could call them that, yes," Miles said slowly, "though we usually think of only the reeve's guards as soldiers—and the Protector's Own Army, of course."

"So he has an army, does he? And none of his ministers do?"

"No, sir, although each of them can call up his reeves and their guards, if he needs to."

"But if he did, the Protector's Army would crush them." Gar nodded slowly. "What do they usually do, these Protector's soldiers?"

"He sends them against highwaymen and bandits, sir, if they've grown too many for a reeve to tackle."

"Enough duty to keep them more or less in shape, not enough to take them away from him for very long," Dirk summarized. "Of course none of the ministers would dare to defy him."

Miles stared, scandalized at the very thought of someone fighting the Protector!

"So the civil service starts with magistrates . . ."

Miles interrupted. "By your leave, sir, the first examination makes a man a clerk. Many never get past that; they spend their lives running a village for magistrate after magistrate."

"They get to stay put, huh?" Dirk looked up keenly. "And get to stay with the same wife, too. I'll bet a lot of them never even try for the second exam."

"If they do, though, they become magistrates?" Gar asked.

"Yes, sir—and the third examination makes a man a reeve, though he has to have done very good work as a magistrate before he's offered the chance."

"A system designed to operate on merit alone," Gar said

thoughtfully, "and apparently open to anyone who can pass the examinations—but the sons of the officials are always better trained, and far more likely to score high."

"More to the point," Dirk said, "the examiners probably know those sons or knew their fathers' friends, and pass them while they flunk applicants who don't have connections."

"You're judging by Terran history," Gar said, "but I do have to admit that most methods of corruption were invented on old Earth. In practice, the system is open to new blood only if some of the old blood dies out."

"And I expect there are quite a few peasants who'd be more than willing to help it die."

Miles looked up, scandalized again. Would these two never be done speaking treason?

But it did make a man think. . . .

CHAPTER 6

Orgoru stole down the weed-choked lanes, looking about him in quick glances, marveling at the golden glow the sunset drew from the stone all about him— stone, every building stone, some white, some bluish, most gray, some even rosy. Wherever roofs were level, grass and trees sprang, some so thick they must have been a century old or more. Here and there, a building had tumbled, strewing blocks across the road—a full, wide road! inside a town!—but no other stones had fallen. Most of the buildings still stood, tall and proud, and completely intact.

Still, there was something unearthly, something weird and eldritch, for so vast a place, built for so many people, to be so completely empty; Orgoru hadn't seen a single living being larger than a fox, and that in spite of his calling out again and again, "Hello! I am Orgoru, Prince of Paradime! Will no one bid me welcome?" For so he knew men of royal station must speak.

But no one answered.

After a few hours, Orgoru began to feel a little foolish. As the dusk gathered, he was feeling very glum. He gathered some scraps of wood, started to lay a fire next to a wall, then realized that the smoke would char the stone and took up his sticks again, walking around the building until it blocked the wind from him. There he laid his sticks a few feet from the wall, took flint and steel, and kindled a fire. Its glow cheered him a little, especially since chill was wrapping about him with the gathering night. He folded his legs and sat, gazing into the flames, sad and morose. So there weren't any glorious noble people after all! But if not, where were they? For he knew he was one of their own kind! And what could have made the noises the man had heard?

Ghosts . . .

Orgoru shivered and glanced about him, feeling the first thin tendrils of fear. He told himself that ghosts who laugh and make music aren't apt to hurt people, but the thought didn't convince him.

A small gray form appeared out of the darkness, bounding toward him. For a moment, Orgoru's heart jammed in his throat. Ghosts . . .

Then it passed through the light from his fire, and he stared after it. Only a rabbit! The sight of it waked sudden, ravenous hunger; his fist closed around a pebble—but he had never been a poacher, and threw the stone away with disgust. A prince, hunt rabbits? Prey upon the weak and defenseless? Never! A boar perhaps, a wolf certainly, but not something so small and harmless. He watched the rabbit bounding away into the night while his stomach scolded him, and knew he would have to find some food. With a sigh, he rose, and went seeking in the shadows, where wind-blown soil had gathered in the angles of buildings, to find leaves that he knew, and dug up their roots and tubers. He brought an armful back to his fire and tossed them in to roast, keeping a few that didn't need to be cooked to begin his meal. Teeth crunched into a carrot, and he reflected wryly that such grubbing in the dirt was scarcely fitting for a prince—but what could he do? Even princes must eat, and he remembered an old tale about a king hiding from his enemies in a farmer's cottage because he had just lost a battle. His imagination instantly raised the picture of the end of the story—the king casting off his forester's tunic and hood, appearing in golden brocade and ermine. . . .

Something moved in the shadows.

Orgoru spun about, dropping the carrot, heart hammering.

They came forth from an archway between mounds of tumbled stone blocks, tall and lean, graceful and slender, caparisoned in garments of rare and costly cloth—brocade and damask, silk and lawn, ruby and amethyst and gold and royal blue and silver and emerald, glittering with jewels, their hair held by coronets and tiaras, a dozen lords and ladies in clothing whose modesty and economy of line bespoke breeding and elegance. At their head paced a tall, proud man in blue and silver, his raven hair bound with the coronet of a duke—and Orgoru couldn't believe it, couldn't comprehend the fact that at last, at long last, he was hearing the words, "Welcome, fellow of our kind. Welcome, noble man and nobleman. I am the Duke of Darambay. Will you favor us with your own name and station?"

"See, now? It pays to wear your locks long!" Dirk finished smoothing the false moustache down and stepped back to admire his handiwork. "If you hadn't had hair to spare, we couldn't have made you such a natural-looking moustache!"

"Skilled work." Gar nodded critical approval. "Between the moustache, and everyone remembering you as wearing your hair down past your collar, you'll stand very little chance of being recognized, even if your magistrate has sent couriers to all the nearby villages."

"But my clothes," Miles objected.

Gar coughed into his fist, and Dirk said delicately, "I hate to have to be the one to tell you, Miles, but your tunic and trousers aren't exactly unique."

Miles frowned up at Gar. "What does he mean?"

"He means that all the men your age wear pretty much the same clothing," Gar said. "I'm afraid there really isn't all that much that's individual about yours, Miles."

"Oh." Miles looked down at his body, surprised that he had never noticed. "Well, that's lucky now, isn't it?"

"Sure is." Dirk mounted his horse. "Jump up behind, Miles. I think we're ready to ride through that town."

Miles caught his hand and swung up on the horse's rump, trying to suppress his fear of being so high. Not of horses, of course—he'd been harnessing and currying plowhorses most of his life, and even riding them when the magistrate wasn't looking—but guardsmen's mounts were a different matter entirely, and much taller. Dirk clucked to the beast, and Miles clung for dear life. "I wish we could go around the town."

"Yes, but if we did, that would be as good as putting up a banner announcing that we're trying to hide something," Dirk pointed out. "I'm afraid we're going to have to brazen it out, Miles."

It was a real village—half a dozen streets branching off from the high road, a small courthouse, half a dozen shops, even an inn. The people glanced up at the sound of hooves, then glanced quickly away.

Dirk frowned. "What're they afraid of?"

"Us," Miles told him, "or rather, you." He had overcome his surprise at two such shrewd men being so ignorant about small, everyday things.

"Because we're dressed like soldiers, you mean? Look out—official."

The man with the hip-length robe stepped out from the gateway of the courthouse and raised his staff—in greeting, Miles hoped. The villagers automatically shied away, looking suddenly wary as he approached.

"Bailiff," Miles muttered.

"Good day, guardsmen!" The bailiff's eyes were small in a broad face, broad because he had let himself go to fat—but Dirk saw quite a bit of muscle beneath it.

"Good day, bailiff," Dirk said, reining in his horse. "I trust all is peaceful."

"It is indeed, guardsmen." The bailiff held out his hand. "But you know the Protector's law. I must ask to see your travel permits."

"Of course." Dirk handed his down; so did Gar.

The bailiff looked from one to the other, frowning. "This isn't the regular form."

"It wasn't our business to ask," Dirk told him, while Gar just sat by with a half-smile, looking menacing. "Privately, though, I think my magistrate was rather angry at losing two men."

"Yes, I can see that, and I suppose these will do." The bailiff looked up with a gleam in his eye. "I'll take them to our magistrate!" He swept an arm toward the two-story building a hundred yards down from the courthouse. "Dine at our inn, sirs, on the Protector's coin—this may take some time, as the magistrate is deep in his books over a knotty point of law."

"It sounds quite uncomfortable," Gar said sympathetically.

The bailiff looked up sharply—and with confusion; he didn't recognize humor, at least not in regard to his duties. "No, our inn is quite well appointed, guardsmen. Rest you there." He turned away, started toward the courthouse, then stopped, frowning, at the sight of two women standing in the street and chatting. He started toward them, calling, "What're you doing, wasting the daylight in idle gossip? Get along with you now, back to your housework!"

The women didn't even wait for him to finish his sentence, didn't even say good-bye—they scurried away, heads down.

Gar frowned.

"Yes, I think dinner at an inn sounds very pleasant, don't you?" Dirk said, with an edge to his voice.

"Undoubtedly," Gar said, and kicked his heels to start his horse toward the inn—but his eyes stayed on the bailiff as he strode into the courthouse.

They came up to one of the women who had been chatting, still hurrying down the street. A man fell in beside her and snapped, "I *told* you not to gossip where the bailiff might see you!"

"He had those strangers to think about," the woman retorted. "If you had any worth as a husband, you'd have gone to ask him a question, and given us time to say good-bye!"

"If you were a decent wife, you'd never embarrass me by calling down the bailiff's notice!"

Gar rode on by, his face hard.

"What of all that big talk when we married?" another woman railed at the portly man beside her as they came out of a shop. "You were going to learn to read, you were going to study! You were going to become a bailiff yourself, if not a magistrate!"

"When did I have time?" the man snarled. "Not once I was married, with you expecting me to dance attendance on you as soon as you were with child!"

"Oh, so I'm to blame for giving you children, am I!"

"Do all your married couples quarrel?" Dirk asked as they passed the argument.

Miles shrugged. "Most, sir, yes."

"What would you expect, if you had to marry whatever woman a judge ordered you to?" Gar said harshly.

Dirk ignored the question and asked Miles, "Is there a lot of infidelity? People having affairs with somebody else's wife or husband?"

"Oh, no, sir!" Miles said, shocked.

"Surprising." Gar frowned.

"Not considering the punishment, sir."

"Which is?"

"Amputation."

"Of what?" Gar raised a hand. "Never mind—I don't think I want to know. The same thing applies with unmarried people, I assume."

"Oh, not if they go on to marry," Miles assured him.

"Great," Dirk said sourly. "So all a girl has to do is con a man into bedding her, and he has to marry her—and they can spend the rest of their lives fighting and hating each other. Or a boy who really wants to marry a girl, manages to get her drunk and into bed. Then they *have* to get married, and spend the rest of their lives making each other miserable. Really great system, yeah."

"I wonder if it has that much worse a track record than people who choose their own mates by falling in love," Gar sighed.

Miles looked up, staring in amazement. People choose their own mates? By love? It was true that there were always a few who fell in love before the reeve could tell them who to marry—but only a few.

"Yeah, they used to say that marriage is like buying a pig in a poke," Dirk growled. "You never knew whether you had a mangy scruffian or a prize specimen until after you got it home and opened the poke sack."

"Yes, I've heard that," Gar mused, "heard that you never really know what kind of person you've married until after the wedding, when the two people no longer have to impress each other, and drop all pretense. Surely they mean 'after the honeymoon.' "

"I hear that sometimes it starts on the wedding night." Dirk shook his head. "If that's what marriage is like, I'll stay single all my life!"

Miles stared even harder, scandalized and thrilled. What a wonderful thought, not to marry at all!

They tied their horses and stepped into the inn. Gloom enfolded them after the glare of the sunlight; Gar and Dirk stood still, waiting for their sight to clear. The aromas of an inn surrounded Miles, and he sniffed eagerly. Straw and wood polish, ale, and the heavenly scent of roasting pork! Surely guardsmen lived well, if they were given meat every day! He had been in an inn before, but only when business had taken him to the reeve's town—four times in his life. It was a rare and thrilling experience.

"Your pleasure, guardsmen?"

Miles looked up, startled. The landlord was taller than Dirk, six feet or so, and with only a small paunch. A fringe of pale yellow hair surrounded his bald scalp, and he was wiping his hands on his apron.

"Ale and meat, goodman," Dirk said, "and a table by a window."

The innkeeper nodded. "I'll have the flowing bowl to you directly, guardsmen." He swept a hand toward the common room. "Choose what table you will." Then he turned away to the kitchen, calling, "Guests, my dear! Meat for the guardsmen and their choreboy, if you will!"

"Indeed, my love!" caroled a voice from the kitchen. "The roast is almost done."

"Your mouth is open," Gar informed his friend.

"What . . . ? Oh! Yeah!" Dirk turned away, reddening. "Sorry. Just kind of strange to hear 'dear' and 'my love' after what we've been seeing."

Only two groups of men sat at table; Gar and Dirk had a wide choice—so why did they choose the corner farthest from the door? True, they were by a window—but why did they sit with their backs to the corner, instead of facing the panes? Even more mystifying, they went on with their talk as they sat, not even seeming to think about what they did. Strange indeed!

The landlord came up with a tray, three bowls on it. "Your ale, gentlemen. I'm sorry it's an old brewing, but the reeve hasn't sent me my ration of barley and hops yet. It was a bad harvest last year, of course, but his clerk says it will come any day now. As to your food, my wife will have—".

"Your meat, guardsmen! One side, husband!"

The innkeeper stepped aside quickly, then took the plates from his wife's tray and set them before the men. He gave her a quick kiss on the cheek as he turned away, hurrying back to the door, where two more men were just coming in.

Dirk stared, stunned, and Gar said, "You seem fortunate in your marriage, goodwoman."

"Aye, sir." The landlady, pretty even in her mid-forties and her plumpness, blushed a little. "He has been a good husband to me these twenty-seven years, thanks to kind fortune."

"Or to a good match. You seem to have been as good to him, and as loving."

"How could I be less, with so gentle and affectionate a man?" she said, keeping her voice low and her gaze downcast.

"I haven't seen very many couples as happy as you two," Dirk said. "In fact, none."

"It's so strange." The woman shook her head. "We seem to be such ordinary people, but when I hear what other folk have to bear, I realize we're rare indeed."

"How did you do it?" Gar asked.

The wife shrugged. "We've done our best to be kind to one another, sir, but that hasn't been very hard. I was lucky enough to fall in love with the man the reeve chose for me, and luckier still that he fell in love with me."

"Maybe the reeve knew you well enough to choose wisely," Dirk suggested.

"No, it couldn't have been that. We hadn't met the reeve very often, only the usual ceremonies, when each of us had to stand before him at seven and again at fourteen, that he might witness we were well and thriving, and his clerk register that we had passed from infant to child and again from child to adult. And the man who appointed us to wed one another was the fourth reeve we'd known."

Dirk shivered. Miles wondered why—surely the custom couldn't be strange to him. After all, it was the law.

"But the reeve knows all about everyone in his county," the landlady went on, "and chose us wisely, by our good fortune. You did want bread with your meat, did you not?"

"Of course," Gar said politely, and took the dark brown loaf she held out. "Thank you, goodwoman."

"Oh, I love to watch folk enjoy the food I've cooked, sir! Call if you need anything else!" She turned and swept back to the kitchen.

"Two very lucky people," Gar said, watching her go.

"And you think it's sheer luck, huh?" Dirk asked, watching his face. "Of course, it could be keen insight into character and good record-keeping."

"Then why're so many of them so miserable with each other?" Gar turned back to the table and shrugged. "The net of probability occasionally scoops up a treasure. If a few marriages are absolutely deplorable, the bell curve balances them with another few that are heavenly."

"But most of them are varying degrees of the mixture of good and bad? Yes, I think so." Dirk shrugged. "Just hope I draw one that's closer to the happy end than the miserable one." His face darkened. "Come to think of it, I won't get married if it's not."

"And you're the one who said we can only guess!" Gar said, with a hard smile.

Dirk shrugged. "If you're both head over heels in love, you're starting with all the advantages you can have—if both people are being as honest about themselves as they can be."

"Even then, it's a gamble." Gar warned.

"I know, but at least you're playing with better odds. No, I won't settle for anything less than head over heels."

Listening wide-eared, Miles thought privately that Dirk would never marry, then—but he was scandalized that the man seemed to think he had a choice. Had he fallen in with a couple of madmen?

"So their happy marriage is just good fortune," Gar summarized.

"No, it took a lot of effort, too," Dirk corrected. "You heard her—they both tried as hard as they could to be kind to one another."

"They're good people," Miles murmured, frightened at himself for intruding.

Dirk nodded. "Yes. That helps. Still, I'd have to say it was mostly luck—or Providence."

Gar frowned, his gaze suddenly keen. "Come to think of it, they didn't mention Providence, did they? Or the saints, or God."

Miles wondered what the unfamiliar words meant.

"No," Dirk said slowly, "and now that you mention it, even here on the ground we definitely haven't seen anything resembling a church." He turned to Miles. "Have we?"

Miles stared, completely at a loss. "What's a church?"

CHAPTER 7

That's what I thought." Dirk waved to the innkeeper. The man looked up over a double fistful of tankards to give Dirk a quick nod, then turned away to another table, distributed bumpers of ale, and came back to Dirk, wiping his hands on his apron again. "Your pleasure, guardsmen?"

"Our hearts are in need of uplifting, mine host," Dirk said. "When and where can we find services?"

The innkeeper looked surprised, but said, "Ah, you're in luck, sir! The magistrate will lead the philosophy discussion tomorrow night! He'll remind everyone of the basic ideas of their duties to the State, and its to them, for half an hour, then go on to more advanced ideas for those who want to stay."

"Bad fortune!" Gar said. "I would very much like to hear that—but we'll be on our way before nightfall, or surely tomorrow morning."

Miles devoutly hoped they'd be out of town long before then.

"That's the trouble with being assigned to travel," Dirk agreed. "It keeps us from attending discussions as frequently as we'd like."

"Indeed," Gar agreed. "Why, we haven't been to a single session since that one a month ago." He turned to Dirk. "The one about the falseness of religion, wasn't it? I wanted to learn more."

The innkeeper looked interested. "What does 'religion' mean? We've never heard of it at our services."

"The magistrate didn't quite make it clear," Gar admitted.

"No wonder you wanted to hear more! It's a refreshing change from hearing the same ideas again and again every few years. One grows hungry to learn more—but I know we have to be constantly reminded of the need for government and the logical reasons why a people need a Protector to shield them from the worst excesses of human nature."

"Yes," Gar agreed, "and the need for that Protector to have weapons to use against the wicked, so he can prevent them from hurting the good folk."

"As you guardsmen do," the innkeeper agreed, "but that's why we common folk mustn't have swords or pikes ourselves, for the wicked mustn't be able to win against the Protector of the good folk."

"So that the number of the wicked will always grow smaller," Dirk said, "which is why people need to strive for good and righteous behavior."

"I see the services aren't just boring talk, to you," the innkeeper said with a tone of respect. "I must confess, guardsmen, that I was surprised that you actually wanted to attend services—but I'm impressed, though, with your desire to learn. You must be born to magistrates' lives, or better."

"Why, thank you," Dirk said with a smile, "though you're no slouch yourself, when it comes to an interest in learning."

"My love!" his wife cried across the room, exasperated. "Are you talking philosophy again? We have customers!"

"At once, my dear!" the innkeeper called. Then to Gar, Dirk, and Miles, "If you'll excuse me, guardsmen . . ."

"Of course! Don't let us keep you from your business."

The innkeeper bustled off, and Gar turned back to them with a very thoughtful look. "So magistrates preach political ideas, rather than having ministers preach morality. The Religion of the State, you might call it."

"Not too far from a state religion," Dirk said with a sarcastic smile. "Probably mixed in with some real philosophy to keep people from plunging into despair."

"But 'the State' means 'the Protector' in practical terms," Gar pointed out, "so in effect, the Protector has no rival for the people's loyalty."

"Of course—he couldn't stand the competition." Dirk turned to frown at Miles. "You can go if you want to—you're not a slave, at least not to us. But we're not really as crazy as we sound."

"I—I didn't think you were." Miles was plastered back in his chair, sweat beading his forehead. "But I beg you, sirs, speak softly! If the bailiff or one of his watchmen were to hear you, we'd be clapped in irons and thrown in the gaol in a moment!"

"We'll try to keep it down," Dirk promised.

The innkeeper hurried back. "My common room is nearly filled, guardsmen. Would you mind if a few others shared your table?"

"No, not at all," Dirk said quickly.

Miles tried to shrink into the wood of the chair.

Four peasants in work-stained clothes sat down between Gar and Dirk on the one side, and to Miles's left and right on the other. They eyed Dirk and Gar warily as they sat, giving the impression that they would rather be at any other table in the inn—but this was the last one left with any room. "Good day, guardsmen!" one cried, trying to be cheerful. "What news?"

"Nothing worth noticing," Gar grunted. "The Protector still takes half your crops, tells you who to marry, and won't let you have a sword to defend yourself. What could be good?"

The peasants stared at him in alarm. So did Miles—but Dirk glared at him in warning.

"Why, the magistrates tell us when to rise, when to sleep, and when to eat!" Gar grumbled.

The peasants began to edge away from him.

"I've been lucky enough to escape three shrews," Gar boasted, "because the Protector transferred me from reeve to reeve just in time. A man needs a woman, though! All right, I'm glad it wasn't the wrong woman—but couldn't the reeves hurry up and find me the right one? Have they no insight, no caring?"

Miles felt as though he had melted and was sliding out of his chair—or at least wished he were.

"It will be a hot afternoon, I think, Corin!" one peasant said, very loudly.

"Educated, do they call themselves?" Gar growled.

"Aye, Merkin, but I see clouds piling up in the west," Corin called back. "I dare hope for rain by nightfall!"

"They know less about people than a plowman!" Gar snapped.

"Rain tonight would be good indeed," Corin projected. "The crops need it—and so do I!"

Dirk tried to lean around the man between himself and Gar.

"Oh, am I in your way?" the man said brightly. "Excuse me—I'll find another seat!"

"And I!"

"And I!"

"And I!"

That quickly, they were alone.

"I don't think the bait drew any hawks," Dirk said, thin-lipped.

"Master Gar," Miles gasped, "if you wanted the table to yourself, why didn't you just say so?"

"That's not what he wanted," Dirk said, standing, "but I think we'd better leave the table to *them.*" He headed for the door. Gar, looking disgusted, thrust himself to his feet and followed. So did Miles, with frightened glances to left and right. Maybe he *should* find other road companions. . . .

"Charge it to the magistrate," Dirk told the innkeeper, and the man nodded, not quite able to hide his relief at seeing them walk out the door.

As they came out, Miles breathed a long, shaky sigh of relief. "I had thought we were dead men—or at least ones clapped in irons!"

"Listen to the man on the scene," Dirk advised Gar. "I know we need a place to spend the night, but the jail isn't it."

Even on the verge of panic, Miles noticed that Dirk had a strange way of saying "gaol." He made it all one sound, "jail," instead of two, the way Miles said it: "jay-yul."

"All right, so it was a good idea that didn't work," Gar growled. "Maybe nobody else is willing to admit their discontent that openly—but if we could stay the night, I'll bet one or two would come up and ask me if I was angry enough to do anything about my complaints."

Miles began to tremble. Dirk noticed and asked, "Do you think anyone would ask that, Miles?"

"No, sir," Miles said fervently. "They're too much afraid of the Protector's punishments, and too fond of life. Besides, they'd fear you might be a Protector's spy, trying to tempt them into treason!"

"An agent provocateur?" Gar nodded heavily. "I shouldn't be surprised that they use them." He turned toward the courthouse.

Miles gasped and hung back. "You can't think of going in there! Not after what you've been saying!"

"Why not?" Gar countered. "They probably haven't heard, and even if they have, I'll just tell them I'm one of the Protector's spies you were worried about. Come along, Miles—we have to have our travel permits approved, don't we?"

As they rode out of town an hour later, Gar nodded with satisfaction. "Sometimes a man who insists everything be done by the book can be useful."

"I never dreamed he would insist on giving us proper permits!" Miles was still dazed.

"At least he gave us the originals back," Dirk said, "so we can safely burn them. We shouldn't have any trouble with guardsmen trying to stop us now."

"It can be useful, the bureaucracy of a police state," Gar admitted.

"Police state?" Dirk looked up, interested. "You think it's that bad, huh?"

Gar shrugged. "There's a very elaborate apparatus to catch fugitives, and the punishments for breaking the law, or even disobeying authority, are quick, severe, and public, to serve as a warning to would-be lawbreakers. Certainly that constitutes a police state. Besides, can you doubt it, after the way those peasants reacted to my complaining?"

"No, not really," Dirk sighed. "So we're dealing with a dictatorship, a police state headed by a Protector commanding a legion of reeves, who in their own turn command magistrates, who give orders to bailiffs, who boss a small army of foresters and watchmen. In addition, the Protector has his own personal army, and the reeves each have their own troop of guards. I haven't counted, but I suspect that, if you mobilized all those policemen and soldiers, you'd have a total army that would be overwhelming."

"Certainly enough to overwhelm any rebellions that might crop up," Gar said, "not that they'd get the chance, with secret police everywhere. On the positive side, though, the Protector's job isn't hereditary. None of the official positions are."

"No, but they might as well be. Sure, the system is supposed to be open to anybody who's smart and able—but in practice, the children of the officials are the only ones able to pass the exams. No free public schools, so most people can't afford to read and write, which incidentally makes them easier for the Protector to control. The few who do manage to scrape together the money to go to school, mysteriously fail the exams."

"It could be that their educations aren't as good as the teaching the officials' sons get," Gar pointed out.

"Yes—'sons.' " Dirk's mouth twisted wryly. "So you've noticed there aren't any female officials, huh? And yes, it could be that the sons of magistrates get superior educations, because the Protector provides it—but it could also be that all the officials in a district learn who each other are, and who their children are, in spite of that five-year rotation. They'd feel it's their duty to the last man who held the post to take care of his children, so they'd learn who all the officials' children are in their district—and when it came time for the exams, they'd make sure they didn't pass anyone else's son."

Miles managed to pull himself up from the depths of horror long enough to say, "There are a few farmers' sons who do pass the examinations—always a few."

"Yes, the ones who are so brilliant that the officials would be taking too much of a chance to let them slip through the net," Gar agreed. "There are those inspector-generals roving about in secret, after all. An examination board wouldn't want one to talk to a few townsfolk, then examine their records and find indisputable evidence of corruption."

"Right—it has to be disputable," Dirk agreed. "So okay, no son inherits his father's position—but he does get into the ranks of the officials, and proceeds to rise."

"Many don't ever become reeves," Miles objected.

"Sure. If your father never got beyond magistrate, he can't pull strings to have you promoted. The only sons who would get promoted to reeve, are the ones whose fathers made it to the top rank."

"So the Protectorship really is won by merit," Gar inferred, "at least the merit of backroom politicking and influence-peddling."

"Yeah, that does prove some ability at manipulating people, and that's a large part of running a police state," Dirk agreed. He shook his head in wonder. "How do you suppose these people ever dreamed up such a system?"

"I don't," Gar said. "I suspect the first Protector inherited a civil service from the colonial days. Bureaucracies are like living creatures, after all—they fight to survive no matter what happens. When Terra cut off the outer colony planets, and they couldn't get high-tech equipment or outside funding anymore, the bureaucracy found it was in danger of becoming extinct, since it no longer had Terra's laws and proclamations to enforce."

"So it developed its own boss," Dirk concluded, and nodded bitterly. "Yeah, that makes sense. A period of chaos, with the civil service desperately trying to maintain order in a sudden, drastic depression, skilled people having to become farmers, and reinventing the horse-drawn plow because the machines ran out of fuel—sure, a strong man would rise and conquer town after town until the rest realized they'd better join him voluntarily. Then he'd march into the capitol, and the bureaucrats would shout for joy because somebody had come to give them orders to carry out, and keep their jobs going."

"And everyone was so happy to have the chaos over with that they welcomed any government, no matter how severe," Gar said. "But give the system its due—it does provide a very orderly society, and no one seems to starve."

"Yeah, all the body-needs are met," Dirk agreed, "food, fuel, shelter, safety—but the emotional needs aren't, and people get twisted inside trying to satisfy cravings they're told they shouldn't even have."

"Yes—love, support, self-fulfillment." Gar nodded. "No system can provide those, though, Dirk."

Miles wondered why his face suddenly seemed so hungry, his eyes so despairing.

"No, but they can at least give you a hunting license," Dirk answered. "Some systems do give you the right to try to be happy, at least to the point of letting you stay single if you don't fall in love. But that requires a minimal amount of freedom, and here there's so little personal liberty that only the lucky are happy."

"Yes, by sheer chance," Gar said, "when they should have the choice of striving for happiness themselves." He sighed. "I suppose we do owe them that much, don't we?"

"No," Dirk said, "but we're going to give it to them anyway."

"Be welcome among us," the duke said, extending a hand, his manner courtly and gracious.

Orgoru clasped his hand and rose, overawed. "I—I thank Your Grace," he stammered, "but how did you know me for what I was?"

"Your nobility fairly shines from you," said a beautiful older lady, coming up to stand by the duke. "How could we mistake it?"

"Still, we needed some proof," the duke said.

"You have shown it to us."

Orgoru turned to look where the voice had come from—and stood, frozen. She was young, she was graceful, she was the most beautiful woman he had ever seen—and she was praising him! "Your respect for the city, refusing even to darken its stone with the smoke of your fire, and your mercy in sparing the life of the rabbit who might have made your dinner, show the nobility of your spirit!"

"Come, join our revelry," the duke bade him, and the brilliantly dressed men and women closed ranks around him. "Sound, music!" the duke commanded, and a harmony of flutes, sackbuts, hautboys, and viols sprang up around them. Orgoru looked about with quick glances, but saw no musician. A chill enveloped him, the chill of fear of the supernatural—until he remembered that these lords and ladies were so noble that even the spirits themselves would delight in pleasing them. The apprehension vanished, and he walked in their midst, giddy with pleasure as they sang a song of welcome. The beautiful maiden caught his eye; she cast him a roguish glance, then turned away, head high, making a point of ignoring him.

Orgoru grinned, understanding the game and, for the first time in his life, beginning to enjoy it.

They paraded to the center of the city, and the younger lords and ladies began to dance and cavort in their joy at discovering one more of their number. The moon had come out and turned all the buildings to silver, set against the midnight blue of the sky. They danced down streets of glowing pavement between walls adorned with bas-reliefs and mosaics toward a vast circular plaza. There, where all the grand boulevards met, a great hill rose with one grand broad way climbing its side. At its top stood a tall, round building of alabaster, its dome gleaming in the night, its portals thrown wide, light streaming out, light and music. The glad crowd swept into it, and Orgoru gazed about him in wonder renewed, for all the walls were inlaid with precious stones, all the panels of the dome were painted with scenes from stories he had heard as a small child, told as fairy tales, but which he had realized held a great significance in themselves. Surely that was Venus with Adonis, that Cupid stealing upon the sleeping Psyche, that Narcissus in love with his own reflection!

But it was to a flat wall that they led him, an alcove at one side of the great curving wall that was decorated with curlicues of gold about a mosaic of jewels, a mosaic that showed no picture of a living creature, but only curves and lines in a composition that took his breath with its beauty.

Then a voice reverberated from it. "Good evening, my lords and ladies. Who is this visitor you have brought me?"

Orgoru stared, frozen in shock. His hair tried to stand on end.

The beautiful maiden seemed to understand; she clasped his arm and whispered, "Our Guardian seems rather fearsome when first you meet him, but he is our mainstay and our comfort, our guard and our provider."

Orgoru didn't quite understand what manner of spirit spoke to him, or could live inside a wall—but he did know that he didn't dare appear frightened in front of so beautiful a damsel. He squared his shoulders and gave what he hoped was a gentle, reassuring smile with a bit of gratitude thrown in—and more than a hint of awe at her beauty. He must have succeeded in some measure, for she blushed and turned away.

"Our visitor has come to live among us, Guardian," the duke said. "He tells us that he is the Prince of Paradime—but we must ask that you cloak him in the glory that suits his rank."

"Certainly," the Guardian agreed.

"Step into the booth," the beautiful damsel told him. "You will feel nothing, but the spirit will take your measure and give you fresh clothing to replace the rags of your disguise."

"I will do whatever you ask," Orgoru said, looking deeply into her eyes, "if you will only tell me your name." Where had they come from, such words, such courtly phrases? Orgoru had never had a way with girls!

But this was no mere girl—she was a lady born, perhaps even a princess! He found that nothing tied his tongue, that he knew how to address a woman who deserved the title of lady;

he found that her gaze on him was admiring as well as flirtatious, and perhaps it was that which unbound his tongue.

She blushed and lowered her eyes, but she said, "I am the Countess Gilda d'Alexi, Prince. May I know *your* name?"

"I am Orgoru," he said simply, then stepped into the booth fearlessly—or seeming to be; his heart hammered within his breast.

He felt no touch, he heard no sound, but in a minute's time, the Guardian said, "Your day's attire waits in the closet in your suite, O Prince—the Azure Rooms in the east wing. Go forth to rejoice."

Orgoru obeyed, feeling that he had missed something somewhere—but he stepped out of the booth, and the Guardian's voice sounded all about him: "It is even as you have guessed, my lord Duke. He is indeed one of your own kind, and belongs among you in this city."

The countess's eyes glowed, the duke cried with delight, and all the lords and ladies cheered. They set off toward the east wing with Orgoru in their midst, singing with joy.

CHAPTER 8

W elcome among us indeed!" cried the duke. "And in proof of it, here is your own suite—the Azure Rooms! Put your hand to the panel, for no one else's will open it now."

Wondering, Orgoru touched the door. It swung open to reveal a huge room with cream-colored walls and deep blue trim and curtains. Even the people in the pictures on the walls wore blue clothing, and they were all lords and ladies, gods and goddesses, with a few servants here and there to remind him of his station in life.

"Enter, Your Highness, enter!" the duke urged.

"Yes, enter," the countess echoed, with smoldering eyes. Orgoru looked into them, swallowed heartily, and entered.

The crowd tumbled in with him, vying for his attention as each showed him a new marvel.

"This is your sitting room. Here you can be alone in luxury as befits your station!"

"Behold your hearth!" An older noblewoman gestured at the small fireplace in the corner. "You'll never need it for more than decoration, of course—these rooms stay warm all through winter, cool all through the summer!"

"If you wish to dine," said a tall young man in scarlet clothes, "here is your table." He touched a horizontal bar in the wall, and it slid out, extending legs to become a table indeed. "Only speak aloud what you wish to eat, and you shall find it on the table when it appears!"

"It seems a pretty picture-frame, does it not?" Another beautiful young noblewoman—they were all beautiful, all these people, as he had known they would be, but none seemed as beautiful to him as Countess Gilda—gestured at an ornate but empty picture-frame. "But speak the word, and it will fill with moving images, images that show a whole story. Picture! Show me *The Romance of the Rose!*"

The picture came to life, with gloriously clad men and women moving about, straight and courtly, the very paragons of gentility. Orgoru fixed the title of the picture in his memory—he felt lumpen and awkward among these people, and wanted to make sure he knew how to move properly.

"Though there are also books!" A fellow prince gestured toward a floor-to-ceiling case filled with leather-bound editions.

"Amazing!" But Orgoru's stomach sank—how could he admit to these cultured people that he didn't know how to read?

"This is the most marvelous of all!" The countess plucked a slender volume from a waist-high shelf, opened it, and held it before Orgoru. "See! It speaks!"

He stared down at a pointed shape with a crossbar, while a voice from the book intoned, "This is the letter *A*, sometimes pronounced 'ah.' "

"A treasure," Orgoru said with feeling, and his heart went out to the countess. How gracious, how tactful of her, to show him that he had the means to learn to read at hand! And how deep her insight, to know that he needed it!

She closed the book and slipped it back onto the shelf, then turned to a door, saying, "Here are more wonders." This door opened at her touch, and the crowd ushered him into the chamber. It was half the size of the sitting room, floor hidden by another azure carpet with designs of leaves and flowers, with a huge four-poster bed centered in one wall. Orgoru gawked, imagining lolling in such luxury when the most he had ever known was a pallet stuffed with straw. He felt a hand touch his, and looked down to see Countess Gilda smiling up at him with mischief in her eyes. He stared back, frozen, pulse hammering, but she laughed and spun away to another door. "Your dressing chamber!"

They hurried him in, still vying with one another to show him its wonders. There was a cupboard that made the dirt fall from him, a tub that filled with hot scented water by itself (they assured him that it was safe, and baths within its waters were restorative and were delights in themselves), and another cupboard that always had clean garments for him (old ones dropped on its floor simply disappeared by morning). Instead of a razor, there was a cream to spread on his skin, and when he wiped it off, his beard would be gone—and would stay gone for a month!

"Refresh yourself," the duke invited, "then come join us in the great hall. Only say where you wish to go, and a spot of azure will appear on the wall, and move before you to guide you to us."

"Do not make us wait long," Gilda breathed, reaching out to touch him one last time as she stepped through the door.

They all went out behind her, laughing and joking, rejoicing that there was one more nobleman among them—and another of royal blood, too! Orgoru's heart overflowed with gratitude to them all, for taking him to their collective bosom so quickly, and without question. Yes, surely he would come to join them as quickly as he could! But not in these peasant clothes, this disguise that had helped him escape from bondage. He closed the door to the dressing chamber, kicked off his heavy shoes and his tunic, and stepped into the cleaning booth.

He was amazed how fresh and new he felt when he came out, and that without a drop of water touching his skin! He wiped away his beard as they had shown him, then opened his closet—and discovered doublet and hose that were so beautiful they took his breath away. They were silver with azure embroidery and a short azure cloak with azure boots. Over them hung a short linen garment that was strange, but after puzzling over it for a little, he drew it on and up about his hips, where it clung as though alive. It was a strange and not entirely pleasant sensation for a man whose loins had always gone ungirded, but if it was the custom here, he would accept it. Then he pulled on the glorious doublet and hose and stood in front of his mirror, amazed at the transformation. Here was no dumpy unkempt peasant, but a tall, lean aristocrat with shining hair and a severe, handsome but noble face that he scarcely recognized as his own.

He strode to the door, feeling ready to take his rightful place among the glittering people.

When the sun neared the horizon, Gar turned off the road into a small woodlot. "Time to think of camping, my friends."

"It does look like the best shelter we're apt to find," Dirk sighed. "Of course, there *might* be an inn at the next village. . . ."

Miles shuddered. "By your leave, sirs, I'd rather not stay at an inn. I know it's foolish of me, but I feel as though if I stay a whole night within reach of the Watch, they're more likely to catch me." Again, he was amazed at his own temerity in speaking to gentlemen before he was spoken to.

But they didn't seem to notice. "I can understand that all too well," Dirk said, "and I'd have to say you're smart. Sure, staying in the woods for a whole night is considerably safer— fewer faces to see us, and much less chance of a forester happening by."

"Especially the foresters who're chasing us," Gar agreed.

Fifty yards from the road, the underbrush tapered away, leaving large patches of clear ground under thirty-foot spruce trees; their lower branches were bare. Gar drew rein. "This will do for a campsite. Miles, would you go seek wood, please, while Dirk and I pitch the tent?"

"S-surely, Master Gar." Miles went, amazed that the big man had asked, rather than commanded.

However, he had begun to become as much afraid of trav-cling with them as of traveling alone. The way Master Gar was talking, he'd have the Protector's spies down on him in a week or less, with the guardsmen in tow—and the punishments for speaking treason were every bit as bad as those for refusing to marry. Worse in immediate pain, just as bad in ruining a man's life—what little was left of it would be spent in the Protector's mines. So Miles began to gather wood, then gathered more and more, working his way farther and farther from the campsite. He was careful to hold on to his armload of sticks, though—if Gar or Dirk came looking for him, he would rather seem to be too stupid to know when he had enough kindling, than to have them realize he was trying to escape.

Of course, there was no reason for him *not* to leave—they had said, more than once, that he wasn't a prisoner, that he was free to go whenever he wanted. They might not even chase him—but Miles didn't want to take chances.

"Ho!" A hard hand clapped down on his shoulder. Miles cried out and twisted, excuses coming to his lips—and saw not Dirk's face, but a stranger's, under a forester's green cap with the red feather showing he commanded a band. Two more hands seized his arms from behind, and the firewood flew clattering.

"Light," the forester commanded, and someone unshuttered a dark lantern. Several other shapes loomed near, and Miles's heart sank. How he wished he had stayed with Gar and Dirk now!

Gar and Dirk . . . He remembered how they had played with the minds of the men who had stopped them. Maybe he could talk his way out of this, convince them he was a traveler whose permit had been stolen, lost now, and hungry . . .

Then a figure with a hip-length robe and chain of office stepped into the lantern-light and, though shadows made the face grotesque, Miles recognized the bailiff of his village. His stomach hollowed; lying would do no good now.

"Is this your man?" asked the chief forester.

The bailiff shook his head. "Mine was clean-shaven and long-haired; he might have trimmed his mop, but he could never have grown so thick a— No, wait!" He squinted, then reached out and yanked the moustache loose.

Miles cried out with pain.

"By the Protector, it *is* you!" the bailiff cried. "Thought you'd be smart to cut the hair from your head and glue it onto your face, did you?"

"No, actually," said a deep but mild voice. "That was *my* idea."

The bailiff whirled, startled—then looked up, and up, to Gar's face. He took an involuntary step back, overwhelmed—and Miles saw his chance. He stuck out a foot; the bailiff went sprawling. The foresters cried out, and the hands on Miles's arms loosened. He tore himself free, spun, and stuck out a foot again as he shoved with all his might. The forester who'd been holding him howled as he fell. The bailiff looked up, saw Miles leaping toward the darkness, and shouted with anger. Then his voice choked off as Gar lifted him by the back of his collar, holding him out at arm's length.

As one, the foresters turned on Gar. Dirk lashed out a kick, and one man fell; Gar threw the bailiff into two more, but three others drew swords and charged him, shouting.

Safe in the dark, Miles swerved and spun about. These men had saved him once, and had just done it again. He couldn't leave them to fight his fights for him. He caught up his heaviest stick of firewood and ran back, just as Gar's huge fist sent two men sprawling. The bailiff was struggling to his feet, lugging out his own sword. Miles struck with the club, and the bailiff fell senseless. Miles felt a moment's anguish; he had known the man since childhood, and he'd often been kind. Then panic surged, for Miles had struck an officer, and knew he'd hang if he was ever caught.

Better not to be. He turned to see the last forester slashing at Gar; the big man caught his blade on a knife big enough to be a short sword. Miles shouted; the forester whirled about, startled, and Miles swung his stick. The man fell, but three more foresters were struggling back to their feet. They all fell on Dirk as the smaller of the two targets.

Gar yanked two of them off the ground by the scruffs

of their necks. Dirk blocked the third's swing with his own sword and slammed a fist into the other man's chin. He fell, unconscious.

"What about you two?" Gar held them up so their faces were level with his. "I know you have to report what you've just seen, but if I let you go, will you promise to take the rest of the night getting home?"

The men both glanced at the bailiff and the chief forester, and saw they were out cold.

"You could say you've been lamed and had to limp," Dirk suggested helpfully. "We could even make it true."

"No, no! We'll manage to lean on one another!" one man choked out. "Only let us free!"

Gar set them down gently. They pulled their necklines free of their larynxes and took deep, rattling breaths.

"Of course, we'll keep your swords," Dirk said.

They glanced at one another, not at all happy about it, then held out their weapons, hilts first.

Dirk took them and passed one to Miles. "Be off with you now."

The two foresters limped off into the night, leaning on one another, doing a very convincing job of looking maimed.

"They'll bear word," Miles warned.

"So will the others, when they come to," Dirk told him.

"And we're not about to kill men who're only trying to do their jobs and be loyal to their ruler." Gar rubbed a sore arm. "Ouch! That 'holding 'em at arm's length' stunt is impressive, but it *hurts*."

"You . . . you saved me again," Miles stammered.

Dirk shrugged it off. "What are friends for?"

Miles felt as though he were about to drown in guilt. Here he had been trying to run away from them, and they had fought for him!

"Well, we're outlaws now, too," Dirk told him. "Of course, we were outlaws before, but the bailiffs didn't know that."

"And those foresters you let go will bring the reeve's guards down upon us!"

"Can't be helped," Gar said. "We'll have to hide now, like

any other outlaws, and I'm afraid we can't wait to reach these Badlands of yours. What's the best hiding place that's close?"

"You're in it." Miles spread his arms. "The woods. All the woodlots hereabouts are like streams, flowing into the huge lake of the forest. We have only to make sure we stay among the trees, and we'll reach the depths soon enough. Of course, the foresters might find us even there . . ."

"And are very likely to find us before we get to the forest," Dirk said grimly. "Well, let's fetch the horses and find a deer trail. If it has room for stags, it has room for mounted men."

Half an hour later, Miles led them through the woods and toward the forest. He had only been in this particular woodlot once before, seeking shelter on the way to the reeve's town, but he remembered it well enough to know how to go toward the deeper forest. As he went, he wondered how Dirk and Gar had come to be near when he needed help.

Because they had been following him, of course—to make sure he wasn't captured. They had realized he had been gone too long, and had set off to make sure he hadn't run into trouble! Another tidal wave of guilt swamped Miles.

Orgoru came into the great hall, and found the tables set. His fellow aristocrats laughed and chatted with one another, and he could see that flirtation was a well-established game among them.

"Welcome, Prince of Paradime!" called a tall, middle-aged man with a crown on his head.

Orgoru halted and stared.

"Ah, how well you look, now that you are refreshed!" The Duke of Darambay swooped down to catch him by the arm and lead him to the crowned man. "Your Majesty, may I present Orgoru, the Prince of Paradime! Orgoru, kneel to your sovereign, King Longar!"

Awed all over again, Orgoru knelt to the tall man with the high and noble forehead, the Roman nose, whose royalty fairly shone about him. "Your Majesty! I . . . I thank you for your hospitality!"

"Gladly given," rumbled the kingly voice. "Welcome among

us, Prince of Paradime! Tonight we celebrate, rejoicing that a new brother is come among us! My lords and ladies, to the festive board!"

They sat and began to dine, laughing and chatting, and using their silverware so easily and naturally that they scarcely seemed to be aware of it. Orgoru did his best to imitate them, blushing more than once when he reached for a fork of strange design but saw his neighbor take another, or used his knife in his right hand when they used theirs in their left. No one seemed to notice, though, and if they did, they only smiled, amused but also as though at a fond memory, and Orgoru realized all over again that he was only going through what all of them had undergone when they had finally been restored to their own kind, after a lifetime of exile. Strange that none of them seemed to have been born here. . . .

The conversation flashed and glittered about him, filled with allusions to stories and sciences that Orgoru had never heard of. He resolved to read every book in his room, and quickly, too.

"I think that perhaps my courtiers spend too much time in pleasure," King Longar rumbled. "We have the Guardian to teach us anything we wish to know, after all!"

"Yes, but learning, too, is pleasure, Your Majesty," a young prince said (Orgoru could tell his rank by his coronet, larger than the duke's).

"I can only praise such pleasuring," the king rejoined, "though I certainly cannot object to the sorts you seek from one another, either."

Orgoru looked about the table to see what he was talking about, and noticed how many men were kissing ladies' hands or counting their fingers, how many long lashes were fluttering, and how many ladies peeked over their fans at men across the table.

Finally the ordeal of the meal was over, and the duke introduced Orgoru to four young noblewomen, one after the other, each beautiful, none so beautiful as Countess Gilda. Lady Amber was tall and graceful, asking, "Will you dance the gavotte with me, Prince?"

"I would be delighted," Orgoru stammered, "but I don't know the dance."

"Why, then, I will teach it to you! Only lead me out!"

The floor of the great hall was polished to a glow, and the dancers took their places as the music began. Lady Amber taught him the gavotte, with good-natured jokes to cover his clumsiness; the young Duchess of Dorent made him practice the dance, with lighthearted teasing about his long years in exile having robbed him of courtly graces; Lady Louette taught him the minuet, and he practiced it with the Marquise of Corobaer—but it was Countess Gilda who taught him the waltz.

She teased him into gracefulness, rallied him into remembering the steps, and by the end of the tune, he was whirling about the floor with her body pressed close to his, blushing furiously and laughing at her jests, breathless with exertion and desire.

"I am wearied, I must confess," she told him. "Come, let us find something to drink."

"As my lady wishes," Orgoru said, and followed her to one of several niches in the inner wall. "Chablis," she said into the air, and slid back a little door to take out a goblet bedewed with condensation and brimming with a white fluid. She told Orgoru, "The punch is quite good tonight," and he took the hint, saying, "Punch," to the air, and wondering what drink could sound like a blow. Then he slid the door back and removed a small round cup with a handle scarcely big enough for a single finger. Turning back to look at the throng, he almost dropped his cup, for as the couples whirled by in the waltz, he saw several joined mouth-to-mouth as they swung, several others caressing openly.

"Surely you're not shocked by the behavior of noble folk," Countess Gilda protested. He turned to deny it, but saw the wicked gleam in her eye. "Come," she said, and led him behind a tall tapestry that hung from the curved wall. In the dark recess behind it, she reached up to cup a hand around the back of his neck and pull his head down, and not very far, for she was almost as tall as he. He resisted for only a startled moment, then bent to find her lips with his—and learned how wondrous a kiss could be.

When they parted, she laughed, with a little breathless giggle. "There now! I've taught you two things, and only one of them the waltz!"

Orgoru opened his mouth to protest that he had kissed a woman before, but before he could lie, she was leading him out into the hall again, just as the dance ended and several couples left the floor. She stepped back into the circle, holding up her hands and saying, "Come, my prince. Perhaps you can practice both new skills at one time."

Orgoru stared a moment; then his pulse leaped, and so did he, back to the circle to catch Countess Gilda giggling to him. Behind her, he noticed several couples leaving the hall arm in arm, but he had no time to be amazed or scandalized, for the music began again, and off they went into a mad, intoxicating whirl, body to body, mouth to mouth.

He was so caught up in the wonder and excitement of it all that he never noticed there were no servants, other than the magic spirits who did everything to serve them, never noticed that the only living people here were all aristocrats. It seemed so right, so fitting, and he would frankly have resented any peasants who intruded.

It also never occurred to him to wonder what would have happened if he had failed the tests of these city people, or if the Guardian hadn't pronounced him to be of their kind. He was only glad that he was, at last, where he belonged.

CHAPTER 9

It was a long, cold night for Ciletha. She had thought to carry flint and steel, and finally built herself a small campfire, but was afraid to make it too big, for fear it might attract foresters. So she huddled close to it, trying to draw what little warmth it gave, listening to her stomach rumble—the berries had been few, and many hours ago. Finally she drifted into sleep. She knew it had to have been sleep, because when Orgoru said, "You have been a good companion, Ciletha, but you must go your way now, and I must go mine," then turned and disappeared into the night, she awoke weeping. She looked about, frantic, but saw no trace that he had ever been there, then remembered that he had gone through the gate in late afternoon. She managed to sleep again, but woke from shivering and stared glumly at the gateway, convinced that Orgoru had met his fate. Grief overwhelmed her, and fear of going on without him.

Something moved against the pale forms of stone.

Ciletha stared. Could it be Orgoru?

More forms moved in the darkness, and torches appeared, showing light over a glowing assembly—but what a sight!

Ciletha stared, unable to believe her eyes. She thought she had never seen so many dumpy, short, and lumpen people in her life—and certainly had never seen such a hodgepodge of clothes! They were of all manner of shapes and styles, all extravagant, exaggerated. Oh, any one costume was gorgeous, of expensive, luxurious cloth and brilliant in color, but so many jewellike tones together clashed and jarred and almost hurt her eyes in their dissonance.

Then Orgoru stepped out from among them.

Ciletha stared in disbelief. He wore a doublet and hose of blue and silver with an embroidered cape of the same colors; his hair was curled over his brow, and his eyes were alive with excitement. A sob caught in her throat as she dashed to meet him. "Oh, Orgoru!"

He ran to catch her hands, grinning from ear to ear. "Ciletha! Oh, it's so wonderful! I wish you could share it!"

The word "wish" chilled her. She glanced past him at the squat, soft-looking people, outrageous in their garish costumes, prancing toward one another with glad smiles, pacing with controlled steps that seemed somehow to be parodies of the movements of magistrates and reeves, their chins tilted high, looking down their noses at one another, tittering and smirking as they glanced at her. Suddenly she understood: she could not share this life with him, because she could never want to. "I— I'm glad you've managed to find what you want, Orgoru."

"Everything I've ever dreamed of! Lords and ladies, people of beauty and nobility, of refinement and culture! Look at them, Ciletha! Aren't they magnificent?"

She looked, and shuddered.

Orgoru frowned. "What's wrong?"

"It's been a cold night." She wondered how he could possibly see these clowns as being noble. But she couldn't bring herself to disturb his waking dream; she forced a tremulous smile and said, "There are certainly none like them in all the world, Orgoru. How lucky you are!"

"Lucky indeed! So have no fear for me, Ciletha—I am where I have always wanted to be! Oh, I hope you'll find your heart's desire, too, just as I have!"

A tall, rawboned young woman began to move toward Orgoru, with a flirtatious glance that seemed ludicrous on her long, lantern-jawed face.

"Thank you, Orgoru." Ciletha forced the words through lips gone suddenly stiff. "I'm so happy for you, my old friend! See, I'm crying with joy!"

"How good of you, Ciletha! How generous!" Orgoru caught one of her tears on his finger and kissed it.

The courtly gesture seemed incongruous in so earthy a man that she managed to force a smile. "Good-bye, Orgoru. May you find every happiness!"

"Good-bye, sweet playfellow."

The "sweet" almost undid her; she turned away and stumbled off into the night, fighting back tears. She glanced back over her shoulder, but Orgoru had already turned away to rejoin his strange companions, who went mincing and laughing away, though they looked as though they should waddle.

Ciletha fled blindly into the night. When their laughter had died behind her, the tears burst forth. She stumbled through the darkened woods until she collided with a tree and leaned against its reassuring bulk, sobbing with heartbreak and finally admitting to herself that she had fallen in love with the bumbling but sweet idiot—who, of course, did not love her. She herself was scarcely beautiful, but Orgoru, once you looked past the poor grooming and clumsiness, was good-looking, at least in the face—or would be, if he weren't so plump. No, of course he'd never noticed her as a woman—and never would have. No wonder that it was only after he was lost to her that she could admit she loved him.

When they were a mile or two from the unconscious foresters, Dirk, Gar, and Miles managed to scrape together a quick camp, cutting pine boughs for beds. Each mounted watch in turn while the others slept, but there was no sign of pursuit, no trace of a night-patrolling forester, and the breeze bore them no faint belling of hounds.

They rose with the sun and hurried on through the woods, as fast as horses could go—a fast walk, but not tiring as quickly as humans would have done. They used every device they knew to break their trail, and though the hounds might eventually find them, they would be very long in doing so.

By evening, they had come among huge old oaks and elms that towered high above them, leaving very little light for the underbrush, which stayed low and thin. There Miles slid off Gar's horse with a grateful sigh, groaned at the pain in his legs, and told his companions, "We've come to the deep woods. We'll be safer here than back near the road, but not really safe for very long."

"Which means not at all." Gar looked around. "Can you think of a good place to hide within the woods, Miles?"

The peasant shook his head. "There are tales of hidden caves with great treasures, whole villages of outlaws, and lost cities overgrown by the forest, sirs, but nothing that I could really believe in."

"Not surprising—those are motifs common to folktales in many places." Gar frowned, looking about him.

A crashing in the underbrush, feet coming closer—Gar and Dirk spun their horses to face the disturbance. Miles whirled to face it, too, aches and pains suddenly forgotten.

She burst through the wall of a thicket, running with a limping step and sobbing breaths, looking back over her shoulder in fear, and Miles stared, stiff with amazement. He had never seen a woman move with such complete and utter femininity. He was so stupefied that he didn't even bring up his staff, and the woman slammed right into his chest. Then he did bring up his arms, but she shoved herself away, lifting her eyes to stare at him.

By itself, there was nothing remarkable about her face. Her features were regular, her mouth rather wide, a sprinkle of freckles across her cheeks and the bridge of her nose, her chestnut hair wildly disheveled—but Miles stared again, and found himself entranced.

Then her mouth opened in a scream, and Miles had to hold his arms very loosely about her, enough to keep her from running, not enough to frighten, as he pleaded, "No, lass, don't fear! We're friends, we'll protect you from whatever—"

The brush came crashing down, and "whatever" burst out—six stocky men in stained and ragged tunics and hose, encrusted with dirt and grease, four with week-old stubble, three with unkempt beards. They plowed to a halt when they saw two mounted guardsmen facing them, and a peasant thrusting their woman-quarry behind him as he brought up his staff.

"Just go your way now," Gar said quietly, "and none of us will have anything to worry about."

The biggest outlaw's face split in a gloating grin. He gave a harsh laugh and cried, "They fear us, lads!"

"But they're guardsmen!" the youngest quavered.

"We're all dead men if we're caught anyway! What matter the death of a guardsman? Out upon them!" He yanked out a rusty sword and charged Gar with a howl. His mates took life and charged behind him, shouting bloody murder.

Gar didn't even draw his sword; he swung his horse aside and leaned down to hook a huge fist into the leader's head as he went by. The leader stumbled and fell to his knees.

Two men pounced on Miles, shouting for the woman, one with a staff and one with a sword that had so many nicks it was nearly a saw. He spun his own staff up to block, then slammed the butt down on the sword. It cracked, and the outlaw stood staring foolishly at the six inches of blade left to his hilt.

One outlaw snatched his bow off his back and strung it while another charged at Dirk with a spear, shouting. The spearhead stabbed straight toward Dirk's heart—but he leaned aside, caught the shaft, and yanked hard. The man stumbled into the horse's side and fell. Dirk spun the spear about, shouting, "Archer!" and throwing, hard.

Another outlaw leveled his quarterstaff like a lance and ran howling at Gar. The big man caught the end of the staff, braced it against his knee, and let the butt catch the outlaw in the belly. He sat down hard, gagging, and Gar yanked the staff free.

Miles's other attacker shouted in anger and swung his staff high. It was a beginner's mistake, and Miles took full advantage of it, shooting his own staff end-on into the man's belly before he could block. The outlaw folded over in pain and sat down hard as Miles danced aside, staff back up to guard, looking about him for more enemies.

The archer was just coming to his feet, bow strung and pulling an arrow from the quiver. He heard Dirk's shout and looked up, staring, then yelped with fright and ducked aside. The spear missed him by inches.

Gar shouted, whirling the staff over his head like a windmill, his horse moving toward the leader. The man yelped in fright, scrambled to his feet, and ran for the underbrush.

Dirk shouted again as he spurred his horse, charging down on the archer. The man howled and fled back into the trees. Dirk pulled up his horse just short of the thicket and turned it back, in time to see two more outlaws running for the bracken. Two others lay unconscious.

Miles looked about him, saw no more enemies moving, and dropped his staff, turning to open his arms for the fugitive. "There now, lass, you're safe. We won't let them get at you."

She stood frozen a moment, lips parted as though uncertain whether to cry out in terror or in joy. Then she sagged against Miles's chest, whole body racked with huge sobs. Dazed, he folded his arms about her, amazed at how wonderful she felt there. He had never held a woman before. He looked up helplessly, but only saw Gar nodding in grave approval. Miles took heart and turned back to murmuring the sort of inanities his mother had used to soothe him when he was very small: "There, there, it'll be all right now, we won't let them get you," and, "Hush, now, hush, there's no need to cry, we're all your friends here," until finally she gulped, pushed him away a little, and wiped streaming eyes on her sleeve. She looked up at him through her tears with a tremulous smile. "Thank you, goodman! I can't ever thank you enough."

"You just did." Where had that gallant phrase come from? "But it wasn't me alone who fought for you, lass. These kind gentlemen did more than I."

"Not this time, we didn't." Dirk was grinning. "You scored just as high as we did, Miles."

"Are you Miles, then?" the woman asked, looking up wide-eyed. "I'm Ciletha."

"I'm charmed to meet you—and by you." The words seemed to roll off Miles's tongue with an ease he'd never known. "Now I'm glad I had to flee from the bailiff."

"Flee?" Ciletha drew back a little. "What for?"

"For refusing to marry the woman his master had chosen for me, and she hated the notion more than I did," Miles told her, "though I have to admit I didn't come right out and say no to the magistrate—I just left. But what sent you to the wildwood, poor thing?"

Ciletha lowered her gaze. "I came with a friend, who was looking for the Lost City. He found it, and chose to stay there."

"Lost City?" Gar edged his horse closer, suddenly very intent. "That sounds like a good place to hide from the hounds and the foresters. Can you take us back there?"

"Why . . . I don't know, sir." Ciletha looked about her, confused. "I've been turned so much about and about while I ran from those fiends . . ." Privately she shuddered at the idea of going back to those strange, ugly, garishly dressed people—but the forest had proved more dangerous than the ruins, and with friends to protect her . . .

Somehow, she knew that Miles would protect her with every ounce of his strength. The knowledge spread through her with a warm reassurance. Why he would, she refused to think—but she knew she was safe with him. Perhaps his friends were to be trusted just as much—but had they fought to save her, or to win her? Surely they wouldn't betray Miles, though.

"Think," Gar urged. "Was the sun behind the city, or behind your shoulder?"

"Behind the city," Ciletha said without hesitation, "but it was the moon, sir—I've been wandering for days now, I think only four of them. Who can find the moon under all these leaves, though?"

"He has an unusually good sense of direction," Dirk informed her.

"Ciletha, these are my masters, Dirk and Gar," Miles said.

"Friends," Dirk said quickly. "Just friends, Miss. We don't own him. Pleased to meet you."

"And I." Gar inclined his head in greeting.

"They aren't really guards," Miles explained, "just wearing the livery as disguise. They're from very far away, and don't know a lot of our customs."

"Are other counties so different?" Ciletha asked, looking at the horsemen with wide eyes.

"We're from farther away than another county, I'm afraid," Dirk said.

"Let's ride while we talk," Gar suggested. "If the moon was behind the city, it should be this way."

"Yeah, well, that takes care of east versus west," Dirk said as he pulled his horse around to fall in beside Gar's, "but what do we do about north versus south?"

"Oh, I'm sure we'll find some sort of landmark," Gar said easily.

Dirk shot him a calculating glare. "Yeah, I'll just bet you will." He turned back to Miles and Ciletha. "Coming, folks? Miles could ride with Gar, and you could ride with me, Ciletha."

"I'd just as soon walk," she said quickly, so of course Miles said, too, "I'll walk."

"Suit yourself," Dirk said. "Horses can't go much faster than people in a nighttime wood, anyway." He turned to face forward again, leaving the two locals to follow.

"What of this lad who brought you into the wood?" Miles asked. "What was he like?"

"Oh, no taller than you," Ciletha said, "and pudgy, most would call him. But he had large eyes, of the most beautiful brown you could think, and a cute little nose between high cheeks, with generous lips. He's generous within, too, is Orgoru, though most folk won't let him show it."

Her tone was so warm that Miles knew she must be in love with the lout, and felt a stab of jealousy that surprised him— but he realized that, though Ciletha wasn't beautiful, there was something of elfin charm to her face, to the shape of her nose and the tilt of her eyes, and beauty in those large orbs and their long lashes. He felt his own heart move strangely, and wondered if he were himself falling in love.

A stick cracked, and Ciletha froze. The horsemen halted,

too. After a moment, Gar said, "Only a badger." He clucked to his horse and moved on.

The others followed, but Ciletha's eyes were wide, apprehensive. "Please, lad, let's not talk. Those bandits might hear us and come back—and bring a bigger band."

Miles smiled. "They'll hear the horses in any case, lass, but I'll admit that hooves might belong to deer. Nay, as you'll have it."

They went on in silence, following the horses.

Miles couldn't help sneaking covert glances at Ciletha whenever they passed through a patch of moonlight. Dirty and ragged though she was, there was some elusive quality about her that held him fascinated. His attention seemed to make Ciletha uneasy, so he whispered, " 'Ware, now—there's a root ahead."

She recovered her composure and smiled. "I see it, lad. Don't worry yourself about me—I've been a poacher seven years and more."

"You?" Miles stared, for women were rarely poachers.

"Aye, me. My father was ailing all that time, and I knew he needed meat." Her tone hardened. "No, I didn't leave him—he left me, through the gate of death."

Miles was startled, even shocked. "Don't blame him for it, lass. It's not as though he chose it."

"Oh, I know, I know," Ciletha said, "but his going left me without protection against the magistrates, or the town boys who wanted my father's house."

"Ah. Well, I can see you'd be angry, then," Miles said, "and I've no doubt your father is, too—angry at the death that sundered him from you."

"What are you saying?" Ciletha stared. "You talk as though he were still alive in his grave!"

"No, but I've heard some folk say that the spirit lives on after the body dies," Miles said slowly, "and it tries to move about in the world, if its business isn't done."

"Ghosts?" Ciletha breathed.

"Aye, the ghosts of our nursery tales. No one ever asks what happens to the spirits of those whose life's business *is* done, though," Miles said, musing. "Wouldn't there have to be some-place for them to go and rest, some Spirits' Home?"

"I suppose there would," Ciletha said slowly. "It would have to be a happy place, wouldn't it? For everyone there could have that pleasant feeling that comes from a task well-finished."

Gar rode on, listening to the two young folk behind him reinventing religion, and smiled. Dirk caught his eye and winked.

Then, distant and so faint it might have been imagination, they heard the first elusive baying of the hounds. Miles stopped, galvanized even though the sound faded away again. Gar grinned. "They've followed the false trail we laid."

"That'll delay them a few hours," Dirk said, "but they'll still catch us by morning. Can't you find this city a little faster?"

"We're moving directly toward it," Gar told him, "and it's not very far away. Ciletha must have been going in circles when she left it, and certainly when the bandits chased her."

Ciletha looked up, startled, and Miles touched her hand, giving her a reassuring smile. "It's the natural thing, lass, in a strange wood." He turned back to the path—and saw a skeleton moving toward them in the scraps of moonlight that filtered through the trees.

CHAPTER 10

Miles would have run, but Ciletha cried out in fear, and he leaped to place himself between her and the skeleton. Gar and Dirk only stared, though, and Dirk said softly, "Well, would you look at that!"

"At a guess," Gar said, "I'd say this Lost City was left over from the original colonists."

"Left over for five hundred years! Amazing that it's still working!"

Miles stared, and Ciletha cried, "What nonsense are they talking?"

Gar turned back and gave them a reassuring smile. "Nothing to worry about, folks. It's just a machine."

"Machine! Machines are huge ungainly things, like mills! This is a walking skeleton, a spirit of the dead!"

"Not at all," Gar told them. "It's a robot, a moving statue."

"But where did they get a power source that would keep this thing going so long?" Dirk asked. "And how do they keep it working?"

"We are recharged every day, sir," the skeleton replied, "and automated machines manufacture spare parts according to the templates on file."

Ciletha gave a little shriek, and Miles nearly shouted in fear. "How can you say it's not a spirit," Ciletha cried, "when it talks?"

The featureless skull swiveled toward her, and the skeleton said, "This unit is equipped with a vocoder and a computer, sir, and is programmed to respond to human questions."

"Nonsense," she whispered. "It's a ghost that talks nonsense!"

"There must be some reason to it somewhere," Miles said, trying to sound reassuring. "If Gar and Dirk say it makes sense, it must—somehow."

"What do you do if those humans attack you instead of asking questions?" Dirk asked.

"We immobilize them, sir."

" 'We.' " Gar frowned. "How many of you are there?"

"Three hundred, sir. Half recharge by day, half by night."

"Sentry duty?" Dirk tensed. "What are you guarding against?"

"Large animals, sir, and bandits—and others who might wish to enter the city to prey upon its people, or to find a living without working. That is our original programming."

Gar frowned. "You obviously don't take us for bandits."

"No, sir. You have made no threatening movements, and though you carry weapons, you are clearly not coming in attack mode, nor with enough companions to constitute a threat."

"It isn't really a skeleton," Miles whispered to Ciletha. "Its head doesn't have eye or nose sockets."

"No," she said, eyes wide in wonder, "and it doesn't have ribs, just a sort of flattened egg. But Miles, it gleams like polished steel!"

"Yes, it does," he answered, "and I think it must be. I thought the old tales were just children's stories!"

"You've guessed rightly," Gar told the robot, "we're not bandits. In fact, we're fugitives looking for shelter. Can you take us into the city for the night?"

"I'm sure hospitality can be arranged, sir. Please follow me."

The robot turned and walked away. Gar and Dirk clucked to their horses and followed, beckoning Miles and Ciletha along. They stared, then ran to catch up. As they slowed again, Ciletha asked, "What kind of men are they, these friends of yours, not to be frightened by that . . . thing?"

"Very strange men," Miles replied, "though they've saved me from the bailiff's men twice, and seem to be thoroughly good in every way. But I have to help them, too, because they don't know very much about everyday life."

"They seem to know enough about magic," Ciletha said, with a wary glance at the skeleton.

"They'd be the first to tell me that it's not."

"Would you believe them?" she asked, with a skeptical glance.

"No," Miles confessed. "Not really."

They followed the robot for hours, or so it seemed, until the canopy of leaves suddenly fell away, leaving only isolated trees, and letting the moonlight bathe the stone towers that loomed high in the night.

The companions stopped involuntarily, catching their breath. The stone glimmered in the moonlight, giving the im-pression of a fairy city, a magical realm. Even though the towers were festooned with flowering vines, and every flat surface held its crop of brush and at least one small tree, the illusion of enchant-ment held.

The robot paused, turning its "head." "Why do you stop?"

"To appreciate beauty," Dirk told it.

The silvery skull nodded. "Yes, a human concept. I confess that the word is meaningless noise to me, but the referent seems to take hold of your species at the oddest times."

"And this is a very odd time," Gar agreed. "We would like to see this treasure from a closer vantage point, sentry."

"Of course, sir. This way."

The robot found a trail where they could have sworn there was none. They followed slowly, scarcely able to take their eyes from the soaring towers.

"You've seen this before," Miles said.

"Yes, but its spell still catches me." Ciletha smiled up at

the glowing spires. Light glittered in her eyes—or were those tears? "Maybe I won't be afraid to go in, with friends about me."

"Oh, we're certainly your friends." Miles stopped himself from saying that he wanted to be much more, then was amazed to realize how he felt about a woman he had only just met. "What was there to fear, though?"

Ciletha shuddered and would have answered, but the underbrush about them suddenly ceased, showing them a very wide gap in a high and gleaming wall.

"This is the gate," the robot said. "Welcome to the city of Voyagend."

"Voyage's End—for a ship full of colonists." Gar traced the line of the hill within the walls. "See how the buildings rise tier upon tier to the highest towers?"

Dirk nodded. "The ship's still there, just buried. Think they planned it that way?"

"Almost certainly," Gar replied. "After all, they didn't have enough fuel to lift off again. Why not make their years-long home part of the landscape? That way, they'd always have it with them."

Miles and Ciletha listened with wide, wondering eyes.

"That right, sentry?" Dirk asked.

"You have guessed correctly, sir," the robot said. "Will it please you to enter?"

"Hard to say," Dirk said slowly.

Faint on the night breeze came the belling of hounds.

"On second thought, it would please me very much. Take us in, sentry."

The robot led the way through the gate.

"Sentry," Gar said, "there may be some men following us with dogs. Discourage them, will you?"

"Certainly, sir. I will cover your trail with a mild solution of petroleum derivatives—but I don't think you need fear. These people may have discarded religion, but they are still superstitious."

"Needs will out," Dirk muttered.

"Certain primal drives always find expression," Gar muttered back.

"What on earth are they talking about?" Ciletha wanted to know.

Miles shook his head, bewildered. "I don't have the faintest idea."

Gar suddenly reined in his horse. A pace behind him, Dirk asked, "Ghosts?"

"Not many, at least," Gar answered, "and not malevolent."

If he had been alone, Miles would have run right then. With Ciletha beside him, though, he didn't dare.

She looked about her, wide-eyed. "What's he talking about? I don't see anything, not even those odd dumpy people!"

Miles looked down the long, broad, silent boulevard, glancing at each of the buildings. "If there were ghosts, I could believe they'd flock here," he said slowly, "but I don't see anything."

"Would it matter if we did?" Ciletha's voice trembled. "Where else could we hide that the hounds wouldn't follow?" Her grip tightened on his arm, and truth to tell, it gave Miles as much reassurance as it seemed to give her.

Dirk pointed to the ruins of what looked like an ancient Greek temple, high above them on the hilltop. "That's high ground, and it should have back exits."

"A good choice," Gar agreed. "Sentry, can you lead us there?"

"Of course, sir," the robot said, and struck off along the boulevard. Gar and Dirk followed, so Miles and Ciletha had no choice but to go along, though Miles's stomach hollowed farther with every step.

The boulevard led straight to a wide circular plaza that radiated a dozen streets. Without the slightest hesitation the robot went to the one that sloped up toward the "temple."

"Odd to rise so," Dirk commented.

"Yes, sir, but that straight climb was useful. Children used to delight in it when snow fell."

Ciletha laughed, almost breathless. "How can I fear a place where children used to go sledding?"

"I can't, either." Miles grinned. "Especially if their ghosts are happy."

"They are," Gar called out ahead.

Miles frowned, and Ciletha asked, "How can he know if a ghost is happy?"

"He's teasing us," Miles told her. "There aren't any ghosts." He hoped he was right.

The street ran straight up the hill. "They banked this into a long, gentle slope when they buried the ship," Dirk offered.

Gar nodded. "They were building a toboggan run, not a roller coaster."

"Their secret language again," Ciletha sighed.

Miles looked at her and grinned. She was amazingly resilient—or very brave. Or both.

Up they climbed, up and up between buildings tinted rose and blue and gray in the moonlight. Empty windows stared down at them, but the buildings seemed to smile. More happy people than miserable ones had lived here. Behind them, the belling of the hounds became louder and louder. Miles couldn't help but feel safe here, though.

Finally the ground leveled off, and they stood in a great circular plaza with the great templelike structure towering before them. A long, long stairway led up to a doorway decorated with bas-relief carvings, but its grade was so shallow that Miles didn't think it would be terribly tiring to climb.

"You must leave your horses here," the robot told them.

"Makes sense." Dirk dismounted and tied his horse's reins to a nearby marble post. "Let's go."

Gar dismounted too, and the companions climbed up toward the temple. The going was easy, but it was a long, long way at a constant climb, and Miles's legs began to ache. He kept glancing at Ciletha with concern, but she seemed to have less trouble than he, only breathing heavily as she went, and he could appreciate that.

Finally the stairs ended, and the pillars of the temple loomed above them, far higher than they had seemed from the ground below. Miles stared up at them, awed.

Then the voices of the hounds broke into a frenzy.

"The animals have come out of the forest and struck your trail," the robot informed them.

Miles turned, his stomach sinking—and saw bolts of lightning strike down from the towers, sheeting between the city and the hunters. He cried out in dismay, "I didn't mean that people should die so I could escape!"

"None have died," the robot informed him, with such total assurance that it raised the hairs on the back of his neck. "The energy struck far before them, but it has been enough to give them pause. You may hear what they say." It made no move, but voices suddenly spoke, floating above the steps before them. The hounds barked and whined in fear, and a man's voice called, "The hounds won't go ahead now, bailiff."

"I don't blame them," said a heavy voice that Miles knew. "Let them go, forester! If they've fled to that place, they're as good as imprisoned."

"Aye." The voice became muffled, as though the man had turned his back. "Anyone who would flee here of his own free will, must be like all the rest of them."

"Yes," said another. "If they chose this place, what difference? Here or in the madhouse, it's all the same."

The noises of the dogs, and the men's calls to them, faded, then stopped abruptly.

"Directional sound," Dirk offered, "automatically adjusting the focal point."

Gar nodded. "Parabolic audio pickups buried in the wall, at a guess. And that lightning would give them a good reason to stay away."

"It would scare *me.*" Dirk turned to the robot. "How did the city know to keep them out, sentry?"

"Why, sir, because you had told this unit you were being chased."

"So." Dirk looked up at Gar, interested. "If we tell one part of the city, we tell it all. Central computer somewhere?"

"That sounds likely," Gar agreed. He turned to Miles. "Why would our coming in here be the same as being imprisoned in a madhouse?"

Miles could only spread his hands, baffled. Ciletha shook her head, equally at a loss.

"Why not ask the people who live here?" Dirk asked softly.

They turned and looked into the "temple." Soft lights had come to life, showing them the line of dumpy-looking people in gorgeous clothing, stepping out to gather in the doorway of the temple.

Orgoru was suspicious of the strangers, as were all his fellow aristocrats, but when the Guardian told them the newcomers were being chased by a bailiff and his foresters, Orgoru felt pangs of sympathy. Then, when the moving picture on the wall of the great hall had shown them the foresters turning away, and they had heard the foresters say the fugitives belonged in the city, King Longar cried, "That is reason enough to trust them, at least enough for a night's hospitality!"

"After all," said an older duke, "the Guardian will tell us whether they really are our kind, or not."

"Then let them stay one night," King Longar pronounced, with regal largesse. "Orgoru, Prince of Paradime, the greeting is yours to give, since you are the newest come."

Orgoru felt a surge of elation that overcame his shyness of strangers. "I thank Your Majesty." He turned with the rest of them, following the king to the portal of the palace.

There he stopped, as they all did, waiting till the strangers turned to see them, and beginning to feel indignant because they seemed to be rapt in gazing out at the moonlit buildings, preferring them to the aristocrats. Finally they did turn, and froze. Orgoru smiled, feeling confidence return as the strangers stood staring.

"Orgoru, relieve their fears," King Longar said.

"I shall, Majesty." Orgoru stepped forward, hand raised to greet the newcomers. "Welcome to the city of Voyagend."

The youngest of the three stepped between Orgoru and the woman, but the tallest raised his hand and his voice. "I thank you for your welcome."

"I am Orgoru, Prince of Paradime." Orgoru made his smile as reassuring as he could.

The woman leaned out from behind the short man, staring, and Orgoru finally saw her face clearly. "Ciletha!" Then he was running out through the portal, princely dignity forgotten, to throw his arms about her. "Ciletha, you came back after all!"

"Oh, Orgoru!" Ciletha cried. Then her voice broke; she sobbed and clung to him.

The youngest stranger's face darkened, and he turned away, but the tallest held him by the shoulder.

Orgoru looked up over his old friend's head, stroking her hair, but remembering his duties as welcomer. "Who are you who seek our refuge?"

"I am Magnus, cousin to the Count d'Armand and heir to the Lord High Warlock of Gramarye," Gar said.

Orgoru stared. Behind him, he heard a rustle of excited comment. No wonder; these folk were their own kind after all!

"Show-off," the middle stranger muttered.

"My apologies." Gar inclined his head and gestured toward Dirk and Miles. "I am slow in my courtesies. These are my companions, the Duke Dulaine and the Marquis of Miles. I thank Your Highness for your hospitality."

Marquis? Gar must be mad! Anyone could see that Miles was no more than a peasant! Miles glanced at Dirk for support, but saw that the other companion was only nodding with slow approval, and Miles's mouth went suddenly dry. Was Dirk mad, too?

No. Of course not. These men were experienced travelers, and knew how to meet the situation. Miles tried to relax, but he couldn't help wondering why Gar had introduced himself as Magnus.

They took their places at the festive board, the visitors at the head table with the king, since they were of noble rank, and Orgoru with them, since it was he who had greeted them. Miles told himself sternly that he had no right to feel downcast; Ciletha had shown no interest in him other than friendship.

Gar picked up his cocktail fork as the bowl of prawns appeared at his place. He pretended not to notice that several of the "aristocrats" hesitated over the choice of silverware, then imitated their older neighbors. Gar turned to Orgoru, who was just picking up his cocktail fork after a glance at the king. "Ciletha tells us that you are only newly come to this city, Prince."

"Indeed," Orgoru replied. "Like so many of my fellow aristocrats, I was reared in hiding, disguised as a peasant." He gestured toward the table with a self-deprecating smile. "We are clumsy and have much to learn that our peasant hosts couldn't teach us, but we learn quickly." The smile became more firm. "I have already improved my carriage and bearing considerably."

"Carriage?" Miles asked in an undertone, not wanting Ciletha to hear. "He walked on his own two feet! And how could a human body have bearings?"

"Same word, different meaning," Dirk explained, equally low-voiced. "By 'carriage and bearing,' he means the way he stands and walks—the way he holds himself."

"How strangely they twist words," Miles said.

"Have you indeed!" Gar's voice was warm with admiration. "How have you learned so quickly?"

"Oh, by watching the other lords and ladies, of course," Orgoru said, "but also by the magic picture in my suite."

"Magic?" Dirk's interest pricked up. "Does it show moving images?"

"Indeed it does," said Orgoru. "I told it to show me pictures of lords and ladies moving about, and it presented me with a story called *King Richard II*." He grew sad. "A tragic and noble story it is, of a right royal king overwhelmed by a base traitor and slain in his prison."

"And the lords and ladies in it moved most elegantly," Gar summed up. "But as I remember the play, there are peasants in it, too."

"Oh, most surely, my lord!" Orgoru grinned. "They're clumsy and ungainly in their movements, very much as I was when I came here. The Guardian showed me pictures of myself as I was when the others first brought me into this palace. Already I find them most amusing."

"Yes, quite." Gar glanced at Dirk. "Recorded pictures of events, you say? Who is this 'Guardian'?"

"All have met him, but none have met him," Orgoru said cryptically. "He is a spirit that lives inside a wondrously decorated wall. You shall speak with him yourself before this night is over."

Miles noticed that he didn't mention their having any choice. He glanced at Ciletha, and his heart twisted, for he saw she was suffering, and no wonder—Orgoru had scarcely paid her any attention since he'd greeted her, and kept making eyes at the tall, rawboned woman with the long face. She responded with roguish glances that looked frankly ridiculous in a woman of her size.

Gar noticed. "But tell me, Prince, why there are no children to be seen in this city. I see from the flirtations going on around this very table that your courtiers are certainly aware of one another romantically; do they never have sons or daughters?"

Orgoru stared, frankly at a loss. King Longar saw, and stepped in with an explanation. "Love-games are constant, Count, and affairs are frequent—they combat the ennui which is the aristocrat's constant bane."

"I trust there are few marriages, then, or questions of honor would be rife."

"My lords and ladies seldom marry," the king confirmed, "and somehow no children are born of the affairs. The few children born of the marriages are always stolen by elves, alas."

"Elves?" Gar's interest focused. "Are you sure?"

The king shrugged impatiently. "Who can be sure, with elves? But the babe is laid to sleep in its cradle, guarded by several lords—for they are quick to serve one another in such wise, I assure you. In the morning though, no matter how wakeful and alert they are, the child is gone. What could it be but the work of elves?"

Gar and Dirk exchanged a glance; then Gar turned back to the king, nodding.

"Thank you for enlightening me, Your Majesty." Gar

inclined his head, as though the short, fat little man had a real aura of royalty about him, rather than looking like the village brewer.

"It was a pleasure," the king said, with a condescending air that was ludicrous in so cuddly a body. He turned back to the table, and other conversations, with his back straight and chin high, and an air of nobility that contrasted so wildly with his physical appearance that Miles was hard put not to laugh.

"Tell me, my lord," said Orgoru, "what does your father the Lord High Warlock do, to merit such a title?"

Gar launched into a very elaborate explanation that made absolutely nothing clear, then managed to ask question after question that drew responses from everyone else at the table, their eyes brightening and excitement entering their voices as the conversation roamed over history, literature, and politics. When the meal ended, conversation went on, the "lords" and "ladies" forming little knots of discussion, even though music called them to dance.

The tall, rawboned woman with the long face hearkened to that call, though, and swept over to Orgoru. Since he'd been glancing at her every few minutes, he noticed her immediately, and turned to give her a courtly bow. "Countess Gilda! May we have your opinion on the Hussite Wars?"

"Perhaps later, Prince," the countess said, "but at the moment, I could not stand still; the music animates my feet."

"Does it so? Why, then, allow me the pleasure of this dance!" Orgoru swept her up in his arms and swirled away with her onto the floor.

Miles and Ciletha, stranded at the high table, stared. "Did he always know that dance?" Miles asked.

"No! He never knew any dance! He has learned it in just these last few days—as he has learned to bow, and to hold his head with that slight tilt, to stand so straightly and walk so lightly!" Tears stood in her eyes. "But who is that horse who calls herself a countess? Who is she that plays at being a creature from a children's tale? How dare she take him!"

Miles stared at her, then felt a rush of hope—she might be in love with Orgoru, but he felt no more than friendship for her, might even be in love with this "countess"! He felt shame, too, that he should be pleased at something that caused Ciletha pain, but there was no point in hiding it from himself—Gilda gave Miles an opportunity with Ciletha, and he had to admit to himself that he had already fallen in love with her. It was a strange and thrilling feeling, for he had never been in love before. He turned back to watch the two dancers—still easy to single out, though other couples were coming out on the floor to join them—and saw the sparkle in Gilda's eye, saw the answering gleam in Orgoru's, heard her hearty laugh and his throaty chuckle.

Ciletha, too, saw the interplay. She gave a choking sob and rose, turning away from Miles and rushing out of the great hall.

Miles stared after her, taken aback. Then his heart overflowed with pity for her, and he leaped up to follow.

CHAPTER 11

M iles chased the sound of Ciletha's footsteps through
half-lit halls and around two corners before he found
her leaning against a wall, crying her heart out. Then
what could he do but hover anxiously? She looked up and saw
him, though, stared almost in fright a moment, then threw herself into his arms, sobbing as though her heart would break—
which it very well might.

Finally the sobs slackened, and she moaned, "Let me go
mad, too! Wouldn't Orgoru fall in love with me then?"

Miles stood frozen, staring over her head at the wall. Of
course! She was right, very right! Living their lives as though
in a fairy tale, learning to bow and mince and dance in elaborate rounds—of course they were insane! Who else could live
so? How else could people who were clearly peasants think
themselves to be kings and duchesses?

But if insanity let them live in luxury, without working, who
wouldn't want to go mad?

Fear stabbed, fear at the thought of Ciletha becoming one of
those painted, posturing, artificial creatures. "Cupid shoots his
arrows where he will, Ciletha," he said softly. "People who are

clearly right for one another, usually fall in love with somebody else."

Ciletha stilled a little, but still quivered. "You don't think she's right for him, then?"

Miles had to be careful here. "How much do they have in common, besides their madness? Oh, I've seen boys in my village fall in love, all right—but rarely with the good women who would be so good for them! It's always the minx who turns their heads." He frowned, not liking the next thought. "Maybe it's better to let the reeves choose for us, after all."

"No!" Ciletha pushed herself away enough to glare up into his face. "To have to try to be a wife to a man I loathe? Never! If anyone has to plan my life, it'll be me!"

"Planning seems to have very little to do with it," Miles said, with irony.

"Beauty does, though," Ciletha said.

They were both silent a moment, thinking of Orgoru and Gilda. Then Ciletha said, "Perhaps not, though."

"I'm sure he sees her as beautiful," Miles said, "even as she seems to see him as handsome."

"He is, in his way," Ciletha said, her voice small.

"Maybe," Miles said, "but I don't think that's the handsomeness that Gilda sees."

Ciletha frowned up at him. "You mean that they actually see different faces, different bodies, from the ones we see? Surely that can't be."

"Maybe," Miles said slowly, "but I saw a picture in my childhood, when my parents took me to stand before the reeve, and I remembered it very well—a bright, colorful image of a knight and a dragon, hanging in front of a house. I remembered it for years, and when I'd had a terrible day and was trying to sleep, I'd think of that picture, and it gave me an odd sort of comfort. But when I was fourteen, they took me to the reeve's town again, and I saw the picture once more. It was all wrong—the knight was standing, though I remembered him as kneeling, and held a spear, not a sword. The dragon was much smaller, not really surrounding the knight with its coils—in fact, it didn't have coils, and it did have wings, though I hadn't remembered them. To cap it, at fourteen, I knew the house for what it was—a tavern, and the picture was the sign that hung over its door."

Ciletha stared; then she burst into laughter and pressed a hand up to his cheek. "Poor Miles! How dreadful that must have been!"

"Meeting reality always is," Miles confessed. "But I still have the picture my memory made up, there in my mind, where I can always look at it."

Ciletha frowned. "I see what you mean," she said slowly, "that the woman Orgoru sees may have a lot in common with the Countess Gilda we see, but is far more beautiful, and far more graceful."

"Oh, she's graceful enough," Miles said. "None of them are clumsy. They all have the magistrate's walk, the tilt of the chin—but it looks wrong on them, somehow. Not 'graceful,' perhaps, but 'stately.' "

"Certainly not alluring." Ciletha's voice hardened. "Though I'm sure that's how Orgoru sees her."

"Yes, and she probably sees him as tall and lean, with a noble brow and Roman nose."

Ciletha smiled, then gave in and let a giggle out. "Yes, she probably does. I can see how you might be right, Miles."

Miles thought the delight he felt at hearing her laugh must have been far more than he had any reason to feel. He couldn't keep the smile in, though, and said, "Right or wrong, I'd rather not go back there right now. Do you think we can find a door that leads out? I'd like some fresh air—and the ruins shouldn't be too frightening by night."

"Not as long as we don't see another of those skeletons." Ciletha didn't really seem to find the prospect very frightening. "Let's stay close to the palace, though."

They found the door, and the plaza outside was so wide that they could wander as much as they wanted and still be fairly near the building. They didn't see any robots, but they did see plenty of stars. They began to talk about how vastly far away the sky must be, and Miles told her the silliness he'd heard from Gar and Dirk, that each of those points of light was a sun, that some even had worlds circling them, and that it would take the Protector's fastest courier thousands of years to ride from one to another. She laughed with him, first at the notion of a horse galloping between the stars, then at the absurdity of each star being a whole sun. Then she quieted, though, and told Miles she had heard a story like that in her childhood, that stars held other worlds around them, and that their ancestors had come from such a world, so very far away.

Then they began to really think how far it must be between stars, if that tale were true, and that led them to thinking of eternity, of how long the world might last beyond their deaths, and of course that led them to talking about whether or not their ghosts really would live on after their bodies died.

So they spent an hour or two in one another's company, passing the nighttime hours discussing the great questions that confront the young, and when at last they went back into the palace, each was smiling, but each felt a little sadness that these few hours together, alone, were over.

Countess Gilda decided on a bit of variety, and accepted another lord's invitation to dance, though she kept glancing at Orgoru as she did, no doubt hoping to see him jealous—but before the green-eyed monster could come upon him, Gar and Dirk had buttonholed him near the refreshment table.

"You seem to be one of the younger lords," Gar commented. "How did you come to be here?"

"Like all the others, I was raised in hiding for fear of my father's enemies," Orgoru began. He didn't mean to go on for very long, but Gar and Dirk asked him question after question, and seemed to be so genuinely interested that he found himself telling them the story of his life, in detail. He was just finishing when Countess Gilda came back in a swirl of skirts, pouting. "So you have missed me not at all, sir!"

"I have missed you most fantastically," Orgoru said quickly, "and only my talk with these gentlemen has soothed my spirits."

"I do not believe you! You would as soon talk to them as dance with me!" Gilda turned on her heel to flounce away.

Orgoru caught her hand and pressed a quick kiss upon it, as he had watched the other lords do. "Oh no, sweet sunrise, don't leave me in the darkness of longing!"

"Well, I'll abate my severity," Gilda said, turning back with a sunny smile. "You may dance with me, then."

"You are so kind and generous!" Orgoru cried, and led her out onto the floor.

"As I thought," Gar said, watching them go, "delusions of grandeur."

"Yes," Dirk agreed, "but it's charitable not to disillusion him. After all, he's not hurting anyone here—and do you really think he'd be able to lead a successful life outside?"

"True—and it's a kindness to shelter him here. A great kindness, especially considering that all the rest of them seem to be suffering from the same syndrome."

Dirk nodded. "Just a matter of time before they'd start going around giving orders and expecting to be treated like royalty."

"And being beaten for their pains. Who knows how they might end?" Gar asked.

"Rhetorical question, I hope," Dirk replied. "They'd be ostracized or exiled, and die young."

"Yes," Gar said heavily. "So why not let them all gather here, where a central computer can keep them alive? They can be happy, of course—but they can't have children."

"A gold-plated insane asylum." Dirk nodded. "How about those few children who are born, but are stolen by elves?"

"The human sentries are sedated, and robots take the babies," Gar said immediately. "I hope they leave them on the doorsteps of cottagers who want children."

"Probably—always a few woodcutters living alone in forests. But children who were raised here, would never be able to leave."

"Yes—they'd certainly never have a normal upbringing, or learn how to fend for themselves," Gar said. "It's a great kindness, if you think of it that way."

"It also supplies a purpose for a computer that's been abandoned by its civilization," Dirk pointed out.

"Yes." Gar nodded. "I gather we're going to be meeting that

computer soon." He looked up as Miles came drifting back with Ciletha, both with heady smiles, carefully not looking at one another—but their hands touched.

"The hour grows late, milords," a young nobleman said, coming up to them. "You must be wearied after your travels. May I show you to your rooms?"

Dirk bit back surprise that an aristocrat would do a porter's job—after all, there weren't any servants here, just "aristocrats." While he was still biting, Gar said gravely, "Why, yes, thank you. That would be most kind."

Each had a suite to himself or herself, of course. When they had bathed, cleaned their clothes in the "shower," and dressed again, Dirk and Gar met in Gar's sitting room. Miles tapped on the door a few minutes later. Gar let him in, smiling. "You seem to have had a good evening."

"Yes." Miles smiled, letting the glow show. "Ciletha's a most wonderful woman, sirs." His brow creased. "How sad that she's in love with that lout Orgoru!"

"Sad indeed," Dirk said with a knowing smile. "You'll have to do something about that."

Miles looked up in surprise, then began to smile again, slowly.

" 'Lout'?" Gar asked. "Strange way to talk about a lord!"

"There are no lords or ladies in the whole world," Miles said flatly, "only in tales for children. This Orgoru's no more noble than I am, and I've seen his kind in my own village. There're the ones who can't do anything, so they try to pretend they're better than anyone else—either that, or they just give up, eke out a living hauling and digging, and die young." He saddened. "Maddening though they are, I suppose I'd rather they tried to lord it over the rest of us, and keep getting knocked down for their pains—I wouldn't wish the other kind of life on a dog."

"Not exactly a nice life either way," Dirk said darkly. "Better for him to be here, where he won't bother anybody."

"No, not a bit!" Miles took fire. "What right does he have to live in luxury when he can't even do as much work as I can?

And *what right* does he have to the love of such a woman as Ciletha?"

"Both outcasts in their home village, I suppose," Gar said, "who grew up together, and were each other's only friend."

"Ciletha, an outcast?" Miles stared.

"Men don't always see a woman's real worth, Miles," Gar said, with a sardonic grimace. "In fact, I suspect these poor delusionaries don't see the world as it really is at all."

"Still," Dirk said, "she's bound to become disenchanted with Orgoru, watching him posturing here—and paying court to that poor horse-faced Gilda. Just be there for her, and be patient, and she'll turn to you sooner or later."

"I don't know if I can accept being second choice," Miles said, frowning. "How could I wed her if, all my life, I'd have to remember that she would have chosen Orgoru if she could have?"

"Wait until she knows enough about him to *not* choose him," Dirk said.

There was a knock at the door. Gar went to open it. "Orgoru! Come in. We were just talking about you."

"Why, how complimentary!" Orgoru came in a step. "But I have come to ask you if you are refreshed enough to meet the Guardian before you sleep."

"We would be pleased." But Gar's gaze lingered on Orgoru, who forced a smile to hide his discomfort.

"He's happier the way he is," Dirk snapped.

"True," Gar agreed, "but we need him."

Dirk frowned. "You sure you know what you're doing? The human mind is a pretty delicate thing."

"I know." Gar stared at the madman. "Let me see if there would be any danger here."

Orgoru felt as though the giant's eyes were boring into his mind. Then, horrified, he felt something tickle, moving inside his head, and screamed, a raw hoarse cry, sinking to his knees; he barely heard Gar say, "This would be simple, though, and quite safe. He's very uncomplicated, really—a classic case, needing only . . ."

Suddenly other "lords" burst in, crying, "Who is hurting you?"

"They are!" Orgoru screamed, pointing at Dirk and Gar. "Seize them!"

The false aristocrats jumped on Gar and Dirk. Dirk knocked the first two over with quick jabs, and Gar picked up a couple and tossed them away—but the hall was suddenly full of others, pouring into the room and burying the three men under sheer numbers. Miles struck about him wildly, but the city men leaned aside from his blows or blocked them, then caught his arms and pinned him against the wall. He could only stand and watch his companions being buried, and could only think how senseless this was, for he'd seen them defeat armed foresters. Neither seemed to be fighting terribly hard, and Miles guessed that they must be afraid of hurting the poor madmen. Gar roared and Dirk howled, but the "lords" overpowered them, burying them under sheer numbers.

"Well done." King Longar came waddling through the door, his moon-face grim. "Now take them before the Guardian."

The madmen hustled the three men to their feet and bundled them out the door. As they passed Ciletha's suite, she burst through the doorway, crying, "What's happening?"

"He hurt me," Orgoru panted, coming up to her, "the big one. I felt him poking about in my mind. We're taking them to the Guardian for judgment."

Ciletha stared at him, and Miles, watching, saw realization come into her eyes, realization that Orgoru was even more insane than she had thought. His posturing and pretenses hadn't ripped her veil of belief in him, but his claim that the giant had invaded his mind did.

Then the madmen were hustling Miles on down the hallway, and Ciletha followed, crying, "He can't have done it! He can't have meant any harm! He's a good man, he saved Miles twice and more, he would have saved you!"

"I don't need to be saved," Orgoru snapped at her. "I don't want to be."

Ciletha halted, frozen, her eyes huge, as the implications of

Orgoru's words sank in. Then she ran after them, choking down sobs. They mustn't hurt Miles!

Back into the great hall they went, around and into a sort of alcove, where they stopped. Ciletha halted too, staring in amazement at the jeweled curves and angles inlaid in the wall's surface.

"Great Guardian!" King Longar boomed. "Here are three who would join our court, but have hurt one of our number! Judge, we pray you! Judge whether or not they are true aristocrats! Judge whether or not they are of our kind!"

A voice resonated all about them, making Ciletha jump with fright—but the spirit showed no threat to anyone. "Which of you has it hurt?"

"I." Orgoru stepped forward, still holding his head, and Ciletha felt a stab of pity for him.

"How did he hurt you?"

"He poked about in my mind!"

None of the false aristocrats seemed at all skeptical about the remark. Looking from one face to another, Ciletha was amazed to see complete and total belief.

The invisible Guardian didn't seem to have any doubts, either. "Let me sense their motives."

There was no sound, no movement, but suddenly Ciletha felt as though she were surrounded by something warm and clinging, sinking in through the very bone of her skull. Strangely, though, she wasn't the slightest bit frightened—the Guardian, whatever it was, meant only to help, never to hurt.

Then the sensation was gone, and the Guardian declared, "They are not of your kind, neither they nor the woman."

Instantly, Orgoru cried out, "The woman has made no move to hurt or imperil anyone!"

Ciletha felt a surge of gratitude and affection for her old friend, instantly followed by panic and fear for Miles.

"We thank you, O Guardian," King Longar said, then turned to his courtiers. "Take them out of the palace."

The crowd shouted and surged toward the portal, out through it and down the long, long flight of stairs. There they halted, turning the prisoners to face King Longar, whose face was grim. "You have abused our hospitality, and you are not of our kind. We can't have the vulgar discovering our court and flocking here to overwhelm us."

Miles looked up at more footsteps clattering down the stairs. Dirk looked up, too, and stared. "Laser rifles!"

Gar never took his eyes from King Longar. "So you have actually managed to learn how to operate some of the machinery here."

"Machinery?" The king frowned. "We have magical weapons, and courtiers before us learned which parts of the Guardian's design to push in order to bring them to life."

"We knew the nuclear generators still worked, or the robots wouldn't," Dirk said to Gar, "and some mad genius learned how to punch the right buttons to connect them to machines."

Every "aristocrat" stiffened, their faces turning ugly, and King Longar's voice was heavy with menace. "Mad? Do you say we are mad?"

For answer, Gar turned to him and asked, "Does the Guardian make the lightning sheet from the top of the wall when enemies come near, or have you learned how to do that, too?"

The tension stretched so thin that Miles thought it would break him when it snapped. Then Longar exploded. "I can't believe the gall of this man! Three magical weapons are trained on him, and all he can do is ask questions! Have you no common sense, vagabond, no fear?"

Gar gave Dirk a questioning glance. Dirk shrugged. They both turned back to Longar, shaking their heads as Dirk said, "Not really, no."

The "noblemen" stared at them, astounded. King Longar burst out, "Why? How can you not fear?"

With a sudden surge, Gar kicked out, sending the men who held his legs sprawling. He landed in a crouch, bowed with a snap, and the two who had held his arms went tumbling over his head, slamming into half a dozen of their fellows.

At the same moment, Dirk doubled his whole body, pulling the men who held him closer together, then drove his elbows back as he shoved with both feet. The men who held those feet dropped them, clutching their stomachs and gagging; the arm-holders clung on long enough for Dirk's feet to hit ground, when he elbowed them again. They let go, and he whirled to kick at the men holding Miles's knees. They fell, howling, and Miles set down his feet with a shout of triumph. He strained forward, and the men holding his arms shouted, pulling backward. Then Miles leaped back as hard and as far as he could, swinging his arms forward with all his strength, and the two collided with each other. Free, he turned to swing at the nearest aristocrat. The man sprawled backward into two more who were running forward.

The whole court shouted and charged at them.

Lightning split the night, and everyone froze, turning to see Dirk and Gar holding two rifles with a third at Gar's feet. "Grab it, Miles!" Dirk snapped.

Miles sprinted to them and caught up the weapon. He had no idea how to use it, nor had need to—he only needed to keep it from the madmen.

"We're going to leave now," Gar said gently. "Please don't try to follow us. I assure you, we know how to use these weapons, and we know they can scar these walls, even burn through them. We'd rather not see that happen."

He left the other threat unspoken: that the beams could burn through people, too.

"But—but we are noblemen!" King Longar cried. "How can you have defeated us so easily?"

"Because we're trained soldiers, Your Majesty." Dirk's voice was gentle somehow, even sympathetic. "Ciletha? You can come with us—or you can stay here."

The madmen turned toward the woman, their faces ugly.

"No!" Orgoru cried. "She is good, she is gentle, and not to blame one whit for what these men have done!"

But the dark looks stayed on the madmen's faces, and Ciletha shuddered, suddenly realizing how unpredictable they might be. Quickly, she ran to Miles.

"Don't follow us, now," Dirk warned. "Miles, Ciletha, turn and go."

Miles offered his arm as he turned around. Ciletha took it, heart pounding, and they walked slowly down the boulevard leading to the gate, with Dirk and Gar backing up behind them, rifles pointed a little above the heads of the silent, frozen band of madmen, standing there with the moonlight silvering their ludicrous finery.

CHAPTER 12

Gar and Dirk kept their word—they went on out through the doorless gateway and into the forest for more than a hundred yards. There, though, Gar held up a hand and stopped. The others did, too. They stood a moment, listening. Inside the city, they heard shouting.

The pause was enough to tear the shreds of composure Ciletha had left. She turned away from the men into the nearest pool of shadow and wept bitterly. But strong arms folded about her, and a hard-muscled chest moved to touch her cheek. She clung and sobbed, knowing it was Miles, knowing she could trust him not to think ill of her.

"Hush, now," he soothed. "We're safe—they won't find us here. We've lost them."

"And I've lost him forever!" she wailed. "Orgoru will never love me now!"

The arms and chest went very still, and Ciletha caught her breath, suddenly realizing that she didn't want to lose Miles, too—but he loosened, and his hand began to caress her back again. Her whole body shuddered with a huge racking sob of relief, and she could let the tension out in weeping again.

"Think they'll find some more of these portable cannon?" Dirk asked.

"Of course, or they won't dare chase us," Gar told him.

The shouting wasn't quite so far away now.

"Aristocrats!" Dirk sneered. "Sure they are, running in a mob just like the peasants they really are!"

"Be fair—I've seen aristocrats form their own mobs, too." Gar looked up as Miles and Ciletha came back into the moonlight, his arm about her shoulders. "Functional again? Good, because we have an ambush to lay."

"Ambush?" Ciletha stared. "Aren't we trying to escape them?"

"Only for the moment," Gar answered. "Right now, I want one of them alive and unhurt—preferably Orgoru."

"Orgoru?" Fear for her friend seized her. "Why him?"

Gar must have heard the fright in her voice, for he said, "Don't worry, maiden, we won't hurt him—just the opposite, in fact. Your friend has a sickness of the heart and mind, and I mean to cure him."

The fear deepened, fear of having her own insight confirmed. "He's not mad!"

"Orgoru is mentally ill," Gar told her. "They all are. They all suffer from a malady called 'delusions of grandeur.' Here they can wallow in their delusions without anyone to hamper them, for the Guardian takes care of them and protects them. It's kind in its way, but it would be kinder still to cure them and let them take up useful, productive lives in the real world again."

"Sure of that, are you?" Dirk said sourly.

"Let them decide when they've had a chance," Gar countered.

"But why do you care?" Miles asked, bewildered.

"Because I've spent the last few weeks trying to find an underground—a band of people organized in secret, with the purpose of overthrowing the Protector and his armies."

"So that's why you were talking so foolishly in that inn!"

"If you think that was foolish," Dirk said, "You should have heard the things I've heard him say in other, uh, countries. He's calmed down considerably."

"How is it you're still free?" Miles asked, round-eyed.

"We're quick," Dirk explained.

"We made far fewer mistakes once you were there to explain local customs for us," Gar told Miles. "I've finally admitted that there is no underground—but I still want to overthrow the iron rule of the Protector, and let the people choose their own form of government, one that will let them select their professions, travel when and where they will, and choose their own mates."

Ciletha gasped with delight and fear, awed by the giant's audacity.

"What has all that to do with this city of madmen?" Miles asked, bewildered.

"They could *be* my underground—if I cure their delusions first."

"Be kinder to leave them mired in mania," Dirk muttered.

"Perhaps—but their country needs them. Think, my friends! In their efforts to become aristocrats, they've already learned the accent, the bearing, and the manners of the magistrates! And they know something of literature, science, and the arts— I led the conversation into many different areas at dinner, and the ones who had been here awhile knew the basics of all the main areas of human thought! They even know something about their Protector's laws and procedures, though they'll have to learn a great deal more."

"Their Guardian computer will probably be willing to give them teaching materials," Dirk said, beginning to be fascinated in spite of his native caution.

"Exactly! Though we'll have to teach them something about hand-to-hand combat, and strategy and tactics, too—these magistrates seem to have to be minor generals. But when they've learned, we can send each one out to replace a real magistrate who's been reassigned."

"Yes, and some of them might even work their way up through the bureaucracy!" Dirk's eyes lit with enthusiasm.

"But what of the genuine magistrates who were on their way to take up those posts?" Miles objected. The idea was too vast, too audacious for him.

"The real replacements can be easily waylaid and held captive in Voyagend," Gar told him. "I have a notion I can persuade them that a more liberal government would be in their best interests—especially if they saw the chance to return to their favorite wives and stay with them, and visit their other children."

"Can magistrates really care so much for wives and children?" Ciletha wondered.

"Once they're allowed to stay with them? Sure!" Dirk said. "Don't underestimate the paternal instinct."

"But if these false magistrates of yours come to power, they'll command the bailiffs and the watchmen!" Miles exclaimed. "If they become reeves, they'll command armies!"

"Yes," Gar said, "and once they have command, they can recruit and train agents who can talk the soldiers into believing in human rights!"

"What are 'rights'?" Ciletha asked, caught between excitement and bewilderment.

"The idea that there are some things that are right for all people to do or try to do, simply because they're born human," Gar explained. "Everyone has a right to stay alive, or to try to; everyone has the right to be free to run his own life, unless he tries to take that right away from other people—tries to murder or rape them, or steal what they've spent a lifetime saving, or so on."

"Even the right to choose her own mate?" Ciletha asked with sudden hope.

"Definitely that! In this country, that needs to be written down as a separate law!"

"Throttle your rockets, Space Ranger," Dirk said, suddenly wary. "The Protector reassigns those magistrates on a five-year rotation schedule. Do you really want to spend the next sixty months of your life on this planet? Remember, before you answer, that there are people starving on other worlds while they're waiting for you."

"No one's waiting for me," Gar scoffed, then suddenly turned sad for an instant before he swept Dirk's objections aside with a broad arm. "If these people can learn to become agents, they can learn how to run a whole network of cells! They can do the day-to-day administration on their own. We'll come back in five years, to oversee the overthrow!"

"Overthrow!" Ciletha gasped. "Is it really necessary to overthrow the Protector?"

Gar calmed amazingly, turning to her with a gentle smile. "Absolutely necessary, young woman. The Protector is a dictator ruling an entrenched bureaucracy, and neither will give up a jot of power if it can possibly help it. Indeed, both will fight to their very deaths to hold on to every bit of power they have."

"But they have given us safety and kept us fed and housed!"

"Yes." Miles nodded, seeing Ciletha's point. "Surely we can keep what's good in this government!"

"Why, you can indeed," Gar said, looking at his guide with new respect. "You'll have to change the masters—the Protector and his reeves, at least, and maybe the magistrates and inspectors-general, too—but you can keep the actual machinery of running the country, the 'bureaucracy' as we call it. It's so entrenched that you probably couldn't eliminate it, anyway—the local village mayor would ask the city mayor what he should do, and the city mayor would ask the county's governor, and so forth."

"So why not keep calling them magistrates and reeves? But you can choose who they'll be," Dirk said earnestly. "Everyone gets to say who they want for the post, and the person who gets the most voices, gets the job, too."

"You would choose the Protector in similar fashion," Gar added, "though you shouldn't call him 'Protector'; he might develop ideas about seizing power. No, call him 'president' or 'premier' or 'prime minister' or 'First Citizen' or some such, and give him only the power to carry out whatever policy the reeves decide on, when they're all gathered together."

Dirk nodded. "When they go home, though, each reeve has to answer to a gathering of all his magistrates, and each magistrate has to let the people of his town or village tell him what they want him to do."

"Is it possible?" Ciletha breathed.

"It is! I can feel it! It is!" Miles squeezed her hand.

"But why 'him' and 'he'?" Ciletha asked, frowning. "Why might not women be magistrates?"

Miles turned to stare at her, stunned by the outrageousness of the idea.

"No reason at all," Dirk said promptly, "except that the people have been ruled by men so long that it will take them a generation or two to get used to the idea. By the time you're fifty, though, you should be able to run for office. Probably won't be elected, but your daughter might be."

Ciletha gave him a wistful smile. "If I ever have a daughter."

"You must!" Miles declared, and caught her hand, then suddenly turned grave. "It will be very dangerous, though. If the Protector's spies catch us before we overthrow him, we'll be tortured and executed."

"It's not for the fainthearted," Dirk agreed. "Is it worth your life?"

Ciletha and Miles looked at one another, hands clasped. Then both cried, "Yes!" together.

That decided, they found a trail and followed it to a spot where a huge boulder thrust up amidst the brush and trees, overgrown with lichens and vines. Miles noticed squared-off corners and decided it must be a stone left by the city's builders. Dirk hid him behind it, then climbed to a branch overhanging the trail. Gar stepped into the brush on the other side of the path and disappeared.

"You won't hurt him, will you?" Ciletha said to Miles in a shaking whisper.

Miles felt a stab of jealousy, but assured her, "No, lass, for your sake alone, I'd not hurt him. As to Dirk and Gar, they need him alive and well for their own reasons."

"Could he truly become the first false magistrate?" Ciletha wondered.

"Hist!" Miles laid a hand on her arm, tensing and looking back along the trail.

The shouting had stopped abruptly when the mob came to the edge of the woods, but they were muttering to one another so loudly, and cracking so many twigs as they went, that there was no danger of missing them. They came into a patch of moonlight, ungainly, plump men, or ones so scrawny they seemed almost cadavers, oddly graceful in their finery. They crept past the boulder with loud shushing of one another and a veritable racket of crushed sticks and dried brush, Orgoru in their midst. Suddenly he stopped, frowning about him.

"Go on, Orgoru!" hissed the Earl of March.

"Pass me." Orgoru stared into the bushes, frowning. "I'll bring up the rear."

"As you will," the earl grumbled, and went on, beckoning the men behind him to follow.

Orgoru didn't, though. He stood frowning off into the brush, and Ciletha wondered what he had heard. Suddenly he came to himself, realizing that the mob had moved on down the trail. He turned to follow—and Gar stepped out of the underbrush, catching him with one arm across his chest, pinioning Orgoru's arm and clapping a pad of cloth over his mouth. Dirk leaped out to catch Orgoru's flailing free hand and press something small against the wrist. Orgoru tried to scream through the cloth, then went suddenly limp.

Ciletha dashed from the underbrush. "Is he . . . is he . . . ?"

"Asleep." Gar hoisted the unconscious Orgoru to his shoulder. "Only asleep, lass. Frightened, I'm sure, but not hurt one bit. We can't cure him here, though, where the others are sure to come back. Let's find a cave."

They found one halfway around the city wall, where a dead pine had fallen against another huge leftover building-block. Dirk cut away inner dry branches with his sword, then cut fresh boughs from another tree to make a pallet. Gar laid Orgoru on it, and Ciletha crowded close to see for herself that his color was good, and his chest rising and falling. She relaxed with a sigh of relief—Orgoru did indeed look as though he were asleep.

"Watch if you wish, but don't talk." Gar sat down cross-legged beside Orgoru and closed his eyes.

"He's not kidding about keeping quiet," Dirk said. "What

he's going to do is very hard, and takes every ounce of concentration he can muster. If you don't want him to hurt Orgoru by accident, be absolutely quiet—and if you can't, go take a walk until Gar's done."

"I shall be a very mouse," Ciletha promised.

But the steadfastness of the gaze she fixed on Orgoru lanced Miles with jealousy. As quietly as he could, he crept out of the lean-to and went to walk in the night, trying to calm his heart and find peace for his soul. But he couldn't help glancing back—and saw Dirk standing by the boulder, watching for the mob. It struck Miles as a good idea, and an excellent excuse for staying away from Ciletha and Orgoru. He began to prowl about the lean-to, a self-appointed sentry.

Little Orgoru tripped, stumbled into the table. His mother's only vase crashed to the floor. "What was that?" she cried, and came running. Orgoru flinched away from her, trying to make himself as small as possible, knowing the beating that was coming. . . .

But she only said, "Oh! My vase!" and seemed to wilt, as though all the spirit had gone out of her. She sat down heavily on the bench, threw her apron over her head, and began to cry.

Orgoru stared, unable to believe his good fortune. This wasn't how he remembered it (but how could he remember something that hadn't even happened yet?). Surely she would beat him when she was done crying! But her sobs went on and on, tearing his heart, and he dared to creep closer, finally to touch her and stammer, "I—I'm sorry, Mama."

Her hand reached out; he shied, but it only rested lightly on his head. "It's all right, all right, Orgoru," she said through her tears. "It was an accident, an accident. These things happen; vases break." Then she wailed into her apron, a whole new torrent of tears.

Orgoru couldn't bear her grief. He clasped her hand with both of his own. "Don't cry, Mama. I'll make you a new one."

He did, too, scooping the clay from the riverbank, molding it with his hands, and drying it in the sun. Something within him knew that it looked a fright, but he preened with the pride of accomplishment anyway, and his mother was delighted. "Oh, what a wonderful boy! How thoughtful of you! How pretty it is!" It must have been his intentions that pleased her, though, not the vase itself. He wondered why she never put a flower in it, but when he grew up, he realized that not having been fired, the vase would have melted with the water. By that time, though, he had made a few pennies from odd jobs, and from pelts sold after hunting season, and had bought her a new vase anyway. But she packed the old one away for her memories.

"You've done a good job with the mare's cabbage and thistles, Orgoru."

Seven-year-old Orgoru lifted his hoe and looked back over the row of plants, feeling pride expand in his chest. "Thank you, Papa."

"But you still have half the weeds left in that row."

Orgoru stared in confusion. "Which ones, Papa?"

"These, Orgoru." Papa's big hand parted broader leaves from narrow. "These are common grass, but the narrow ones are wheat. Chop the grass stems out."

"All right, Papa!" Orgoru bent to his task, chopping the grass stems, eager to please his father. Strangely, he seemed to remember that Papa had screamed at him until he was red in the face, then clouted him on the side of the skull until his head rang and he saw stars—but that must have been a bad dream, for Papa had just been gentle in his teaching.

He didn't have a hoe in his hands that fall, when the children came running after the grown-ups, tired from reaping and binding sheaves all day—but the children, in spite of having done their share of binding, still had energy enough to run and shout.

The blow took Orgoru full in the back. He stumbled, nearly fell, but managed to catch his balance in only a few steps. He turned to see who had struck him, fighting down anger. . . .

Clyde grinned down at him, a head taller and two years

older, with his friends grinning behind him. "Sorry, Orgoru," Clyde said. "I stumbled."

Stumbled! It was no accident, and they all knew it—but Orgoru fought down his temper and said, as his mother had taught him, "That's all right, Clyde. I stumble, too, now and then."

"Stumble like this?" Clyde slammed a fist into Orgoru's chest. He staggered back, and the other boys shouted. So did Orgoru as he caught his balance and charged back at Clyde, fists pumping as his father had taught him. Then anger calmed a little, and he realized that the other boys had formed a circle around the two of them, shouting. His stomach sank as he realized he was going to take a beating, for Clyde was the best fighter in the village for his age. But he couldn't cry off now, for the grown-ups were turning back to supervise, and Orgoru would rather have suffered a hundred beatings than have his father ashamed of him.

The punch came. Orgoru blocked, but Clyde was so strong that his fist clipped Orgoru's chin anyway. Orgoru staggered back, keeping his guard up and managing to block two more punches while his head cleared, then throw himself into a desperate right cross. It was so unexpected that he caught Clyde on the side of the head, and the bigger boy reeled backward while his friends shouted angrily. Orgoru followed with three quick punches, but Clyde rallied and came back with a punch to the stomach. Orgoru blocked, but the fist came through anyway because Clyde was so much stronger than he. The block had taken most of the force, though, so Orgoru only had to hold his breath while he slammed out two more punches.

It went on for five minutes before Orgoru fell and couldn't get up because he was fighting for breath. He struggled, hearing Clyde gibe at him—but the boy suddenly went silent, and big rough hands were helping Orgoru up. "Well fought, my boy," said his father. "I'm proud of you."

"Proud!" Orgoru stared upward at the fond, smiling face, for it hadn't happened this way, Clyde had beaten him to a pulp, and Papa had taken him home, grumbling about his weakling son and demanding to know why Orgoru hadn't fought better.

But it *was* happening, Papa was smiling with pride and saying, "There's no shame in losing, Orgoru, especially when the boy is bigger and older than you. Besides, you'll be a better boxer with each fight. Come home to good beer, lad—you've earned it."

It was Orgoru's first taste of beer, and the next day, the other boys greeted him with smiles, and treated him with greater respect afterward. They never became great friends, but at least they weren't enemies.

So it went, Orgoru reliving each harrowing, painful episode from his past and a good many ordinary, everyday scenes with his parents. The other children accepted him as an equal, even if he seemed to be nothing out of the ordinary, and if he misbehaved, his parents scolded him, but more often they praised him and told him how special he was to them.

Each time, what was happening warred with a memory of humiliation and censure, but Orgoru was quick to accept these new and wonderful versions of life. When he left his village, it was to become a forester in the next county, and his parting from his parents was bittersweet, filled with pride as well as tears.

While patrolling the woods one day, he found Voyagend. The noblemen welcomed him, hailed him as the Prince of Paradime, and the ladies flirted with him, but he found it all less than wonderful somehow, hollow in some way, unsatisfying.

Then, his first night in the city, he fell asleep, and in the darkness of his dream swirled something small and white, something that swelled and grew until he realized it was coming closer and closer. He began to be able to make out features, then to realize that the swirling was a long beard and longer hair that eddied and drifted like seaweed in the tide— but this was no pier piling or boulder they engulfed, it was a face, lined and old, with thin lips and a blade of a nose, a high forehead and eyes that seemed to pierce right through Orgoru, through him and into his very soul.

"Who are you?" Orgoru cried in fear.

The old man's voice echoed inside his head, though his lips never moved: *I am the Wizard of Peace, and I have come to tell you the truth about yourself.*

Fear surged up in Orgoru, fear without reason or source, but it rose and rose and crested in panic until he realized he was screaming, "No! No! Never!"

CHAPTER 13

B ut the old man went on mercilessly. "You are not the Prince of Paradime, but only Orgoru, the son of a plowman. You are the true son of that miserable peasant and his wife!"

"Don't dare to call them miserable!" Orgoru shouted. "They were good and kind, they were wise and patient!"

"Then you should be proud to be their son."

Orgoru stared, caught between longings—to really have been the son of two such wonderful people, and to be the Prince of Paradime, whose false parents had ridiculed and beaten him.

"Yes, you wish to be the son of two such good people," said the Wizard, "and now you see the goodness that was hidden within them, and the goodness that might have been brought out if theirs had been a good and joyful marriage, not a forced coupling that both resented. But you can also see the goodness within Orgoru, that trust and fellowship can bring forth."

Orgoru hung motionless in his dream, suspended between hope and bitterness.

"Have the courage to be what you truly are," the Wizard

bade him, "and the greater courage to strive to become what you dream of being."

"There are no lords or ladies in the Protector's land," Orgoru said, with lips and tongue gone suddenly dry.

"No, but there are magistrates, and their wives and children. You know as well as I that the reeves and ministers live as elegantly as the aristocrats of children's tales, and that their children are almost certain to become reeves and ministers in their own turn, or the wives of reeves and ministers."

"Do you say the reeves and ministers are the noblemen of this land?" Orgoru asked, still parched.

"They are the equivalents, yes."

Orgoru lay unmoving still, his thoughts racing.

"Be what you are." The Wizard's ice-blue eyes pierced to Orgoru's core again.

And suddenly, miraculously, Orgoru was. He was simply and only Orgoru, the son of a peasant, and could accept the fact. But within him burned the desire to become in fact what he had been in pretense—one of the aristocrats of his world. Within him was now a granite core of determination. He would learn to read and write, he would learn the Protector's laws and procedures, he would become a magistrate!

Then wonder grew and filled him, wonder that he could now see that the Prince of Paradime had been only pretense, wonder that he could accept the truth of his own state.

"Yes, you can regain your life of luxury," the Wizard told him, "but *noblesse oblige*—nobility imposes obligations. You must earn your rank by fulfilling the duties that go with it— securing the welfare of your fellow peasants. Then you shall become a magistrate or reeve in reality, instead of a prince in illusion."

Orgoru groaned as the memory of the gilded life he had just begun to lead overwhelmed him, of the beautiful women and noble men whom he would no doubt now discover were really very ordinary. "I'd prefer the illusion!"

"Then you may have it," the Wizard declared, "*if* you first help your fellow peasants to win their freedom. Help them to overthrow the Protector, become one of the new magistrates who serve the people rather than their overlord, see the new government firmly established—and I will send you back into your delusion. But you must earn it first."

Orgoru stared. "What is this talk of overthrow? Of new magistrates?"

But the Wizard had begun to shrink, and Orgoru realized he was receding, going away. "Don't leave!" Orgoru cried. "Tell me first!"

"Ask the giant," the Wizard said. Then he shrank abruptly to a little white ball, racing away from Orgoru, becoming only a dot that winked out, and was gone.

Orgoru hung suspended in darkness with hope blooming in him. If there was truly a chance to bring down the Protector and the vicious magistrates who served him, then there would really be a chance for Orgoru to become a magistrate himself! But how was this all to be done? The Wizard had said to ask the giant—but which giant? Where? How would Orgoru find him?

"Where?" he cried, flailing about. "Where is he?" His arm struck something solid. He turned to look, and saw brown trouser thighs with huge hands resting on them. Looking up, he saw Gar looming over him, huge against darkness, and realized *he* was the giant!

Then Orgoru realized that he was awake.

He opened his mouth to demand Gar tell him how to over-throw the Protector—then realized that the giant was swaying, eyes still closed, sweat streaming down his face. His eyelids opened; he looked down at Orgoru with unutterable weariness and said, "Forgive me, but I can't tell you now. Please rise from that bed, for I need it."

Orgoru stared, not understanding, not even knowing he had been on a bed.

Then Dirk came up beside Gar, reaching down toward Orgoru. "Up, my friend. He has cured you; he has earned his rest."

Orgoru understood enough to seize Dirk's hand and scramble to his feet. Gar swayed, then leaned, then fell, crashing down onto the bed of pine boughs, his eyes closing.

Orgoru stared. "Why is he so tired?"

"Because he has just finished a very hard task," Dirk explained, "and on top of that, he was worried about your health, after that blow on the head."

Orgoru felt his head, frowning, but found no lump. "I don't remember being struck."

"You were," Dirk assured him, "where it counted most. You understand what you have to do now?"

"Only in broad outline," Orgoru sighed, "but I will undertake it, for the reward promised me. What must I do first?"

"Nothing much," Dirk told him. "Go back into the city and pretend to be the Prince of Paradime still—but whenever anybody wakes up from delusion, talk to them and reassure them. When you've all been cured, we'll tell you how to overthrow the Protector and the magistrates who have become corrupt. Then we'll start your training."

Training? Orgoru wondered what kind of training he could mean.

Distant shouts came thinly through the dead pine needles. Dirk raised his head. "Your friends have found out you're missing, and are coming back for you. Actually, they've been searching for you, and for us, all night. Tell them you fell and hit your head, and just woke up. Come on."

He led the way out of the lean-to. Orgoru stared at it in surprise; he hadn't known he was in it. He also hadn't known how much time had passed, but the forest around him glowed with the twilight of false dawn. Then he looked up, and saw Ciletha standing next to the stocky man he remembered as Gar and Dirk's servant. What was he really?

"Orgoru!" Ciletha cried in a voice that was half a sob, and ran to him. Orgoru held her against his chest, bemused, amazed at her embrace, beset by a feeling of newness, as though he had never seen the world before. *Is this what it's like to see everything as it really is?* Aloud, he soothed, "Don't worry, Ciletha. I'm all right. In fact, I'm better than I've ever been."

She pulled back, staring up at him, face stained with tears. "Are you . . . are you still . . . ?"

"The Prince of Paradime?" Orgoru smiled and shook his head. "No. I'm cured of that."

But why was the stocky man—Miles, that's what his name was!—why was he standing so stiffly, looking so grim?

The shouting was coming closer. "I must go," Orgoru said, and stepped away from Ciletha with a quick pat on her shoulder.

"This way." Dirk led him between a huge old elm and a hickory. He stopped halfway through and faded back out of sight. Orgoru saw the dim trail and stepped forward just as the "aristocrats" burst into sight.

Orgoru was shaken to his core. Admittedly, their finery was torn and bedraggled from briars, and from leaves laden with dew—but the colors were so garish! And the people were so common! Moon-faced or gaunt, short and round or tall and skinny—where were the elegant forms he remembered?

Was this how he really looked?

The thought was almost enough to send him back into madness, but a fat little man with a full crown came bustling up to him, and a voice he recognized demanded, "Prince of Paradime! Where have you been?"

Orgoru stared. Could this rotund commoner really be King Longar? But where was the imposing stature, the commanding mien?

He shook himself and forced a smile. "I must have struck my head on a tree branch as I searched for you, Your Majesty, for I've only just now waked up, and my head aches abominably." The first part was true, anyway.

"Well, let us rejoice that you are restored to us!" King Longar reached up to clap him on the shoulder.

Up? It should have been down! He'd been taller than Orgoru—at least in delusion.

"Come, back to the city!" the king called to his noblemen. "It's a great victory, for we've driven off the invaders and rescued one of our own!"

The men gave a single, unified cheer, and turned back toward the city. Orgoru jostled along in their midst, forcing himself to smile and bow and joke with them about their wonderful night's work. He knew that the tale of this adventure would swell till a whole army took the place of Gar, Dirk, and Miles, and Orgoru would be torn from their evil clutches before the aristocrats fought the army into a rout. Looking about, he could see that they believed it already, and it hadn't even been put into words.

It frightened him that he could understand them so well—but the Guardian had been right, he was one of their kind.

If the Guardian was real.

Real or not, Orgoru resolved to hold fast to one bit of delusion—his image of himself as tall and lean, graceful and cultured, with a noble brow and wise face. When he stopped to think about it, he knew he was only a plump, dowdy, very ordinary looking man—but he didn't intend to stop to think about it if he didn't have to. His unthinking image of himself as aristocratic, would help him become the magistrate, then the reeve, that he knew he could be!

When the Protector was overthrown.

As they came back into the city, though, another shock awaited him. Why he should have thought the women wouldn't look any different, when the men did, he didn't know—but they were different indeed, tall, short, fat, cadaverous, lumpen and plain, with moon-faces and horse-faces and squints and warts. They cried welcome to the men as they came into the palace, and some ran to embrace their lovers. Orgoru watched in shock until one tall, rawboned woman came hurrying up to him and, in the voice of Countess Gilda, cried, "Welcome back! Oh, I feared so for your safety, for your life, my prince!" She threw her arms about him, but Orgoru stood frozen, trying to reconcile the beautiful countess of his delusion with this long-faced, lantern-jawed woman.

Gilda thrust herself away, staring up at him in alarm. "Why are you so cold, my love?"

With a stabbing pain, Orgoru felt the image of beauty wrenched away from him—but he looked into Gilda's eyes, those huge, limpid, lovely dark blue eyes, and knew that one element of her beauty, at least, was real.

Perhaps her conversation was, too, her intelligence and her

wit. His pulse quickened with the thought, but he still couldn't bring himself to really embrace this tall, ungainly creature. Silently, he thanked all good fortune that he hadn't started a real affair, and certainly that he hadn't married yet!

Orgoru prowled the halls of the palace in the early light of the next morning, pausing to listen at every door, prepared to explain, if anyone came upon him, that he had waked in the middle of the night and couldn't sleep again, so he had gone to take a walk and try to regain sleepiness. Part of the story, at least, was true.

As he stopped by Countess Gilda's door, he heard sobbing.

At once, compassion flowed, and all his revulsion fled. He tapped on her door. The sobbing stopped.

"It's Orgoru," he called softly.

There was only one sobbing gasp from within.

"Orgoru only," he explained, "not the Prince of Paradime. Not to you—now."

There was a burst of footsteps, and the door flew open; he found himself staring into Gilda's tear-streaked face. She looked him up and down with a look of disbelief. "You? Orgoru? But . . . but how . . ."

"This is how I really am," Orgoru told her gently. "Look closely at my face! Do you see nothing of the Orgoru you knew?"

"Some . . . something," she managed.

"I woke crying out yesterday morning," Orgoru told her. "May I come in?"

"Yes! At once! Before anyone sees!" Gilda pulled him into the chamber and shut the door quickly, then turned and leaned against it, bosom heaving—and Orgoru realized that not all the delusion had been false. "How . . . how did you . . ."

"I dreamed of all the worst wrongs of my life being righted," Orgoru told her. "I dreamed of an old man who called himself 'the Wizard of Peace,' and made me see myself as I really am—only Orgoru, the son of peasants. I nearly fled back into madness then, but he had shown me enough that was good about myself that I held on to sanity."

"I, too!" Gilda gasped. "I dreamed of other boys and girls treating me kindly, including me in their games, even dancing with me when I grew to young womanhood! I found I dared to see myself as I was, and not shrink in disgust!"

Orgoru nodded. "Then the Wizard told me I could earn real nobility by rescuing the common people from this dictator who rules with with an iron rod, the Protector."

"I . . . I too," Gilda said, her tone faltering.

Orgoru looked into those large, fine eyes, and realized that she wasn't so plain after all—even though her face was streaked, and her eyes red with tears. "Brace yourself. None of the others look as you have seen them. King Longar is short and fat."

"How . . . how did I look to you?"

"Shorter than you are, voluptuous, and stunning in your beauty." Orgoru knew that lies wouldn't serve. He took a step closer, frowning. "But looking closely, looking into your eyes, I see that not all of that beauty was a dream."

Gratitude flashed across her face, chased out by a sardonic grimace. "I know what I am, Orgoru. I've looked in my mirror. Don't lie to me, for it did not."

Yes, there was something of her old wit left there, and certainly . . . "Your intelligence is as great as I remember it."

"Oh, is it really! And what man ever found a woman attractive for intelligence?"

"I," Orgoru told her truthfully, "and most of the men here, I think."

She stared, hope rising in her eyes.

"We all of us value wit, at least," he told her, "men and women alike."

"Then there *was* some shred of truth in that delusion," she whispered.

"Some," he told her. "When the shock of seeing the others for the first time wore off, I watched them move, watched them dance. Their gracefulness is no illusion, nor their posture and bearing. They have all learned to move like the aristocrats in the magic pictures, and that grace remains. It's learned, but it's there."

"Then the Wizard spoke truly? We *can* learn to be real lords and ladies?"

"Our land's equivalent, at least," Orgoru told her, "reeves and their wives."

Suddenly she almost collapsed, and he sprang to catch her, to hold her up. "Give me my madness again!" she sobbed into his chest.

"We shall have to earn it," he told her sadly, "and to earn it, we have to become what we only played at being."

Her body firmed; the tears dwindled, and she looked up at him. "We shall, then," she said, with the same iron resolution that now made up his core. "I may never be able to be beautiful, but I shall become a lady in fact."

"You already are," he whispered.

That afternoon, Lord Saunders woke from his nap sobbing. Orgoru was prowling the halls and came upon him before he had been alone long. The two men commiserated, then resolved to hurry the overthrow along, so that they could earn their return to madness.

The next morning, Lady Rijora awoke weeping, and Gilda went to comfort her. King Longar woke crying out that afternoon, and Saunders and Orgoru comforted him. Thus, one by one and ten a day, the deluded folk awoke to sanity, and longed for madness.

By the end of the month, everyone in Voyagend had dreamed of the Wizard, and the Wizard had assured them all that the giant would tell them how to overthrow the Protector. They welcomed Gar and his companions back into the city, albeit nervously, and while he was recovering from the exertion of curing them, they spent a nervous night trying to socialize in their old style, but all very obviously trying not to feel uncomfortable with these plain, drab, ordinary-looking people whom reality had shown them. Toward the end of the evening, Miles found Dirk and said, "Master Dirk . . ."

Dirk gave him a warning glare. Miles sighed; the man was right. "Dirk, we must do something, and quickly! They're so repulsed by the sight of one another that we may very well see them trying to go mad again!"

"A lot more chance than I'd like to take," Dirk agreed. "After all, *wanting* to get well is one of the biggest assets in recovery. Well, I'll catch them before they all go to bed." He stepped out into the middle of the room and called, "Music, stop playing!"

He could have waited until the end of the dance, of course, but the computer stopped the music in mid-bar, and it drew the people's attention to him more sharply than any amount of shouting could have done. They stepped apart from their partners with ill-concealed relief and turned to stare at the giant's friend.

"I know you all want to start learning how to overthrow the Protector," Dirk called out. "Well, even though Gar is still recuperating, we can start without him."

A murmur went around the room, apprehension and excitement mixed. Dirk waited for it to calm, then went on. "The first part is learning to live by the same schedule the magistrates do, and the second part is to learn to fight, so you can tell your bailiffs how to command their watchmen—or your armies, if you rise to reeves. So everyone wakes at nine o'clock tomorrow, and we'll work our way earlier and earlier until you're up with the sun."

A massed groan rose from the quondam aristocrats.

"I know, I know, but it's necessary," Dirk answered. "How many magistrates have you seen who slept in till noon? So up at nine tomorrow, and we'll start the day with a light breakfast, then a few basic lessons in hand-to-hand combat."

"But what shall the ladies do?" Rijora called.

"Do?" Dirk said blankly. "Why, get out there with a quarter-staff, of course!"

A hum of shocked talk went up. Dirk waited a moment, then held up hands for calm. "Let's make this clear for everyone— you're not going out for a Sunday picnic. Everybody who's in on this scheme is very likely to be attacked at some point, and you'd all better know how to defend yourselves. In some ways, it's even more important for the ladies! So up at nine, now, and that means you ought to be getting to bed as quickly as you can!"

He didn't need to add "alone"—even longtime lovers were shying away from one another now. They dispersed, and Dirk took Miles and Ciletha for a visit to Gar.

His suite was as grand as the rest, with full computer support. Dirk stopped in the sitting room and said, "Wait here. I'll call you if he's up to talking." They nodded, so he went to tap on the bedroom door.

"Come in," Gar called.

Dirk stepped in as Gar called, "Lights, low," and the lights glowed to life enough to show him lying in the four-poster bed, rising up on one elbow. "How are things, Dirk?"

"Tense." Dirk started to sit down in the bedside chair he'd been using a lot lately, then hesitated. "Did you eat today?"

"I think so." Gar rubbed his eyes. "I stumbled over to the dispenser and had some oatmeal the last time I woke—but the sun was shining then."

"Yeah, that was this morning. Think you can stay awake long enough for some chicken soup?"

Gar nodded, so Dirk went to the dispenser and brought back a tray. As Gar sipped, Dirk said, "They're full of nervous energy, so I figured I'd better channel it before they deliberately try to go mad again."

"Wise." Gar nodded. "What will you do?"

"Wake them up at nine, for starters. Then a few light calisthenics and some basic self-defense techniques—how to fall and roll, block a punch, that kind of thing. Might start with quarterstaves."

"Enough to raise morale, at least. How fit is Miles to help you?"

"I've been giving him and Ciletha lessons in my spare time, which I seem to have a lot of lately. They're both ready for their green belts, and Miles is an expert with the quarterstaff, so I won't be out there alone."

"Helpful." Gar said. "Any luck with the Guardian?"

"Well, it didn't say no." Dirk had spent half an hour in front of the decorated wall, trying to get a definite answer from the computer. "Says it wants to talk to you personally, when you're ready."

"It didn't order us out of the city, then?"

"Didn't even try. From the odd comment here and there, I gather it thinks we're the best thing to happen to these people since they started coming here. But it wants to make sure we're both aiming in the same direction as it is, so it needs a conference."

"It can probably manage that right here." Gar looked up at the ceiling and called, "Can you hear us, O Guardian?"

"Yes," the surrounding voice said instantly.

Dirk jumped half a foot and came down oozing adrenaline.

CHAPTER 14

"Y̶ou have not requested confidentiality," the voice explained.

"So if I ask you to turn off your audio pickups, you will?"

"Correct," the computer confirmed.

"I don't think many of the inmates thought of that," Dirk muttered. "Must have picked up a lot of interesting sounds."

"I don't think it's possible to shock a machine," Gar told him, then raised his voice again. "Shall we confer now?"

"The timbre of your voice, and the amount of time you spend sleeping, indicates that you are not yet in proper condition for such a meeting."

Gar nodded. "Fair enough. But tell me this—can you provide teaching materials for all the people here?"

"Yes. They will be provided via the viewscreens in their suites."

"May I compliment you on the quality of the frames you provide for them."

"Thank you, but human designers deserve the credit, not I. What subjects will you be requesting?"

"History, both Terran and local; literary classics; military strategy and tactics; local laws and bureaucratic procedures . . ."

"I am quite out of date in that subject—by several centuries, in fact."

"Yes, but you can teach them the basis from which the modern ones are derived. As to making the knowledge current, we'll see what resources we can rustle up."

Literally, Dirk thought.

"Oh, a whole host of subjects," Gar said, suddenly sagging back on the pillow. Dirk suppressed the urge to jump to take his pulse.

"I see you are too tired for further talk," the Guardian said. "Call me at need. For now, good night."

"Good night," Gar replied, his voice weakening.

"I'll let you sleep in a minute," Dirk said slowly, "but in the meantime, I was just wondering . . ."

"Yes?"

"Well, your exhaustion is part of the answer, but only part."

"Glad to hear it. What's the question?"

"If you can cure mental illness so easily . . ." Dirk began, then stopped and said, "Let me revise that. If you can cure mental illness so quickly, why don't you do it more often?"

"In the first place," Gar sighed, "I can't. Most mentally ill people are far more complicated than these, with several disorders all twined together. In the second place, even if I could, I'd have no right. It's a matter of invading somebody's mind, you see, and sick or not, I have no right to do that without their permission."

"No, you don't," Dirk said slowly. "What gave you the right this time?"

"Necessity," Gar sighed, "which means that I really had no right—but it was that, or forget about these people gaining their freedom, and I didn't have any right to do that, either."

By the end of the week, all the recruits had learned how to fall without hurting themselves, and how to deliver and block a punch and a kick. The few who hadn't learned to read, had made a good beginning from the lessons the Guardian supplied them, and Dirk had started teaching them the basic outline of the history of their planet.

In the first session of that class, people began to ask questions about where their ancestors came from, and were astounded to learn that the fairy stories about other worlds were true. That led to a lively discussion about which childhood tales had been true and which fantasy; Dirk helped resolve it by telling them which fairy tales came from medieval Terra, and which countries there—so by the end of the week, they had a very general outline of Terran history and geography in their minds, and an even more sketchy outline of the history of space colonization.

Dirk had also learned which of them were very intelligent, and that no one was anything else. He asked the Guardian about that.

"How come all your inmates have such high IQs?" he asked the decorated wall.

"Because those who weren't would have felt inferior here, and that would have deepened their delusion," the computer voice told him.

Dirk felt a cold chill inside. "What did you do with them?"

"Sent them to the city of Firstmark. The computer there cares for them as I care for mine."

"Oh, really." Dirk pricked up his ears. "I take it Firstmark is buried in the forest, too?"

"It is indeed."

"Just how many lost cities are there?"

"Five," the computer answered. "Firstmark and Secondmark are for people of moderate intelligence. Thirdmark is for people of low intelligence, but Fourthmark holds delusionaries of high intelligence, too. I did not think it wise to have more than three hundred people in each city."

"So there are more than a thousand people ready to become subversives, not counting Thirdmark," Dirk said slowly, "and there are only a dozen living cities, and maybe four hundred towns, in this whole land."

"You should have a potential labor force equal to half the bureaucracy, if I guess rightly from what you have told me of it."

Dirk nodded slowly. "If Gar's health holds up, yes. Half should be enough for a revolution."

"Quite adequate," the computer agreed.

By the end of the third week, Gar had recovered enough for his conference with the computer. It was very distressed to learn that the bureaucracy it had served had become the tool of a dictatorship, and was completely in favor of overthrowing the Protector, provided that it could be done with very little bloodshed. Gar explained the plan, and the Guardian approved it.

So the former delusionaries kept on with their training in weapons in the morning, then retired to their chambers to learn literature, history, psychology, mathematics, general science, music, strategy and tactics, and political science, then went on to learning the root legal code from which the Protector's laws were drawn. The computer was also able to teach them the bureaucratic procedure that was probably the basis for the current government. The people confirmed the resemblance from their own experience with magistrates and reeves.

Very quickly, they began to form study groups, to discuss issues that confused them. Dirk explained to them that they could talk to the computer anywhere within the palace, and was amazed to find that the machine could explain a dozen different concepts to a dozen different groups at the same time. In those discussions, the Guardian revealed that the Protector was originally chosen by vote, and that everyone was born with rights—an alien concept which the cured madmen accepted eagerly, since it confirmed the ideas Gar and Dirk had given them.

As soon as the educational program was set up, Gar and Dirk left for Firstmark—which the Guardian had explained was short for "first market." Dirk gave the original settlers high marks for organization, but negative marks for creativity.

Miles was astounded to find himself left in charge of Voya-gend, but even more surprised to find the people coming to him to answer questions and resolve disputes. He was most sur-prised to find that he knew the answers and could settle the dis-putes fairly. Apparently Gar and Dirk had taught him more than he had realized.

CHAPTER 15

Two years passed, with Gar and Dirk returning from their journeys for brief visits; they were constantly on the road, overseeing training in all four cities. As the former inmates' minds grew, they hammered out their own idea of what a government should be. The bailiffs would be appointed by the magistrates, as they always had been, but to become a magistrate, men and women would have to pass examinations, then be appointed by the Protector, but would have to be approved by vote of the people in their villages every year. The reeves would be elected by the magistrates from their own number, but would have to stand for a vote of confidence from the people of their shires every year. The Council of Reeves would be elected by all the bureaucrats together from the ranks of the reeves; the Council would elect the ministers from their own ranks, and people would elect the Protector from the ranks of the ministers.

Thus, to qualify to vote for the reeves, they had to initially pass examinations. To stand for office as a reeve, or minister, they had to prove themselves by years of service, and for Protector, by more years of service as a minister.

Once they knew how they wished to reshape their government and why, Gar began to give them their assignments within the underground, so that they could undergo advanced training. Those most adept at music were appointed to be minstrels, given subtly subversive songs to sing, and special training as secret agents, to keep all the false magistrates in touch with one another. The women, knowing they couldn't become magistrates, were given very specific training on how to influence other people—persuasion and soft propaganda. The men, already trained as potential magistrates, now learned how to be secret agents, too, learning the cell system, codes, and infiltration techniques.

Meanwhile, Dirk sent out minstrels with forged travel permits, to listen more than they sang until they learned of magistrates scheduled for reassignment. By the time the first such agent came back to the City in high excitement, knowing the time and place of the rotation, the first false magistrate was ready to go—Orgoru.

The sun was barely risen as Orgoru came out of the city dressed in magistrate's robes to meet the false bailiff and the dozen men dressed in watchmen's uniforms.

"Farewell! Oh, fare you well indeed!" Gilda cried, and threw her arms around Orgoru's neck. "I was among the first to greet you when first you came—let me be among the last to bid you good-bye!"

"Good-bye—until I see you again." Orgoru took her into his arms, amazed that so bony a woman could feel so soft in his embrace—then even more amazed as she pulled her head back enough to turn, and kissed him full on the lips. It was a lingering caress, and for a moment, closing his eyes, Orgoru saw again the beautiful countess. Then he drew away, smiling with affection, for they had shared many long talks about right and wrong, and the fate of their country, in the last two years, and he had become almost as fond of common Gilda as he had been obsessed with the beautiful countess. "Good-bye until I see you again," he said, "and may all go well for you."

"Send word as soon as you know you're safe!"

"I will," he promised, and turned away quickly to mount his horse, before he could feel greater temptation to take her with him. Mounting, he turned back, and was surprised to see Ciletha standing by the gate, hand lifted in farewell, eyes bright with tears. Orgoru gave her what he hoped was a reassuring smile, then turned away to his horse and his men.

It never occurred to him to wonder why Ciletha had come to see him off, or why she should be teary-eyed. They were old friends, after all.

He did wonder, though, if he really wanted to trust his life to that grim-faced Miles. What the deuce did the man have against him, after all? But his master Dirk was going too, leaving Gar and Ciletha in charge of the city—Ciletha in charge! an amazing thought!—so Orgoru mounted his horse and rode off to ambush a magistrate.

They stopped at a place where a dusty country road joined the high road that led to the town of Greenthorpe. They had passed out of the forest, but huge trees overhung the crossroads. Orgoru looked around, frowning. "This isn't too good a place for an ambush, Master Miles."

"It's as good as we're going to get," the peasant growled.

Orgoru glanced at Dirk, but the master only nodded and turned pointedly to Miles.

Miles sighed and explained. "The trees are large enough to hide our raiders, both behind their trunks and in their branches. We don't really expect to need them, though."

"I know—the custom is for the outgoing magistrate to send watchmen to the halfway point, to meet their new master," Orgoru said. "I take it this is that point."

"Not quite—not by a league. That's close enough so the new magistrate won't be surprised to see us, but far enough away so that the Greenthorpe watchmen won't come this far—though Nathan will watch half a mile down the road, and bring us word if they do."

Nathan touched his forelock and jogged away toward the south. Orgoru watched him go, marveling that this man, two years before, had thought himself to be Lord Saunders. "So we'll deceive," he said, "not ambush."

Miles nodded. "We'll only ambush if we have to."

Ryan, formerly Lord Finn, went down the northern road toward Atterborough, from which the new magistrate was coming. The others sat down, ate, and rested, two napping and two awake, until Ryan came jogging back. "They're coming! A mile away—I saw them from high in a tree!"

"Stations, quickly," Miles ordered.

Andrew (the erstwhile Count Parlous) and Douglas (the quondam Duke River) climbed up into the trees and disappeared among the branches. Gar and Orgoru stepped behind a tree trunk. Orgoru heard the whisper of arrows laid against bows, and hoped, for the sake of the real magistrate and his men, that they would believe the deception.

Ryan paced nearby, nervous and unable to hide it. He wore ordinary peasant clothes, as a coachman would. Miles and Dirk, though, were dressed in watchmen's livery, and sat leaning against the tree trunk, gossiping and yawning. Orgoru couldn't believe his ears—their intended victims nearly upon them, and the men were discussing government!

A voice hailed them from far down the road.

Miles came to his feet, Dirk right behind him. They waved at the approaching carriage with its two riders and extra horse, then waited smiling until the coachman drew the carriage up. The magistrate, a heavyset man in his forties, gave them a smile, and the gray-haired coachman called, "Are you from Greenthorpe?"

"The Greenthorpe escort we are," Miles lied cheerfully. It went against all his upbringing, but Dirk had impressed upon him how important it was. Besides, they *were* planning to make sure a magistrate got to Greenthorpe—just not this one.

"Then we'll be pleased to let you escort our master." The coachman climbed down from the carriage and came around to gaze up at the magistrate. "You've been a good master, Magistrate Flound, and I envy the folk in Greenthorpe. Fare you well with them."

"Fare you well," Flound said with a sad smile, "and I hope

your new master is a good one. Give him a chance, Holstin—
he's quite young yet, and is apt to be sharp in his nervousness."

"Weren't we all!" Holstin held up a hand, horizontal, palm
downward. Flound let his own hand rest on it for a moment;
then Holstin stepped aside so that the two riders might
exchange good-byes, and receive the laying-on of the magistrate's hand in farewell.

It was enough like a blessing to give Dirk a start. He wondered if it was the only form of touching that ritual allowed
between a magistrate and his men.

The farewells done, Miles climbed up on the box and took
the reins. He clucked to the horses and drove off at a sedate
pace. Flound looked back once, with a fond smile, then turned
his face resolutely toward the future—but Dirk, riding close
beside, noticed tears in his eyes.

They rode, Ryan and Dirk on either side, for half a league, to
the intersection where Orgoru stood hidden. There Miles said,
"Whoa!" and pulled in the horses.

Flound leaned forward, frowning. "Why have you stopped?"

"Because this is as far as you go, Your Honor," Dirk
answered. "Climb down, please."

Flound looked up in shock. "You're outlaws!"

"I'm afraid so," Dirk said with a sympathetic smile, "but we
don't mean—"

Flound sprang at him.

He slammed into Dirk, knocking him from his horse and
grabbing frantically at the saddle, but didn't quite manage to
hold, and fell himself, half on top of Dirk. He scrambled to his
feet and pulled a short club from under his robe. Dirk leaped
up, too, and swung an uppercut. Flound blocked with the club,
then swung it with a shout.

It was a fast blow, but Dirk ducked under it, coming up to
shoot a quick punch at the magistrate's jaw. Flound blocked
with his left and swung the club again. Dirk leaped back, but
the club seemed to follow him somehow, and caught him on
the left shoulder. He ground his teeth against pain and grabbed
for the club with his right hand.

Ryan leaned down from his saddle to catch Flound around

the throat, but the magistrate danced aside and chopped viciously with the club. Dirk snatched his hand away, and Miles sprang down to throw his arms around the magistrate from behind. Flound kicked back sharply, and Miles cried out at the pain in his shin. The distraction was enough; Flound twisted away, and swung his club at Miles's temple.

Orgoru shouted as he caught Flound's arm and yanked it back, enough so that the club missed. The magistrate yanked hard, but Orgoru held tight to his wrist and turned the palm up, yanking the sleeve of the robe high.

Flound finally took a good look at Orgoru and stared, thunderstruck by seeing magistrate's robes.

In the second he was frozen, Dirk pressed a small bulb against his wrist.

That brought Flound out of his stupor with a shout. He slammed a kick into Orgoru's stomach. Orgoru managed to block, but that only took some of the force from it, and he doubled over in pain. Flound yanked his arm free and turned to face Dirk, breathing hard and swinging his club in a whirring circle.

Then, suddenly, his eyes rolled up and he slumped to the ground.

"Thought that drug would never kick in," Dirk panted as he came over to pick the club from nerveless fingers.

"We didn't know," Miles said, eyes wide. "I swear to you, Mas—Dirk, I never knew magistrates hid clubs beneath their robes!"

"Neither did I," Orgoru said, and Ryan echoed him and added, "I never knew they'd been taught how to fight, either!"

"Then it's a good thing we taught *you*." Dirk handed Orgoru the club. "Keep that with your blackjack now, and use the club first if you have to use anything, since that's what they'll expect you to have."

"I shall," Orgoru said. "Good fortune that you taught me single-stick play!"

"Good fortune indeed," Dirk agreed, "but we can't trust to luck. From now on, the real magistrates won't even get this much of a chance. We can't have somebody winding up dead, can we?"

"Not if we can help it, no," Orgoru said, slightly shocked at the idea. "After all, this isn't war."

"Yet," Ryan said heavily.

"Well, into the carriage with you," Dirk told Orgoru. "You still have a reception committee to meet."

"Yes! Thank you for this help, Dirk." Orgoru turned to Miles. "And thank you, too, Miles."

"It's I should be thanking you," Miles answered, with the first real smile he had ever given Orgoru. "He would have cracked my head if you hadn't stopped him."

"I can't have a highly trained agent stopped by a feeble old magistrate, can I?" Orgoru returned the smile.

"No, and you can't stop, either," Dirk told him. "Up into the carriage with you."

As Orgoru climbed, Nathan came running up the southern road from his sentry post. "Horses! The Greenthorpe party must have gotten impatient!"

"Or can't see their milestones," Dirk said dryly. "You ride escort, Nathan. I'd better keep His Nibs here, until you boys get back." He reached up to clasp Orgoru's hand. "Good luck!"

"Thank you," Orgoru said fervently, then sat back, his heart pounding, as Miles started the horses.

They came to the trio from Greenthorpe in only a few hundred yards. The Greenthorpers reined in, and Miles drew the carriage to a halt. Orgoru, his heart in his mouth, gave them a smile that he hoped had just the right degree of condescension. "Are you the men from Greenthorpe?"

"Aye, Your Honor," one of the watchmen saluted.

"I am Magistrate Flound. Will you escort me to my new post?"

"We'll be delighted, Your Honor!"

Ryan climbed down off the box and came around to the side of the carriage. "Farewell, Magistrate. You've been a good master to me."

They reenacted the scene they had just watched the real

Flound play out, then turned their mounts, Miles on the spare horse, and rode away.

"Onward, goodmen," Orgoru said with a genial smile, and leaned back as his new coachman drove him off to the biggest sham of his life.

The carriage stopped in front of the courthouse, and the coachman hopped to open the door. Orgoru climbed down, smiling his thanks, and followed the man to the doorway, where a portly man in a bailiff's short robe waited.

"Bailiff Tundro, may I present Magistrate Flound."

"Greetings, Your Honor." The bailiff gave him a little bow. "Welcome to Greenthorpe."

Something within Orgoru thrilled to that. "Greetings, bailiff, and thank you for your welcome. Please introduce me to the rest of the staff."

Tundro looked slightly surprised, probably at the word "please," but led Orgoru inside and introduced him to the servants, who insisted on laying out a light supper, then drawing his bath.

Bathed, fed, and thoroughly scared, Orgoru locked himself in the library, hauled down the first volume in the Code of Laws, and started speed-reading frantically.

CHAPTER 16

Thus Orgoru was the first to become a magistrate, and stalled during the day while he read law books frantically at night, to learn the updates for the last few hundred years. When he was sure of procedure, he started catching up on business and getting to know the people. He was aware that he only had six months to find a wife and marry. But the people seemed to accept him, and though his clerk gave him a raised eyebrow on occasion and had to fix his mistakes fairly frequently, the staff seemed to accept him as genuine, and after the first few weeks, he began to calm down. Still, a terrible homesickness overwhelmed him every night, homesickness for Voyagend and the other cured inmates who had become his friends in reality as well as delusion.

After the first month, though, he had a very pleasant surprise. At the end of the court session, the bailiff told him, "There are two people newly come to Greenthorpe, Your Honor, a merchant and his sister. They wish to file a complaint against a neighbor, for their father died a month ago, and the neighbor laid claim to half the goods in their warehouse."

Orgoru sighed; he hadn't really learned much about business, and would have to trust to common sense. Besides, he'd already found out that if you just asked enough questions, people frequently answered their own while answering yours. "Very well. I'll meet them in the study. Please tell Varjis to bring tea."

"Yes, Your Honor."

Orgoru went into the library, threw himself down in a leather-covered chair, and sighed. He hadn't realized that being a magistrate involved so much work. Then the door opened, and he looked up—to see Jules, the erstwhile King Longar, and Gilda!

He couldn't help himself; he stared, and surely Bailiff Tundro must have noticed it before he said, "Merchant Ruhle and his sister Gilda."

Orgoru recovered and forced a bland smile. "Sit down, won't you? Thank you, Tundro."

"Of course, Your Honor."

Orgoru was sure Tundro's sharp eyes hadn't missed anything, but for the moment, he didn't care. He bolted from his chair and caught Gilda in a bear hug. "Oh, thank you, thank you, my friends! It's so good to see you, so good!" He let her go and turned to pump Jules's hand. "Thank you a thousand times!"

"We couldn't let you languish by yourself any longer," Gilda said, "so we trumped up an excuse to visit."

"Sit down, sit down!" Orgoru suited the action to the word, gesturing at chairs. "Be comfortable! Tell me, what news from home?" His eyes widened as he heard himself call Voyagend "home," but it really was, far more than the village in which he'd grown up.

"All goes well," Jules told him, "though very busily. The minstrels are sending back lists of which magistrates will be transferred when, and Gar has driven Miles crazy by setting him to keep records of each of them, then choosing which man to send to replace which magistrate. Every week we send out two more men to become officials, and three or four women to find ways to marry genuine magistrates, or to take positions as nurses that will help them subvert soldiers." He grinned. "It's quite a hive of activity, I can tell you."

"And the magistrates they send back, the real ones?" Orgoru asked, with a bit of guilt.

"They're furious, which means they're well in every other way," Gilda told him. "Gar has sent them all to live in that great long block of a building that is all living apartments, and appointed Bade—you remember, the former Duke of Despres?"

"Of course." Orgoru nodded vigorously. "Surely *Bade* isn't going to be head jailer, not with his hatred of officials!"

"He has more reason to dislike them than most of us," Jules admitted, "considering what they did to his family. But the Guardian wouldn't let him mistreat them even if he planned to, and his hatred will keep him vigilant to make sure none escape."

The door opened, and the maid came in with a tea cart.

"I really don't think the man has reason enough to hate you," Orgoru said. "Can't he understand healthy competition between businessmen?"

They gave him blank stares, then realized he had switched topics to the official reason for their being there. "He seems to be one of those who has to win at all costs," Jules said, "and takes any competition as a personal attack."

"Yes, that will do nicely, thank you," Orgoru said to the maid, who curtsied and left, closing the door behind her.

Gilda caught her breath. "You do that so well! Just like a real magistrate!"

"I *am* a real magistrate," Orgoru said, "or at least, I have to think that way, or I'll fail completely."

Jules frowned, concerned. "Be careful, Orgoru."

"Don't worry, I won't fall back into delusion." Orgoru looked about him and grimaced. "Believe me, if I were going to, I wouldn't choose this!"

"Being a lord was so much more pleasing." Gilda handed him a filled cup.

Orgoru stared at it in surprise. "Forgive me! I should have poured."

"There's certainly no need." She handed a cup to Jules, then poured one for herself, set down the pot, then looked up past Orgoru's shoulder. "Oh! What a lovely garden!"

"Yes, isn't it?" Orgoru turned to look. "One of the compensations for the stresses of the job. It's excellent for relaxation at the end of a long day—and for helping think through a problem." He turned back to her. "Would you like to walk in it?"

"I'd love to." She set down her cup.

"Jules?" Orgoru asked.

The former king waved away the invitation. "I've had enough walking for one day, thank you. You two take your time—I'll find plenty of company in your biscuits and tea."

"As you wish." Orgoru rose and held out his hand. "My lady, will you walk?"

Gilda came to take his arm, giggling. "Those courtly phrases sound so strange now!"

"But they come so naturally," Orgoru said, as they went out the French doors into the garden.

They strolled down the pathway, Gilda saying, "It really is lovely."

"Not as lovely a sight as my first glimpse of Voyagend, that first night," Orgoru sighed. "That was magical indeed."

"Fantastic, one might almost say." Gilda smiled.

Orgoru laughed. "Yes, a fantasy indeed!" He turned to look into her eyes. "And so were you—luscious and lovely, the most beautiful woman I had ever seen."

"You were so tall," she said, "and lean, and handsome."

"No! Was I really?" Orgoru laughed.

"Indeed you were—gauche, but so very handsome!"

"Whereas now," Orgoru said ruefully, "I am graceful and at least somewhat cultured, but plain and lumpen!"

"Certainly not lumpen," Gilda said sharply, and squeezed his biceps. "Dirk's physical training has given you a great deal of hard muscle."

He smiled at her. "It gave you almost as voluptuous a figure as you had in my delusion." He was amazed to feel a flicker of the old passion.

"In *my* delusion, you filled me with desire," Gilda leaned closer to him. "Seeing you as a magistrate kindles it anew."

The flicker blew into a blaze. "In me also," he said, and leaned closer himself. Their lips touched, very tentatively at first, brushing one another enough to tickle, to raise shivers. Then the kiss deepened and lasted a long time indeed.

When they parted, he embraced her, amazed to find himself trembling, delighted to feel her trembling, too. "Come, sit!" He stepped away and gestured her to a bench. She sat—but he knelt and said, "Marry me, Gilda! Please marry me!"

She stared, even though it was what she had hoped for, had burned for. "But . . . but I am plain and gangling!" she protested.

"You will always be beautiful to me, for I've seen you through the eyes of the Prince of Paradime. You still have all the charm, grace, and wit of the Countess Gilda—and I've fallen in love with you all over again."

"Oh, Orgoru!" She leaned forward, clasping both his hands. "But will it last?"

"Oh, yes," he said, looking deeply into her eyes. When he saw that she still hesitated, he said, "Come, my love! You know that I have to marry somebody soon, to stave off suspicion. Will you leave me to the clutches of some illiterate, clumsy village maid?"

"No, never!" She smiled fondly. "Far better that it be someone you trust."

"And love," he breathed, then stretched up to kiss her again. When they parted, he caught his breath and said, "Still, if you have any doubts, I promise not to make physical advances."

"Oh, do you indeed!" Gilda cried. "Am I so ugly after all that you can't bear to touch me, then?"

"You know the falseness of that from my kiss," Orgoru protested. "Be assured that I do want to touch you, and very badly, too."

"I certainly hope you will not do it badly!" Gilda exclaimed.

Orgoru spread his hands, laughing. "Come, now! You will be angered if I don't, and angered if I do!"

"Not if you do it well," she returned, and leaned down with a lazy smile. "If you think you can, and really want to, prove it!"

He did. She wasn't angry.

When they parted, Orgoru moaned, "Marry me, sweet lady, or forever after know yourself to be cruel! Will you marry me, sweeting?"

"Yes," she whispered.

This time, their kiss lasted and lasted, until Jules finally came to the window, alarmed that they had been so long silent—but what he saw made him smile, and eased his fears for them immensely.

Miles was hard at work in the palace office—it had been the sitting room of his suite, but the records had overflowed, and he had been forced to move—when a voice called, "Hail the conquering hero!"

Looking up, he saw Jules coming through the door and looking very proud of himself. He grinned and leaped up, coming around his desk. "Hail, hero! What have you done?"

"Escorted Gilda to see Orgoru, and I assure you, he was very glad to see us, and very hungry for news."

"But he was well?"

"Well? He was thriving! Now he's even better."

"News from home did that much good, eh?" Miles asked, grinning.

"News from home—and Gilda. Ask me where she is, Miles."

Miles lost his smile. "Where is she?"

"She stayed with Orgoru! They started talking about old times, and fell in love all over again! They mean to be married in a month!" Jules frowned. "Why the face of calamity? Don't you understand, boy? They're engaged!"

"Oh, I understand well enough!" It was the strangest mix of emotions Miles had ever felt—elation that Orgoru was no longer his rival, but real, deep fear at what effect the news would have on Ciletha. "Whatever you do, don't tell her!"

"Her? Who? Gilda? I think she knows."

"No—Ciletha!"

"Don't tell Ciletha? Whyever not?"

"Yes—why not tell Ciletha?" The lady herself came through the doorway, slender and light as though blown on the wind.

"This lamebrain seems to think I shouldn't tell you Orgoru and Gilda are engaged." Jules turned to her, frowning—it was very deflating to have his wonderful news treated as a tragedy.

Worse, Ciletha didn't treat it as much of anything. "Are they really?" she asked with a polite little smile. "How wonderful for them!" Then she went to Miles's desk and laid some papers on it. "The reports from Fourthmark, Miles. Dirk said you'd want them."

Jules scowled. "No one seems to care much about romance anymore. If you'll excuse me, I'm tired and hot from my trip. I'm going to my suite. At least the tub will appreciate me!"

"Thank you very much for the news, Jules," Miles said hastily. "Believe me, you don't know how important it is!"

"I do. I'm glad you have some hint of it yourself." The former king went out, not much mollified.

Miles turned to Ciletha anxiously.

"I'm all *right*, Miles," she insisted. "Anyone who knew those two knew this would happen some day."

"But . . . but it doesn't . . . grieve you?"

"Grieve me? No." She looked up at him, exasperated. "How blind can you be? I fell out of love with Orgoru two years ago!"

It was the first time she had admitted she'd been in love with him.

"Then—you don't really care?"

"Care? I'm glad for my old friend. I hope they'll be happy." Then, suddenly, her eyes brimmed over.

Miles reached her in one step and swept her into his embrace. She wept into his chest, gasping. "I don't know why . . . I'm crying. . . . I don't care . . . about him . . . anymore. . . ." Then she raised a tear-stained face to him. "I suppose I'm mourning the past, what little good there was in it."

He gazed down into her face gravely for a moment, then quite deliberately kissed her.

It started as a short, light kiss, but it deepened and lasted amazingly. When he finally lifted his head and drew breath, astounded and stunned, Ciletha gave a little, happy sigh and laid her head on his chest again. "I thought you'd never do that!"

"I never would have dared, until today." He stroked her hair, gazing over her head, feeling the most delightful sensation steal over him. "I would tell you to take heart, but you already have—*my* heart."

"And you took mine long ago, you silly man! Didn't you see that I'd fallen out of love with Orgoru and in love with you?"

"I'm blind," he whispered.

"Then you'll have to work by touch," she said, and raised her head for another kiss.

They forgot to close the door. Sometime later, Jules stumped by, bathed and trimmed. He stopped to stare in at them, then turned away, shaking his head and muttering about something in the air.

Miles stared. "You want me to do *what*?"

"To coordinate all the efforts of the underground," Gar said patiently, "to keep track of what everyone's doing, and if anyone makes a mistake, send someone to fix it."

"We're asking you to be chief rebel, Miles," Dirk said, smiling. "We're asking you to boss the revolution."

Miles sat down hard, staring blankly in front of him. It was just good luck he'd had a chair handy—or maybe that was why they had come into his study and told him at his desk.

He looked around at the room, not even seeing the velvet drapes, the tapestry, the gilded moldings, the fireplace, or the graceful, damask-covered furniture. "Chief rebel?" he asked, stupefied.

"Yes," Gar said. "Why do you think we had you take care of the records and send people out, then interview them when they came back?"

"You were training me for the job!"

"Very successfully, too," Dirk agreed. "You're ready for it, Miles—and we're ready to go find other oppressive governments to overthrow. You can handle everything here for the next four years."

"Don't worry," Gar said. "We'll come back for the actual revolution."

Miles's mind seized on something trivial. He gazed at a random note on his desk. "Isn't it an amazing coincidence that the peasant you chose for a guide should prove to be the man you want to lead the revolution?"

"No coincidence at all," Dirk snapped. "Why did you think we chose you for a guide, out of all the outlawed peasants in the land? Why do you think we kept you with us?"

"You have the intelligence to do the job, and the strength of will to hold the position," Gar told him. "Besides that, you can think quickly enough to handle an emergency."

"We've taught you all we can," Dirk said. "You can do the job—and you're the only man on the planet who can."

"Me? An illiterate peasant, oppose the Protector and all his soldiers?"

"You," Dirk said, "and a thousand false magistrates, not to mention the soldiers our agents are subverting at the rate of twenty a day. They may not know the word 'revolution' or our intention to overthrow the Protector, but they won't fight to stop you."

"Just remember that you have to keep the real magistrates penned up until after the revolution," Gar cautioned. "They know how to flatter and fawn, and they're very likely to convince you of their loyalty—then turn their coats the second they're free, and bring back an army to destroy you."

"The magistrate who does that will become a minister overnight," Dirk agreed.

Miles nodded. "I'll remember." Then he shook himself. "Wait a minute! I haven't even said I'll do it yet!"

"Well?" Dirk said, hands on his hips.

"Will you?" Gar demanded.

Miles's gaze strayed. "I'll have to talk to Ciletha first." He braced himself for exasperation, but they must have known more than he thought (when didn't they?)—for Dirk only nodded, and Gar said, "Of course you must."

He met Ciletha for their usual walk in the park—the captive bureaucrats had been very indignant at having to clear away the vines and overgrowth enough for the robot gardeners to begin work again. Now he met Ciletha there every evening, even if they'd been together at their desks all day, to enjoy the cool air and gaze at the ponds and flower beds.

"You're quiet tonight, my dear," Ciletha prodded.

"Yes. I—I have some . . . some very important news, Ciletha," Miles said.

When he fell silent, Ciletha suppressed a sigh and said only, "Go on."

"Gar and Dirk came to see me today . . ."

He stopped again. Ciletha pressed. "What about?"

"They want me to be chief rebel. They want me to lead the revolution."

"Chief rebel! Oh, how wonderful, Miles!" Ciletha planted a huge kiss on his lips. Instinct took over, and he embraced her, amazed.

Suddenly she broke the kiss and pushed herself away, eyes wide with horror. "Miles! The danger! If they catch you, they'll torture you to draw everyone's name from you. Then, when they've milked you dry, they'll draw and quarter you!"

Miles shuddered at the thought of the dread, slow punishment and put it from him resolutely. "I know, Ciletha. I can't take that risk without your understanding. I'm foolish enough to think my life affects yours, after all."

"Foolish! Oh, you dear boy, no! You *are* my life now!" The horror lifted from her suddenly, and her smile was like the sunrise. "Come, now. We both knew we were wagering our lives for this. We all do. If the Protector's spies catch us, we'll all be tortured and hanged—but we can't go back now."

Miles frowned, thinking of it for the first time. "No, we can't, can we? Even if I took you back to my home village and presented you to the magistrate as my fiancée, he'd still have me flogged, set me to years of hard labor—and probably forbid our marriage, to prove that no one can defy the Protector." He shuddered. "No, I think I'd rather have a real death than a living one."

"I would, too," she said softly, "and we can only be slain once."

"Yes, we can, can't we?" Miles smiled at her, realizing all over again what a unique woman she was. "But I'm far more concerned for you than for myself, Ciletha. After all, I'm the one who dragged you into this mess."

"I dragged myself into it," she told him sternly, "or blundered into it, rather—blundered into you and Gar and Dirk that dark night. But I chose to stay—and I choose to stay now."

"Well, yes," Miles said, "but you wouldn't have done so if it hadn't been for me."

"I thought you would never realize that," she whispered, swaying very close to him. He stared at her in surprise, then realized her meaning and took her in his arms to kiss her again.

When they came up for air, he whispered, "I love you, Ciletha."

"So you have told me," she replied. "Do you finally believe that I love you, too?"

Miles smiled as joy swept him again. "I could only hope for that," he said, "but never believe it."

"Believe it, then!" she scolded; then, swaying right up against him and half closing her eyes, "What will it take to *make* you believe it?"

He kissed her again and came up smiling. "A wedding," he whispered. "Marry me, and I'll believe you love me."

Ciletha gave a sigh of mock exasperation. "The lengths I must go to, to make you see what is clearly before you! Well, if I must marry to make you trust me, then I will."

He gave a shout of joy, then kissed her again. When he drew back, he said, "But I haven't asked you properly," and dropped to one knee. "Will you marry me, Ciletha?"

She gave him a mock cuff on the ear. "Yes, you blockhead!" Then more softly, "Yes, you wonderful, handsome man, I will marry you."

They kissed again. Then she pushed herself away, suddenly very serious. "But not until this revolution is won or lost, Miles. It would be horrible to bear children and see them chewed up by the Protector's forces. If we win, then I'll marry you." She frowned, suddenly worried. "You did mean to have children, didn't you?"

"Oh, yes," Miles breathed, and the kiss was even longer this time.

When Miles lifted his head, though, concern shadowed his face. "I didn't tell Dirk and Gar that I'm not the only person who knows who all the rebels are, and where. I'm very frightened for you, my love."

"Well, then." Ciletha wrapped her arms around him and pressed her head into his shoulder. "You'll just have to take very good care of me, won't you?"

"Why, yes, I will," he said, his smile returning, and pressed a finger under her chin to lift her head. "I won't let you out of my sight, my love."

"Well," she said, "at least not at night," and kissed him again.

So it was that Ciletha stood beside Miles on top of a hill in the very first predawn light a week later, wondering what Dirk and Gar were waiting for, but too polite to ask.

"How do you write out your records?" Gar asked one more time.

"In ink that runs if it gets wet," Ciletha said patiently, "and we keep a tank of water nearby, to dump in the records if our sentries tell us soldiers are coming."

"Infiltrate the secret police if you can," Dirk reminded them for the tenth time.

"We will if we can find them," Miles told them patiently. "You don't know how sorry I am to see you go, and how glad I'll be to see you come back!"

"Thank you." Gar smiled warmly. "But you don't really need us any more. This revolution will run itself now—it's like a boulder that's been pushed off the top of a hill. If nobody stops it, it'll knock down the castle at the bottom."

"It would take a very great deal to stop a boulder going that fast," Dirk seconded, "especially since this boulder gets bigger as it rolls."

"Good-bye." Gar reached down to embrace Miles, then Ciletha, and came up with that fleeting trace of longing flickering over his face.

"Farewell indeed!" she told him. "Until you come back to us!"

"We will if we live," Dirk promised, "and we intend to. Go now, you two. Leave us to our transportation."

"Go on," Gar said, still smiling.

Miles took Ciletha's arm in his. Together they turned and started down the hill. They heard nothing, saw nothing, but as they reached the bottom, something made them turn and look up.

They saw the huge golden disk hovering over the hilltop, and Dirk and Gar climbing up the ramp it had lowered to them. They disappeared inside; the ramp lifted, and the disk rose.

Miles and Ciletha stood staring at it until it was long out of sight.

"Now I believe our ancestors came from another star," Miles whispered.

Ciletha shook herself and turned away. "Come, beloved. We have a Protector to overthrow."

CHAPTER 17

She remembered being the Lady Rijora, and in her dreams, she still was—but in the light of day, she knew herself once again as just plain Bess.

Plain indeed! Where Lady Rijora's mirror had shown her a finely chiseled face with large blue long-lashed eyes, fair complexion, and a veritable mane of golden curls, Bess saw a moon-round face with close-set brown eyes, skin scarred by pimples, and framed by straight lank brown hair. The layers of fat had faded with Dirk's combat drills and the Guardian's diet, though, and she bore herself with grace, back straight and step light. Her tongue kept the lady's accent as well as her hands remembered the gestures of refined conversation, and the ways of using the tableware for an elaborate formal dinner. Even more, she remembered the tricks of wide-eyed flirtation, of sidelong glances and the tilt of a head and the bat of eyelashes so well that she didn't even need to think of them.

Less obvious, and much to be hidden, was the knowledge of literature that their deluded court had learned from the Guardian, and the seriousness of the lessons Gar and Dirk had taught—of history, of law, of the workings of society and government, and of the human mind. It was knowledge to be hidden, yes, but also to be used for asking the occasional question that stimulated conversation, and made it much quicker for her to learn from its interplay.

The townswomen eyed her with suspicion as she walked down the high street with her basket on her arm, and she heard more than one mutter, "Who does she think she is, putting on such airs?"

Without even thinking, the words leaped to her tongue: *I am the Lady Rijora, peasant. You forget your place.* She bit them back in time, though, only tossing her head in reply—and that little gesture brought angry murmurs from other women all along the way.

At least I'm attracting attention, she thought, but with her heart in her throat. She meant to be noticed, surely enough—but what would happen when she was?

A man in livery, carrying the staff of a watchman, stepped up to her, his face carefully neutral. "Good day, goodwoman."

"Good day, watchman." Her heart rose into her throat.

"Let me see your travel permit, please." The officer held out his hand.

"Of course." She rummaged in her basket and held out the packet, her heart hammering, no matter how calmly she smiled. This was the first crisis—whether or not her forged papers would pass inspection. The Guardian itself had made them, of course, feeding them out of a slot in the wall, and had reassured her that it had shaped them after real papers that a wanderer had brought only five years earlier—but how much could change in five years? Certainly she had!

The papers, though, had not—or so it seemed. The watchman read them through in a minute, nodding in satisfaction. "So. You are Bess of the village of Milorga, come seeking your third cousins." He looked up, frowning. "Your magistrate does not say why you seek them. Do you need to live with them?"

Bess noticed the dangerous glint in his eye—the official on the watch for single folk who should be bound into marriage.

That was her intention, but she didn't have the same partner in mind that he seemed to have. "No, sir—it's just that my grandmother has only this last month learned that her brother lived long enough to wed, when he was mustered out of the Protector's service."

The watchman stiffened; service to a Protector's guardsman, retired or active, held a high priority.

"Gram is old and frail," Bess went on, "and wishes to see her niece or nephew, if she has such, and their children, if there are any. Mama must tend the old woman, so I am sent to seek our relatives."

"A good deed," the watchman said piously, "but why here in our town of Grister?"

"It's the last place Grandma knew of my great-uncle being sent," Bess explained, "and she hopes that his family will be here, of course, but if not, she hopes that someone here might still remember where he went."

"Sent here." The watchman thrust out a lip, looking thoughtful. "He was assigned to be a reeve's guard, then?"

"Yes, sir, but his reeve sent him to organize the Watch for the magistrate of this village."

"A common thing, when a magistrate is new to his office and has just begun his first assignment," the watchman said, nodding. "Indeed, the officer who commands us is just such a reeve's man, for our new magistrate is very young, and newly sent to begin his career." He couldn't help a hint of condescension coming into his voice.

Bess couldn't keep a thrill from her heart. She knew very well that the magistrate here was brand-new, and very young, as such officials went, only in his mid-twenties. In fact, that was why Miles had sent her.

"What was your great-uncle's name?" the watchman asked.

Bess was well prepared for that question—indeed, well prepared for any question having to do with her fictitious family. "Raymond, sir. Of Milorga."

The watchman shook his head, frowning. "I don't know the name, and I've lived here all my life. We can ask, but I doubt that anyone will recognize it. I think you'd better come to the courthouse, young woman, and see if young Magistrate Kerren will consent to look in his record book for you."

"Thank you, sir," Bess said, and sighed. "I didn't really expect to find his family here. I am hoping for some hint of their whereabouts, though."

"It is likely to be a long search, through many villages," the watchman said with sympathy. "Come, maiden. Let me take you to our magistrate."

Bess went willingly—very willingly indeed. She didn't *have* to marry the young magistrate, of course—Miles had made it clear that he wouldn't ask that of any woman. But if he wasn't too repugnant, and if she could bring herself to marry without love, she could do a great deal of good for the cause. He had been quick to remind her that, since she came to it by assignment, it didn't need to last any longer than any magistrate's marriage—and between the Guardian and the knowledge Dirk had taught them all, she knew quite well how to keep from becoming pregnant.

Unless she wanted to, of course.

Bess was more than willing. What else did life hold for her, now that the Wizard had waked her from her lovely dream? For a moment, she felt a lash of savage anger at him, for tearing away her sweet insanity—but she let it pass, knowing that holding to her anger, treasuring it, would only undo her. She was restored to real life and had to make the best of it—and she wouldn't be the first woman to marry for reasons other than love. She was no virgin—the affairs and love-games of the deluded court had been real enough in that respect, and she had joined in with a will.

Still, the thought of marriage was exciting, though also frightening. Besides, the magistrate was young. She intended to be his first wife, and if the revolution succeeded, perhaps his only wife.

If he was desirable.

Spring had come around again. The trees around the Green-thorpe courthouse were heavy with blossoms, and the people of the village wore their brightest clothing as they filed in through the open gates, to take up their places all around the doorway. Musicians played—viol, gamba, and lute, with a flute, a hautboy, and a bassoon giving the music richer accents with their wooden instruments.

The bailiff and the most prominent merchants stood to the left of the courthouse door, richly clad. At the right stood the masters of the trade guilds, more soberly dressed, but with their chains of office making them every bit as grand as the merchants.

The orchestra paused, then played more loudly, a solemn march, as Orgoru came out of the courthouse door in his most formal velvet robes, his own chain of office dimming all others by its luster. The crowd murmured in anticipation as the march picked up tempo, remaining stately but with a more joyous tune. The people in the gateway parted, and six village girls came walking down the path dressed in light pastel gowns with flower wreaths in their hair. After them came Gilda, clothed in white, a crown of flowers holding the veil that covered her face.

The bridesmaids parted, stepping to either side. Gilda paced between them, and if there were a few glares of jealousy and, here and there, a muttered remark that would have been more fitting for a cat than for a village matron, surely they may be excused. After all, every woman between the ages of fifteen and fifty had secretly been hoping to wed the new magistrate, and for an outsider to walk off with the prize was certainly reason for bitterness.

Orgoru stepped forward, hand outstretched, and Gilda stepped up to the broad threshold beside him.

The music ended with a bright flourish, and the bailiff stepped forward, cleared his throat, and thumped his staff for silence. "Friends and neighbors! Hark and hear! It is the office of the magistrate to perform weddings, but when the magistrate himself is being married, his bailiff has the honor of conducting the ceremony—and so I do!"

He turned to face Orgoru and Gilda, beginning the long sequence of questions that made it as sure as anything could that the two people before him knew what they were getting into, and were braced for the worst as well as expecting the best. Nothing could really guarantee a happy marriage, of course, and there was nothing to stop a couple of youngsters from simply memorizing the questions and the answers without stopping to think what they meant—but the challenges the bailiff read off would at least give all but the worst hotheads time for second thoughts.

In the case of marriages the magistrate himself ordered, of course, the ceremony was much shorter.

Finally the questions were done; finally the bailiff called out, "I now pronounce you man and wife!" and Orgoru lifted Gilda's veil to kiss her. The crowd cheered, and if among them was a vagabond with his lute slung across his back and his pouch at his side, why, the more shouts that praised the happy couple, the luckier their union would be.

The orchestra broke into a triumphant wedding march as their magistrate and his new wife turned to wave at the crowd, then led the way down the path toward the gates, and the tables that had been set up outside, filled with food, and the kegs of wine and beer that stood beside them. They shook hands with each of their guests, which included the whole village and most of the surrounding farm families.

As the vagabond came through, one or two of the villagers may have noticed the bride giving the vagabond a quick peck on the cheek, and the magistrate leaning forward to whisper in the vagabond's ear as he shook his hand. "Thank you for coming, Miles! It's so good to see you here!"

"I had to come to wish you well, Orgoru," the secret chief of the rebels whispered back, "and I do, with all my heart!" He gave Orgoru's hand a last pump, and moved on. The magistrate smiled after him a moment.

"What is it, husband?" Gilda said, low-voiced and blushing.

"I think Ciletha may have become closer to our friend Miles than we knew," he murmured back, then turned to shake the next hand, while Gilda glanced at Miles's back, her eyes glowing with shared happiness.

The little orchestra took up dance tunes, and when they tired, a farmer stepped forward with his bagpipes. The celebration lasted until the sun went down, and no one begrudged the vagabond a bite or a glass of wine, especially since he began to play his lute when the other musicians tired. When they caught their breath and began to play again, he danced with the village girls, and only he seemed to be surprised at the strange woman who stepped from the crowd to dance with him.

So Orgoru and Gilda were married, and Miles and Ciletha danced at their wedding, and though the revolution might be long in coming, they certainly seemed to be enjoying the waiting.

After the wedding, Orgoru closed the bedroom door on the last of the well-wishers, took Gilda in his arms, and kissed her. Then he stepped a little away and said, "Remember, we don't have to make love if you don't want."

"Of course I want to," she said, "and you yourself are the sweet reason why. But if you need any other reason, remember that without your children, I'll have no claim on the Protector's living after you're reassigned. Worse, everyone will think I'm barren, and I'll be sent to the frontier farms—though, truth to tell, I'd resigned myself to spinsterhood before I came to Greenthorpe."

Confused, Orgoru said, "But we're going to overthrow the system and be able to stay together for life!" *Or die trying,* he thought, though he didn't mention that out loud.

Gilda beamed at him and said, "I know."

Orgoru stared at her until he realized she had only been playing her role to the hilt; then he began to smile again.

Gilda laughed and said, "There, I see you've begun to understand the game. Now kiss me, handsome prince."

Nonetheless, Orgoru was ready to take a few weeks seducing her. Gilda, however, had more immediate plans.

Dilana's magistrate was older, much older—but so was Dilana. From being the grand duchess of the deluded, she had become a matronly, though lean and angular, widow of a peasant who had died at the hands of bandits with their two sons—at least, so far as the magistrate knew.

They sat in his study, the garden a swathe of color beyond the windows, complementing the rich wood of the paneling and his desk. The velvet upholstery of chairs and settee might have been taken from those flowers, so well did the whole blend. For a moment, Dilana marveled that every courthouse in the land could be identical right down to the finishing of each room. Its purpose was clear—to make the magistrates feel at home, when they were always strangers in new towns. Still, the familiar setting could only lighten homesickness, never cure it completely.

He nodded, frowning as he read her papers. It was reason enough to start a new life, far from the scene of her bereavement, and the memories of past joys. He laid the papers aside with a sigh. "Yes, surely, Goodwoman Dilana. You're welcome among us, and I'm sure there will be many people who will be glad of your skill with herbs."

Dilana knew better than to bat her eyelashes or cast coy glances from the corners of her eyes, knew how false such gestures would seem coming from a mature woman—but she did lower her gaze to her hands, folded in her lap. "It was good of Magistrate Proxum to speak so well of me."

"No more than you deserve, I'm sure," Magistrate Gorlin said. "I haven't met this Proxum, but a magistrate knows quality when he sees it."

Was he speaking of the mythical Proxum, or himself? Dilana dared hope, and murmured, "Magistrate Proxum is quite young, sir."

"So his judgment is not fully formed, eh?" Gorlin smiled, amused. "Still, people cured are people cured, Goody Dilana. Even a man in his twenties couldn't mistake that."

"My skill couldn't heal my husband, though," Dilana said, affecting infinite sadness, "nor my sons."

"But you couldn't come to them in time." Gorlin leaned forward to touch her arm in reassurance. "Loss strikes us all sooner or later, mistress—and though I haven't suffered the death of a spouse and children, three wives and six babies have passed from my life as surely as any grave could take them. You know that we aren't even allowed to write letters to those we leave behind us, don't you?"

"I do, sir." Dilana muffled her voice and, to her own surprise, felt actual tears start to her eyes. "It must be some slight comfort to know that they still live—but I can see that it would be slight." She strove to pack as much sympathy behind the words as she could.

"Slight indeed." Gorlin sat back with a sigh. "But we must go on, mistress, we must still seek life. There are too many who may need the help we can bring, too many whose lives we may yet enrich, for us to seek to end our sorrows for loss alone."

"Yes, we must go on." Dilana looked up, her heart really aching for the poor magistrate and the loss he had suffered. Now it was she who reached out a hesitant hand to reassure and comfort. "At least you, having passed through it thrice before, know why life must go on, know it by experience."

"I do that." Gorlin took her hand with a gentle smile. "When I left my first wife, I was plunged into sadness that darkened all the world about me—but I pressed on to my new duties, out of sheer faith that the people had need of a magistrate."

"I am sure they did," Dilana said softly, thrilling to his touch, to the caress of his voice. "There are people you have protected from bandits, weak folk whom you have saved from the oppression of their stronger neighbors."

Gorlin let out a massive sigh. "It's so good to talk to someone who has seen, and knows by living!"

Dilana blushed and lowered her gaze again, taking her hand away. "There are virtues in experience that nothing but some time spent living can bring, Magistrate Gorlin."

"Yes, virtues of understanding and sympathy." Gorlin took her hand again. "It will be very good to have you here among us, Goodwoman Dilana."

"You flatter me, Magistrate Gorlin."

"Well, yes." Gorlin's melancholy cracked into a smile. "And I intend to. Call me William, Mistress Dilana."

"Why, thank you, Magis—William." Dilana looked up in surprise. *Now* she batted her eyelashes. "But I have no private name to give you; I am only Dilana."

"Then I shall call you Dilana indeed." Gorlin caressed the hand he held.

The courthouse looked exactly like the one in Bess's home village, which gave her a sense of reassurance, but didn't surprise her at all. Everyone knew how a courthouse was supposed to look: big and square and built of warm yellow brick, with a roof of tile instead of thatch exactly divided by four dormers, and real glass in the big rectangular windows. She didn't know that identical courthouses all across the land made the power of the government seem to be everywhere, and invulnerable.

The watchman led her through the big double doors into the usual vestibule, fifteen feet by ten, and turned to his right, through a smaller set of double doors that led into the courtroom. The magistrate sat behind the bench, two feet above everyone else in the room, looking far too young for so exalted a position—and would probably have looked intimidated by it all, if he hadn't been frowning darkly at everyone. Bess's heart sank until she realized that he was probably scowling to hide a feeling of being too small for the task.

The watchman gestured her to a seat on a bench along the wall and whispered, "I'm afraid you'll have to wait, maiden. He must hear other petitions first."

"Of course," Bess whispered back, and settled herself with complete composure. Bess she might be, but the self-assurance of believing herself to be a lady of quality still hung about her, belying the simplicity of her homespun blouse, bodice, and skirt.

The watchman straightened and signed to the magistrate. Bess was a bit nearsighted and didn't want to squint, so she couldn't make out the details of his face, but at least he seemed not to be as ugly as a bull. At the third try, the watchman caught the official's eye, and the magistrate nodded slightly. He didn't interrupt the current petitioner, though—a bearded middle-aged man asking for more time to pay his overdue taxes. It seemed the summer had been hard, and the crops not what they should have been, and he also seemed to feel the need of going into great detail about it all. Bess sighed and settled herself to be patient. There were several other people waiting—she counted eight, but from the way some of them glared at one another, she suspected there were only five cases. Still, the ones involving arguments were apt to take quite a bit longer.

The bearded man took long enough. Finally he paused for breath, and the young magistrate said wearily, "Yes, the season has been hard, farmer. Your tax is reduced to twelve bushels of wheat and one bullock."

The farmer stared, taken aback, then began to smile.

"Next year, though, if the weather is good, I'll expect you to make up the shortage, or at least part of it, and the rest the year after."

The smile faded.

"Clerk, note it," the magistrate said, and the clerk, older than the magistrate by half and probably his guiding hand for these first few years, nodded and bent to his pen.

The farmer swallowed, ducked his head. "I thank Your Worship." He stepped over to the clerk's high writing desk, pulling his hat on.

The waiting petitioners rustled as they sat forward eagerly. The magistrate turned to them and said, "Watchman Goude waits to tell me of the young woman he has brought in. I shall hear her next, so that he may go about his rounds."

The petitioners muttered in indignation, and Bess sat forward, surprised and suddenly nervous.

"Come now, maiden, he won't bite you," the watchman said kindly, but with a glint of amusement in his eye. "Let's stand before him, shall we?" And he kept his pace beside her all that long way, or so it seemed, up to the magistrate.

They stopped the customary four feet from the bench, and Bess looked up in surprise. *Why, he's handsome,* she thought, *or nearly.*

Handsome enough, surely, with dark hair around the rim of his judge's hat, and regular features below, with a straight nose, strong chin, and large eyes—or at least, large for a man. He was perhaps a year or two younger than she herself. She was a little old to be unwed, but perhaps he didn't notice— though he did seem to be noticing everything else about her. His glance took her in from head to foot, lingering on her face, then her hands and her basket. He seemed faintly puzzled. "Good day, goodwoman."

"Good day, Your Honor," Bess replied. Her stomach churned with nervousness.

"Why is she here, watchman?"

"She is newly come to our town, Your Honor," Watchman Goude explained. "She tells me her errand is to seek out relatives that she has newly learned might be here."

"Newly learned?" The young magistrate bent his gaze upon her, and Bess was surprised how penetrating that gaze seemed. Uneasily, she realized that this magistrate was probably nobody's fool, and might be harder to deceive than she had planned.

He pursed his lips in thought. "How is it you have only just learned of your relatives' whereabouts, young woman?"

A good question, in a land where everyone needed travel permits. Bess launched into her explanation. "I am Elizabeth from the village of Milorga, Your Honor, though my folk call me plain Bess."

"Not so plain as all that," the magistrate said thoughtfully, and Bess's heart skipped a beat.

"My grandmother had a son and a daughter, Your Honor," she said. "The daughter stayed in Milorga and wed my father. The son went to the reeve to become a soldier, and soon found himself in the Protector's town. He wrote home for a number of years, but his letters came more rarely as time went by, and finally stopped altogether. Grandma was afraid he had died, but

Papa and Mama assured her the reeve would have written to tell her if he had. So we have dwelt for many years, not knowing whether he was alive or dead—but this last Midwinter Day, a peddler came to our town, and when we asked after Uncle Raymond, as we always do, he said he had been arrested by a Raymond of Milorga when he passed through Grister, some years before."

"Arrested?" The magistrate frowned. "For what?"

"A goodwife had accused him of giving her three yards of red ribbon, Your Honor, instead of five, and it *was* only three, when the magistrate's clerk measured it—but Uncle Raymond had seen her old hat bedecked with red bows, and told the magistrate of it."

"Had he indeed!" The magistrate smiled, amused. "Did the magistrate unwind the bows and measure them?"

"They had no need, or so the peddler said—anyone could see there was at least six feet of ribbon in those bows, if not eight."

"They must have been huge indeed."

"Why, I remember that now!" Watchman Goude exclaimed. "Goody Prou—Ahem! The woman in question was in a temper for weeks. Maybe it was lucky for your uncle that the reeve called him back to service the next week, damsel. He had scarcely been here a fortnight."

"Really!" The magistrate looked up, interested. "Why was he called away so soon?"

"I can't say, Your Honor—we never ask, when it's the Protector's business."

The magistrate gave a quick nod. "No, of course not." He turned back to Bess. "You have reason to think he might be your uncle?"

"Only from his name and his birthplace, Your Honor—but there can't be all that many Raymonds of his age who came from Milorga. It's a large village, but still a village, and everyone knows everyone else."

"He was the only Raymond who was, say, forty-five years old, then?"

"No, Your Honor, there were three—but the other two are still there, and have been all their lives," Bess answered. It was hard to meet the judge's eyes—so penetrating, so warm a brown, so sympathetic, that they started something quivering inside her. Meet them she did, though, standing her straightest with shoulders back and head high. "Watchman Goude was good enough to tell me that you might look in your book for me, to see where he went."

"We might do that, yes," the magistrate said slowly, "but I must not stall this court session to oblige you. I have little free time today—but if you will discuss the matter with me over dinner, I may be able to find a few minutes then."

Bess's heart skipped a beat, and the other petitioners stirred, muttering in indignation about one of their number being invited to dine with the magistrate, and a stranger at that! She didn't hear any lewd suggestions, though—there was that much advantage to being plain. "Why, thank you! You do me much honor," she said.

The smile he gave her was brief, but dazzling. "At sunset, then, in my chambers." He turned to the clerk. "Eben Clark, will you bring the book for the year Raymond of Milorga was with us?"

"I will, Your Honor." The clerk met his magistrate's gaze squarely, and though his face was expressionless, his eyes were shrewd.

Bess turned away, her heart pounding. Fate had given her the chance she had hoped for, far more quickly and easily than she could have believed. She was bound and determined that she would not waste it! Plain or not, loved or not, she would marry Magistrate Kerren!

But she hoped, at least, for friendship.

Bess came back to the courthouse as the sun was setting, pulse drumming, drawing deep breaths to calm herself. Desperately, she reminded herself that the marriage didn't need to last more than five years. Of course, for that five years, she had to make herself so pleasant a companion, so indispensable to Magistrate Kerren's comfort, that he would begin to trust her, would take her ideas seriously, and would eventually change his own ideals of government to come into line with hers. It had been happening as long as history, she reminded herself—even in the Bible, that book the Guardian had taught them that had explained so much that was mysterious in ancient Terran literature—men coming to accept the ideas of the women they loved. This was her part in the revolution, in bringing the ideal of rights to the people of her land, of rights for *all* people, even women; it was what she could do to work toward a better world.

Then, after that, the Wizard would send her back into her wonderful dreamworld of nobility and luxury. . . .

The guard at the door knocked for her, and the portal opened. A butler gave her a short nod. "Maiden Bess. You are expected. Follow me."

He turned away, and she followed as he'd said, trying not to resent his coldness, even rudeness—not a single "please," not a word of welcome.

The hallway was paneled in wood waxed to a golden luster, wood also used for ceiling beams. A chandelier hung from its center, cut-glass pendants refracting the light of the candles to fill the space. Bess stared, and made no attempt to hide it—awe would be expected of a village girl, for few ever saw the magistrate's living quarters in the courthouse.

The dual door at the end of the hallway stood open to show a huge dining room with a table long enough for twenty. Bess's heart skipped a beat—was she to have dinner with the magistrate in that virtual cavern?

Apparently not—the butler led her down its length, then through a single door at the end of the side wall. She followed, stepping through into a much smaller room, only twelve feet square, with a table that could seat only four. Broad windows to her right looked out onto a manicured garden, golden in the sunset. Large landscapes in gilded frames echoed the garden's peace on the other three walls. It felt cozy after the cavernous dining room, but still spacious.

Magistrate Kerren was sitting at the table facing the window, caressing a wineglass with his fingers. He looked up as he heard them enter, and was already beginning to stand as the butler said, "Maiden Elizabeth of Milorga, Your Honor."

CHAPTER 18

"Thank you, Willem." The magistrate smiled, then asked Bess, "Will you join me in drinking wine, maiden?"

"I will, and gladly, Your Honor." Bess had to hide a smile at the memory of her mother's warning not to drink wine with strange men. It had proved true, of course, but surely Mama hadn't thought of her bibing with a magistrate!

"The burgundy, if you would, William." The magistrate gestured to the seat opposite his own. "Sit, if you will, maiden."

"Thank you, Your Honor." She sat, reflecting that the master was far more polite than the servant. Maybe Willem felt the hint of rebuke, because he set the wineglass beside her even as she sat. "Thank you," she said, eyes downcast, and knew from the warmth of the magistrate's tone that she had guessed rightly.

"Thank you, Willem. You may leave us now," the magistrate said.

The butler bowed and left. Bess sat straight in her chair, raising the glass to inhale the wine's fragrance. She let her breath out in a happy sigh; there had been little enough wine in her life in the last two years. The aroma blended perfectly with the beauty of the garden before her, and in spite of the tension of her situation, she felt herself beginning to relax. She sipped the wine, let it roll across her tongue, and swallowed, savoring the flavor of a sun-drenched summer past, then looked up to see the magistrate gazing intently at her. She blanched, then lowered her gaze in confusion, angry with herself for dropping her guard so easily.

But it seemed to have been the wisest course of action after all; the magistrate noted, "You have tasted wine before, maiden, and know how to make that taste last."

"Oh, yes, Your Honor," Bess said, improvising quickly. "My father was a wine-maker, and taught us all that gulping wine was nearly a crime."

He looked her up and down in a quick glance, though, and said, "That may be so, but the straightness of your posture, the way you hold yourself, the tilt of your head, speak of breeding and culture. How have you come to behave so much like a lady of refinement?"

I watched visual recordings of real ladies. But Bess couldn't say that, of course. She improvised again. "When I came of age to marry, Your Honor, no man offered—so I went with several other young folk to the city, and found service with the family of a wealthy merchant. I mimicked his wife and daughters, and the housekeeper schooled me in proper carriage and behavior so that I could serve at dinners when the master entertained other people of consequence. I had learned fairly well when the reeve and his wife came to dinner, and the next day, they commanded me to come serve them."

The magistrate had been listening with growing concern. Now he leaned forward intently and asked, "Did they treat you well?"

"Why . . . yes, Your Honor." Bess stumbled over the words, for halfway through the sentence she realized he was worried that she might have been molested, forced to go to bed with the merchant or the reeve. "Both merchant's wife and reeve's lady were courteous and thoughtful mistresses. I scarcely saw their husbands, and their children were . . . well, as children are."

"Imps and angels by turns." The magistrate sat back, nodding. "I'm glad to hear life went so well for you. But you didn't find a husband, so you went back to your home village?"

"Yes, Your Honor, when my mother's health weakened and she needed someone by her. I'm her only child, so it came to me to go tend her. But she became quite well with me there."

"No doubt simple loneliness was the cause of it." Magistrate Kerren frowned. "How will she fare, now that you have left her again?"

"Well enough, I hope, for I don't mean to be gone very long. If we can find Uncle Raymond, I can go home to tell Mama so that she can write to him. Have you found any trace of him, Your Honor?"

"Yes, Eben Clark found the entry in the book." Magistrate Kerren picked up a scrap of paper and handed it to her. "He was called back to the Protector's Town, and I have no doubt he was scarcely there before he was reassigned." Before she could even ask, he said, "Eben Clark has already drafted a letter asking the provost where your uncle has been sent. It will go out with tomorrow morning's post—but you'll have to be patient, maiden. It could easily be three weeks before we have an answer, perhaps two months."

"I could expect no sooner." Bess leaned forward, reaching out to Kerren but not too far. "Oh, thank you, Your Honor! Thank you again and again for going to such trouble for me, a poor stranger!"

"I am more than pleased to have been able to help." Kerren's smile was warm, then turned bleak. "You'd be surprised how rarely we are able to really help any one citizen with such a problem."

Bess's heart went out to him; the man really cared about people, not just power. "Please tell me if there's any way in which I can show my gratitude!"

"Why, there is." Kerren's smile came back as his gaze met hers. "Dine with me and tell me of your joys and sorrows, so that I may be a little less lonely for a while."

"Why . . . gladly, Your Honor." Bess dropped her gaze to her wineglass. "But everything I've done is very ordinary. I can't think any of it would be very interesting."

"I've found that most people's lives have moments that would interest anyone." Kerren lifted a small silver bell and rang it.

The butler came in. "Your Honor?"

"We'll begin the meal now," Kerren replied.

"Very good, Your Honor." The butler signaled, and a maid came in with a tray. She placed bowls of soup before them, and Kerren picked up his spoon as he said, "Begin with your family. You have mentioned your mother. Was childhood happy?"

"Oh, very happy, Your Honor!" Silently, Bess blessed the research department—in this case, Lord Corel, or Corin, as he really was. Corin had written out a full description of everyone he could remember in his hometown of Milorga, including the Raymond who had joined the Protector's Army, and his widowed sister with her poor, sickly daughter. Gar had sent someone back to Milorga to see what had changed in the years Corin had lived in the Lost City—who, Bess didn't know, but it couldn't have been Corin, for whoever it was had asked questions that every villager would have known: Did the widow still live in her cottage? Had Raymond come home? He or she had brought back the answers: The widow still lived, but her daughter had gone away shortly before—no one knew where—and there were dark mutterings about walking into the woods late at night.

Raymond's fate was unknown—but another agent had somehow discovered that he had been sent to put down an uprising that had cropped up overnight around a deranged shepherd who claimed people's lives were controlled by supernatural beings. An astounding number of people had pledged loyalty to him, finding that his delusions explained the bleakness of their own lives and held some hint of making them better. When the magistrate had tried to arrest the shepherd, his people had fought back fiercely, repelling his watchmen. The magistrate had sent to the reeve for help, but the people had fought the reeve's troops to a stalemate, and he had called for more help. The Protector had sent every man who could be spared within a hundred miles of the uprising. Raymond of

Milorga had been one of them, and had died on the battlefield. Since the commanders hadn't known much about their hastily gathered soldiers, no one had thought to write a letter of sympathy to his sister back home in Milorga.

Bess had read the tale, shedding a few tears for the poor, lonely mother and her simpleton daughter. She had some notion of how they must have felt, outcast and ignored. Now, though, she could tell Magistrate Kerren these bare bones of a life, sure that if he thought to send to Milorga to confirm her tale, he would indeed find a widow whose daughter had left town, and if the local magistrate there had no record of her going, why, such things could be easily lost—an absentminded clerk forgetting to jot an entry in a book, or a preoccupied magistrate forgetting this particular detail. In any event, he would probably not want to admit that one of his villagers had left without his leave and not been caught. As to Raymond, if Kerren did indeed learn his fate, there would be no one to contradict Bess's version of it.

So she prattled on, telling him of her own growing-up, and filling the tale with amusing little anecdotes, some of which had really happened, using all the graces and artifices she had learned during the glittering dinners of mock lords and ladies. Kerren laughed, and asked questions and made comments; she could almost see the tension leaving him in wave after wave.

Fish followed soup, and meat followed fish. Gradually, Bess became the questioner, and Kerren's answers became longer. Bess threw in the occasional observation of her own: "Surely the Protector can't have an endless supply of magistrates, Your Honor."

"No, there are only a thousand fifty-three of us," Kerren replied, looking surprised; most peasants assumed the Protector's men were infinite in number. "But there are two hundred twelve reeves to whom they answer."

The conversation ranged over politics, history, and literature, even making forays into art. Kerren seemed to grow more and more surprised with every answer.

"Where did you learn to read, lass?"

"Oh, the magistrate's clerk was good enough to teach me,

sir, so that I could read to my grandmother when she could no longer get about much. I've read all his books to her in the last few years—except the ones about law, of course."

"Of course." The magistrate looked dazed. Pleased, but dazed.

Over an after-dinner cordial, the two of them grew quite philosophical, speculating about how the world might have come to be, how people had grown upon its surface, and whether there could be any kernel of truth underlying the myth that all their forebears had really come down from the stars above.

When it was quite dark outside, and both of them were feeling a bit dazed, the butler came in and said, "The maiden's chamber is ready, Your Honor."

"My chamber!" Bess sat bolt upright in wide-eyed surprise and open alarm—and secret elation. "Your Honor, I can't impose on your hospitality!"

"Where else will you stay?" Kerren pointed out. "You have no relatives here, and you must stay two months, so you surely won't have money enough for an inn."

"I can find work . . ."

"I shall not forbid it, but I don't think you'll find many openings just now. In any event, the courthouse has a guest wing, and you shall surely be one of my guests until you can make other arrangements."

"Well . . . if I really will not be putting you out . . ."

"The Protector provides."

"But I must do something to earn my keep."

"Why, yes." The young magistrate smiled and caught her hand. "You shall dine with me every night."

Bess smiled and dropped her gaze, blushing. "Magistrate, I shall be honored!"

"And I shall take great pleasure in your company." Magistrate Kerren dropped her hand with a smile. "Of course, we might run out of conversation. Do you think two months will be long enough?"

Two months was more than enough.

* * *

Dilana listened with full concentration as Magistrate Gorlin told her about the case that had come before him that morning. He didn't look at her, only gazed at the garden while he spoke, his brow furrowed, and Dilana's heart went out to him because of the pain in his voice. She made sympathetic noises from time to time, and couldn't help noticing, with the back of her mind, how dear Gorlin's profile had become to her in the last few months.

He certainly wasn't handsome, though she could see that he might have been in his youth. For a man in the fullness of middle age, though, his chin was too small for the fleshiness his face had taken on, his nose too big, his lips too full. But they were sensitive, those lips, showing every trace of the pain he was feeling; staring at them raised familiar sensations within her, and she was delighted to find that she could feel them still.

From their conversations—almost daily—she had come to know how deeply he cared for the people he'd been sent to govern, how much he shared their pains, but how cautious he was about sharing their joys. He was a lonely man, and seemed determined to remain so for fear of the grief of parting that he knew must come in a few years. He hadn't remarried yet, and was dangerously close to the end of his first six months in this assignment, at the end of which he had to marry somebody, anybody.

Dilana had already pondered the riddle of why he had never been promoted to reeve, then found that he had only applied once. He could have been afraid to try again, not wanting to be turned down—but she thought it more likely that he wanted to work directly with the people of a single village, not order fifty other magistrates, only seeing the actual people he governed when they appealed a legal case to him.

She was becoming impossibly fond of the man. Why couldn't he see it!

"That two sisters should be ready to tear each other apart over a single cow their father left, the one thing of all his belongings that he didn't will to one or the other!" Gorlin shook his head with sorrow approaching grief. "It makes me glad magistrates can't own their own houses or furniture, and not much else but the clothes on our backs and the money we've saved!"

"It's certainly not what their father could have wanted," Dilana agreed. "Of course, I suppose he could have been one of the cruel ones who delights in causing trouble, one of the few who die cackling with delight over the way people will fight over their estates."

Gorlin shook his head again. "From all I hear about him, he was a good man who prided himself on providing for his wife and children. What could have set them against each other so?"

"I have found," Dilana said slowly, "that when such quarrels grow so tall, their roots are deep in the past."

Gorlin looked up in surprise. "What an insight! But what manner of roots could they be?"

"Jealousy," Dilana said, "and envy." She remembered her own childhood and shivered. "He might have favored the one over the other, so that the first grew steadily prouder of his regard and more jealous in not wanting to share it, while the worm of envy bored deeper and deeper into the other's heart." In her own case, she now knew, that worm had bred the delusion that she wasn't her father's daughter at all, but the cuckoo-child of a distant prince.

Gorlin nodded, his eyes glowing. "Of course that would explain the bitterness within them! The first is trying to hold on to everything of her father's that she can, thinking them to be signs of his love, while the other is frantically trying to grasp whatever last shreds of him she may!"

Dilana explained. "If she couldn't have his love while he was alive, she can at least have his goods now that he is dead."

"And now that I think of it, he left most of his belongings to the younger sister, and only a few to the older! Fool that I am, I thought it was because the elder's husband was richer than the younger's!" Then he frowned. "Still, how does that help me judge between them? I can't give one cow to two women! I've already suggested that they sell the beast and split the money, but both raised a howl at that."

"Of course," Dilana said softly, "if wealth isn't really what each wants."

"Yes, certainly," Gorlin agreed. Then he grinned, thumping the arm of his chair in delight. "We'll give them each something of their father's! He already left his bull to the younger—I'll insist it be bred to the cow, then hold the beast in escrow until the calf is born! The elder sister shall have the cow, and the younger shall have the calf bred from both her father's beasts!"

"That won't content either one of them," Dilana warned. "Each wants her father all to herself, and if she can't have him, at least she can have what belonged to him."

"Then I shall decree the calf to be his, since it came from both his beasts, and they shall have to be content with my judgment, or go to the reeve!" He chuckled. "I wouldn't be surprised if they both start claiming the calf, saying that the other sister can have the older animal!"

"Why, so they shall!" Dilana exclaimed in surprise. "Then neither of them can complain if you give the cow to the other!"

"No, they can't, can they?" Gorlin turned to her, his eyes warm with ardor. "What a gem you are, to see so easily into their hearts!"

Dilana blushed and lowered her gaze. "I'm only remembering what I've seen happen all my life, Your Honor."

"Then I must have that memory by me, or I'll misjudge again and again!" Gorlin rose from his chair, towering over her, reaching down to take her hand.

Dilana gazed up at him, letting her hand follow his willingly, her heart thumping.

Gorlin sank to one knee and spoke deep in his throat. "I knew I would have to ask this again, but I never thought to really want it—yet I do, and more than ever! Fair lady, will you marry me?"

"Oh, yes, Your Honor," Dilana answered, her voice faint, then fainter still as his lips came to her own. "Yes, William, yes."

* * *

One by one, the real magistrates were kidnapped away to the Lost City and the care of Bade, the Guardian, and its skeleton staff, who kept them soundly caged and explained why their imprisonment was necessary. Of course, they had the free run of a whole city, even if it was in need of a bit of maintenance, and most of them were more than ready for an extended vacation anyway. Indoors, at least, they had genuine luxury, more than they had ever known, complete with gourmet food and fine wines, so they recovered from their initial indignation pretty quickly, and only one or two made any attempt to escape.

The rest bent their efforts to studying the new system the rebels were trying to put into place, and to figuring out how to use it to their own advantage.

In their places, false magistrates frantically learned all the details of their new jobs, then settled in to doing their best as administrators, and to gradually swaying their guardsmen to their new beliefs in individual rights and personal freedom. Year by year, more and more of the magistrates and reeves were really cured madmen.

There weren't enough of them for all the positions, of course—so the cured madwomen spread throughout every province, working their way into the affections of real magistrates, as Bess and Dilana had done. In Voyagend, they had learned from the Guardian how to make conversation and to carry themselves as real women of the upper class; they had learned to speak in cultured tones, to walk and move with grace and style. After being cured, they had learned history, politics, literature, the arts, and the sciences from the Guardian. Plain or not, they had huge advantages over village lassies when it came to catching the attention of educated men.

Most of them married magistrates and reeves new to their assignments. The others became servants in official households and gradually came to know their employers better and better. A reassigned magistrate couldn't take his wife and children along, but no rule said he couldn't take along a female servant whom he had found especially useful—and when he settled into his new village, he was quite likely to choose a woman he already knew and whose company he enjoyed, for his next wife.

The inspectors-general were more difficult, for the obvious reason—nobody knew who they were. Still, it was possible to make guesses, possible to assign teams of men to follow travelers and join merchants' caravans, and one inspector-general after another went to the Lost City. Bade and the Guardian found that they were much less likely to accept their imprisonment willingly, though, or to be swayed to the ideas and ideals of the New Order. After all, they had given up more to gain their current rank in the Old, and that rank was very high; each of them had very real hopes of becoming Protector, or at least a minister. They had labored all their lives to achieve it, and weren't about to throw it away by eliminating the Protector and his office, nor the system in which they held so much power.

Miles conferred with the Guardian, and finally sent the inspectors-general to a separate ruined city, one guarded much more closely by its computer and robots. For them, at least, the imprisonment was real—still luxurious, but nonetheless real. Women came to join them, though—women who weren't very pretty, but knew how to use cosmetics to make the most of the looks they had; women who walked gracefully and spoke in cultured tones, women who knew the arts and the sciences, who could talk with the exiled inspectors-general about history and politics. Gradually, even these hardcase adherents of the Old Order began to think there might be something to be said for the New.

"Your Honor, come quickly!" The butler appeared in the doorway, looking harried for once. "Magistrate Plurible is coming! He's sent a runner ahead; he's only a mile away!"

Magistrate Athellen—formerly Lord Llewellyn in delusion—looked up from his desk, face ashen. Usually visiting magistrates sent word ahead, and he had plenty of time to prepare, but this surprise visit scared him thoroughly. In desperation, he fell back on the stratagem he had used before. "Tell

Constable Garrick and Watchman Porry to come into my study, quickly! Tell Mistress Paysan to prepare a quick tea! I'll hurry and change into my formal robe!"

"I must assist Your Honor!"

"There's no time! You set the preparations in motion!" Athellen bolted from his desk.

The formal robe still held the blackjack and dagger hidden in its folds from its last such use—in fact, Athellen had begun to take comfort from knowing they were always there. He shaved quickly, ducked back into the empty study to prepare the teacups, and was out in front of the courthouse five minutes before the coach rattled around the curve of the road.

The horses stopped, and the footman jumped down to open the door. Magistrate Plurible stepped down and toward Athellen, arms spread wide, a smile of greeting on his face, a smile that froze, then died as he saw who was waiting for him.

Athellen's worst fears had come true—but he remembered what Miles had told them all to do if this happened. After all, sooner or later, some of them were bound to meet people who knew the man they were pretending to be. It was just Athellen's bad luck that it had been sooner.

He stepped forward with a broad smile. "Magistrate Plurible! You do me great honor!" Then, close enough for Plurible to hear a whisper, Athellen hissed, "Yes, I know I'm not who you expected to see, but there's an excellent reason, and no one else must know of it!" Aloud, he fairly trumpeted, "Come into my study, and take refreshment!"

Sudden dread filled Plurible's face, but it was quickly masked. He whispered, "As you say, Inspector."

Athellen turned away, arm in arm with Plurible, hiding a surge of elation. The man had assumed he was an inspector-general impersonating a magistrate—and whatever reasons there might be for such an action, they had to be horrible.

And kept secret. . . .

They came into the study. "Take a seat, Your Honor!" Athellen waved his visitor to a chair as he went around behind the desk. "May I introduce you to my trusty Constable Garrick and Watchman Porry!"

The two officers bowed. Plurible nodded to acknowledge them as he sat, then turned back to Athellen. "What does all this mean, Inspector? I know I can't be told all of it, but surely you can give me some small hint. Is my old friend Athellen in trouble?"

"I wouldn't like to use such a word," Athellen said, and rang the small bell on his desk. A side door opened, and the butler ushered in a maid, who set down the teapot.

"Explanations must wait till you have a cup in your hand!" Athellen insisted. "You have been traveling all morning, at a guess, and need refreshment!"

"It would be welcome," Plurible said reluctantly. Clearly, he would rather hear the news first, but dared not say so. He took the cup and sipped. "Now, sir?"

"Yes, now." Athellen took a long sip, playing for time, then sat back and said, "Not in trouble, no. Your old friend Athellen, though, needed . . . a rest."

Plurible stiffened in alarm. "A collapse?"

"I would rather call it exhaustion," the fake Athellen said, "but it's bad for morale for people to know of it—so when it came time for reassignment, we sent him to a secluded retreat, and I took his place."

"Thank heavens it could be managed so neatly!" Plurible sighed. "Is he recovering quickly?"

"I hope so, but no one has told me anything."

"Of course, of course," Plurible muttered, and sipped again. A quick glanced showed Athellen the thoughtful look on his visitor's face. At a guess, Plurible was revising his estimate of the fake Athellen's rank downward from inspector-general to one of the second-rank bureaucrats who kept all the records of the land and coordinated all the reeves—specifically, one of the group of troubleshooters who were always kept ready for such occasions. No one knew for sure if they really existed, but nobody really doubted it, either. Plurible sipped again, then asked, "What will you tell the people here when he has recovered?"

"Oh, we'll arrange a mid-term reassignment, and explain that another magistrate died unexpectedly," Athellen assured him. "Of course, it's possible the doctors will insist he take the whole five years as a vacation; I've heard of it happening."

"Yes. . . . To write his . . . impressions of . . . duh peeble he . . . hazzz governed." Plurible sipped again, then looked up, blinking bleary eyes.

"I think the journey has tired you out," Athellen said, fairly oozing sympathy. "Perhaps you should nap before dinner."

"Nnno, nnno! Mid . . . day . . . zleeb? Nev . . . nev . . ." But Plurible's eyes closed, and he slumped in his chair.

Porry stepped forward just in time to catch the teacup before it fell. "How much of the drug did you put in his teacup, Your Honor?"

"Enough." Athellen rose. "Put him to bed, and watch over him. Then, Porry, go into the forest and . . ."

"Hoot like an owl and tell the forester who answers that we need a replacement." Porry nodded. "I remember, Your Honor."

"Good." He watched the two men carry the magistrate out, then rang the bell again. The butler came in. "Your Honor?"

"Are my watchmen making Magistrate Plurible's men comfortable, Satter?"

"Quite comfortable, Your Honor." The butler's face showed his disapproval. "They're already half drunk."

Athellen nodded with satisfaction. "Tell the watchmen to keep it up, and tell Plurible's men that their master has suddenly taken ill and gone to bed in one of my guest rooms. They have the afternoon to relax, but they must stay in the courthouse compound. They will probably be staying the night, so tell the bailiff to make arrangements."

"As you will, Your Honor." Satter's tone left no doubt as to *his* opinion of the events, but he bowed and left to carry out his orders anyway.

Athellen sank into his chair with a sigh. The crisis was past, and successfully survived—or the first stage, of it, anyway. Still, he didn't doubt that the men the Guardian would send would successfully cart away Plurible and his drunken watchmen, leaving a new and false Plurible in his place. Athellen heartily hoped he would never again meet someone who had known the real Athellen.

CHAPTER 19

Dilana glanced up from her embroidery, watching her husband furtively. It was winter, but he sat gazing at the garden beyond the window anyway. It was pretty enough, she had to admit, even buried under snow—or would have been, on a sunny day, but this one was overcast, and so was William's face. Considering the case he had before him at the moment, that wasn't surprising. She laid down the stretched linen, folded her hands in her lap, and said, "Would it be so bad as all that if young Charyg became a cabinetmaker?"

William looked up with a start. Then he smiled and reached out to touch her hand. "How did you know what I was thinking?"

She returned the smile, clasping his hand. "You were quite upset about it when you came to dinner yesterday, and have been gloomy ever since. It's not hard to guess. Come, husband—what harm in the boy's going to apprentice to old Wizzigruf, if it makes him happy?"

"Perhaps because it would make his father sad."

"Only for a while. He thinks the boy is taking a step back in the world, after all. But when Toby Charyg becomes a guild-master, I suspect his father will be quite proud of him."

"*If* he becomes a guildmaster," William cautioned.

Dilana shrugged. "The lad has talent, we've all seen it in the scraps of wood he's carved and the knickknacks he's made for his mother. That cradle he gave his sister for her wedding was nearly a work of art. But even if he doesn't, husband, isn't it right for the lad to be happy?"

"Not if it makes his father gloomy."

"If old Charyg really loves the boy, the lad's happiness will make *him* happy," Dilana pointed out, "and if the boy is sad being a merchant, that will make his father unhappy, too—and probably angry. They'll quarrel, maybe even come to blows. No, surely it's right for the boy to be happy."

"Happiness isn't something that's right or wrong," William grumbled. "It's simply good luck."

"If that's so, I've been very lucky indeed." Dilana squeezed his hand, then let it go.

He looked deeply into her eyes and smiled. "I too," he said softly, "and I see what you mean, for it's *very* right."

"Then surely we all have a right to try to become happy."

"*Have* a right?" William frowned. "Odd phrase, that."

Dilana was suddenly tense; this was the delicate moment, and she hadn't been able to see it coming. She turned to look out at the garden, choosing her words carefully, deliberately changing their meanings. "Surely something that is right, is something that we have, my husband. But some of those 'rights' are ours simply because we're born. Everyone has a right to try to stay alive, for instance, and to defend himself or herself against thieves and murderers."

"Yes, that's true; certainly I can't deny it," William said slowly. "But life is something that happens to us whether we want it to or not, my love—though our parents may have some choice in the matter."

His hand caught around hers again, and she looked up to meet the warmth of his smile with a glow of her own.

"Happiness, though, doesn't come with the first breath of life," William went on. "It happens to you, or it doesn't. Even those who choose their own mates often make mistakes; you can do all the things that you think will bring happiness, and still find yourself sunk in gloom. It's not a right."

"No," Dilana said slowly, never looking away from him, "but you can *try* to be happy. Surely that much is a right, at least."

William's look turned thoughtful. "Perhaps," he said slowly, and turned to gaze out at the garden again. "Perhaps . . ."

Watching his face, Dilana breathed out a silent sigh of relief. It had been a very difficult moment, but she seemed to have managed it fairly well. Except, of course, that he was now deep in thought, though she seemed to have rescued him from his dark mood.

Still, she also seemed to have thrown away an intimate moment that might have led to a night of ecstasy. She sighed again, and reminded herself that they all had to make sacrifices for the Cause.

The night fulfilled its promise, though, and more. The next day, William gave his judgment: that young Charyg should be apprenticed to the village cabinetmaker. Then he took old Charyg into his study for a long, long talk. The merchant emerged looking somber, but no longer angry—and very, very thoughtful.

Later that spring, Dilana astounded both William and herself by conceiving. She was nearly forty, but somehow she survived the birth of her first child, and was amazed that William seemed overjoyed, even though the baby was a girl, not a boy. Three years later, he was having long "conversations" with their daughter, which generally meant listening to her prattle as she sat on his knee. Little by little, Dilana began to mention the rights baby Luisa had gained by virtue of being born, and as the result of William's and her own decision to encourage that event. William assured her that he was thoroughly aware of his responsibilities to the child—but bit by bit, he began to believe that women's rights had to be stated as clearly as men's.

Thus the genuine magistrates who stayed in office talked of human rights with their new wives, and slowly, little by little, began to think of some changes to the government, ways following from that idea of individual human rights. Miles found that, although he didn't have enough madmen to replace all the officials, he didn't need to.

"You don't really think you can hold us here if we really want to go, do you?" Magistrate Flound said with a hard smile.

"Oh, yes," Bade said, his voice soft as velvet. "Yes, I think we can hold you here no matter how badly you want to leave."

"A mere five of you?" Flound scoffed. He sat back with a sneer of contempt. "Against five hundred of us?"

"Five of us, and the Guardian with its thousand robots." Actually, there were only a hundred robots on duty at any one time, but they moved around so often and so quickly that Bade was sure none of the magistrates could count them. "They could hold you fast even without we five jailers. In fact, we're only here to watch for trouble signs the Guardian might not catch."

It was certainly true that the master computer had never had to be a jailer before. The madmen had all wanted to stay.

Bade still wanted to stay, too, but not to wallow in delusion anymore. Hatred burned white-hot within him, and he wanted to be in Voyagend to visit the revenge of imprisonment on every magistrate brought to him. He would never forget his father's angry shouts at Lado, their village magistrate, because the man had kept the father's money, while turning Bade out of school for learning too slowly. (But what he had learned, he had learned well!) He would never forget the sight of his father in the stocks, with neighbors jeering at him and throwing rotten vegetables, the moldy pulp dripping down over half of Papa's face. He would never forget his mother's tears, or her loud arguments telling Papa to stop pushing the boy.

But Papa hadn't been pushing Bade—he had only tried to give him the chance for the learning he so loved. Here in the Lost City, Bade had found that chance, and had spent hours in a learning carrel every day, with the Guardian feeding him pictures and words on a viewscreen, stopping to explain anything that he didn't understand. He had still learned slowly, though not as slowly as with a village teacher who snarled and berated his students. The Guardian told him now that he knew as much as any magistrate, though he was behind in local events by a few hundred years.

Now, of course, Orgoru and the other impostor magistrates were sending back law books and history books, and their own observations on the intrigue that underlay it all. Little by little, Bade was catching up.

So he gave back hard smile for hard smile and told Flound, "You couldn't want to break out of this city more than you do already. There isn't a one of you who doesn't ache for the reward and career boost that would come from telling the nearest reeve all about us rebels in this city, and letting the Protector's spies know about our agents all over the land."

Flound lost his smile, glaring in hatred at Bade.

The glare satisfied Bade's need for revenge—a little. He leaned back in his chair, crossing his legs. "Yes, the Guardian hears everything you say, Flound."

The magistrate's eyes sparked anger at the impertinence of this peasant, addressing him without his title.

"Everything you say," Bade went on softly. "You can't plan an escape attempt without its knowing—and if the Guardian knows, I know."

It wasn't true, of course—the computer had audio pickups in every room in the city and quite a number in outdoor public places, but scarcely everywhere. It was quite possible to find some sheltered nook, some end of an alley, where the computer couldn't hear—but it wouldn't hurt for Flound and his lackeys to think the machine knew everything.

"How do you think the Guardian knew enough to send his skeleton to push you back, when you tried to climb the wall in the dead of night last week?" Bade asked.

Flound's glare was a dagger, and Bade grinned in return, knowing the magistrate's stomach was sinking as he began to believe the computer *had* overheard his planning with his score of confederates. Of course, the robot who had stopped them had really only been on sentry duty, making his rounds by a randomized schedule—but Flound didn't need to know that. The man left Bade's office with a snarl, and Bade allowed himself to feel the warm glow of triumph.

The house stood as near the wall as any, for a thirty-foot width of clear pavement circled inside the wall all around the city. But thirty feet was close enough for Flound's purpose. Of course, the house was made of stone, like all the buildings that still stood in the ruined city—a very strange, ruddy stone, warm to the touch, but stone nonetheless, for what else could it be if it were so hard? The floors were made of the same stone, all flat, all one piece, and Flound marveled that the ancient builders had been able to find or cut such large sheets of rock. Maybe the old tales were true, maybe the ancients really had secrets of building, miraculous tools and methods that had been lost!

But the house was built around a courtyard, and the courtyard was paved with flagstones. Oh, Flound had found only a mass of weeds, but had dug down beneath them, then cleared away the dead herbage, exulting. Flagstones they were, though carved into beautiful shapes and fitted together like a puzzle— but separate stones, and the weeds sprouting between them, showed there must be dirt below!

No one objected to his moving in and making the house his own, neither Bade nor the Guardian nor any of its "robots," as Bade called them—its strange smooth-boned eerie skeletons with their heads like eggs, with jewels for eyes, jewels that Flound had already learned could shoot out spears of light, spears that burned and cut like swords. He told himself he didn't fear the creatures, but he was very glad they didn't object to his taking the house for his dwelling, or to his having a dozen friends in to talk and drink every day.

To talk and drink, six of them, while the other six dug beneath the flagstones, boring a tunnel under the plaza toward the wall. Then that six would come up and wash in the amazing streams of water that sprang at a touch from the wall into the huge tub, and the next six would go down, each taking his turn at shoveling, each taking his turn at filling the baskets and hauling them out. The pile of earth mounded high around the walls of the courtyard, but who was to see except Flound and his friends? He congratulated himself on his cleverness, and kept on digging.

"Surely Flound and his friends must have realized that any city protected by a wall would have constant searches for sappers undermining that wall!" the Guardian protested.

"They might have thought of it," Bade agreed, "but the only such searching they know of, is men walking around the wall with long rods to thrust into the earth. They don't see your robots walking around with probes, so they assume you're not checking."

"I forget that such intelligent men know nothing of sonar," the Guardian sighed. "Are you sure you won't let me teach them, Bade?"

"Not until the revolution is over, and won," Bade said in an iron tone. "They have us outnumbered, after all. Let's keep them at every disadvantage we can."

"If you must," the computer said with a tone of resignation. "But it goes against my twelfth programming directive, Bade."

"Yes, a teacher by instinct as well as training." Bade smiled without mirth. "I definitely can't complain, since I've benefited so much by your instruction. But you have directives of higher priority, Guardian, one of which is to keep these men imprisoned for the security of the movement which is trying to restore the freedom you were programmed to protect."

"Someone somewhere must have taken the concept of order in society too far, when the people fell out of contact with me," the computer lamented. "Still, you are correct, Bade—we must keep them in. Surely, though, we can let them know that their tunnel will be closed before they can use it."

"No, let them think they have succeeded." Bade's mouth drew into a thin, cruel smile. "Their disappointment will be all the sharper, and they will be that much less likely to try again. We must convince them that you're unbeatable, Guardian. Our fight is virtually won, if they stop trying."

"I confess I do not understand human thought processes well enough to disagree with you, Bade," the computer acknowledged. "From what little I do know, though, it seems quite cruel."

"Oh, it is," Bade agreed, "but the suffering they would cause if they escaped, would be much more cruel by far."

It was a good excuse, he realized, but acknowledged that it was just that, an excuse, and nothing more. The truth was that he would enjoy seeing the dismay and hurt on their faces, when they finished their tunnel and found it was useless. Revenge on one magistrate was sweet, but revenge on them all would be far more satisfying still.

They had to tunnel down quite a bit, for sure enough, the wall was deeply set in the earth. Finally they were ready for the final bit of digging, under the six-foot width of the wall and up. They waited for a night without a moon, gathered in the house during the day, and laughed and joked loudly, clinking glasses and giving all the evidence of a party. As darkness fell, they lit the lamps, kept the party going for another hour, then gradually slackened the noise, put out one lamp at a time, and finally gave the appearance of a sleeping house, filled with saturated partygoers who hadn't bothered to go home—sensible enough, when none of them really had a home here.

Then, in the middle of the night, they went out to finish their tunnel.

Flound himself dug the last few feet to the surface with a will, grinning like a demon, filling basket after basket, which his comrades passed back from man to man until they dumped it in the courtyard, then passed it back empty. The shovel bit and shoved through. Flound held back a cry of triumph as he quickly battered at the hole, widening it, pushing back the edges, pounding the grass down with the back of the shovel . . .

. . . and paused as he saw two long, thin gleaming legs stretching up from the edge of the hole. With a sinking heart, he followed them up to the crosspiece that served as hips, the flattened tank that served as ribs, the pipe-thin arms and skeletal hands, and finally the ruby-eyed egg of its head.

"You really must not come out, Magistrate Flound," the robot said.

Flound stared in horror while his friends jostled close, asking, "What is it? Why have you stopped?" Then the two who could see around him saw the robot, and moaned.

"How . . . how did you know?" Flound croaked.

"We could hear your digging, Flound." Bade stepped up just behind the robot.

"That is a drastically oversimplified description of sonar," the robot objected.

Flound glared pure hatred at Bade.

The jailer permitted himself a very small smile. Inside, though, his elation soared.

Flound wouldn't be able to accept losing, though, Bade reflected as he paced to the top of the wall hours later, watching the city begin to glow in the false dawn. Flound would have to keep trying, especially since it had become a contest between himself and Bade. His pride would make him engineer a much more serious breakout attempt, or Bade misread his prisoners completely. They were all intelligent, and most of them were aggressive and competitive, too. Keen minds joined with restlessness and the bitterness of defeat. They would never be able to accept prison like gentle sheep. The next try would be massive and violent, and some of the magistrates might die.

Part of Bade looked forward to that with an almost greedy anticipation—but part of him felt the shame of not doing his job well. He was supposed to be a jailer, not an executioner; Gar had been very insistent on the importance of none of the magistrates being hurt. He said it was vital to their success that the rebels seem to be not villains, but rescuers—and for that, all their prisoners had to come out alive and well cared-for. Bade had to find some way to make them satisfied with their captivity.

How? He bent his mind to the task for hours, thinking in his slow but methodical way. As evening came on, he left his office, not wanting the robot with the dinner tray to find him—he wasn't hungry, being too deeply embroiled in thinking, in trying to find the answer to the puzzle. He could have asked the Guardian, of course, but he had begun to realize that the machine had its limits, and one of them was in looking into people's hearts and understanding how they felt.

He paced the battlements as the sky darkened. The moon had risen when he asked himself why *he* was happy to stay here, guarding sullen and hostile men. There was the revenge, of course, but by itself, that couldn't have been enough. No, there was something else, something more, and if he were honest with himself, he would have to admit—

The answer sprang into his mind, and he stopped, staring into the night, then began to feel jubilation rise within him— for he had realized that he was enjoying this puzzle-solving very much, then remembered that he always had. He was not only willing, but eager, to stay and be jailer, because he enjoyed the constant competition, the constant need to outthink the hated magistrates.

If he were willing to stay because of the pleasure of the contest, wouldn't the magistrates be willing, too?

Of course, his challenge was keeping them penned in. What other challenge could he find for them, other than the need to break out?

Learning. They all enjoyed learning, or had the drive to force themselves to it to gain their goal. He could spread a veritable forest of knowledge before them, and give each of them a hunting license.

First, though, he had to give them a reason to go hunting, a quarry to chase.

What could a band of bureaucrats want, that would make them willing, even eager, to buckle down to the work of learning facts they had never known existed?

The answer burst into his mind like a lamp flaring into brightness.

* * *

The merchant's face was dark with anger as his wagon rolled into town. The driver was silent, eyeing the merchant beside him warily.

"Stop here!" the merchant commanded, and the driver drew up in front of the courthouse. People stopped and stared, and a guard came hurrying up. "Here now! Keep your load going! You can't just stop in the middle of the road!"

"Stop where he tells you," the merchant told the driver, then leaped down from the wagon and strode toward the courthouse, anger in every stride. Caught between two rule breakings, the guard dithered a minute, looking from one to the other. The driver gave him a sympathetic look, and the guard's head snapped up in indignation. "Wait here!" he snapped, and turned to dash after the merchant. But it was too late, the man had already gone through the door, and by the time the guard caught up, was already telling the bailiff, "Tell the magistrate I wish to see him!"

"Indeed." The bailiff gave him a bland nod and waved the guard away. "And who shall I say requires to see Magistrate Lovel with no word of warning?"

"Branstock, a merchant in cloths and notions! Be quick, man, or your chance may be gone and the trail grown cold."

The bailiff suddenly became much more attentive. "What trail?"

"The trail of the bandits who robbed me! If they hadn't thought my anger amusing, they might well have taken my life, too, and that of my driver! Do you mean to laugh at such matters?"

"I assure you, sir, I do not. Ho, Breavis!" The bailiff waved to someone in the courtroom, and a man with ink-stained fingers came out. "This is Breavis Clark, clerk to Magistrate Lovel," the bailiff said by way of explanation. "Clark, this merchant is Branstock, with a report for His Honor that I don't think he'll want to delay. Will you show him in?" Then, to Branstock, "Your pardon, merchant, but I must hurry away to set my men on the trail of these bandits. I shall speak to your driver while you speak to the magistrate. Good afternoon!" He nodded and turned, walking quickly.

"Well, that's something, at least," Branstock said, looking a little mollified.

"I assure you, sir, we don't take banditry lightly in this township," the clerk told him. "Follow me, please." He led the way to the magistrate's study. "Wait," he advised, and the magistrate looked up through the open door, looked up in inquiry. "Your Honor, a merchant who wishes to lodge a complaint," the clerk said. "He was robbed within your township. Bailiff Jacoby has gone to attend to it, but Branstock still wishes to speak with you."

"Yes, certainly, come in at once." The magistrate rose.

The clerk stepped aside to let Branstock in. "Thank you for seeing me, Your Honor," he said, and Breavis frowned, for the man didn't sound anywhere nearly as respectful as a merchant should when speaking to a magistrate. But his tone seemed not to matter to Magistrate Lovel—or if it did, it served as some sort of signal. His face went rigid at sight of the merchant, and he said, "Close the door, please, Breavis Clark."

Clark did, but with misgivings. It wasn't unheard of for the magistrate to go behind closed doors with a visitor, provided he were male, but never at first meeting. Unless . . .

His stomach sank. Could this very ordinary seeming merchant be an inspector-general?

It would explain the magistrate's reaction to his tone, instead of the rebuke Clark had expected from official to merchant— but by what signal had Lovel recognized the secret inspector?

No doubt by one only magistrates learned. Whatever the case, there was one thing of which Breavis Clark was certain— he would never really know for sure.

The magistrate waited for the door to close, then threw his arms around the merchant. "Miles! Praise Heaven! At last someone I can truly talk to!"

Miles felt the trembling in the man's arms, and knew all over again the fearful tension under which his agents lived. "Poor, brave soul, to live so much apart from your own kind! But your wife, Lovel—isn't she, at least, a consolation to you?"

Lovel stepped back to hold him at arm's length. "A mighty consolation to be sure, but not one with whom I can share the truth about my work. She *is* beginning to wonder why she hasn't become pregnant, though."

"Let her wonder," Miles advised. "If you start to love her, our enemies will have enough of a hold over you—but if you had a baby, they would really be able to twist you by threatening the child."

Lovel nodded. "And if we fail, she can always claim she was deceived, quite truthfully, and find another mate—but if she has a baby by an impostor, she'll have a much harder time remarrying."

"And the State, of course, won't support the child of an impostor," Miles nodded.

Lovel released him and gestured to a chair. "Sit down, sit down, and I shall ring for tea!"

"It would be pleasant," Miles admitted, sitting, "but before you do, I had better tell you the details of the mythical bandits you're sending your bailiff to track."

"Yes indeed! What will he find when he reaches the place with all his men? And where is that place, by the way?"

"A mile outside the town, on the main road. They'll find the tracks of a dozen horses—we had to unharness our beasts and ride them back and forth, and off into the woods, six times—and a few bits of cloth on the bushes. The tracks disappear into a river. When your men don't find the bandits themselves, you can send to the magistrates all around you, and three of them will tell the same story. . . ."

"Japheth, Orgoru, and Minello." Lovel grinned, sitting behind his desk. "We have to stick together, don't we?"

"We do indeed." Miles smiled. "That should be enough. You can call for tea now."

"Of course." Lovel leaned back to pull on a rope. The door opened, and he said to the guard who looked in, "Tea, strong and dark! Quickly, tell her!"

The guard nodded and closed the door, with a frown to

answer Miles's glare—but a frown that gained a distinct look of foreboding before the panel shut to hide him.

"What of the others?" Lovel asked. "Tell me all the news!"

Miles launched into a brief account of all the agents he had seen in the last month. "Etaoin's bailiff and watchmen are all beginning to agitate with *him* for guarantees of safety for the peasants, and Lucia's first child was born in October. Her husband is already seeing that women . . ."

The door opened, and the maid came in with the tea.

". . . must be able to march through your township without worrying about assaults on their virtue," Miles went on without missing a beat. "Even if you have the bandits in your gaol, can you guarantee the good behavior of your town's young men?"

"Not guarantee, of course—no one ever can," Lovel replied as the maid put down the tea tray, wide-eyed. "But we've only had two charges of assault since I've been here, and both those young men have been scourged and pilloried, so I doubt anyone else would be eager to imitate them."

Miles nodded, back in character as Branstock. "Let's hope not. Still, bandits daring to waylay travelers so close to the edge of your town aren't the most encouraging sight."

The maid poured the tea.

Lovel waved away Branstock's objection—and the maid. She curtsied and went out as he was saying, "I have no doubt the bailiff and his men will . . ."

The door closed behind the maid.

". . . have the men in irons soon enough," Lovel finished, then doubled over in silent laughter. So did Miles.

When they had managed to recover themselves, Miles wiped tears from his eyes and said, "What a pair of charlatans we are!"

"More than a pair of us, Miles," Lovel chuckled. "Many more, I hope."

When Branstock left the courthouse in the middle of the afternoon, Lovel came out of his study looking somber. "Tell the bailiff to see me as soon as he returns," he told his guards, and when the bailiff came home to report failure—the trail of the bandits had mysteriously disappeared—Lovel told him gravely, "We seem to have overlooked some rather serious matters, bailiff," and went on to give him a list.

The bailiff, of course, immediately summoned his watchmen and proceeded to give *them* a lecture—so there was no question about it in anyone's mind, and by noon of the next day, everyone in town knew that "merchant Branstock" had really been an inspector-general—in disguise, as they always were.

The tinker strolled along the high road, his pots and pans clanking and clattering to the rhythm of his steps—and to that rhythm, he sang,

> "Oh, mistress mine, where are you roaming?
> Oh, mistress mine, where are you roaming?
> Oh, stay and hear!
> Your true love's coming . . ."

He'd been singing it for the last mile and was growing very tired of it when at last a band of men in worn homespun clothing stepped out of the woods to surround him. "We'll have those pots and pans, tinker."

"Oh, spare a poor man, sir!" the tinker cried, and backed away—straight into another bandit, who chuckled in his ear and clamped a hand on his arm.

"All right, then, we'll take you, too!" the first bandit cried, and the men surrounded him, forcing the tinker into the trees, squalling protests.

When they were a few hundred yards from the road, though, the bandits let go of the tinker, and their leader ducked his head in greeting. "Well met, Miles."

"Well met indeed!" Miles sighed. "I could have sworn I'd go hoarse from singing that dratted song! I thought you had men guarding every mile of roadway in this district."

"Every mile, yes—but you had to pace half that mile before you passed me," one of the other bandits said. "I recognized the song, though, and knew that you wanted a conference right away."

"That I did," Miles sighed, and swung his pack off his back. "What a relief!" He rubbed sore shoulders.

"What did you need to tell us?" the bandit leader asked.

"Send word to the city—Reeve Plumpkin in Dore Town will be replaced next month. His replacement will be Magistrate Gole, coming from Belo Village."

"He'll be driving up the south road, then." The bandit leader's eyes glittered—they didn't get a chance to place one of the cured madmen as a reeve very often. "We'll be ready for him—and we'll hold him until the city can send us a man to take his place. Where's Plumpkin going?"

"North to Milton Town. Rumor has it that he'll be promoted to inspector-general."

"What a coup that would be!" one of the bandits breathed.

"A blow for the New Order indeed," Miles agreed, "so tell the city to send two men." Then the glow died from his eyes, and hunger replaced it. "Tell them to send Ciletha, too, to meet me a mile outside of Grantnor."

A few of the men gave lascivious grins at that, but the leader only looked sympathetic. "Of course, Miles. No doubt she'll have a lot of news for you." He glared darkly at the bandit who opened his mouth with a ribald look on his face. After a moment, the man closed his mouth and lost his leer.

Ledora had tried to catch a magistrate, but one of the local girls with less mind and more beauty had caught him instead—so she had found a place as a cook with a reeve's guardsmen. The Reeve's Guard was a small army a thousand strong, and as she dished food onto their plates, she heard them talking about comrades who were ill. She spent her free hours seeking out the sick ones and curing them, and before long, she had become the army's nurse. That gave her time alone with men who were feeling too poorly to try to molest her, but well enough to listen to the occasional word she dropped about the ways in which they were all just virtual puppets of the

Protector and his reeves and magistrates. The soldiers turned thoughtful as they recovered, and now and again at mealtimes, she heard them discussing the ideas she had planted. Her bosom swelled with pride at the good work she was doing for the New Order, and she prided herself on how quietly and secretly she had done it—until the heavy hand fell on her shoulder.

CHAPTER 20

Pain bit through her thumbs, and Countess Vogel woke up screaming. She looked about her frantically, looked up at the stone walls, the smoking torches, the strange, macabre machinery with the brown stains, and the bare-chested men in black hoods.

She also saw the gaunt man with the burning eyes, dressed likewise in black—black robes, round black hat, even a black stone in his ring. He leaned forward over her, demanding, "Tell us what you know!"

"I know nothing!" she cried. "How did I come here? Fiend, you have kidnapped me!"

The man nodded at someone behind her head—she realized she was lying on her back with her hands bound above her coiffure—and the pain bit into her thumbs again. She screamed; the man nodded, and the pain eased. She lay gasping in terror.

The man saw, and nodded, pleased. "Tell us what you remember, Nurse Ledora."

"Nurse? What nurse? I am the Countess Vog—" The black-robed man nodded again, disgusted, and she broke off, screaming. The pain lasted longer this time, and when he nodded again to ease it, and she had managed to stop her screaming, he said, "Look about you, and see how much worse the pain could be." He pointed. "That is a rack, to stretch you and hold you stretched until your bones begin to pull apart from one another. That is the iron boot, to hold your foot imprisoned for days until the pain becomes excruciating. That is the iron maiden, and that is the cangue and that is . . ."

He listed them all for her, and she turned to jelly within— but she could only protest, "I am no one but the Countess Vogel, and know nothing but dancing and dalliance!"

"I am the Questioner Renunzio." He nodded at the unseen torturer, and pain bit through her thumbs again. Over her scream he bellowed, "Tell me what you remember, nurse!"

Nurse . . .

Ledora spun about to stare into the stern face of a bailiff she had never seen, a face that spoke and said, "Nurse Ledora, I arrest you for sedition and treason against the Protector and the Realm!"

"I remember a hard-faced man who arrested me!" she cried.

"Before that!" that same hard-faced man snapped.

"Before that . . . before that . . ."

"You were a nurse!" he thundered.

Yes, Ledora had been a nurse, had talked with wounded soldiers about human rights, about people being subject only to themselves, but how did Countess Vogel know that? It must have been a dream. . . .

Even as this was a nightmare.

"Did you tempt men into treachery!" Renunzio thundered.

"Ledora did!" the countess screamed. "It was Ledora!"

"You are Ledora! You are the traitor! You must suffer the punishment!"

"I'm not Ledora! I'm the Countess . . ."

Renunzio struck her mouth with the back of his hand. "You are the nurse Ledora, and your lies shall do you no good!" He twisted about and commanded a torturer, "Take off her shoes!"

She felt her shoes being ripped from her feet, and cried out in fear. Renunzio snapped his fingers at the torturer, and a thin rod smacked across her soles. Ledora screamed, terrified and amazed that it could hurt so much.

"What did you tell the soldiers!" Rununzio thundered.

Ledora bathed the soldier's brow, telling him, "All men have the right to live without fear of the Protector making them disappear in the night! All men have the right to be free—to decide for themselves what work they will do, who they will marry, and to stand up for themselves if someone tries to hurt them, or their wives or children! All men have the right to make these choices for themselves, so that they can at least try to be happy!"

"Rights!" the countess screamed. "I told them that all people are born with rights that no government can take away from them!"

One of the torturers looked up, startled, and behind the mask, his eyes grew thoughtful.

"Sedition!" Renunzio snarled. "Treachery! Who taught you these vile notions?" He snapped his fingers again.

The wand struck her soles, the thumbscrews bit deeper, and poor Countess Vogel, confused and terrified, cried out the first memory that came to her mind. . . .

She sat in a room with many other men and women who had been lords and ladies (but how had they become anything less?), and before them stood a young man wearing peasant's clothes, saying, "One by one, the men will go out to take the places of magistrates and reeves, and the women will go out to try to fascinate and marry other officials, then teach them very slowly about the New Order. Those who can't, will become nurses to the reeves' soldiers, and teach the fighting men about human rights and self-government, little by little."

"And what will you do, Miles?" one of the other women asked.

"I shall disguise myself as an inspector-general," the man answered, "and go from magistrate to magistrate, telling you all what progress we're making, and helping where I'm needed—or calling for help from the city."

"Who told you!" Renunzio thundered. Pain bit again in hands and feet both, and the countess screamed, "Miles! Miles told us!"

"Us?" Renunzio pounced on the word. "Who else? Who else?"

"All the lords! All the ladies! Count Lorif, and Prince Parslane, and the Grand Duchess Kolyenkov, and . . ."

"Her wits are going," one of the torturers muttered.

"Silence, fool!" Renunzio snapped. "I will say when she's in danger of breaking! Woman! Where is this Miles you speak of?"

"Anywhere! Anywhere!" she cried. "He's an inspector-general! He could be anywhere!"

"An inspector-general!" Renunzio stared, his eyes bright with unholy excitement. "A real inspector-general, or an impostor?"

"An impostor! We were all to be impostors, every lord and lady of us! But it was all a dream, just a dream!"

The torturer swung his rod up for another blow, but Renunzio stopped him with a raised hand. "One more, and her mind *will* be worthless junk. Take her back to her cell. With a few days' rest, she may tell us more."

The word ran through the revolution's cells that Ledora had been taken. Nurses melted away from reeves' bands overnight, and in the Protector's Army, no man spoke of anything but his duties and his home. Miles disguised himself as a beggar and went into the forest to work his way back to Voyagend. He stared into his campfire in the night, trying to ignore the fear that seemed to wrap itself about him, trying not to panic at every slightest sound, the cry of the owl, the call of the night-bird, the rustle of a badger in the underbrush, the snap of a twig . . .

The snap! He whirled about, swinging an arm up to block, and saw the two foresters looming over him for a split second before pain exploded through his head, and he sank down into the safe, warm, darkness.

* * *

Miles came to with a splitting headache. The caution of the outlaw made him lie still, opening his eyes just enough to peek through the lashes. Stone, gray stone all about him, dimly washed by light high on the wall. . . . A stout wooden door bound with brass, a tiny hole at eye level for a standing man. . . .

He knew a prison when he saw one.

But he kept looking and wished he hadn't, for his gaze led him to a gaunt, black-clad man with ravenous eyes who sat beside him on a low stool.

"Come now, I know you're awake," this apparition said, quite companionably. "Open your eyes, and let's get on with it."

Miles lay still, hoping the man was bluffing.

"I heard the change in your breathing," the man insisted, "and I've sat by the beds of enough traitors to the Protector so that I know the difference. Come, you're wasting time, my time, your time, and"—his voice stayed quite mild, even casual—"you may not have a great deal of time left. So be a good fellow and open your eyes, eh?"

Reluctantly, Miles opened his eyes completely, and was relieved not to see any torture instruments, nor any of the dreaded men in black masks. "My head aches abominably," he muttered.

"Aches? Well, let it serve as a lesson, for other parts of you will hurt far worse if you don't answer my questions with the truth." The tone was still quite mild, making Miles shiver with dread. "I am Renunzio," the human vulture went on, "and my task is to make you renounce indeed—renounce the treachery you have committed, or renounce life. It is, lamentably, your choice—lamentable because I'd far rather have true answers than your mutilated corpse."

Miles knew better than to claim it wasn't true, that he hadn't even thought of treachery. "Water," he croaked.

"Yes, a few drops, for you're no use to me if you can't talk," Renunzio told him. He reached down and brought up a tin cup, then scooped an arm under Miles's shoulders and yanked him upright with astonishing strength for one so skinny. The pain rocked through Miles's head in waves; his stomach lurched and the room darkened about him. He wouldn't even have known the cup was there if it hadn't pressed hard against his lips and tilted. Water flooded into his throat; he coughed, drowning for a moment, and shoved the cup away, coughing still. When he was done wheezing, he realized Renunzio had done as he said—only a few drops had actually stayed in his mouth. The rest soaked the front of his shirt.

"This is my case," Renunzio informed him. "I am the spymaster who began to suspect your plot from hearing the reports my agents brought of the talk circulating in the Protector's Army. I put on a uniform and walked about, listening myself, and found that men who had never breathed a word against the Protector, but who fell ill and went into hospital, uttered sedition with great excitement when they came out. I suppose I shouldn't have been surprised, for I've long known that treason is a disease, and one anyone may catch. Still, I was surprised, so I feigned illness myself, and while I lay abed in hospital, a nurse named Ledora began to speak to me of a strange notion called 'rights.' Would you know of this?"

Words of denial leaped to Miles's tongue, but he remembered all of his tormentor's cautions and said warily, "I've heard the idea spoken."

"Yes, and spoken it yourself, too, and loudly and long, I'm sure—but we'll hear of that later. For now, all you need to know is that we arrested the woman and put her to the question. She denied it all, of course, even though I told her I'd heard it myself, from her own lips. We put the thumbscrews on her, and the most amazing thing happened."

Miles shuddered at the tone of wonder in the man's voice, at the eagerness with which he spoke of torture—but he saw Renunzio was waiting, and thought it best to humor him in small things. He took his cue and croaked, "What?"

"She went mad. For a while I thought she was shamming, but the thumbscrews and the baton on the soles of her feet wouldn't make her admit to being Ledora again. She insisted she was some sort of countess, though anyone could see she was only a peasant, though I'll admit she's a graceful one."

Is! Miles's heart leaped with relief, but he was careful to keep the look of foreboding that had been growing within him.

"I might have thought she was lying," Renunzio went on, "if she hadn't answered every question I asked—and with no more pain than thumbscrews and baton, though I had to watch my phrasing. Asking her what she had done was useless; asking her what she remembered did the trick."

Miles let the look of foreboding deepen to impending doom.

Renunzio leaned forward and hissed, "Five years! She told us this rot has been growing for five years! It's amazing that it hasn't infested the whole of the army—or perhaps it has. There was no way to tell how far it stretched, for before she was strong enough for a second bout of questioning, she fell sick with some sort of brain fever. Again, I would have thought she was faking, but every other prisoner in that wing fell ill, too—it's obviously some sort of epidemic, and only one brave cook is willing to go in to shove food to those madmen."

Relief washed over Miles, though he tried hard not to let it show. The cook must have been a convert to the New Order, and had laced the prisoners' gruel with some sort of herb that made them rave, made them temporarily mad.

At least, he hoped it was temporary.

Renunzio leaned even closer, breathing his words right into Miles's face. "So, since I can't ask her—I'll have to ask *you*."

Ledora had told Renunzio a bit more than that, it seemed—he threw out random bits and pieces as he talked with Miles, enough to make him sweat with worry, not enough to give him any idea of the limits of the torturer's knowledge. All he could be reasonably sure of was that the nurse hadn't told Renunzio the identities of any of the substituted officials, for he hadn't received word of any arrests before he was taken himself, and as he paced the dungeon hallway with the inquisitor, none of the groans he heard seemed to be in familiar voices.

But why had Renunzio taken him out of his cell? Two guards marched behind them, and Miles went down the corridor side by side with the torturer, not daring to resist too much, but feeling the fear gather and build within him.

"She told us about you, of course," Renunzio said for the tenth time, "told us the leader of the traitors was one Miles, who was masquerading as an inspector-general. It took quite a bit of searching, mind you, for inspectors-general disguise themselves as all manner of wanderers. We brought in a hundred vagabonds, at least, and found three of them to be real inspectors-general indeed, which took some fast talking—but finally we found you." He gave Miles a toothy grin. "Or are you going to try to tell me you aren't the leader of this foul little nest of traitors?"

Miles chose his words carefully. "I don't think I'll try to tell you a single word, Renunzio, since you won't believe anything but what you want to hear anyway."

"Oh, but you will," the vulture purred. "And you're wrong about what I won't believe. Come watch!"

He clamped bony talons around Miles's upper arm and dragged him through the door at the end of the hallway. The guards followed.

They stepped into a nightmare.

The room was windowless and dank, filled with vile smells, lit only by the orange flames in half a dozen braziers, each of which held pokers and branding-irons and other instruments that Miles didn't want to know about. A man was strapped down to a table with a wheel at the end, arms stretched tight above his head, groaning. He was naked except for a loincloth.

Renunzio came and sat by the victim, smiling. "Hurts a bit when you've lain stretched out like that all night, doesn't it? But I promise you the pain will be much worse, my chuck, if you don't tell us what we wish to know."

The victim eyed the irons heating in the brazier and moaned, "Anything!"

"Ah, you wish to cooperate! Still, let us be a bit more sure that you'll tell us the truth. Torturer, fit the thumbscrews on him."

"I'll confess! I'll confess!" the man cried.

"Confess that you lay in wait for the Protector and struck at him with a sword?" Renunzio asked.

"Yes, yes! I'm not so much a fool as to deny it!"

"Of course not, since a dozen guards saw you do it, before they beat you senseless and dragged you in here. But *I'm* not so much a fool as to think you were able to sneak into that shrubbery by yourself, or forge your own sword, either. Who helped you?"

"No one!" the would-be assassin cried in mounting fear.

Renunzio gestured. The torturer turned the screw, and the prisoner howled with pain. Renunzio made a chopping gesture, and the torturer backed off the screw. "Tell me their names," the inquisitor urged.

"I . . . I can't think of any," the prisoner panted.

"Surely you can," Renunzio coaxed. "Bring a hot iron, to brand it on his memory."

The prisoner screamed even before the iron touched him, screamed raw and hoarse as it bit his skin. As the iron came away, Renunzio asked, "Was it Okin Germane?"

Miles started with dismay. Okin Germane was a Protector's Minister!

"Who?" the man gasped.

Renunzio signaled to the torturer again.

When he could stop screaming, the criminal gasped, "Yes! Yes, it was Okin Germane!"

"Liar!" Renunzio snapped. "Okin Germane is the most trusted of the Protector's Ministers! He would never move against his master! Now tell me the truth!" He gestured again, and the torturer moved in.

So it went, with Renunzio playing a fantastic, warped guessing-game with the prisoner, wherein the man on the rack had to guess whether or not to agree with the inquisitor, and Miles became more and more sick within as he watched. Finally he realized that Renunzio was drawing it out far longer than necessary, just to make Miles realize how horrible the torture could be. Guilt struck deep then, but there was nothing he could do to stop it.

But perhaps there was! "Stop, stop!" Miles cried. "Let him die! I'll tell you everything I know!"

"That you will, but it's not your turn yet," Renunzio chuckled, and gestured to the torturer again.

That sickened Miles more than the torture itself; that struck the terror more deeply into him than the victim's screams—the pleasure Renunzio took in his work. He could only watch from then on, sick and weak with the pain of the poor thing that writhed and shrieked before him.

Finally Renunzio must have been satisfied in some strange way, for the creature on the rack gargled an answer, and the inquisitor nodded. "So I thought," he mused, "so I thought." He turned to the head torturer. "Take him off the rack, and prepare him for his execution." He rose from the stool, sighed as he stretched, then came over to Miles and clapped a hard hand on his shoulder as he led him wobbling out of the chamber. "A waste of time and effort," Renunzio sighed, "since his 'confession' will probably turn out to be bogus, merely something he said to make the torture stop, telling me what he knew I wanted to hear."

"Knew" because Renunzio had prompted him, Miles realized, and the names the inquisitor had used were those of high-ranking officials—the High Bailiff of the Protector's Guard, a general of an army in all but name; three ministers; and one he didn't recognize, but felt sure was a man of high rank and great influence. True or not, Renunzio now had evidence to use against them, evidence which he could horde, claiming he needed to wait for opportunities to prove it by the testimony of other such prisoners, but really waiting until a chance came to use it as a weapon in the constant intrigues within the top echelons of government, to gain greater power and rank himself. Miles realized the man had decided to become a minister, though not by the usual route of examinations and years of successful administration.

Renunzio watched Miles's face, waiting for the thoughts to register. The rebel leader fought to keep his face expressionless, but the inquisitor must have seen something, for his eyes brightened with delight. "Past experience has shown me that would-be assassins like that usually act alone," he said, "crazed by grief, bitterness, or some other cause. I would rather you told me willingly, so that your words might be more trustworthy." But the gaze he turned on the rebel leader belied his words, so bright was it with avarice.

"Why did you keep him in agony so long, then?" Miles asked, quaking inside.

"Why, to give the Watch time to gather the citizens to view his hanging, of course! And to make sure there were enough marks on his body to scare our good citizens so thoroughly that none of them will dare try to assassinate our beloved Protector, or to work against him in any way. Come, for you too must see!"

And come Miles did, for the guards bundled him after Renunzio, through an iron gate and past sentries, up three flights of dank stone steps, through a brass-bound portal of six-inch-thick wood and past another sentry, down a lightless tunnel to another door with a small barred window, out between two more sentries and into a huge courtyard, open to the city itself, where three major roads debouched into a vast plaza. It was crowded now with people, merchants in the plain broadcloth of their warehouses, tradesmen in their aprons, and housewives in theirs, some with utensils still in their hands. Ordinary people they were, common people, and Miles could see only the leading rank of soldiers at the back on the side nearest him, but knew they were there behind the people all about, having just herded them from their shops and houses.

They stood in glum silence, those people, or with a low, apprehensive murmur. It was a grim crowd, but Renunzio signed to a watchman who stood on an iron-railed balcony above, and he signed toward the crowd. Here and there, voices began to chant, "Traitor! Traitor!" and the rest of the people, knowing what would keep them alive and what would see them arrested, began to chant with them. The noise grew, gained a life of its own, and even people who hated this event (which included most of them) found themselves chanting with anger and even eagerness, "Traitor! Traitor! Hang up the traitor!"

Renunzio seized the back of Miles's head and yanked, turning his face upward. "Look!" he commanded, and Miles couldn't very well disobey, since his gaze was already on the top of the castle wall.

There, an iron beam jutted out from the stone with a rope curling from its end back to the parapet. As he watched, guards shoved a man stumbling to the edge of the wall, and Miles saw that the rope was tied around his neck. One guard struck him in the belly, making him double over, so that he couldn't help but see the huge fifty-foot drop before him. It was the would-be assassin, and he began to scream at the sight below. He screamed even louder as a hard boot struck him, sending him plummeting off the edge, screaming in terror, a scream that ended very suddenly.

At the last second, Miles wrenched his head about, trying to turn his eyes away, but Renunzio's claws held him in an iron grip. "That is your fate," he hissed, "unless you tell me what I wish to know."

Miles stared at the poor, pathetic body above him, at the raw welts and livid brandmarks. "Yes," he gasped, hating himself for it. "Yes, I'll tell you. I'll tell it all."

"Good man." Renunzio patted him on the back, quite gently, and as he turned Miles away to go back into the prison, the rebel leader couldn't help the horrible surge of guilt that came with the suspicion that Renunzio wouldn't have made the poor felon suffer nearly as much if he hadn't been trying to scare Miles into surrender.

Which, of course, he hadn't done. Miles had made as much of a show as Renunzio had. He didn't expect it would take the inquisitor long to realize that what he was hearing was as complete a fiction as any minstrel would sing—but the more time Miles could buy, the fewer of his people would be taken.

For the revolution was finished now, he knew—defeated, without a single stroke against the Protector. His last order had been for everyone to flee to the forest and the mountains. The longer he could draw out Renunzio's game, the more of them would escape to safety.

Miles screamed as the branding iron bit into his chest. It was even worse than the pain that raged through every joint, for Renunzio had left him stretched out on the rack only overnight. The worst of the burning pain eased; he saw the iron rising away and lay staring in terror and amazement that it could have hurt so much.

"I don't believe a word of it," Renunzio chuckled, gazing down with glee into Miles's eyes. "A city of madmen in the forest? Ridiculous! Do you think I'm fool enough to believe a fairy tale like that?"

"But it's true!" Miles protested. "The knights cured them of their madness, taught them how to be magistrates and reeves, and sent them out to take office in place of the real ones!"

Renunzio's mouth thinned with scorn; he waved to the torturer, and pain stabbed through Miles's toes. He had no idea what they had done, couldn't see down far enough, but the pain was so intense it nearly made him faint. The inquisitor saw and gestured to a torturer, who dashed water into Miles's face, ice water, and the shock almost made him pass out, then brought him a clearheadedness he regretted.

"Worse and worse!" Renunzio hissed. "First a city of madmen, then two knights who can magically cure their madness, and finally a spirit who lives within a wall and teaches the madmen in a matter of months what real officials take twenty years to learn! Can you do no better than that, dear Miles?"

The worst of it was that he meant the "dear"; the rebel leader's pain made him precious to Renunzio, made him feel some sort of bond between them.

"I—I'll try," Miles gasped. His terror at the pain hid his elation. He had gambled on telling the truth first, sure that Renunzio would think it a lie. Indeed, if Miles hadn't lived through it himself, he would have thought it a fairy tale, too.

Something seared his arm, a brief sharp pain that made him cry out, then clamp his jaws shut, ashamed when the pain was so small compared to the rest.

"Just to claim your attention," Renunzio explained. "Now, let's begin with those two knights, shall we? What were their names?"

"Sir Dirk Dulaine," Miles gasped, "and Sir Gar Pike."

Renunzio frowned, and Miles braced himself for pain, but the inquisitor only said, "I would think 'Gar Pike' was a lie, if

'Dirk Dulaine' weren't coupled with it; the name almost makes sense. And where are they now, these two champion traitors?"

"Gone back where they came from," Miles said.

Renunzio's eyes kindled with avarice again. "And where is that?" he purred.

Miles braced himself; the man wasn't going to like the truth. "The stars—in a ship that flies."

Renunzio's face went rigid, eyes burning with rage, and he raised a hand to gesture—

Something boomed against the torture-chamber door.

Irritated, Renunzio looked up, lowering his hand. He nodded at the guard, who pulled the door open.

Two watchmen stood there, one so tall he had to stoop as he entered—and Miles fought to keep his face contorted in fear while hope leaped in his heart.

"What matter is so great as to make you disturb my work?" Renunzio demanded.

"An order that you bring the prisoner before the Protector himself," the shorter man answered, "without the slightest delay!"

Miles went limp with relief.

CHAPTER 21

The huge sergeant slouched into the torture chamber behind the ordinary-sized one.

"I've almost brought the man to the point of telling me all I—the Protector wishes to know!" Renunzio glared. "What possesses him to need the fellow right now? This is a devil of an inconvenient time!"

It struck Miles as a very convenient time indeed.

"I don't ask questions," the smaller man said. "Let him up now, if you please."

A disgusted torturer moved to unbuckle the straps that held Miles down.

But Renunzio held up his hand. "Wait! I don't need to follow that order unless I see it in writing! Show me the written document, guardsman!"

"If you must," the smaller guard growled, and pulled a rolled parchment from his belt. He stepped down next to the rack and handed it to Renunzio, who unrolled it, scowling.

The guardsman struck him on the head with something small that only made a smacking sound. Renunzio's eyes rolled up;

he toppled off his stool. The paper floated to the floor, but as it went, Miles read the single word *Surprise!*

The chief torturer recovered from his own surprise with a shout of anger and turned to fight off the invaders.

There really was no contest, though. The torturers were strong, immensely strong, and brutal—but they were used to striking men who were tied up or tied down, and couldn't fight back. The guardsmen, though, were seasoned soldiers, used to fighting men who fought back, and were armed into the bargain.

The guard blocked the chief torturer's haymaker and drove his own fist into the man's belly, and the chief doubled over with an agonized grunt. His two assistants leaped for the guardsman with a shout, but the giant sergeant wrapped a hand around the neck of one and yanked him off the floor. The smaller guard whirled to face his attacker, who stabbed at him with a white-hot poker—but the guard struck it aside with his halberd and whipped the butt around to crack the torturer's head.

The giant pulled the hood off his strangling captive and gave him half a dozen slaps with a hand the size of a dinner plate. The torturer's head rolled back, and his eyes rolled up.

But the smaller man was already unbuckling Miles. "We had to come back a little early," he confided. "On the last planet we visited, the new king turned out to be a reformer, and had very good bodyguards."

"Of course," the huge one said, "anyone who claimed that Dirk had something to do with the old king's abdicating would have been telling vile lies."

"I don't have the slightest idea what you're talking about," Miles said fervently, "but you have no idea how glad I am to see you both!"

"I think we can guess." Gar frowned down at his feet, then took a small jar out of the pouch at his side. "This should ease the pain a bit."

His touch, at least, made it worse. Miles ground his teeth to hold back a howl. Dirk was busy unscrewing something above his head. He took Miles's hands out gently and brought his arms down to his sides. Miles groaned with relief.

"Sorry," Gar said, "but it really will feel better when I'm done."

"No, no! I was groaning at having my arms back." Miles realized how ridiculous that sounded, but before he could say so, Gar straightened up, screwing the lid back on the jar and slipping it into his pouch. The fire in Miles's feet cooled instantly, and he groaned again, then said quickly, "What a blessing!"

"You'll have to stay off them for a few days." Gar's voice was tight with anger. "Up with you, now! We need that bed for the next patient!" He scooped Miles up in his arms and deposited him on Renunzio's stool. "Keep your feet up."

Dirk steadied Miles while Gar hauled Renunzio off the floor with much less gentleness than he had shown the rebel leader, and laid him down on the rack. Miles bit his tongue to keep from protesting; he knew what was coming.

Sure enough, Gar shackled Renunzio's ankles and wrists, then turned the wheel until the unconscious man lay stretched out on his own bed of pain. Gar stepped back, surveyed him critically, then decided, "There's no real tension on him."

"Gar," Dirk said, voice shaking, "this is beneath you."

"Just a *little*," Gar qualified. He moved the wheel two more notches, then nodded, satisfied. "No damage, and no pain—yet. But I think he'll have a very rude awakening. Gag him, Dirk."

He turned away, and Miles realized he hadn't put the gag on with his own hands because he couldn't trust himself not to strangle Renunzio. Dirk tore a strip of cloth from the inquisitor's coat and bound it around his mouth. He stepped back to survey his work critically, then offered, "I could jam it down his throat."

Somehow, Miles found the strength to say, "No. Leave him for the guards to find. Your mercy will mean more to them than my revenge."

"A good point." Dirk turned back, pulling a jar of salve and a roll of bandages out of his own pouch. "I think we'd better give your thumbs a little ease, too."

As he bandaged them, Miles looked up just in time to see Gar finish tying the chief torturer into a chair that was bolted to the floor under a bucket with a hole in the bottom. Drops of water struck his head, about one every two seconds. Miles looked around and saw the man's two apprentices bound into torture machines of their own. Gar stepped back to survey his handiwork. "Neat enough, I think. Gag them, will you, Dirk?"

As Dirk bandaged the apprentices' mouths, the giant turned back to Renunzio, scowling down at him. The inquisitor moaned and turned—or tried to. He froze as he realized he was bound, and his eyes flew open. He took in his situation with one quick glance, then stared up at the huge man who towered above him, resting one hand on the wheel. Renunzio went stiff with terror.

Gar saw and nodded, satisfied. "Yes, he'll have punishment enough for the time being. We'll leave him for you to judge, Miles, after we usher in the New Order."

Renunzio's gaze flew to Miles, saw the somber, weighing look on his face, and his eyes sickened with horror.

"Enough of him." Gar turned away with sudden decision. "No one could have blamed us if we had drawn and quartered him, but they'll respect you more for leaving him to the process of the Law. Off into the night, now! It's high time we hauled you out of this hole!"

Dirk produced a guard's uniform, and they helped Miles dress in it, though painfully. Then Gar slung the rebel leader over his shoulder, Dirk opened the door, and Gar turned back for one last glare at Renunzio. "Be glad it's Miles who will judge you, torturemaster, and not I. He, at least, has some notion of mercy." Then he turned away, and Dirk closed the door behind him.

In the hallway, Dirk snorted, "Phony!"

"I prefer to think of myself as making an insightful impact,"

Gar returned placidly. "Besides, if I did have to decide his fate, my anger just might get the better of me."

"Might."

"Anything is possible," Gar reminded, "including this revolution—but we'll discuss that after we're back in the forest."

They went up a flight of stairs, and the sentry at the top frowned. "Why can't he walk?"

"They worked on his feet," Dirk said shortly.

"Well, it's your back, not mine," the sentry said, shrugging. He opened the door. "Get on with you, now."

They went on through, and Miles glanced at the man in surprise, then realized that Gar had told him the same story he had fed the warders at the door to the torture chamber. But the guards at the outer door were another matter—if Gar were bringing a prisoner to the Protector, he would only have to go upstairs. Why did the guards step aside without even asking? Come to that, why did they fall in behind, following Dirk and Gar? Miles craned his neck up far enough to see the guards' faces, and felt a shock—he recognized them from the city! Tomlin winked at him, and Miles managed to muster enough poise to wink back.

His stomach felt as though it were being punched with every step Gar took, so he was immensely glad when the giant lowered him into a saddle. "Just hug the horse's sides with your knees, Miles, don't try to use your feet in the stirrups—they'll take a few days more to heal." Gar turned away to mount a huge, rangy gray. Dirk and the guards swung up on extra mounts; then the man who had been holding the horses swung up onto the last one and followed after. Miles rode amazed. "How did you manage to pull together a strike force like this so quickly?"

"It hasn't been as quick as we'd have liked," Dirk said grimly. "We landed two days ago, but it took us most of the first day to work our way out of the forest and into town, then to find a magistrate who was one of our agents. We found him throwing everything vital into a box and calling for his horse; his cell had just received word of your arrest, and the only thing he wasn't sure about was whether or not you could hold out under torture long enough for all of your agents to get away."

"We told him we were sure you would," Gar said, also grimly. "Then we recruited him and started riding for the capital. We ambushed a few Protector's soldiers on the way, gathered a few more of our impostor magistrates who were just packing up, and changed clothes just before we rode up to the castle. Nobody had any problem with our riding in, and it didn't take much to knock out the sentries at the dungeon door. It did take two days, though."

"Amazing speed, and you reached me just in time," Miles said. "Believe me, I can't thank you enough!"

"We didn't quite get there in time," Dirk muttered.

Miles decided to ignore the man's guilt—there wasn't anything more he could do to lighten it. "So the revolution is dead, then?"

"Not at all," Gar said quickly. "Our agent magistrates have all fled their posts, yes, and they all appointed their clerks to run things while they were gone—and the agents who are magistrates' wives have developed great-aunts who suddenly took ill and needed to have them go help, so they should all be safe by now. The agent nurses disappeared into the towns and forests as soon as the first was taken prisoner, and so far as we can tell, only a dozen or so have been lost to the Protector's spies."

Miles blew out a sigh of relief. "I did hold out long enough, then."

"Yes, and you seemed to have held them off with talk long enough to keep them from doing much," Gar said, in tones of surprised admiration.

"More a matter of Renunzio wanting to overawe me, than any good management of mine," Miles confessed. "So our agents are almost all still with us, and ready to hand if we need them—but what can we do?"

"First give me a tally of your strength," Gar said. "How many magistrates and reeves have we replaced?"

"Almost half, and most of the rest have married our agents," Miles answered.

"Very good! How many out of each hundred?"

"Seventy-eight," Miles said without even stopping to think. "Of the remaining twenty-two, twelve have bands of watchmen and reeve's guards who will side with us instead of their magistrates and reeves."

"Your nurses have done well!" Dirk said, almost in awe.

"It has something to do with their knowing more medicine than the Protector's doctors," Miles said, appreciating the irony. "They're ready, though, and even in the Protector's Army, half his soldiers will probably fight for us, not him."

Dirk gave a long whistle, and Gar said, in tones of amazement, "You have done fantastically well, Miles!"

Miles fairly glowed with pleasure at their praise. "Only seeing that they did as you told me, my teachers. What do I have them do now, though?"

"What with the number of agents and the watchmen and guardsmen they command, they're a small army in themselves! Send the word out to have them march on Milton Town."

"The Protector's spies will have warned him," Dirk reminded them, "and he still has *some* soldiers loyal to him. They'll be watching the roads."

"Tell them to travel by night," Gar said grimly, "and to send their foresters before them. If they find soldiers, they can ambush them and steal their uniforms."

"Do they have to kill them, then?" Miles asked, his eyes wide.

Gar rode in silence awhile.

"It's only going to be a few days," Dirk said, "one way or another."

Miles felt a chill seize his back. They could lose, they could still lose dreadfully!

But Gar was nodding. "Yes, and our agents can leave them tied up with a few men to guard them. They'll be stiff as pikes when they're untied, but they'll be alive. Take prisoners,

Miles—but be aware that it will be a fight trying to take them, and some men will die on each side!"

"As few as possible, then," Miles said. "How can we claim to be freeing them, if we kill them? I'll tell my people to keep the survivors alive."

"As good a way to put it as any, I suppose," Dirk sighed. He glanced about him as they rode past the last house. "One advantage to a centralized government, at least—no town feels it needs to build a wall. We're out in the country, gentlemen."

"Time to send word, then." Miles turned to the impostor soldiers behind him. "You've all heard what we've decided?"

"Yes, Chairman," one of the soldiers said. "All agents march on Milton Town. Travel by night with foresters as scouts. Beware of the Protector's patrols, overpower them, tie up the survivors, and leave a few men to guard them. I guess that means feed them and water them, too," he added.

Miles nodded. "A very good summary. Go tell your cells, now!"

"Yes, Chairman!" all five men said, and galloped away into the night.

Miles reined in his horse and sat, stiff and still in the moonlight.

"What's the matter?" Dirk asked softly.

"It's begun," Miles said, almost unable to believe it. "It really has begun!"

"It has, that," Gar said heavily, "and there's no stopping it now."

"But there is!" Miles turned to him. "I could send word out through the network, I could tell them to stop marching, to go back to the Lost Cities!"

"You could," Gar said slowly, "but what would happen then?"

"Why . . . the clerks would keep administering the towns, and the Protector would realize half his magistrates and reeves were gone. He'd appoint new ones, then send his spies out to . . ." Miles's voice trailed off.

"To find your agents, torture them to discover where the rest were, and kill them all," Dirk finished for him. "Then he'd garrison the Lost Cities, set full-time patrols in the forests and Badlands, and never, ever again would there be a chance to even *start* a revolution, let alone win one."

"I wasn't really thinking of stopping it anyway," Miles mumbled. "It was just nice to think I could."

"There comes a point in life when you have to commit yourself," Gar told him, "or drown in your regrets." He slapped Miles gently on the shoulder. "Cheer up! There's every reason to believe we'll win this one, and without much fighting, either! The Wizard who spoke in the minds of our maniacs was a Wizard in the ways of Peace, Miles, or was trying to be! You're committed now, it's win or die, so you blasted well had better do your all-out best to win!"

Orgoru and Gilda rode down the midnight road side by side— the magistrate's decision to ride rather than take his carriage had raised a few eyebrows, but nobody had been about to contradict him. The superstitions of their peasant childhoods loomed up behind them, though, so they traveled closely enough for their legs to touch, and they held hands, looking about them nervously.

"We must be on watch for Protector's men," Orgoru muttered, and Gilda nodded, accepting the fiction.

Then dark shapes bulged out of the roadside shadows ahead, and Orgoru drew up with a choked-off oath, pulling back on the reins of Gilda's mount as he did. The shapes turned their heads with startled exclamations, and swords whicked from their sheaths. Orgoru drew his own, the hair at the nape of his neck standing on end. Fear hollowed him, weakened him, but he held the sword up bravely.

Gilda stayed him with a light touch on his forearm. "Who are you?" she called softly.

"We are the magistrates Loftu and Grammix," a voice called back, caution in every syllable. "Who are *you?*"

Orgoru slapped his sword back in its scabbard with a laugh of delight that verged on the hysterical, and Gilda called,

"Orgoru and Gilda, you great ninnies! Who did you think we were—the Prince of Paradime and the Countess d'Alexi?"

The two other cured maniacs laughed with relief and kicked their horses, pounding toward their friends and throwing their arms about them. When they separated, Loftu asked, "Didn't you get Miles's order for the women to go back to the city to hold it, in case we needed to retreat there?"

"I did," Gilda said, iron in her tone, "but I'm not about to fret and pace and eat myself up with anxiety while I wait to learn if Orgoru lives or dies."

"Neither are we," said a voice behind the two men, and Lala and Anne came riding up.

Gilda laughed with delight and threw her arms around her friends.

"I think we had better get back to marching," Loftu said.

"A good idea; we can trade news while we ride." The glance Orgoru directed toward the women said that if they stayed to talk, they would stay all night. He turned his horse back toward the north, asking, "You were able to marry Lala, then?"

"No, but she married the magistrate in the next village— Dumarque, his name is, and he's a decent man through and through. But when the word came, she thought he would be safer if she went to visit her sick aunt."

Orgoru nodded grimly. "She'll be safer, too, if we lose."

"We won't," Loftu said with absolute certainty. "There are as many of us as there are of real officials, and we have command of the Watch and the Guards."

But Orgoru knew that the watchmen and the reeve's guardsmen wouldn't fight the Protector's soldiers—their childhood "services," magistrate-led discussion sessions, had everyone convinced through and through of the rightness of the government, and the need for all decent people to obey him.

"Word has filtered through the network that almost half the Protector's Army is with us," the other magistrate said.

With them in spirit, yes—but would they be with them when it came to blows? Even if they believed in the rebels' cause, would they dare strike against their fellow soldiers with their officers' sharp swords behind them? Orgoru could only wonder—and be glad he wasn't the soldier who would have to decide.

If it really did come to blows, though, all the rebels had the fighting skills that Dirk and Gar had taught them. They would outnumber the soldiers—but they had no weapons. No matter how he looked at it, the outcome was uncertain. Blood might be spilled in gallons, and he heartily wished his beloved Gilda were far away, safe in Voyagend.

Onward they rode through the night-darkened wood, chatting in low tones—until more travelers loomed out of the shadows at the next crossroads. "Who moves?" a voice called.

"Magistrates of Miles," Orgoru called back, before any of his companions could try to explain.

The strangers laughed with relief and came forward to pound them on the backs.

So they moved through the night, their company growing at every crossroad—and throughout the land, other sham officials rode as they did, gathering into companies, then regiments. They disappeared into the woods and ditches when day dawned, dispersing to sleep, though four or five always stood watch, carefully concealed.

Gilda shook his shoulder. "Orgoru!"

Orgoru came awake on the instant, stared for a disorient second, then looked up into his wife's eyes, striving for calm while his heart thudded in his breast. "What?"

"There's a squadron of riders coming, and they're wearing the Protector's livery!"

"Don't wake the others," Orgoru said automatically. They would be best hidden by sleeping. For himself, he rolled over and wormed his way out of the hollow where they'd spent the night, to peer through the high grass at the road.

There they came, a dozen mounted men, tall and bearded— but the officer who rode at their head was slight and short, and wore his livery as though it were strange to him.

"A Protector's spy," Orgoru hissed to Gilda, "leading soldiers in patrol now, since he's the one who knows what to look for."

"Could they be seeking *us*?" she breathed.

"Probably. They don't usually go in patrols."

"What do we do?"

"Watch where they go," Orgoru whispered, "and see whether or not they come back."

They were both silent as the patrol rode by and disappeared down the road. Then Gilda sighed with relief, and Orgoru felt himself begin to shake. To hide it, he glanced at the sun and said, "Almost midday. Time for my watch and your nap, anyway, my dear."

Gilda settled into the hollow, but she looked doubtful.

Orgoru rested a hand on her shoulder and said softly, "Sleep, beloved. We're in no danger until we come to Milton Town, you know that." He wished *he* did.

Gilda seemed to, though; she relaxed, nestled into the grass, and covered a yawn. Orgoru gazed down at her sleeping face, feeling a great well of tenderness opening within him, and wondered how it had come to exist.

Then he remembered that he was supposed to be watching the road.

Other men and women were on watch all across the country that day. They were the ones who saw the Protector's patrols ride by, marked their direction, and told their fellows when they gathered in the dusk to resume their march. They warmed their rations, ate and drank, then moved off into the night again, following the trails, alert for the soldiers.

Orgoru's company came upon their first patrol not long after the moon had risen. The soldiers were camped by a stream, banked campfires glowing, horses standing droop-headed and sleeping. Ten small tents surrounded the fire; one sentry stood guard, pacing slowly around the circle.

Orgoru waved his men back and held a quick conference. "There are twenty of us to their ten. Let two go to each tent, pull down the poles, and catch them in canvas."

They nodded, some grim, some with grins, but Loftu asked, "Shall I take out the sentry?"

Orgoru started to answer, but Gilda spoke first. "Yes, but wait for me to play my part."

She turned away into the night, and Loftu stared at her, not understanding. Neither did Orgoru, but it wasn't the time or place to argue. They tied their horses and moved forward until they could all see the soldiers' campsite. Silently, several men moved out to either side, surrounding it in a semicircle.

The sentry paced slowly—and Gilda stepped out of the trees into a patch of moonlight squarely in front of him. He froze, staring in surprise and alarm, and she moved toward him, every movement sensuous, her voice low-pitched and husky. "Good evening, soldier."

The sentry recovered, but kept his voice low, as much in surprise as anything else. "Good evening, damsel. What're you doing on the road in the middle of the night?"

"My horse went lame this afternoon, and I've been creeping through the woods ever since, afraid of bandits but hoping for—"

The shadow-shape of Loftu rose up behind the soldier and struck with his blackjack. The soldier stiffened, staring at Gilda in amazement. Then his eyes rolled up, and he folded.

Orgoru stared, amazed at the resourcefulness of the woman he had married. Then pride swept him, and the urge to be worthy of her. He waved to his men and led the way silently out to the tents.

They went two to each canvas, standing, waiting for Orgoru's signal. He raised a hand, then swept it down and yanked the stick out of the end of the tent. His companion did the same at the other end, and the canvas billowed down to outline the form of the sleeping soldier. They dropped to their knees and tucked the canvas under the man's body, and he came awake with a shout of alarm. A dozen other shouts filled the clearing, then curses of anger, but they did no good; willing hands were rolling every single soldier over and over, cocooning them in fabric.

"Stop!" a man bellowed.

Orgoru froze, then looked up.

A slight man in dark livery held an arm around Gilda's chest, a knife to her throat. Orgoru's heart sank—the spy himself! He had slept apart from his men and come running at the shout! Gilda struggled, cursing, but the spy held her as though his arm were iron and called, "Stand away from those tents and keep your arms high, or she dies!"

CHAPTER 22

Orgoru rose and stepped away from the tent instantly, arms rising as his stomach sank—but live or die, he couldn't risk harm to Gilda. More slowly, the other false magistrates followed suit, and soldiers thrashed about, scrambling to free themselves from fallen tents. Several scrambled to their feet, catching up halberds or turning on their captors with roars of anger—but one soldier spun and centered the point of his weapon between the spy's eyes. "Loose her, Captain!"

The spy stared, unbelieving, and Orgoru came alive with hope. "Strike them down!" he shouted, and false magistrates threw themselves on soldiers with a will, wrestling with them for their halberds while their mates came up from behind, pulling blackjacks from their sleeves. They struck, and the soldiers slumped to the ground. The rebels threw themselves on the tents to roll up the soldiers again. Feet and fists shot out, flailing blindly, and a few of the rebels went sprawling, but the rest struck downward themselves, then tumbled the canvas-covered lumps over and over. In a few minutes, the whole clearing was still, if not quiet—there were a great number of groans, and not a little cursing.

But the spy still stood with his knife at Gilda's throat, glaring down the length of the pike at the soldier. "You, a traitor, Mull?"

"I won't marry any but my Maud, Captain, and she's pledged to another," the soldier said stubbornly. "I'd rather go to the gallows for treachery, than spend my life in prison or slavery for refusing to wed."

The spy spat, "Go to the devil, then!" and flicked his hand. The knife shot end over end toward the soldier, who yelped and leaped aside as Gilda crouched and bowed with a snap. The spy howled as he flew over her head. He landed in a heap, and Orgoru was on him, striking with a blackjack. It smacked; the man went limp, and Orgoru turned to reach for Gilda.

But she was already kneeling by the soldier. "Lie still, fellow! It's only a cut, I think, but it should be bandaged for all that!"

"Bless you, ma'am," Mull said, wide-eyed.

"Bless *you,* for my life and hope!" Gilda tore the rip in Mull's sleeve wider. "Yes, it's only a cut. Orgoru, a little aqua vitae!" She took the bottle he handed her and warned, "This will hurt, but it will make sure your wound doesn't fester. Distract him, Orgoru!"

Distract him? She was better suited to that than he! Nonetheless, Orgoru gave it a manful try. "You're with us, soldier. Why?"

"It's as I said, sir—I heard that you mean to declare that everyone has the right to try to be—AAAHHH!—happy, and . . . all that goes with it, so . . ." Mull paused to draw in a long, shuddering breath as Gilda began to wind a bandage around his arm, then went on, "So I couldn't let the Captain stop you."

"Stout fellow!" Orgoru clasped his good hand. "We'll be forever grateful to you, and if we win, you'll be named among the heroes!"

"I'm no hero," Mull gasped. "I won't lie—I'd rather have

slept in my tent all night, and not taken a chance of hanging. But I couldn't watch my hopes for happiness die with you."

"There!" Gilda tied off the bandage and helped Mull sit up. "You'll show that wound to your grandchildren, Mull, and boast of it!"

"Only if I find the right woman, ma'am, and fall in love," Mull demurred, then stared as Gilda turned into the fortress of Orgoru's arms and let herself give in to trembling. He held her close, stroking her hair and murmuring reassurances.

Mull nodded. "Yes, if I have the luck to fall in love as you have, I will have grandchildren. I thank you for your healing, ma'am."

"It's the least we could do," Orgoru said. "I wish there was more."

"Well . . ."

Orgoru braced himself. "Name it!"

"I'm a dead man now anyway, sir, if you don't win, so . . . could I march with you?"

So they marched, down every low road and bypath, men born peasants, grown up to become lords in delusion, and cured to live lying lives as false magistrates. They ambushed the patrols set to ambush them, or saved one another when the patrols were too clever for one group alone. Fifty-three of the magistrates and their men died in the occasional clashes, but day by day, they came closer and closer to the capital, their numbers swelling as watchmen and bailiffs and reeve's men who had heard of the revolution came secretly to join them. It was an army three thousand strong who surrounded Milton Town a week later, with seven thousand more on the road.

Miles fretted, pacing in the indoor gloom of the warehouse near the town gate. "There must be a thousand traps laid for us by now! The spies must have told the Protector that we're rebelling!"

"Not really," Dirk told him. "You told that agent in the Protector's kitchens to feed and water the questioner and his torturers, and to spread the word that they had a real hard case going, and weren't to be disturbed—not that anybody would get all that curious about secret police business, anyway."

"Still, Renunzio must have made reports!"

Dirk grinned. "I forgot to tell you about that last curse Renunzio threw at me before I gagged him."

Miles turned, staring. "Curse? What curse?"

"He hoped I'd spend the rest of my life running flat-out through a nightmare with never a rest or a drink," Dirk said, grinning, "for coming before he'd told the Protector about us."

Miles stared, speechless, but Gar nodded. "It's the way of bureaucrats. Sometimes they hoard up all the good news, instead of giving it to their superiors in bits and pieces. They tell their bosses when they have the whole situation wrapped up and under control, to make themselves look all-powerful and totally competent. They usually hope for promotion. Sometimes they even get it."

"You mean the Protector never even heard about our rebellion?"

"Well, we can't be *sure* Renunzio didn't tell anybody else," Dirk hedged. "Might be he couldn't resist bragging—but I don't think so. He's the kind who wouldn't want to report it to a superior because the boss might steal the credit."

"Of course," Gar said, "somebody might have let him out of that torture chamber by now—but I don't think he was in any shape to make sense."

"You mean we're still secret?"

"I'm pretty sure about it, yes."

"I," said Gar, "am *completely* sure."

"You would be," Dirk growled.

Miles could scarcely believe it. Suddenly a huge weight seemed to roll off his shoulders, and the rock that had seemed to be rolling around in his belly disappeared. He took a deep breath and realized how wonderful it was here in the warehouse. Sunlight filtered through louvered turrets on the roof, casting a magical half-light over the heaped and stacked bales and crates. Scores of different spices perfumed the air. He felt a sudden, irrational surge of affection for the place, and heartily wished Ciletha had been there to share it.

"But the longer we wait, the greater the chance that word will come in from the provinces of an amazingly large number of magistrates deciding to take a vacation." Gar lifted himself off the bale of velvet he'd been using for a seat. "Your couriers tell us we have three thousand men around the city, and our spics in the Protector's Army tell us he only has twenty-five hundred soldiers, plus a hundred town watchmen. I think it's time to strike."

Miles stared at him, the wonderful feeling draining out of him as though he were a wineskin without a stopper.

"Seven thousand more men on the road," Dirk reminded Gar. "If we wait even one more day, we'll outnumber the Protector's forces by a safe margin."

"His castle has high walls, and his guards have halberds, pikes, and crossbows," Gar reminded. "Surprise will give us more strength than numbers—and a better chance of less bloodshed."

The last phrase decided Miles. "Fewer dead is worth the risk." He felt decision crystallize within him. "Yes, Gar, let's strike."

Gar's eye gleamed with pride as he watched his chief rebel. "Well enough, then. Tell your couriers to have your magistrates ready to march into the city at midnight."

Miles frowned. "But the Watch will find them!"

"Will they?" Gar asked. "Or will *they* find the *Watch*?"

The first twenty magistrates came in during the day, dressed as peasants. As dusk gathered, they hid in alleys, and when night fell, they came out to hunt.

A squadron of watchmen passed the mouth of an alley, talking in bored tones. " 'Extra vigilance,' the bailiff says! And why? Just because there are thousands of men marching up from the south!"

In the shadows at the alley mouth, two "magistrates" exchanged surprised glances.

"As though a mob a hundred miles away could have anything to do with us here!" another man scoffed.

"Mob?" a third man said with a laugh. "Magistrates! How

can puffed-up magistrates be a mob? Especially when they say they're only coming to talk with the Protector because they're so disturbed about marriage!"

"Why would magistrates be upset about weddings?" the first man scoffed. "They have more of them than any other kind of man!"

"Something about there not being enough good marriages," a fifth man said. "Even so, he's sending a thousand soldiers south."

"Yes," said the sixth. "He says it's to escort . . ."

The watchers heard no more, mostly because they stepped out of the alley and stepped up behind the watchmen, hands chopping down, stiffened into blades, making muted smacking sounds. Four watchmen dropped. The other two turned, mouths opening in alarm, but the "magistrates" leaped forward, stiffened fingers driving into bellies. The two watchmen doubled over, unable to talk, and blade-hands chopped again. Then, still silently, the "magistrates" pulled them back into the alley and began tying them up.

"So the spies finally went out at night and found the rest of us," one of the "magistrates" muttered.

"Yes, but it sounds as though they gave a good enough excuse to confuse the issue."

"And the Protector," said a third. "He doesn't want to chop down his civil service if they're not really going to make trouble."

"They don't seem to know our full strength, at least," the first man said, "or he wouldn't think a thousand men would be enough."

"A thousand?" asked the fourth man. "That would be enough, all right—if the men they were going to meet were real magistrates. They'd only be armed with batons, after all, and they can't know as much about fighting as real troupers. Then the thousand soldiers could claim to be an honor guard, but the mob would still realize they had to watch their step."

"Well, that's a thousand troops fewer for us to worry about tomorrow," said the first man. "Let's get going to the turnpike. We've taken out our squadron."

All over the city, the scene was repeated. Sometimes the Watch managed to call for help, and the commando-magistrates had to fade back into the shadows, leaving the unconscious bodies as bait for the next squadron that came on the run. Sometimes the watchmen were too quick, injuring a commando before they were struck down. There were even two squadrons who knocked out the commandos and ran back toward the palace, shouting the alarm—but half a dozen groups of commandos converged on them and stopped their shouting. When it was over, two commandos were dead and half a dozen wounded—but none of the watchmen had been killed, though several would take a few weeks to heal.

Meanwhile, commandos crept up on the bored sentries who guarded the turnpikes on the major roads in and out of the town. There were no city walls, and any number of men could have slipped in between the houses and warehouses that bordered it—but the Protector wasn't worried about a few foot-pads, since the Watch patrolled the streets so well. No, the turnpikes were there to make sure all incoming merchants paid their import taxes, and that all legitimate travelers showed their travel permits. The turnpikes barred the roads at sunset. Anyone who arrived too late had to seek lodging in one of the many inns outside the town, and wait for the officials to come on duty again in the morning.

Sentries guarded those turnpikes, of course, and though three thousand people could have come in between buildings and down alleyways, it was far quicker to march openly down the main roads—so commandos crept up behind the sentries and knocked them out. One or two turned at the wrong moment and swung their halberds at their attackers, so there were another couple of commandos wounded and a few more shouts at the edge of the city—but the waiting rebels swarmed through the turnpikes and knocked out the sentries themselves.

When the sun rose, all the watchmen lay tied up and moaning in cellars and warehouses, with a man and a woman rebel each to tend their wounds, give them a little water, and assure them that, though they would have a hungry day, they'd be released the next morning—if all went well. If it didn't, they might have to wait a bit longer.

That same sunrise woke the Protector, for he earned his pay twice over. He was haughty, but he had some right to be—for, though he was the son of one Protector and the grandson of another, he took pride in forty years of long days and hard effort working his way up through the ranks of the civil service from small-town magistrate to Protector in his own turn. His brothers had failed to rise so high, and lived now in this very town, where they could at least have permanent families—and live where he could keep an eye on them. But he had worked hard to achieve what he had, and worked hard still, rising with the sun and laboring at his desk and in his audience chamber until midnight, keeping track of everything that happened in his realm, and issuing a constant stream of decisions about any problems that arose.

Now his valet threw the curtains wide—and froze in astonishment, the sunlight streaming past him to the Protector, who was just rising from his bed. He frowned and asked, "What is it, Valard?"

"The square, Protector! It's full of men!"

"Let me see!" The Protector pushed Valard aside and stepped up himself to look down upon the square in front of his palace. It was jammed from edge to edge with heads wearing the notched caps of magistrates, faces staring up at the palace in expectation.

The Protector stared back, speechless and frozen. Then he turned from the window in a royal rage. "How on earth did they manage to slip past my soldiers! What the devil are they doing here? No, I know you don't know, Valard—but help me dress! I must confront them instantly, and learn what they want!"

It was a measure of the man's character that his first thought was to confront the danger that awaited him. It was only as a second thought that he said, "Tell the Captain of the Guard to send his men out around the square, behind the library and the treasury and the secretariat, then through the alleys between them to surround this crowd. Oh, and make sure the palace wall is fully manned, of course."

He burst out of his dressing room in his most imposing robes and with his chain of office glinting richly on his breast, the Captain of the Guard beside him, listening to the last of a stream of orders. "—and have them await me in the audience chamber!" the Protector finished. As the man nodded and hurried off, he snapped to another official who stood near, "How stand the provinces?"

"Messages have just come, Protector," the man said quickly. "Rebel magistrates have led mobs against reeves' castles in Autaine, Grabel, and Belorgium . . ."

"Three-quarters of the realm!"

"Yes, Protector, but the reeves and their guardsmen have put them down. There were only a handful of malcontents, of course, and the people themselves joined in their overthrow."

The Protector nodded briskly. "That is well. Now if only the people of this city come to overturn *these* rebels. . . . Open the windows!"

The valet threw open the French doors that let onto the balcony, and the Protector stepped out—and felt as though he had run into a solid wall of sound. The massed shout of "Liberty and rights! Liberty and rights!" slammed into him, repeated over and over until he staggered away from it, dazed and panting. The valet quickly pulled the windows shut, and the Protector gasped, "What the devil do they mean? There is only one right! How can there be more? And what nonsense is this about liberty? Personal liberty is chaos and the door to suffering!" Then, recovering himself, he roared, "Who taught them this nonsense?"

No one answered. For a moment, the hall was quiet. Then a footman stepped forward to say hesitantly, "Protector . . . there are three men awaiting you in the audience chamber, and one is clothed as a magistrate. . . . They ask to speak with you about 'mutual concerns.' "

"Concerns?" The Protector stared; then his brows drew down, and he shouted, "They had best be concerned indeed! How did they come into my audience chamber?"

"No . . . no one knows, sir," the man faltered. "The men you had sent to wait for you discovered them there."

The Protector stood rigid, staring at the man, and for the first time, he felt cold tendrils of fear. He shook them off, spun on his heel, and hurried toward the audience chamber with a snarl.

He burst into the chamber with footmen and men-at-arms scurrying after him, and brought up short, staring. The room was a hall with a fifteen-foot beamed ceiling, the Protector's high chair and bench at one end and banks of seats at the other. Between them stood three men, two seeming very small compared to the other, who must have been seven feet tall if he was an inch. He was dressed as a soldier in doublet and hose, but no livery, only russet cloth. One of the ordinary-sized men was dressed in the same fashion, though in leaf-green, and the third man was dressed as a magistrate.

Facing them was a row of ministers, gowned even more sumptuously than reeves or magistrates. Seeing them filled the Protector with renewed confidence. He waved the footmen and men-at-arms away, suspecting that what transpired here would be something he would not want to have leak out by gossip.

One sergeant lingered. "Sir . . . your safety . . ."

"The ministers will ward me! Out!"

The sergeant's face expressed his misgivings, but he left. The Protector marked him for preference—here was a man who knew both loyalty and obedience.

As the door closed behind the men, he rounded on the intruders. "How did you get in here?"

"We came by night," the one dressed as a magistrate replied.

"Came by night! Into the Protector's palace? How did you get past my guards?"

"Very carefully," the other short one answered, and nothing more.

The Protector's eyes narrowed; he felt his emotions calm to ice. He had played this sort of game before, many times before, and these were men half his age, who certainly could not be as skilled at it as he was. "Who are you?"

"I am Miles." The shortest one bowed slightly. "These are my companions, Dirk and Gar."

"What have you to do with this rabble out in the street?"

"They aren't rabble, Protector, but men who have served you as magistrates and reeves for as many as five years."

Reeves, too! That shook the Protector, but he kept it from showing. "Why did you come here?"

"To confer with you, Protector, about policies that give us great concern."

"Politely phrased," the Protector said, thin-lipped, "but I know demands when I hear them, and your mob in the square has told me what those demands are—liberty, which would cause this realm to tear itself apart, and 'rights,' whatever that may mean!"

"It means that we feel the people must have guarantees of their safety written down, Protector, as the fundamental laws of the land—matters which it is right for them to decide for themselves, and which no government should force upon them."

That rattled the Protector. He couldn't stifle a gasp of shock. "You want to change the foundation of the Law of the Realm!"

"We feel that is necessary," Miles said, almost apologetically.

"Then I shall build you the finest gallows in the land, for you must be the grandest traitor ever to walk! You must know that I would rather die than agree to such a change!"

At last the giant spoke. "We hope that will not be necessary, sir."

The Protector turned on him, face swelling with rage. "You had better believe that won't be necessary, though your own deaths are another matter!"

The third one spoke up. "You might not say that if you heard which rights we wish to guarantee, Protector. They're modest enough, after all."

"If your 'rights' restrict the power of the state to hold itself together, they're scarcely modest!" The Protector turned to him, eyes narrowing again. "But have your say, sir! What's your list?"

"First, that all people have the right to try to be happy."

The Protector sifted through the words in his mind, frowning, trying to find the barb in them and failing. "It seems harmless enough," he said grudgingly. "What next?"

"That everyone has the right to choose their spouses for themselves, and the government can never make them marry someone they don't want."

"But by that law, there would be many who would never marry!"

"Yes, Protector," Miles said evenly, "and there would be many who would find that loneliness is less miserable than a loveless marriage."

"But the realm would have fewer people, which means fewer crops, less income from taxes!"

"Fewer people yes, but happier ones," said the smaller of the two strangers. Dirk, was that his name? "Happier people might be more productive."

The words had a seductive ring, and the Protector frowned, storing them away to chew over when he had time. "That one is worth considering, at least." *And not worth fighting a rebellion.* "What else?"

Miles's eyes brightened with hope. "Everyone is free to worship as they please, and to preach their own religion," Miles told him.

That brought the Protector up sharply. "What is 'religion'?"

"A belief in a god or gods, and worship is talking to them in your mind."

"Fantasy," the Protector pronounced, hands on his hips, "but I see no harm in it, as long as they don't think these 'gods' are real. What else?"

"One that follows from the last, for if people have the right to believe in their religions, they have the right to tell other people about them. Everyone is free to speak whatever they please that won't injure any other person."

"Person?" The Protector jumped on the flaw right away. "Is the government a person?"

"No," Miles admitted.

"Meaning you would have everyone be free to criticize the government—and the Protector!"

"Only as an official," Dirk said quickly. "They wouldn't have the right to say anything about his private life."

"Stuff and nonsense! How a Protector lives his life affects

how well he can govern—and that applies to ministers, reeves, and magistrates, too!"

The ministers glowered and muttered to one another.

The Protector grinned, taking heart from their dislike. "No, I can't agree to that one, young fellows! What else have you to offer me?"

"That everyone has the right to life and safety, and that the government can't take it away from them without a trial by their fellows."

" 'By their fellows'?" the Protector demanded sharply. "What nonsense is this? A trial is decided by a magistrate!"

"The magistrate would still decide the sentence, within the bounds of the law," Miles said, "but the jury of fellow citizens would decide whether or not the accused was guilty."

"Oh, really! And what makes a bunch of plowboys better able to judge than one learned magistrate?"

"It guarantees that no one can be sentenced by one man's whim."

"No, he can be sentenced by the whim of a whole mob! And don't tell me there aren't people unpopular enough to be condemned by their fellows even if they're innocent—I've seen gangs turn against one of their own too often for that, and it's the magistrates who have protected them! No, I can't agree to that 'right,' as you call it, though I'll be glad to tell you why in more detail some other time!"

"Might it be because the law, by limiting the magistrates, limits the Protector?" Dirk suggested.

The Protector turned red. "I have the best interests of the realm at heart, boy, and of every single person in it! If the rest of your 'rights' are as silly as that, you can bring all the mobs you can find, but I'll say no to the last!"

"You haven't *heard* the last," Dirk reminded him. "Can we tell you the next?"

"Yes," the Protector snapped, seething.

"No one can be tortured. Not for any reason."

"No torture? How are we to make criminals tell the truth?" the Protector shouted.

"Torture can't do that," Miles told him. "It can only make them tell you what you want to hear."

"Which is that they're guilty, when we know it already! No, I can't agree to that one, either!" The Protector made a chopping gesture, as though cutting off the discussion. "Enough of this! I can see that most of your 'rights' are tools to injure the realm, maybe even tear it apart! No, I won't agree to them, nor will any of my ministers! This conference is at an end! Send your mob home!"

"I'm afraid not, sir," Miles said, his voice even.

"Oh, really," the Protector said in a voice as dry as hundred-year-old bones. "What will you do, then?"

"If we have to, sir, we'll arrest you and all your men, and put our own government in this palace in your stead."

CHAPTER 23

The Protector threw back his head and laughed, sharply and harshly. "So now we come to the truth of it! It's not the good of the people that you want—it's my power and my palace! But government isn't that easy, young man!"

"I know," Miles replied. "I've been an inspector-general for five years, and all those men outside have been magistrates for at least a year, some for five."

The Protector stared, taken aback. "An inspector-general? At *your* age?"

"Yes, sir."

"Stuff and nonsense, boy! Who made *you* an inspector-general?"

"I did, sir. I kidnapped a real inspector-general and took his place."

The Protector stared at him, the blood draining from his face, and his voice was almost a whisper. "And those men in the square?"

"They kidnapped the real magistrates and reeves, Protector, and took their places, too."

"Impossible! You can't become a magistrate without years of training!"

"Months," Miles said. "I studied very hard in private, and so did they."

"Impossible! Who taught you?"

"The Guardian of the Lost City of Voyagend—and Gar and Dirk here."

The Protector's gaze swung to Gar, and his eyes were windows into death. "So. You're the one who has spread this sedition throughout my realm."

"I have that honor," Gar said with a slight bow. "The seed put down roots quickly, for the soil was very fertile."

"Meaning that the people were eager to believe what you told them—but ignorant people are always quick to believe lies! I'll have you hanged from the castle walls, then chop your bones into pieces so that every magistrate can have one for a charm!"

"I'm afraid that won't be possible, Protector."

"Oh? And why not?" the Protector growled. "I hope you're not counting on that self-taught rabble in the square to protect you from my soldiers!"

"I did have something of the sort in mind, yes."

"Then come gaze upon your downfall, fool!" The Protector strode over to a set of French windows and threw them wide. Instantly, the chant of "Liberty and rights!" slammed in, but he waded through it, stepping out onto the balcony and pulling a bright yellow scarf from his sleeve. He waved it, and the edges of the crowd boiled as soldiers charged out from between the buildings. The doors of the palace opened, and a horde of troopers burst out, laying about them with their pikes and halberds. A cry of fright went up from the crowd, and it pulled in from the edges. The soldiers charged in among them.

"Your men may have faked governing," the Protector said, "but they can't fake fighting."

"No," Gar agreed. "They'll have to do the real thing."

Even as he said it, the rebels began to push back, seizing soldiers' halberds and wrestling them for the weapons—but other soldiers turned and began to fight their own men!

Orgoru was in the forefront of the crowd, shaking his fist and shouting louder than any, when the huge oaken door before him burst open, spewing soldiers who ran at him, halberds leveled. Orgoru cried out in dismay and anger, leaping backward into other rebels—but they were giving way, too, and he staggered against them, but stayed on his feet, remembering that they had expected such an onslaught, and how to deal with it.

"Aside!" he bellowed, and pivoted, following his own order. The halberd-blade shot past him, and he seized its shaft in both hands, pulling hard. The soldier staggered, off balance, and another rebel chopped down at the man's hands with an open palm. The soldier yelped with pain. Orgoru twisted and spun away with the halberd in his own hands while the other rebel yanked the soldier's helmet loose, and a third struck with a blackjack.

Another halberd stabbed toward Orgoru. He parried, shoving it aside with his own weapon, and the rebel next to him pushed it down against the cobbles. The spearhead caught in a crack and the butt jammed back against the soldier's belly. He sagged over it with a grunt, and the rebel struck with a blackjack.

Then there were three soldiers all at once striking at Orgoru, and he whirled his halberd madly, all the reflexes of his quarterstaff play coming to deflect their weapons. He didn't succeed fully—blades tore into his robes, and pain streaked his side and his hip, but he kept up his defense while his fellow rebels worked their way in, seizing pikes and striking with blackjacks. Finally the last soldier dropped, and Orgoru sagged, gasping for breath.

"Look out!" someone cried, and another halberd was jabbing toward him. Orgoru managed to bring up his own weapon barely in time, striking the halberd up, and it cut his cheek as the blade hissed by. Shaken, he struck harder with the butt than he had intended, cracking into the side of the soldier's head. He glimpsed blood before the man sank from sight, and Orgoru hoped he wouldn't be trampled by his own mates. He faced another soldier—the troopers couldn't get at very many of the rebels, because they were at the edge of a huge crowd. But by the same token, there were a lot of soldiers, each eager for his chance as the last one fell.

Each rank of soldiers charged into the crowd, and the rebels opened way for them, then closed in from the sides, shoving halberds down with their bare hands and striking with black-jacks and batons. As one rebel wearied, he fell back, and another took his place—but Orgoru found himself wondering how long they could keep it up. Who would fail first, the soldiers or the rebels?

He heard shouting in front of him, and whirled, then stared in amazement. Soldiers were fighting soldiers! Orgoru cheered, and led rebels in to help.

"Down with traitors!" one soldier cried, and rebels piled onto him.

"Long live the Protector!" cried another, and a rebel kicked his feet out from under him.

But Orgoru braced himself, waiting, and sure enough, another soldier cried, "Down with the Protector!" but the man he was fighting echoed him: "Down with the Protector!"

"How can we tell which is which, Orgoru?" another rebel asked him, bewildered.

"Take them both," Orgoru answered. "We can apologize later."

They did.

The Protector stared. Then he swung about to Gar, howling, "Traitor! You've suborned my army too!"

"Only half of them," Gar told him, "but as you see, I've also taught my homegrown magistrates to fight. I'd guess your soldiers will all be bound tightly in fifteen minutes at most."

For the second time, the Protector felt the stab of fear. He tried to ignore it and demanded, "How will you govern if you tear down my government?"

"Just as we have for the last five years," Miles said. "I told you that we have all taken the places of real magistrates."

"How many of you are there?" the Protector whispered.

"Three thousand here, and five hundred more on the way. With the watchmen and soldiers who have joined them, seven thousand in all."

"Five hundred magistrates and reeves! That's half the officials in my realm!"

"Yes, Protector. We can govern with that many."

"What did you do with the real ones!"

"They're our guests, in the Lost City of Voyagend," Miles told him. "We haven't hurt them, but they're very restless."

"And you think they'll be as glad to govern for you as for me!" the Protector whispered. But the shadow that haunted his face was certainty, for he knew human ambition, and knew the captive magistrates would do just that. He spun about to look out the window again, and saw that the rebels were winning.

"This is how it is throughout the land," Gar said behind him. "The soldiers loyal to you are outnumbered two to one by those we have persuaded to see the glories of the New Order."

"I think not," the Protector snarled. "Far from this city, they will be loyal to me, and have triumphed! I have had messengers tell me this within this last hour!"

"They told you only what you wanted to hear," Dirk said. "They were afraid to tell you anything else, for fear you might not promote them."

"You lie!" the Protector snarled, and, to his ministers, "Seize them!"

The ministers threw off their cloaks, and instead of the gray-haired, reverend statemen they had seemed to be, they appeared as toughened sergeants who drew swords and leaped upon Gar, Dirk, and Miles.

Gar sank to his knees, arms wrapped around his head, and four soldiers fell on him with victorious shouts. Dirk spun about to set his back against Miles's as he whipped out his rapier and Miles pulled a sword and buckler from under his robes. Eight sergeants surrounded them, but paused as the oldest commanded, "Drop your swords, raise your hands, and we'll let you live!"

"Yes, long enough to torture us into telling you everything you already know," Dirk retorted. "Have at you!" He leaped forward, thrusting and slashing, which was very poor tactics, because the soldiers moved to surround him—

Then halted, as a roar filled the chamber. They flicked glances over, astonished, and saw the pile of four of their fellows erupt. Soldiers flew back to strike into the wall and the floor as Gar surged to his feet, shaking them off and drawing his rapier. Before they could recover, he struck the swords out of the hands of two of them, then turned to the third as he scrambled to his feet. The fourth lay unconscious.

Dirk and Miles both struck while their opponents were staring at Gar. Miles's buckler cracked the head of one, and his sword lanced another's shoulder. The man fell back, clutching his wound with a howl as the sword dropped from his fingers— but the other two moved in. Miles backed up—and felt his spine jar against Dirk's, who was facing two men of his own. Two others lay unconscious and bleeding.

Gar struck up the sword of the first man to reach him, then balled a huge fist in his tunic and yanked him off the floor to throw him into his fellow. Both went down with a crash. Gar leaped forward, kicking the sword hands; each man howled with pain, and the blades went flying across the floor. Gar turned to help Dirk.

Dirk wasn't doing too badly. He had managed to catch one soldier with an arm around the throat and hold him as a shield while he parried madly on his right. The other sergeant fell back, clutching a bleeding arm, sword falling from nerveless fingers. Gar yanked both assailants off the ground, and tossed them onto the pile he had started. They landed just as two others were trying to get up, and knocked them back onto the floor.

Miles was already down, bleeding from three cuts, trying frantically to hold off the two blades that darted about him, fending some with his buckler, parrying others. Gar yanked both soldiers off their feet and sent them flying to the discard pile. Two more scrambled to their feet, staggering and woozy, but bringing up swords. Dirk shouted, and they turned to face him. He fenced madly for the minutes it took Miles to scramble to his feet; then Miles shouted, and one of the soldiers turned to face him. He thrust, but Miles parried. He swung his sword up for a cut, but Miles lunged and skewered the man's shoulder. He shouted with pain, and his sword fell. Miles struck his head with the buckler, and the soldier collapsed, out cold. Moments later, Dirk's opponent fell beside him.

"A little help here," Gar called. He was standing by the discard pile, catching soldiers as they scrambled up, and throwing them back. Miles and Dirk came running, and as the next two soldiers stumbled to their feet, they found themselves staring at the tips of two blades. They froze, and Gar knocked their heads together. They slumped, unconscious. Two more of their fellows were also out, their heads having struck the floor instead of a fellow soldier's stomach. The others, seeing the odds against them, hesitated.

"Surrender," Gar said quietly. "You haven't a chance, anyway."

Slowly, the men held up empty hands.

"Lie down on your bellies with your hands behind your back," Dirk directed. "Miles, tie them up."

Miles pulled the men's belts off and began to tie them, wrist and ankle. Dirk joined him, then looked up at a sudden thought. "Where's the Protector?"

Gar looked around at an empty room. "Dirk, finish the job," he snapped. "Come on, Miles."

Miles looked up, startled, then ran after Gar. Distantly, he knew he'd been wounded, but also knew he couldn't let that stop him.

Through the corridors they charged, bowling aside footmen and butlers who squawked with surprise and fear. Down the stairway they galloped, two at a time, out the huge doorway and into—

A melee of soldiers fighting soldiers.

"Through them!" Gar shouted. "Don't stop to fight!"

They twisted and turned their way between battling men,

barely managing to escape edged weapons, and thrust their way into the crowd, where they were surrounded by—

Robes.

They stared around them, appalled. Then Miles cried out, "How are we to find him? Everyone's wearing official's robes!"

"His are richer, and his chain is more massive," Gar called back, "and his robes are purple instead of red or blue!"

Miles called, "How can we find purple among all these blue and red?"

"The other rebels will recognize him as one they don't know!"

"Recognize him?" Miles protested. "There are so many of them from so many different towns that they don't even recognize each other!"

It was true; Miles had done his work too well. Unless some rebel stopped to think what the purple robes meant, the Protector was hidden in a sea of his enemies—and with the fight against the soldiers foremost in their minds, the rebels weren't likely to pay much attention to the color of their neighbors' robes!

"One side! One side!" Gar thrust his way through the crowd, seeking, searching—but in the turmoil of the fight, he couldn't see anything but red and blue. To the center of the crowd he waded, crying, "The Protector! The Protector! Look for purple robes!"

Soldiers looked up and froze in alarm, staring at the giant looming over them. They recovered quickly and turned to fight again—but Gar was already past them, still calling, "The Protector!" Rebels who had never seen Gar, saw and drew back, recognizing him from what they'd heard about the mythical beginner of their revolution. But nowhere did he find the purple robe.

Then a thin cry went up—thin, but echoed and amplified by a dozen voices, then fifty. Gar turned and plowed straight for it. A lane opened for him, rebels pulling back, thrusting soldiers away with their own pikes, straight to the Protector, struggling in the arms of a grizzled sergeant.

Gar plucked him up and held him high, crying, "We have your Protector! Put down your weapons, or he dies!"

All over the square, soldiers looked up in astonishment to see their Protector writhing high above their heads—and the rebels they were fighting struck them down. Then the rebels, too, realized what was happening, and drew back, giving the soldiers a chance to surrender. The soldiers saw the Protector and moaned. Pikes clattered on the paving stones, and soldiers cried, "I surrender! I surrender!"

Gar lowered the Protector to the ground. "You shall be our honored guest for a few days, Protector."

"Yes, until you can work up the courage to hang me!" the Protector snarled, and turned on the man who had caught him. "You, Sergeant Alesworth! You, who were one of my personal guard for fourteen years! Why have you turned against me now?"

The sergeant stared back at him, stone-faced. "Do you remember that I loved my wife, Protector? And that she died?"

The Protector went pale. "Yes. I remember."

"And remember that three months later, you made me marry again?"

"It was for the best! Best for you, and for the realm!"

Alesworth shook his head. "We made each other miserable, Protector, and she turned her misery against my children—but you didn't know about that, did you? No, nor care."

"For that?" the Protector whispered. "Only for that, you have brought down the realm?"

"No, Protector," the sergeant said, "only healed it."

The ceremony took place in that same square, two days later—time enough to clean up the evidence of the fight. As they waited at the door for the Protector and his "honor guard," Dirk surveyed the clean pavement, slightly stained here and there. "Only sixty-three dead and a hundred twenty-seven wounded badly enough for hospital. That's certainly the least bloody revolution you've ever managed, Gar."

"Yes, but sixty-three people *are* dead," Gar said grimly.

282 / Christopher Stasheff

"If this is the best I can do, maybe I should get out of the business."

Dirk shrugged. "Sixty-three because you did lead a revolution, a thousand dead from the secret police and suicide due to misery if you hadn't. More than a thousand, many more, if you count the rest of the years this dictatorship would have stayed in power."

"Maybe," Gar said grimly. "Maybe."

"At least these were clean deaths," Dirk pointed out. "Only one died from torture. Of course, Miles had a little torture, too, but you gave him express healing."

"Yes." Gar frowned. "He never did ask how his feet managed to heal so quickly, just started worrying about all his rebels. That shows either an excellent character, or a revolting degree of faith in me."

"Well, people with faith in you do tend to revolt. . . . No, no, sorry! Hey, here he comes."

They both bowed slightly as the Protector came up flanked by guards, none loyal to himself. He acknowledged their bows with one of his own, mouth tight with irony. "Are you taking me to sign my own death warrant?"

"No, Protector," Gar said, "only the documents transferring power to the provisional government."

"Is there a difference?"

"Oh, yes. At the moment, we're not intending to kill you at all." Gar said it so casually that even Dirk shuddered.

"At the moment," the Protector said dryly. "And if I refuse to sign?"

"Then we shall escort you to your permanent guest quarters. . . ."

"Which you shall do in any case."

"Ah, then," Gar said brightly, "you do realize that we don't plan to execute you."

"Then you are fools," the Protector said simply. "There's no greater threat to a government than a deposed head of state. I might escape, gather men who would rally to me—and there are many, I assure you!—and lead a counterrevolt."

"You might," Gar agreed, "*if* you could escape. We have great faith in our jailers."

"Then you are doubly fools, for there's no prison human hands can build, that another human brain can't find a way to escape."

"Then we must be content to be fools," Gar returned, "for if we violate your right to life, then we betray our own ideals, and build a mortal weakness into our New Order before it's even begun."

"Then fools you are indeed," the Protector retorted, "but I would be a worse fool not to take advantage of your folly. Come, show me your document and I'll sign it! Then cart me away to your prison, so I can set to working out my escape."

"As you wish, Protector." Gar bowed him on. The guards fell in to either side; Dirk and Gar fell in behind him.

"He's right, you know," Dirk said softly. "This kind of mercy *is* foolish."

"Perhaps," Gar returned, equally softly, "but he hasn't met the Guardian and his robots yet—or his human jailer."

A band played a solemn air as the Protector marched to the table in the center of the square, where Miles awaited him. People lined the walls of the surrounding buildings five deep, people hung from every window to watch, and soldiers stood stoutly in front of the crowd, to restrain anyone who became too exuberant—but no one did. There were two thousand people, at least, watching that day, and not one of them cheered or shouted; there was only a constant hum of muted conversation as they talked to one another in wondering tones about the unbelievable event they were witnessing.

Miles bowed as the Protector came to the table and handed him a quill pen. In loud, ringing tones, he declared, "Protector, you have read these documents in the privacy of your chambers. Will you sign them?"

"I haven't much choice, have I?" the Protector said, with full sarcasm.

"You have every choice!" Miles orated. "If you do not wish

to sign, you shall be treated with every bit as much respect as though you did!"

"Or every bit as little," the Protector retorted. "And if I don't, what shall you do then?"

"We shall declare your government to be null and void by the will of the people. Then we shall continue as we have planned, to hold elections. Everyone shall place his 'vote,' a slip of paper containing his choice, through a small slot in a locked box. These votes shall be counted, and the will of the people thus determined."

The Protector yanked the quill from his hand. "Enough! I'll sign. Whatever excuse you find for your rhetoric, it won't be me!"

He bent over the table, dashed off his signature with a flourish, then straightened and handed the pen back to Miles— and the crowd cheered.

They cheered wildly, explosively. Their shouts of joy rang off the marble facades of the buildings all around the square, beating at the Protector, deafening him with rejoicing, and for a brief moment, he looked uncertain. Only for a moment; then he turned back to Miles with a sardonic smile, waited till the cheering had slackened, and cried out in a voice even louder than Miles's, "Now! Take me to my prison!"

He was horrified when the crowd cheered again.

The Protector halted and stared in amazement at the opalescent walls rising high above the trees. "What city is this?"

"One that was lost," Orgoru explained to him. "Our ancestors built it when they first came to this world."

"That's a fairy tale—that our ancestors came from a star!"

"It's quite true, and the biggest of the ships in which they came lies beneath this city—but you'll learn all that from its Guardian, if you wish to."

"Only a fool doesn't wish to learn!"

"Then you'll have every chance you want," Orgoru assured him. "Come, let me introduce you to your host."

"You mean my jailer for the rest of my life, don't you?"

"As you wish." Orgoru stepped forward and gestured to the

stocky man who awaited them in the stone gateway. "Protector, this is Master Bade."

Bade held out a hand, but the Protector's lip curled in scorn. "Come, now! You don't expect me to shake hands with my jailer, do you?"

"I see you have the courage to stare at the unvarnished truth." Bade withdrew his hand.

"Doesn't everyone?"

"Not at all, which is why the harshness of your government drove some of us to seek refuge in delusion. We came here to live a dream life, convinced that we were truly princes and lords."

"A fairy tale indeed! What brought you from it?"

"A giant," Bade said, "but we don't know how."

For a moment, the Protector's eyes fired with hatred. "It seems I owe him even more than I thought."

"Don't let it bother you—he doesn't insist on his due. Will you come up to the top of the wall with me, Protector? I have a sight to show you that may interest you."

"My cell?"

"No, you shall have a palace for a prison. The only hardship is that you shall dwell in it alone."

"Then show it to me quickly, so that I can begin planning my escape!"

"Let me lead you to the last men who said that." Bade led the way onto the top of a tower. The Protector stepped out— and saw a gleaming skeleton. He stared, horrified. "You wouldn't even bury them?"

" 'Them'?" Bade looked up. "Oh, those aren't skeletons, Protector, only robots. Don't worry, in a few days you'll scarcely notice them."

Horror of horrors, the skeleton moved—but the face it turned on the Protector was a featureless eggshell. He shrank back, but noticed how casually Bade went on, and followed him, but with wary glances at the robot, especially as it turned to shadow him.

They came out onto the parapet, and Bade gestured. "There they are."

The Protector looked down—and saw hundreds of men in red robes, with here and there a blue one, even one or two in the plain homespun of a peasant or an inspector-general. His heart sank as he realized he was looking at his kidnapped magistrates and reeves.

CHAPTER 24

Before the horde of magistrates, Bade stood wearing a black robe, though it was decked with silver trim. Solemnly, he raised his right hand; the multitude in front of him rustled as they raised their arms in imitation. "Do you swear loyalty to the Council of Reeves?" Bade asked.

"I do so swear!" the magistrates answered as though with one voice.

"Will you uphold their declarations and enforce their laws?"

"I do so swear!"

"Will you defend and uphold the Charter of Human Rights?"

"I do so swear!"

"Welcome, brother officials of the New Order," Bade intoned. "Leave this city now, to take up your offices under the Reeve of Reeves. Miles, your new Presiding Magistrate, shall soon send you your true wives, those with whom you have felt the actual bond of marriage. Those of you who have found no true wife will not be obliged to take one; you may serve the realm as magistrates anyway. All other wives who do not join their former husbands shall, as we have promised, continue to be supported by the Realm."

The magistrates cheered and began to file out through the gate by which the Protector had just come in. He watched them go, his face ashen.

"All of those men have been my prisoners for at least a year," Bade told him. "Some of them have lived here for five years. With a whole city to roam, they haven't had close confinement to complain of, but they've tried to escape continually, even after I told them that whoever could learn more than the Guardian would be allowed to go free. None did, of course, but they were still trying when Miles sent word that they could go free, and could become magistrates again if they liked. You will have to be ingenious indeed, Protector, to develop a scheme none of them has thought of."

The Protector felt the truth in the words, and felt his heart begin to sink.

"Come, now." Bade beckoned. "Let me introduce you to the Guardian."

The Protector met the bodiless intelligence that greeted him courteously and answered every question he could ask. When he left the chamber, his heart could sink no lower.

Outside the city, Orgoru hurried to join Gilda and the aloof giant who watched their embrace. "It's done," said the former madman.

"Don't tremble so, husband," Gilda said into his shoulder. "You know it's kinder than death, and that we had no choice."

"Or do you think life in the City is so unpleasant as that?" Gar asked.

Orgoru looked up, startled by the implications of the question. "It was quite pleasant," he said slowly, "but we were mad!"

"And I promised you that you could be so again," Gar said gravely, "when you had done the task I asked of you. That work is done, Orgoru, Gilda. Would you claim your reward?"

The two looked at one another, startled. Then Orgoru said slowly, "You mean to make us mad again? To send us back to our illusions, so that I might once again be the Prince of Paradime, and Gilda the Countess d'Alexi?"

"I will, if you wish it."

For a moment, Gilda's eyes were bright with hunger—but she looked at Orgoru, too, in his new blue robe and chain of office, and said slowly, "To be a countess in illusion, or the wife of a reeve and high minister in reality? I think sanity has become sweeter than madness to me, Gar." She caught Orgoru's hands again. "But only as long as I have you. If you would rather go back to madness, Orgoru, I'll go with you."

"But if I have you," he said softly, "I have no need of delusion, for the bitter world has been made sweet by your presence." He stared into her eyes for a minute, beaming, then laughed and leaned away at arm's length. "Besides, to be one of the foremost men of a real realm is at least as sweet as being the Prince of Paradime! Far more work, it's true, but also far more satisfying! Will you stay in reality with me, my love?"

"I will," she said, "till the end of my life," and threw her arms around him.

Gar gazed fondly at their embrace, but felt the old craving grow within him. He solaced it by finding room to wonder if they had not simply found a more pleasant illusion than madness.

Back in Milton Town, Gar made the same offer to all the cured delusionaries. They all refused the return to madness; with even a little success, life was proving more enjoyable than delusion.

"I thought they'd make that choice," Gar confided to Dirk, "but I must admit I had my doubts."

"They seem content to be part of the new power structure," Dirk said, "and to not try to take revenge on the people who made their childhoods miserable."

"There is that chance, when the underdog comes to power," Gar agreed. "I think we had better stay for a month or so, and see how our protégé, Miles, manages."

At the end of that month, they sat on a balcony of the former Protector's palace, with the French windows ajar behind them and the door to their mutual drawing room locked. It would have taken an ingenious burglar indeed to eavesdrop on them.

"Well begun," Gar said, "and well intentioned—but our Miles is taking an awful lot on himself."

"He *has* cleaned up the examinations system pretty well." Dirk sipped his wine. "Of course, he hasn't put in measures to keep it clean."

"I'm sure he'll think of them," Gar replied. "If nothing else, he'll keep the inspector-general system going, as soon as he's sure who's loyal and who isn't. But measures against corruption are always temporary."

"Yes, I know," Dirk said, with a touch of bitterness. "Human ingenuity will always find a way around such safeguards. You don't think there's a permanent cure, do you?"

"Only eternal vigilance, with outbursts of public anger when corruption is found." Gar sighed. "It's unpleasant, but it helps a bit. Of course, so does a periodic housecleaning, and Miles has at least achieved that. The system will probably stay honest for a hundred years, and pretty clean for a century after."

But the first meeting of the Council of Reeves reassured them immensely. After the opening ceremonies, Miles presented bill after bill, asking the Council to approve the reforms he had already put into place, and suggesting new ones to come. The next day, three different groups of reeves each endorsed some of Miles's bills, but not all—and of course, each group had a different set of bills it liked. Then each group submitted some bills of their own. By the third day, each had given itself a name.

That evening, Dirk held up his glass to look at the sunset through the rosy fluid. "Much as I like what our boy Miles is doing, I like what the reeves are doing even better."

"A three-party system." Gar nodded vigorously. "Yes, that will help. Both out-of-power parties will always be criticizing the party in power, and watching it like hawks for any signs of wrongdoing."

"It's certainly more lively," Dirk agreed, "but have we really improved anything? Other than everyone being free not to marry, and able to chose their own mates if they do decide to wed."

"Oh, I think so," Gar said thoughtfully. "The Council of Reeves is about to declare a Charter of Human Rights. The torture chambers have been torn apart, the justice system can't be used as a tool of personal viciousness—did you hear that Miles has even proposed that every verdict be sent to the Guardian for review?"

"Hear it? I suggested it! Meanwhile, the President is accountable to a legislature that's elected by the people—or will be, as soon as they hold their first elections."

Gar nodded. "So all in all, it's probably an improvement on the existing system, if not really a new system. There's every chance that more people will be happier this way."

"So why are you so depressed?"

"Because it *isn't* new," Gar sighed, "and I'm the one who told the Guardian to teach them an overview of human history, not just the annals of this planet alone. I had hoped that they would invent a system of their own."

Dirk shrugged. "So instead, they chose bits and pieces that they liked and put them together to make a new variation. As long as it's right for them, who cares?"

"I do," Gar groaned.

Dirk studied him for a few minutes, frowning, then said, "There's nothing wrong with following in your father's footsteps, Gar—especially if you're doing it by accident."

The elections were actually held on time, and the ballots and all the records were taken to the Guardian for verification. The computer pronounced them legitimate, and the country let out a mass cheer. The score or so of reeves who weren't re-elected weren't so happy, but their replacements were. They switched places, the winners going to the capital and the losers taking their offices in the provinces—and immediately starting the groundwork for their next campaigns. Miles let out a massive sigh of relief, and spent the night celebrating with Ciletha—he was still President.

A few weeks later, they held their first inauguration. It was a solemn and awe-inspiring sight, albeit with something of an improvised nature to it. Gar and Dirk watched, beaming fondly.

Then all that remained was to wait for the newly elected Council of Reeves to draft their Charter of Government—quickly done, since they had been hammering out the details for five years—and incorporating all the safeguards Gar had recommended to Miles. He was delighted that, all by themselves and no doubt due to pressure from the female former lunatics, the reeves added a Grandmothers' Council, which would have to ratify everything the Council of Reeves passed, and might themselves send bills to the reeves. At least, Gar was delighted until he realized that the Grandmothers made the legislature bicameral.

Then, finally, when the Charter had been passed and the new government was firmly in place, Miles left the victory party to take Ciletha out under the stars, turned to her, and said, "The fighting and arguing are done, Ciletha. The new government is in place, and we're still alive and safe."

"Yes, my darling, we are," she whispered.

Never taking his eyes from hers, Miles knelt and asked, "Will you marry me?"

"Yes, my love." Her lips trembled as she bent to give him a long and lasting kiss.

It was a glorious day, with sunlight filling the crisp air of autumn and the leaves a riot of color. The choir sang a song of triumph that sounded suspiciously like a hymn as the bride and groom mounted the platform to stand before the Chairman of the Council of Reeves to exchange their vows. Then, as the crowd filling the square cheered wildly, Miles led his bride to the great doorway of the palace, picked her up, and carried her over the threshold.

The doors closed behind him, but he didn't put Ciletha down—he was too busy kissing her. Finally, she broke the embrace and said softly, "Your arms are trembling, my love."

"Only with desire," Miles said stoutly.

"Nonetheless, please put me down," Ciletha said, "for we have farewells to make."

With great reluctance (even though his arms *were* aching), Miles put her down and turned to his closest guests. He clasped Dirk's hand, then Gar's, as he said, "I thank you, my friends. Ciletha and I would never have married if it hadn't been for you."

"Of course, there's also the minor issue of a government overthrown and freedom won," Dirk said dryly, "not to mention your still being alive to achieve them. But what does that matter against finding your mate, eh?"

"Exactly!" both said at once.

"We were glad to do all that we could," Gar said, "and gladder still that it worked for the best. May you have long and happy lives."

"May all your sorrows be small, and your joys great," Dirk said.

Miles turned somber for a minute. "Will we see you again?"

"Probably not," Dirk said, and,

"Only if you wake up very early tomorrow," Gar said. "It doesn't matter, though. You don't need us anymore."

"We will always long to see you again, though," Ciletha said, extending her hand.

"Perhaps fate will bring us together again," Gar said, but the gaunt longing flickered over his face for an instant, and was gone.

They climbed the hill outside Milton in the predawn light and stood waiting for the first sun-ray to reflect off something high up. As they waited, Dirk mused, "They might have waked up early, and be looking out the window watching us."

"More likely that they haven't slept yet," Gar said, "but if you'll pardon my mentioning it, they have far more important considerations just now than two departing friends."

"You mean each other? Yes, they have." Dirk cast a shrewd glance at his huge companion, saw the longing in his face, and felt its echo within him, which he sternly put down. To distract Gar, he said, "You know, for a man committed to self-determination, you seem to be leaving an awful lot of newborn democracies in your wake."

The naked longing disappeared under Gar's rueful smile. "I'm afraid that's true, Dulaine. I'll reason out why someday."

"Not just now, though, okay?" Dirk pointed upward. "Here comes our ride."

Gar looked up and smiled with relief as the great golden disk spun down.

TOR BOOKS The Best in Fantasy

TOR
BOOKS The Best in Fantasy

LORD OF CHAOS • Robert Jordan
Book Six of *The Wheel of Time*. "For those who like to keep themselves in a fantasy world, it's hard to beat the complex, detailed world created here....A great read."—*Locus*

STONE OF TEARS • Terry Goodkind
The sequel to the epic fantasy bestseller *Wizard's First Rule*.

SPEAR OF HEAVEN • Judith Tarr
"The kind of accomplished fantasy—featuring sound characterization, superior world-building, and more than competent prose—that has won Tarr a large audience." *Booklist*

MEMORY AND DREAM • Charles de Lint
A major novel of art, magic, and transformation, by the modern master of urban fantasy.

NEVERNEVER • Will Shetterly
The sequel to *Elsewhere*. "With a single book, Will Shetterly has redrawn the boundaries of young adult fantasy. This is a remarkable work."—Bruce Coville

TALES FROM THE GREAT TURTLE • Edited by Piers Anthony and Richard Gilliam
"A tribute to the wealth of pre-Columbian history and lore."—*Library Journal*

"No ... no one knows, sir," the man faltered. "The men who